Jane Eyre

Jane Eyre

Charlotte Bronte

and
Wayne Josephson

Readable Classics

Chadwick Publishing
Charlottesville VA 22901

ISBN: 978-0-615-32444-9
Library of Congress Control Number: 2009937410
Readable Classics
www.readableclassics.com
Chadwick Publishing
Charlottesville, VA 22901
Design & Layout: bookdesign.ca
Printed in the United States of America

Jane Eyre

Chapter 1

There was no possibility of taking a walk that day. The cold winter wind had brought somber clouds and penetrating rain. I was glad. I never liked long walks, especially on chilly afternoons. It was dreadful coming home to Gateshead Hall in the raw twilight, with nipped fingers and toes, to be humiliated by my cousins—Eliza, John, and Georgiana Reed.

They were now gathered round their Mama, my aunt Mrs. Reed, in the drawing room. She relaxed on a sofa by the fireside and, with her darlings about her, looked perfectly happy. She had forbidden me from joining the group, saying, "Until you are more sociable and energetic, I really must exclude you from privileges intended only for contented, happy, little children."

"But what have I done?" I asked.

"Jane, I don't like questioners; besides, there is something truly forbidding in a child speaking to her elders in that manner. Be seated somewhere else; and until you can speak pleasantly, remain silent."

I slipped into a breakfast room adjoining the drawing room. From the bookcase, I chose a volume full of pictures and, sitting cross-legged in the window seat, drew the red curtain closed. Occasionally I would look out the window at the dreary November day—a pale blank of mist and clouds, with ceaseless rain sweeping away wildly.

I returned to my book—Bewick's History of British Birds. There were certain introductory pages that, child as I was, I could not pass up. They pictured the haunts of sea fowl—the solitary rocks of the coast of Norway. Nor could I pass up the bleak shores of Siberia and Iceland, with the vast sweep of Arctic ice and snow, and those lonely regions of dreary space. From these death-white scenes I formed ideas of my own—shadowy, like the dreams that float dimly through children's brains.

Each picture told a story, mysterious to my childish understanding, yet deeply interesting—as interesting as the tales that Bessie, the maid, sometimes told on winter evenings, when she happened to be in good humour, and fed us with stories of love and adventure taken from old fairy tales and other ballads.

With the book on my knee, I was then happy—happy at least in my way. I feared nothing but interruption, and that came too soon. The breakfast room door opened.

"Madam Miserable!" cried the voice of cousin John. Then he paused, finding the room apparently empty.

"Where the dickens is she?" he continued. "Lizzy! Georgy!" he called to his sisters. "Jane is not here. Tell Mama she has run out into the rain—bad animal!"

It is well that I drew the curtain, I thought, and eagerly wished he might not discover my hiding place. Nor would he have—he was not quick of mind—but Eliza put her head in the door and said at once:

"She is in the window seat, to be sure, Jack."

I came out immediately, trembling at the idea of being dragged out by Jack.

"What do you want?" I asked, with awkward shyness.

"Say 'What do you want, Master Reed?'" cried John. "I want you to come here." Seating himself in an arm chair, he motioned that I should approach and stand before him.

John Reed was a schoolboy of fourteen years old. I was only ten. He was large and stout for his age, with dirty and unhealthy skin, heavy arms and legs, and large hands and feet. He gorged on food at the table, which made him nauseous and irritable, and gave him bleary eyes and flabby cheeks.

He should now be in boarding school, but his Mama had kept him home for a month or two, "on account of his delicate health." Mr. Miles, the headmaster, suggested that he should have fewer cakes and sweetmeats sent to him from home; but his mother rather thought that John's paleness was due to overwork and longing for home.

John had not much affection for his mother and sisters, and hatred toward me. He bullied and punished me—not two or three times a week, nor once or twice a day, but continually. Every nerve I had was fearful of him, and every bit of flesh in my bones shrank when he came near. I stood no chance against his hatred—the servants did not like to offend their young master by defending me, and Mrs. Reed was blind and deaf on the subject. She chose to never see him hitting or abusing me, though he did both in her very presence, but more frequently behind her back.

As usual, I obeyed John's command and came up to his chair. He spent three minutes thrusting out his tongue at me as far as he could. I knew he would soon strike me and, while awaiting the blow, I pondered his disgusting and ugly appearance. All at once, without speaking, he struck suddenly and strongly. I staggered and, after regaining my balance, stepped back from his chair.

"That is for your rudeness in answering Mama before," said he, "and for sneaking away behind curtains, and for the look you had in your eyes two minutes ago, you rat!"

Accustomed to John Reed's abuse, I never had any thought of striking back; I now prepared for the next blow which would certainly follow the insult.

"What were you doing behind the curtain?" he asked.

"I was reading."

"Show me the book."

I returned to the window and fetched it.

"You have no business to take our books. You are an orphan, Mama says. You have no money—your father left you none. You ought to beg on the street, not live here with gentlemen's children like us, and eat the same meals we do, and wear clothes at our Mama's expense. Now I'll teach you to rummage through my bookshelves, for they are mine. The whole house belongs to me, or will in a few years. Go and stand by the door, away from the mirror and the windows."

I did so, not aware at first what his intention was. But when I saw him lift the book and start to hurl it, I quickly moved aside with a cry of alarm—not soon enough, however. The volume was flung, it hit me, and I fell, striking my head against the door and cutting it. The pain was sharp and the cut bled. My terror had passed, and now other feelings replaced them.

"Wicked, cruel boy!" I said. "You are like a murderer—you are like a slave driver—you are like the Roman emperors!" I had read Goldsmith's History of Rome and had formed my own opinion of Nero and Caligula.

"What! What!" he cried. "Did she say that to me? Did you hear her, Eliza and Georgiana? I'll tell Mama. But first—"

He ran headlong at me. I felt him grab my hair and my shoulder. I truly saw in him a tyrant, a murderer. I don't know what I did to him with my hands, but he called me "Rat! Rat!" and screamed out loud.

Help was near—Eliza and Georgiana had run for Mrs. Reed, who was upstairs. She now came into the room, followed by Bessie and Miss Abbot, the lady's maid.

We were separated. I heard the words, "Dear! Dear! What fury to fly at

Master John!" and "Did ever anybody see such a picture of anger!"

Then Mrs. Reed commanded, "Take her away to the red-room and lock her in there." Four hands were immediately laid upon me, and I was carried upstairs.

Chapter 2

I resisted all the way—a new thing for me—which greatly worsened the bad opinion Bessie and Miss Abbot already had of me. The fact is, I was a bit beside myself, or rather out of myself, as the French would say.

"Hold her arms, Miss Abbot. She's like a mad cat."

"For shame!" cried the lady's maid. "What shocking conduct, Miss Eyre, to strike a young gentleman, your young master."

"Master! How is he my master? Am I a servant?"

"No, you are less than a servant, for you do nothing to earn your keep. There, sit down, and think over your wickedness."

By this time, they had gotten me into the red-room and thrust me on a stool. My impulse was to jump up, but their two pairs of hands held me down.

"If you don't sit still, you will be tied down," said Bessie. "Miss Abbot, lend me your garters; she would break mine."

Miss Abbot bent down to remove from her stout leg the elastic bands that held up her heavy stockings. This took a little of the fire out of me.

"Don't take them off," I cried. "I will not stir."

"Be sure that you don't," said Bessie, and when she had determined that I was really calm, she loosened her hold on me. Then she and Miss Abbot stood with folded arms, looking darkly and doubtfully at my face, wondering about my sanity.

"She never did this before," said Bessie at last.

"No, but it was always in her," was the reply. "I've often told Mrs. Reed my opinion about the child, and she agreed with me. She's a dishonest little thing—I never saw a girl of her age with so much deceit."

Bessie, addressing me, said, "You ought to be aware, Miss, that you are dependent upon Mrs. Reed. If she turned you out, you would have to go to the poorhouse."

I had nothing to say to these words; they were not new to me. This reminder had become a vague sing-song in my ear—very painful and crushing.

Miss Abbot joined in. "And you ought not to think you are equal to your cousins just because Mrs. Reed kindly allows you to be brought up with them. They will have a great deal of money someday, and you will have none. It is your place to be humble and try to make yourself agreeable to them."

"What we tell you is for your own good," added Bessie, in a gentle voice. "You should try to be useful and pleasant; then, perhaps, you will have a home here. But if you become rude and emotional, Mrs. Reed will send you away, I am sure."

"Besides," said Miss Abbot to Bessie, "God will punish her. He might strike her dead in the midst of her tantrums, and then where would she go? Come, Bessie, let us leave her. Say your prayers, Miss Eyre, for if you don't repent, something bad might come down the chimney and fetch you away." They left, shutting the door, and locking it behind them.

The red-room was one of the largest and grandest bedrooms in the mansion, yet very seldom slept in. The bed rested on massive pillars of mahogany and was hung with heavy red curtains. The two large windows had blinds that were always drawn down; the carpet was red; the walls were a soft pink. A cushiony easy chair was white, like a pale throne.

The room was chilly because it seldom had a fire; it was silent, because it was remote from the rest of the house; it was solemn, because it was so seldom entered.

The secret of the red-room, the spell which kept it so lonely in spite of its grandeur, was this—here, in this chamber, my uncle, Mr. Reed, breathed his last breath. Here his coffin was carried by the undertakers' men. And since that day, nine years ago, a sense of dreary respect had kept visitors away.

My seat, to which Bessie and the bitter Miss Abbot had left me riveted, was a low ottoman near the marble fireplace. I was not quite sure whether they had locked the door. When I dared to move, I got up and went to see. Alas, yes. No jail was ever more secure.

Returning to my seat, I passed by the mirror. I glanced at it, and the strange little girl gazing back at me, with a white face and arms and glittering eyes of fear, had the effect of a real ghost. It was like one of the tiny phantoms, half-fairy, half-imp, that Bessie's evening stories described as coming out of the moors. I returned to my stool.

Why was I always suffering, always browbeaten, always accused, forever condemned? Why could I never please anyone? Why was it useless to try to win anyone's favour? Eliza, who was headstrong and selfish, was respected. Georgiana, who had a spoiled temper, was never at fault. John was never punished, though he twisted the necks of pigeons, killed little chicks, set the dogs after the sheep, broke the buds off the choicest flowers in the conservatory, called his mother "old girl", bluntly disobeyed her wishes, tore her silk dresses, and was still "her own darling".

I dared not commit a single fault, I strived to obey every duty, and I was called naughty and tiresome, gloomy and sneaky, from morning to noon, and from noon to night.

My head still ached and bled with the blow and fall I had received. No one had scolded John for striking me; and because I had turned against him to avoid further violence, I was hated.

I could not answer the endless question—Why did I suffer? Now, after many years, I see it clearly.

I was out of harmony with Gateshead Hall. I was unlike Mrs. Reed or her children, opposite them in mood. I was useless to them, unable to serve them or add to their pleasure. If I had been a happy, brilliant, careless, handsome, romping child, Mrs. Reed would have been happier with my presence; her children would have been friendlier; the servants would not have made me the scapegoat.

Daylight began to fade from the red-room; it was past four o'clock, and the cloudy afternoon was becoming dreary twilight. I heard the rain still beating on the window, and the wind howled. Little by little my anger faded; my courage sank and I grew cold as stone. My self-doubt and depression returned. Everyone said I was wicked, and perhaps I was. I thought about starving myself to death—did I even deserve to die? Was the burial vault at Gateshead Church calling me?

In such vault I had been told Mr. Reed lay buried. I could not remember him, but I knew that he was my own uncle—my mother's brother—that he had brought me to this house, as an infant, after my parents died; and in his last breath he had made his wife, Mrs. Reed, promise that she would raise me as one of her own children.

Mrs. Reed probably thought she had kept his promise; and so she had, I daresay, as well as her nature would permit her. But how could she really like a child not related to her, after her husband's death? It must have been most annoying to be tied to a pledge—to replace a parent to a strange child whom she could not love, one who permanently intruded on her own family.

I never doubted that if Uncle Reed had been alive he would have treated me kindly; and now, I began to recall what I had heard about dead men—lying troubled in their graves when their last wishes were not obeyed, revisiting the earth to punish the guilty and avenge those who had been hurt. Then I thought that Mr. Reed's spirit might leave its resting place— whether in the church vault or in the unknown world of the departed— and rise before me in this chamber.

I wiped my tears and hushed my sobs, fearful that any sign of my grief might awaken a supernatural voice to comfort me, or bring some haloed face to bend over me. This would be terrible, and I tried to stifle the idea.

Shaking my hair from my eyes, I lifted my head and looked round the dark room. At this moment, a light gleamed on the wall. Was it the moon shining through the blinds? No, moonlight was still, and this moved. While I gazed, it glided up to the ceiling and trembled over my head. I now believe this streak of light was probably the gleam from a lantern carried by someone across the lawn; but back then, with my mind prepared for horror and my nerves shaken, I thought the darting beam was a vision from the spirit world.

My heart beat quickly and my head grew hot. I heard a sound, a rushing of wings, near me. I felt myself suffocating; I rushed to the door, desperately shook the lock, and screamed.

Steps came running along the gallery, the key turned, and Bessie and Miss Abbot entered the red-room.

"Miss Eyre, are you ill?" said Bessie.

"What a dreadful noise!" exclaimed Miss Abbot. "It went quite through me!"

"Let me out!" I cried. "Take me into the nursery!"

"What for? Are you hurt? Have you seen something?" again demanded Bessie.

"I saw a light, and I thought a ghost would come." I had now grabbed Bessie's hand.

"She screamed on purpose," declared Miss Abbot, with disgust. "And what a scream! If she had been in great pain, one would have excused it, but she only wanted to bring us all here. I know her naughty tricks."

"What is all this?" demanded Mrs. Reed, as she came along the gallery, her gown rustling. "Abbot and Bessie, I believe I gave orders that Jane Eyre should be left in the red-room till I came to her myself."

"Miss Jane screamed so loud, ma'am," pleaded Bessie.

"Let her go," was the only answer. "Let go of Bessie's hand, child. You cannot succeed in getting out by these means. It is my duty to show you that tricks will not work. You will now stay here an hour longer, and I shall only free you if you are perfectly still."

"Oh, Aunt," I screamed. "Have pity! Forgive me! I cannot endure it! Let me be punished some other way! I shall be killed if—"

"Silence! This outburst is most repulsive."

Bessie and Miss Abbot retreated, and Mrs. Reed, impatient of my wild sobs of anguish, abruptly thrust me back and locked me in. I heard her walk away; and soon after she was gone, I fainted.

Chapter 3

The next thing I remember was waking up with a feeling that I had a frightful nightmare. I heard voices, too, and someone was sitting me up, more tenderly than I had ever been raised before. I rested my head against a pillow and felt easy.

In five minutes more, I knew that I was in my own bed. It was night, the fireplace was warm, a candle burnt on the table, and Bessie stood by, and a stranger sat in a chair near my pillow, leaning over me.

I felt a great relief—of protection and security—when I knew that there was a stranger in the room, someone not belonging to Gateshead and not related to Mrs. Reed. I recognized the gentleman as Mr. Lloyd, an apothecary, sometimes called in by Mrs. Reed when the servants were sick—for herself and the children, she called a doctor.

"Well, dear, who am I?" he asked.

I spoke his name and offered my hand; he took it, smiling and saying, "We shall soon do very well." Then he laid me down and instructed Bessie that I was not to be disturbed during the night. After saying he would call again the next day, he departed, to my grief—I felt so safe with him there and, as he left, the room darkened and my heart sank again with unbearable sadness.

"Do you feel as if you could sleep, Miss?" asked Bessie, rather softly.

"I will try."

"Would you like something to drink or eat?"

"No, thank you, Bessie."

"Then I shall go to bed, for it is past twelve o'clock; but you may call me if you want anything in the night."

How polite she was! It gave me courage to ask a question.

"Bessie, what is the matter with me? Am I ill?"

"You fell sick, I suppose, in the red-room with crying; you'll be better soon, no doubt."

Bessie went into the housemaid's apartment, which was near. I heard her say, "Sarah, come and sleep with me in the nursery. I dare not be alone with that poor child tonight—she might die. Mrs. Reed was rather too hard."

Sarah and Bessie both went to bed, and soon the fire and the candle went out. For me, the long night passed with many ghastly fits of wakefulness, full of fear, the fear that only children can feel.

No lasting illness followed this incident in the red-room; it only gave my nerves a shock which I feel even to this day. Yes, Mrs. Reed, you gave me fearful pangs of mental suffering. But I ought to forgive you, for you knew not what you did—you thought you were only curing my bad habits.

The next day, by noon, I was up and dressed, and sat wrapped in a shawl by the fireplace. I felt physically weak and broken down, but my worst ailment was misery, which kept the tears flowing down my cheeks. I should have been happy, for none of the Reeds were at home; but, in fact, my nerves were so raw that nothing could soothe them.

Bessie brought up from the kitchen a lovely tart on a certain brightly painted plate—a piece of china which I had always admired and often asked to hold, but had always been told I was unworthy of such a privilege.

With the precious plate on my knee, I was invited to eat the delicate pastry upon it. But I could not, and put the plate and tart aside.

Bessie asked if I would like a book, and I begged her to fetch Gulliver's Travels from the library. This book had delighted me again and again. I never doubted that one day I might take a long voyage and see with my own eyes the little houses, trees, and diminutive people of Lilliput; and the monster cats and towering men and women of Brobdingnag. Yet now, when this cherished book was placed in my hand, all was eerie and dreary. I closed the book and put it on the table, beside the untasted tart.

Bessie now began dusting and tidying the room. Meanwhile, she sang a song in her sweet voice.

"My feet they are sore, and my limbs they are weary;
Long is the way, and the mountains are wild;
Soon will the twilight close moonless and dreary,
Over the path of the poor orphan child."

By the close of the song, my tears were flowing.

"Come, Miss Jane, don't cry," said Bessie as she finished. But how could she understand my suffering?

Later in the morning Mr. Lloyd came again. "What, already up!" said he, as he entered the nursery. "Well, nurse, how is she?"

Bessie answered that I was doing very well.

"Then she ought to look more cheerful. Miss Jane—your name is Jane, is it not?"

"Yes, sir, Jane Eyre."

"Well, you have been crying, Miss Jane Eyre. Can you tell me what about? Have you any pain?"

"No, sir."

"Oh! I daresay she is crying because she could not go out with Mrs. Reed in the carriage," interrupted Bessie.

"Surely not!" said Mr. Lloyd. "She is too old for such pettiness."

I thought so too. I answered promptly, "I never cried for that—I hate going out in the carriage. I cry because I am miserable."

"Oh no, Miss!" said Bessie.

The good apothecary appeared a little puzzled. He fixed his eyes on me very steadily and, having studied me, said, "What made you ill yesterday?"

"She had a fall," said Bessie, again putting in her word.

"Fall!" he said. "Can't she walk at her age? She must be eight or nine years old."

"I was knocked down," I said bluntly, "but that did not make me ill."

A loud bell rang for the servants' dinner; Mr. Lloyd knew what it was.

"That's for you, nurse," said he. "You can go downstairs; I'll give Miss Jane a lecture till you come back."

Bessie would rather have stayed, but she had to go, because punctuality at meals was rigidly enforced at Gateshead Hall.

"If the fall did not make you ill, what did, then?" asked Mr. Lloyd when Bessie was gone.

"I was shut up in a room, where there is a ghost, till after dark."

I saw Mr. Lloyd smile and frown at the same time.

"Ghost! What, are you a baby? You are afraid of ghosts?"

"Yes, of Mr. Reed's ghost I am—he died in that room and was laid out there. Neither Bessie nor anyone else will go into it at night, and it was cruel to shut me up alone without a candle—so cruel that I shall never forget it."

"Nonsense! And that makes you so miserable? Are you afraid in the daylight, as well?"

"No, but night will come again soon. Besides, I am unhappy—very unhappy—about other things."

"What other things? Can you tell me some of them?"

How much I wished to reply to this question! Children can feel, but they cannot express themselves in words. Fearful, however, of losing this first and only opportunity of releasing my grief, I tried to give a true answer.

"For one thing, I have no father or mother, brothers or sisters."

"You have a kind aunt and cousins."

Again I paused, then clumsily announced, "But John Reed knocked me down, and my aunt shut me up in the red-room."

"Don't you think Gateshead Hall is a very beautiful house?" asked he. "Are you not thankful to have such a fine place to live?"

"It is not my house, sir, and Miss Abbot says I have less right to be here than a servant."

"Pooh! You can't be silly enough to wish to leave such a splendid place?"

"If I had anywhere else to go, I would be glad to leave it; but I can never get away from Gateshead till I am a woman."

"Perhaps you may. Who knows? Have you any relatives besides Mrs. Reed?"

"I think not, sir."

"None belonging to your father?"

"I don't know. I asked Aunt Reed once, and she said possibly I might have some poor relatives named Eyre, but she knew nothing about them."

"If you did, would you like to go to them?"

I reflected. Poverty looks grim to grown people and still more grim to children—they think of the poor only as having ragged clothes, little food, and rude manners.

"No, I should not like to belong to poor people," was my reply.

"Not even if they were kind to you?"

I shook my head. I could not see how poor people could be kind. And then to learn to speak like them, to adopt their manners, to be uneducated— no, I was not brave enough to gain freedom at the price of poverty.

"Would you like to go to school?"

Again I reflected. I hardly knew what school was. John Reed hated his school, and abused his headmaster. But Bessie spoke of young ladies' accomplishments at school—beautiful paintings of landscapes and flowers, songs they could sing, and pieces they could play, purses they could net, French books they could translate. Besides, school would be a complete change—a long journey, a complete break from Gateshead, an entrance into a new life.

"I should indeed like to go to school," was my answer.

"Well, well! Who knows what may happen?" said Mr. Lloyd, as he got up. "This child ought to have change of air and scene," he added, speaking to himself. "Her nerves are not in a good state."

Bessie now returned and, at the same moment Mrs. Reed's carriage was heard rolling up the gravel walk.

"Is that Mrs. Reed, nurse?" asked Mr. Lloyd. "I should like to speak to her before I go."

Bessie invited him to walk into the breakfast room where Mrs. Reed sat. In the conversation that followed, Mr. Lloyd recommended my being sent to school, and it was readily accepted.

That night, I overheard Miss Abbot say to Bessie, "Mrs. Reed will be glad to get rid of such a tiresome, ill-behaved child, who always seems to be watching everybody, and scheming plots behind her back."

That night I also learned, for the first time, from their conversation, that my mother, being a Reed, was as wealthy as Uncle Reed, but my father had been a poor clergyman; that my mother had married him against the wishes of my grandfather Reed, who considered the marriage beneath her; that he was so irritated, he cut her off without a shilling; that after my parents had been married a year, my father caught typhus fever while helping the poor; that my mother caught the infection from him, and both died within a month of each other. When Bessie heard this, she sighed and said, "Poor Miss Jane is to be pitied, too, Abbot."

"Yes," responded Abbot, "if she was a nice, pretty child, one might feel compassion; but one really cannot care for such a little toad as that."

"Not a great deal, to be sure," agreed Bessie.

Chapter 4

A change seemed near; it gave me enough hope to get well. I waited in silence, but days and weeks passed with no mention of my leaving. Mrs. Reed glared at me, but seldom spoke. Since my illness, she had separated me more than ever from her own children. She made me sleep in a small closet by myself, eat my meals alone, and spend all my time in the nursery, while my cousins were constantly in the drawing room.

Eliza and Georgiana, on their mother's orders, spoke to me as little as possible. John thrust his tongue out whenever he saw me, and once attempted to punish me; but I instantly turned against him, striking his ugly nose with the hardest blow my knuckles could inflict. He ran to his Mama, blubbering how "that nasty Jane Eyre" had flown at him like a mad cat. Mrs. Reed stopped him rather harshly:

"Don't talk to me about her, John. I told you not to go near her. Neither you nor your sisters should associate with her."

Leaning over the banister, I cried out suddenly, "They are not fit to associate with me."

On hearing my bold declaration, Mrs. Reed, though she was a rather heavy woman, flew up the stairs, swept me like a whirlwind into the nursery and, crushing me down on the edge of my crib, dared me to leave the room or utter one syllable during the remainder of the day.

Suddenly, without even realizing the words I spoke, I demanded, "What would Uncle Reed say to you, if he were alive?"

"What?" said Mrs. Reed in a whisper. Her cold eyes filled with fear. She removed her hand from my arm.

I knew I was in for it now, but I pressed on.

"My Uncle Reed is in heaven and can see everything you do and think, and so can Papa and Mama. They know how you shut me up all day long, and how you wish me dead."

Mrs. Reed quickly regained her energy. She shook me hard, punched both my ears, and then left without a word. Bessie gave me a sermon for an hour that proved beyond a doubt that I was the most wicked child that ever lived. I half-believed her, for I felt only bad feelings in my heart.

November, December, and half of January passed by. Christmas and the New Year were celebrated at Gateshead with the usual festive cheer—presents exchanged, dinners and evening parties given. I was, of course, excluded from every enjoyment. My share of the celebration was watching Eliza and Georgiana dressed up in beautiful dresses and scarlet sashes, with their hair elaborately done, and listening to the sound of the piano or the harp played downstairs, and watching the butler and footman hand out refreshments.

When I grew tired of all this, I would return to my silent nursery. Though sad, I was not miserable. To speak the truth, I had no wish to be with company, for I was rarely noticed. If Bessie had been kind, I would have enjoyed spending the evenings quietly with her in the nursery; but she would go back down to the kitchen, taking the candle with her, leaving me alone.

I would then sit with my doll on my knee till the fire got low, glancing round occasionally to make sure that no ghosts haunted the dark room. I then quickly undressed and found comfort in my crib. To this crib I always took my doll—human beings must love something and, with no one else to love, I found pleasure in cherishing my shabby doll. I could not sleep unless it was folded into my nightgown; and when it lay there safe and warm, I was happy, believing it to be happy also.

For hours I waited for the company to leave, and listened for the sound of Bessie's steps on the stairs. Sometimes she would come up during the parties and bring me some supper—a bun or a cheese cake—then she would sit on the bed while I ate it, and when I had finished, she would tuck the blanket round me, and kiss me twice, and say, "Goodnight, Miss Jane."

When she was gentle, Bessie seemed to me the best, prettiest, kindest person in the world; and I dearly wished that she would always be so pleasant, and never push me, or scold me, as she too often did. I think Bessie must have been a nice girl. She was pretty too—a slim young woman, with black hair, dark eyes, very nice features, and good, clear skin; but she had a quick temper. Still, I preferred her to anyone else at Gateshead Hall.

It was the fifteenth of January, about nine o'clock in the morning. Bessie was downstairs, my cousins had not yet been summoned to their Mama, and Eliza was putting on her bonnet and coat to feed her chickens. She was fond of selling the eggs to the housekeeper and saving the money. She had a knack for business, not only with eggs, but also in driving hard bargains with the gardener, selling him flowers, seeds, and plants—he had orders from Mrs. Reed to buy everything Eliza had to sell.

Eliza would have sold the hair off her head if she could have made a handsome profit. She first hid her money in odd places, wrapped in a rag, but it was soon discovered by the housemaid. So one day, Eliza, fearful of losing her valued treasure, entrusted it to her mother and charged her an enormous rate of interest—fifty or sixty percent—which she demanded every quarter, keeping her accounts in a little book with great accuracy.

I was making my bed, having been ordered by Bessie to be an under-nursery maid, to tidy the room and dust the chairs. Then, with nothing else to do, I went to the window and breathed on the snowflakes that had frozen to the glass, clearing a space to look outside.

From this window, I saw the gates thrown open and a carriage roll through. It stopped in front of the house, the doorbell rang loudly, and the guest was admitted.

All this meant nothing to me. Then I saw a hungry little robin perched outside my window. My breakfast of break and milk stood on the table, and I took some crumbs to place on the window sill, when Bessie came running upstairs into the nursery.

"Miss Jane, what are you doing? Have you washed your hands and face this morning?"

"No, Bessie, I have only just finished dusting."

Bessie hauled me to the washstand, gave me a brief scrub on my face and hands, combed my hair with a bristly brush, and then hurried me to the top of the stairs and told me to go down directly, as I was wanted in the breakfast room.

I slowly descended. For nearly three months, I had never been called to Mrs. Reed's presence.

I now stood in the empty hall. I stopped in front of the breakfast room door, trembling. I was afraid to enter the room, but afraid to return to the nursery. For ten minutes, I stood in worried hesitation, until the loud ringing of the breakfast room bell decided for me—I must enter.

With both hands I turned the stiff door handle. The door opened, I entered, curtseyed low, and looked up at—a black pillar! The straight, narrow, darkly-dressed gentleman stood erect, the grim face like a carved mask.

Mrs. Reed occupied her usual seat by the fireside; she signaled me to approach; I did so, and she introduced me to the stony stranger with the words:

"This is the little girl about whom I wrote to you."

He turned his head slowly toward me and, having examined me with curious grey eyes that twinkled under a pair of bushy eyebrows, said solemnly in a deep voice, "Her size is small; what is her age?"

"Ten years."

"So much?" was the doubtful answer; and he stared at me for several minutes. Then he addressed me.

"Your name, little girl?"

"Jane Eyre, sir."

"Well, Jane Eyre, are you a good child?"

I was silent, since it was impossible to reply with a 'yes', since I believed otherwise.

Mrs. Reed answered for me by shaking her head, adding, "Perhaps the less said on that subject the better, Mr. Brocklehurst."

"Sorry indeed to hear it! She and I must have a talk," and bending down, he sat in the armchair opposite Mrs. Reed's. "Come here," he said.

I stepped across the rug and he placed me straight in front of him. What a face he had! What a huge nose! And what a mouth! And what large prominent teeth!

"There is no sight so sad as a naughty little girl," he began. "Do you know where the wicked go after death?"

"They go to hell," was my ready answer.

"And what is hell? Can you tell me that?"

"A pit full of fire."

"And would you like to fall into that pit, and burn there forever?"

"No, sir."

"What must you do to avoid it?"

I deliberated a moment. "I must keep in good health, and not die."

"How can you keep in good health? Children younger than you die every day. I buried a little child, five years old, only a day or two ago—a good little child, whose soul is now in heaven. I fear that the same could not be said of you, if you were to die."

I could only cast my eyes down on the two large feet planted on the rug, and sigh, wishing myself far away.

"I hope that sigh is from the heart, and that you repent of ever causing discomfort to your excellent benefactress."

Benefactress! I thought. If Mrs. Reed was called my benefactress, then that must be a bad thing.

"Do you say your prayers morning and night?" continued my interrogator.

"Yes, sir."

"Do you read your Bible?"

"Sometimes."

"With pleasure? Are you fond of it?"

"I like Revelations, and the book of Daniel, and Genesis and Samuel, and a little bit of Exodus, and some parts of Kings and Chronicles, and Job and Jonah."

"And the Psalms? I hope you like them?"

"No, sir."

"No? Oh, shocking! I have a little boy, younger than you, who knows six Psalms by heart; and when you ask him whether he would prefer gingerbread to eat or a Psalm to learn, he says, 'Oh! The Psalm! Angels sing Psalms. I wish to be a little angel here on earth.'"

"Psalms are not interesting," I remarked.

"That proves you have a wicked heart, and you must pray to God to change it, to give you a new and clean one—to take away your heart of stone and give you a heart of flesh."

I was about to ask a question about how that operation would be performed, when Mrs. Reed interrupted, telling me to sit down.

"Mr. Brocklehurst," she said, "I believe I hinted in the letter which I wrote to you three weeks ago, that this little girl has not quite the character and personality I could wish. Should you admit her into Lowood school, I should be glad if the superintendent and teachers kept a strict eye on her and, above all, to guard against her worst fault, a tendency to lie and be deceitful. I mention this in your presence, Jane, so that you may not be a bother to Mr. Brocklehurst."

No matter how carefully I obeyed Mrs. Reed, or tried to please her, my efforts were always repaid with such sentences as those. Now, spoken before a stranger, the accusation cut me to the heart. I felt that she was turning me, in Mr. Brocklehurst's eyes, into a repulsive child, and what could I do to change it? Nothing, thought I, and I hastily wiped away the tears that came.

"Deceit is, indeed, a sad fault in a child," said Mr. Brocklehurst. "All liars will have their time in the lake, burning with fire and brimstone. We shall watch her, Mrs. Reed. I will speak to the teachers."

"I want her to be brought up to be made useful and kept humble. As for her vacations, she will, with your permission, spend them always at Lowood."

"Your decisions are perfectly just, madam," returned Mr. Brocklehurst.

"Humility is a Christian grace, and one that I cultivate in the pupils of Lowood. Just the other day, I had proof of my success. My second daughter, Augusta, went with her Mama to visit the school and, when she returned, exclaimed, 'Oh, dear papa, how quiet and plain all the girls at Lowood look, with their hair combed behind their ears, and their long pinafores— they are almost like poor people's children! They looked at my dress and Mama's, as if they had never seen a silk gown before.'"

"That is exactly what I approve," returned Mrs. Reed. "Had I searched all of England, I could not have found a school more perfectly fitting a child like Jane Eyre. Consistency, my dear Mr. Brocklehurst—I support consistency in all things."

"Consistency, madam, is the first of Christian duties—plain food, simple dress, plain lodging, hardy and active habits—such is the order of the day at Lowood."

"Quite right, sir. I expect, then, that this child will be accepted as a pupil at Lowood?"

"Madam, you may, and I trust she will be grateful for the privilege."

"I will send her, then, as soon as possible, Mr. Brocklehurst; for I assure you, I am anxious to be relieved of a responsibility that was becoming too irksome."

"No doubt, madam; and now I wish you good morning. I shall be return- ing to Brocklehurst Hall in the next week or two. I shall send a notice to Miss Temple, at Lowood, that she is to expect a new girl. Goodbye."

"Goodbye, Mr. Brocklehurst; remember me to Mrs. and Miss Brocklehurst, and to Augusta and Theodore, and Master Broughton Brocklehurst."

"I will, madam. Little girl, here is a book entitled the 'Child's Guide'. Read it with prayer, especially that part containing 'An account of the awfully sudden death of Martha G., a naughty child addicted to falsehood and deceit.'"

With these words, Mr. Brocklehurst put into my hand a thin pamphlet and, having rung for his carriage, departed.

Mrs. Reed and I were left alone; some minutes passed in silence. She was sewing; I was watching her. Mrs. Reed might have been about thirty- seven at the time. She had a short, robust frame, square-shouldered and strong-limbed. Though stout, she was not fat. She had a somewhat large face, with a solid, jutting jaw. Her health was sound as a bell—illness never came near her. Her household was completely under her control; her chil- dren rarely defied her authority; and she dressed well.

Sitting on a low stool, a few yards from her armchair, I examined her figure and studied her features. In my hand, I held the pamphlet containing the sudden death of the Liar. What had just happened, what Mrs. Reed had said about me to Mr. Brocklehurst, their whole conversation, was raw and stinging in my mind. I felt every word as sharply as I heard it, and a passion of hatred and resentment now grew within me.

Mrs. Reed looked up from her work; her eyes settled on mine.

"Get out of the room; return to the nursery," she ordered. I got up, I went to the door, then I came back again. I walked across the room, then came close to her. I gathered my strength and fired this blunt sentence:

"I am not deceitful. If I were, I would say I loved you; but I declare I do not love you. I dislike you worse than anybody in the world except John Reed; and this book about the liar, you may give to your girl, Georgiana, for it is she who tells lies, and not I."

Mrs. Reed's eyes were ice; they continued to stare at me—freezing.

"What more have you to say?" she asked, in the tone of one adult to another.

Shaking from head to toe, thrilled with uncontrollable excitement, I continued, "I am glad you are no relative of mine. I will never call you aunt again as long as I live. I will never come to see you when I am grown up; and if any one asks me how I liked you, and how you treated me, I will say the very thought of you makes me sick, and that you treated me with miserable cruelty."

"How dare you say that, Jane Eyre!"

"How dare I, Mrs. Reed? How dare I? Because it is the truth. You think I have no feelings, and that I can do without one bit of love or kindness; but I cannot live that way—and you have no pity. I shall remember how you violently thrust me back into the red-room, and locked me up there, to my dying day. Even though I was in agony and cried out, while suffocating with distress, 'Have mercy! Have mercy, Aunt Reed!' And that punishment you made me suffer because your wicked boy struck me—knocked me down for nothing. I will tell anybody who asks me, this exact tale. People think you a good woman, but you are bad and hardhearted. You are deceitful!"

After I finished this reply, my soul felt the strangest sense of freedom, of triumph.

Mrs. Reed looked frightened; she lifted up her hands, rocking herself to and fro, and twisting her face as if she would cry. "Jane, you are mistaken. What is the matter with you? Why do you tremble so violently? Would you like to drink some water?"

"No, Mrs. Reed."

"Is there anything else you wish for, Jane? I assure you, I desire to be your friend."

"No, you don't. You told Mr. Brocklehurst I had a bad character, a deceitful personality; and I'll let everybody at Lowood know what you are, and what you have done."

"Jane, you don't understand these things; children must be corrected for their faults."

"Deceit is not my fault!" I cried out in a savage, high voice.

"But you are passionate, Jane, that you must admit; and now return to the nursery—be a dear—and lie down a little."

"I am not your dear; I cannot lie down; send me to school soon, Mrs. Reed, for I hate to live here."

"I will indeed send her to school soon," murmured Mrs. Reed softly, and she abruptly left the room.

I was left there alone—winner of the hardest battle I had ever fought, and the first victory I had ever gained. I stood awhile on the rug, where Mr. Brocklehurst had stood. At first, I smiled to myself and felt elated; but this pleasure quickly faded. A child cannot quarrel with her elders, as I had done, without afterwards feeling regret.

Though I had tasted revenge for the first time, I would now willingly have asked Mrs. Reed's pardon; but I knew, partly from experience and partly from instinct, that was the way to make her hate me twice as much.

I opened the glass door in the breakfast room and went outside to walk in a quiet part of the estate. I leaned against a gate and looked into an empty field. It was a very grey day, an opaque sky, and then snowflakes drifted down.

I stood, a wretched child, whispering to myself over and over again, "What shall I do? What shall I do?"

All at once I heard a voice call, "Miss Jane! Where are you? Come to lunch!"

I knew it was Bessie, but I did not move. She came tripping down the path.

"You naughty little thing!" she said. "Why don't you come when you are called?"

Bessie's presence seemed cheerful compared to my brooding thoughts, even though she was angry. The fact is, after my victory over Mrs. Reed, I did not much care for Bessie's ill temper.

I put my arms round her and said, "Come, Bessie! Don't scold."

The way I spoke to her was more direct, and more fearless, than ever

Jane Eyre

before; somehow it pleased her.

"You are a strange child, Miss Jane," she said, as she looked down at me. "And you are going to school, I suppose?"

I nodded.

"And won't you be sorry to leave poor Bessie?"

"What does Bessie care for me? She is always scolding me."

"Because you're such a shy, frightened little thing. You should be bolder."

"Why? To get more beatings?"

"Nonsense! But you are taken advantage of, that's certain. My mother said, when she came to see me last week, that she would not like a child of hers to be in your place. Now, come inside. I've some good news for you."

"I don't think you do, Bessie."

"Child! What do you mean? What sad eyes you fix on me! Well, all the Reeds are going out this afternoon, and you shall have tea with me. I'll ask the cook to bake you a little cake, and then you shall help me pack your trunk. Mrs. Reed plans for you to leave Gateshead in a day or two, and you shall choose what toys you would like to take with you."

"Bessie, you must promise not to scold me anymore till I go."

"Well, I will. But remember, you are a very good girl, and don't be afraid of me. Don't jump when I happen to speak sharply; it's so annoying."

"I don't think I shall ever be afraid of you again, Bessie, because I have gotten used to you, and I shall soon have another set of people to fear."

"If you fear them, they'll dislike you."

"As you do, Bessie?"

"I don't dislike you, Miss. I believe I am fonder of you than of all the other children."

"You don't show it."

"You sharp little thing! You've got quite a new way of talking. What makes you so bold and strong?"

I was going to mention what had happened between me and Mrs. Reed, but on second thought I thought it better to remain silent.

Bessie added, "And so you're glad to leave me?"

"Not at all, Bessie; indeed, just now I'm rather sorry."

"Just now! And rather! How coolly my little lady says it! I dare say if I asked you for a kiss, you wouldn't give it to me; you'd say you'd rather not."

"I'll kiss you with pleasure; bend down." Bessie stooped and we embraced, then I followed her into the house quite comforted. That afternoon was spent in peace and harmony; and in the evening Bessie told me some of her most enchanting stories, and sang me some of her sweetest songs. Even for me, life had its gleams of sunshine.

Chapter 5

At five o'clock on the morning of January 19th, Bessie brought a candle into my closet and found me already up and nearly dressed. I had risen half an hour before, and had washed my face and put on my clothes by the light of a half-moon. I was to leave Gateshead that day by coach at six a.m.

Bessie was the only person awake; she had lit a fire in the nursery, where she now made my breakfast. Few children can eat when excited with the thoughts of a journey—nor could I. Bessie wrapped up some biscuits and put them into my bag; then she helped me on with my coat and bonnet and, wrapping herself in a shawl, we left the nursery.

As we passed Mrs. Reed's bedroom, she said, "Will you go in and bid her goodbye?"

"No, Bessie; she came to my crib last night and said I need not disturb her in the morning, or my cousins either; and she told me to remember that she had always been my best friend, and to speak well of her."

"What did you say, Miss?"

"Nothing. I covered my face with my blanket, and turned away from her toward the wall."

"That was wrong, Miss Jane."

"It was quite right, Bessie. Mrs. Reed has not been my friend; she has been my enemy."

"Oh, Miss Jane! Don't say so!"

"Goodbye to Gateshead!" I cried, as we passed through the hall and went out the front door.

The moon had set and it was very dark; Bessie carried a lantern. The winter morning was raw and chilly; my teeth chattered as I hurried down the drive. There was a light in the porter's house. When we entered, we found the porter's wife just starting a fire. My trunk, which had been carried down the evening before, stood by the door.

Shortly after the hour of six o'clock, the distant roll of wheels announced the coming coach. I went to the door and watched it approach through the gloom.

"Is she going by herself?" asked the porter's wife.

"Yes."

"And how far is it?"

"Fifty miles."

"What a long way! I am surprised that Mrs. Reed would let her travel so far alone."

The coach drew up with its four horses, its carriage full of passengers. My trunk was hoisted up, and I was taken from Bessie's neck, to which I clung with kisses.

"Be sure and take good care of her," Bessie cried to the guard, as he lifted me inside.

"Ay, ay!" was the answer. The door was closed, and the coach departed. Thus was I separated from Bessie and Gateshead, whirled away to unknown, distant and mysterious places.

I remember little of the journey; I only know that the day seemed to be never-ending, and that we appeared to travel over hundreds of miles of road. We passed through several towns, and in a very large one, the coach stopped, the horses were taken out, and the passengers stepped out to dine.

I was carried into an inn, where the guard wanted me to have some dinner; but I had no appetite, so he left me in a large room with a fireplace at each end. Here I walked around for a long time, feeling very strange, and fearful of someone kidnapping me; for I believed in kidnappers, after listening to Bessie's fireside stories.

At last the guard returned; once more I was placed in the coach, and away we rattled. The afternoon was wet and misty; as it became dusk, the country changed—great grey hills rose up all around. As twilight deepened, we descended into a valley, dark with woods.

At last I fell asleep, but soon the coach stopped, the door opened, and a person who looked like a servant stood there.

"Is there a little girl called Jane Eyre here?" she asked. I answered 'yes' and was then lifted out; my trunk was handed down, and the coach instantly drove away.

I was stiff from sitting so long. I looked about me. Rain, wind, and darkness filled the air. I dimly saw a wall with a door; my guide led me through it, then she shut and locked it behind her.

I now saw several houses with many windows, and lights burning in some. We went up a broad pebbly path to a house, and were admitted by a servant into a parlor with a fire. There, my guide left me alone.

I stood and warmed my numbed fingers over the blaze, then I looked round; the parlor was not as large or splendid as the drawing room at Gateshead, but comfortable enough. I was staring at a picture on the wall, when the door opened, and a woman entered, carrying a candle; another woman followed close behind.

The first was a tall lady, about twenty-nine, with dark hair, dark eyes, and a pale and large forehead; she wore a shawl, her face was serious, her posture erect.

"The child is very young to be sent alone," said she, putting her candle down on the table. She gazed at me attentively for a minute or two, then added, "She had better be put to bed soon; she looks tired." She placed her hand on my shoulder. "Are you tired?" she asked.

"A little, ma'am."

"And hungry too, no doubt. Let her have some supper before she goes to bed, Miss Miller. Is this the first time you have left your parents to come to school, my little girl?"

I explained to her that I had no parents. She asked how long they had been dead, how old I was, what was my name, whether I could read, write, and sew a little, then she touched my cheek gently with her forefinger, and said, "I hope you will be a good child," then dismissed me along with Miss Miller.

Miss Miller looked several years younger than the other woman, and was more ordinary—a ruddy face, and hurried, like someone who had many tasks to do—she looked like what I afterwards found she really was, a teacher's assistant.

Led by her, I passed through several passages till we heard the hum of many voices and entered a wide, long schoolroom, with a great deal of tables, on each of which burned a pair of candles. Seated all around on benches were countless girls of every age, from nine to twenty. They were uniformly dressed in brown frocks of quaint fashion, and long linen pinafores. It was the hour of study; they were engaged in talking about their tasks for tomorrow, and the hum I had heard was their combined whispers.

Miss Miller had me sit on a bench near the door, then walking to the end of the long room, she cried out, "Monitors, collect the lesson books and put them away!"

Four tall girls arose from different tables, and going round, gathered the books and removed them.

Miss Miller again gave the word of command, "Monitors, fetch the supper trays!"

The tall girls went out and returned presently, each carrying a tray of food, and a pitcher of water and mug in the middle of each tray. The food was passed around, and the girls all took a sip of water from the same mug.

When it came to my turn, I drank, for I was thirsty, but did not touch the food—I was too tired to eat—and I saw that it was a thin oat cake cut into pieces.

After the meal, prayers were read by Miss Miller, and the girls filed out in a line of pairs, and went upstairs. Overcome by this time with weariness, I barely noticed that the bedroom was also very long.

Tonight I was to be Miss Miller's bedmate; she helped me to undress, and when I laid down I saw the long rows of beds, each with two girls. In ten minutes, the single light went out, and in the silence and complete darkness, I fell asleep.

The night passed rapidly. I was too tired even to dream. When I opened my eyes, a loud bell was ringing; the girls were up and dressing. Daylight had not yet dawned, and a candle or two burned in the room. I too rose reluctantly; it was bitter cold; shivering, I dressed as well as I could.

There was one wash bowl for every six girls, mounted on stands down the middle of the room. After a long wait, I washed. Again the bell rang; all the girls formed a single file line, two and two, descended the stairs and entered the cold and dimly lit schoolroom. Here, prayers were read by Miss Miller.

Afterwards she called out, "Form classes!"

A great commotion lasted several minutes, during which Miss Miller repeatedly exclaimed, "Silence!" and "Order!"

When it quieted, I saw four girls standing around each table, where one vacant chair awaited a teacher, and a large Bible on each table.

Another bell tinkled; immediately the teachers entered the room; each walked to a table and took her seat. Miss Miller assumed her chair and I stood at her table.

Business now began, the day's prayer was repeated, certain verses of Scripture were said, and then a long reading of chapters in the Bible, which lasted an hour. By the time that exercise was over, the day had fully dawned.

The ever-present bell now sounded for the fourth time. The classes were marched into another room to breakfast; how glad I was to get something to eat! I was now nearly sick from hunger, having eaten so little the day before.

The dining hall was a great, low-ceiled, gloomy room; on two long tables sat large bowls of something hot, which, to my dismay, had an unpleasant odor. When the smell reached the tall girls of the first class, I heard the whispered words, "How disgusting! The porridge is burnt again!"

"Silence!" exclaimed a voice—not that of Miss Miller, but one of the upper teachers, a dark, little person, smartly dressed, but of a gloomy appearance. I looked for Miss Miller and saw her at the other end of my long table. The head of my table was occupied by a strange, foreign-looking, elderly lady, the French teacher, as I afterwards found out. A long grace was said and a hymn sung; then a servant brought in some tea for the teachers, and the meal began.

Famished and now very faint, I devoured a spoonful or two without thinking of its taste, until I realized it that burnt porridge is almost as bad as rotten potatoes. The spoons moved slowly—I watched the girls taste their food and try to swallow it, but in most cases they could not.

Breakfast was over, and no one had eaten. We said a prayer of thanks for what we had not gotten, chanted a second hymn, then left the dining hall to file into the schoolroom. I was one of the last to go out, and I saw one teacher taste the porridge. She looked at the other teachers, their faces showed displeasure, and one of them said, "Dreadful stuff! How shameful!"

A quarter of an hour passed before lessons again began, during which the schoolroom was a noisy commotion, with the girls permitted to talk loud and freely. Everyone complained about the breakfast. Poor things!

The clock struck nine, and Miss Miller stood in the middle of the room, and cried, "Silence! To your seats!"

In five minutes, the disorganized room was now in order, and silence reigned. The teachers now resumed their posts, but still, everyone seemed to wait. Lined up on benches down the sides of the room, the eighty girls sat motionless and erect.

Suddenly the whole school rose at once and a lady entered the room, whom I later learned was Miss Temple—Maria Temple—superintendent of Lowood. As she walked slowly up and down, silently surveying the girls, I studied her. Miss Temple was tall, fair, and shapely, with a stately air and refined features, and brown eyes with a kindness in them. Her dress was purple, with black velvet trimming. A gold watch shone at her waist.

Miss Miller said aloud, "Monitor of the first class, fetch the globes!" Then Miss Temple took her seat before the pair of globes and gave the first class a lesson in geography.

The lower classes, which included me, received an hour of lessons in history and grammar from the other teachers. Next came writing and arithmetic, while music lessons were given by Miss Temple to some of the older girls.

At last the clock struck twelve. Miss Temple rose and said, "I have a word to address to the pupils. This morning you had a breakfast which you could not eat. You must be hungry. I have ordered that a lunch of bread and cheese shall be served to all."

The teachers looked at her with surprise. Miss Temple immediately left the room. The bread and cheese was brought in and distributed, to the great delight and refreshment of the whole school.

The order was now given, "To the garden!"

Each girl put on a straw bonnet and a cloak. I was similarly dressed and, following the girls, I made my way into the open air.

The garden was large, surrounded by high walls. A covered veranda ran down one side. The garden was divided into little flower beds—these were assigned as gardens for the pupils to cultivate, and each bed had an owner. When spring came, the flowers would look pretty; but now, at the end of January, all was wintry ruin and brown decay.

I shuddered as I stood and looked round me. It was an unpleasant day for outdoor exercise—not rainy, but darkened by a drizzly yellow fog. The ground was still soaking wet from the floods of yesterday. The stronger girls ran around and played games, but many pale and thin girls huddled together for shelter and warmth in the veranda; and among these, I frequently heard the sound of a hollow cough.

I had not yet spoken to anyone, nor did anybody seem to take notice of me; I stood alone, but I was accustomed to loneliness. I leaned against a pillar of the veranda, drew my grey coat close about me and, trying to forget the cold which nipped me, and the hunger which gnawed me within, began watching and thinking.

I hardly knew where I was; Gateshead and my past life seemed far away, the present was strange, and of the future I had no idea. I looked round the garden, and then up at the house—a large building, half of which was grey and old, the other half quite new. The new part, containing the school-room and dormitory, had church-like windows.

A stone tablet over the door bore this inscription: 'Lowood Institution. This portion was rebuilt by Naomi Brocklehurst, of Brocklehurst Hall. Let your light so shine before men, that they may see your good works, and glorify your Father which is in heaven. St. Matthew, v. 16.'

Jane Eyre

I read these words over and over again. I was unable to fully understand their meaning. I was still pondering the word 'Institution' when the sound of a cough close behind me made me turn my head. I saw a girl sitting on a stone bench nearby; she was bent over a book, reading intently, and I saw that the title was 'Rasselas', a name that struck me as strange and somewhat attractive.

She happened to look up, and I said to her, "Is your book interesting?"

"I like it," she answered, as she examined me.

"What is it about?" I continued. I hardly know where I found the courage to begin a conversation with a stranger—it was so unlike my nature—but since I also enjoyed reading, I felt a connection with her.

"You may look at it," replied the girl, offering me the book.

I took it, but quickly glancing at the pages, it looked much more dull than the title—there were no fairies or genies, and the printing was too small. I returned it to her; she was about to continue reading, when I ventured another question.

"Can you tell me what the writing on that stone over the door means? What is Lowood Institution?"

"It is this house where you have come to live."

"And why do they call it an institution? Is it in any way different from other schools?"

"It is partly a charity school; you and I, and all the rest of us, are charity children. I suppose you are an orphan—are not either your father or your mother dead?"

"Both died before I can remember."

"Well, all the girls here have lost either one or both parents, and this is called an institution for educating orphans."

"Do we pay any money? Do they keep us for nothing?"

"We pay, or our friends pay, fifteen pounds a year."

"Then why do they call us charity children?"

"Because fifteen pounds is not enough for board and teaching, and the rest is donated."

"Who donates?"

"Wealthy, charity-minded ladies and gentlemen in this neighbourhood and in London."

"Who was Naomi Brocklehurst?"

"The lady who built the new part of this house, and whose son overlooks and directs everything here."

"Why?"

"Because he is treasurer and manager of the institution."

"Then this house does not belong to that tall lady who wears a watch, and who said we were to have some bread and cheese?"

"Miss Temple? Oh, no! I wish it did. She has to answer to Mr. Brocklehurst. He buys all our food and clothes."

"Does he live here?"

"No, two miles away, at Brocklehurst Hall, a large estate."

"Is he a good man?"

"He is a clergyman; they say he does a great deal of good."

"Did you say that tall lady was called Miss Temple?"

"Yes."

"And what are the other teachers called?"

"The one with red cheeks is called Miss Smith—she cuts the cloth for us to make our own clothes, and everything; the little one with black hair is Miss Scatcherd—she teaches history and grammar; and the one who wears a shawl, and has a pocket handkerchief tied to her side with a yellow ribbon, is Madame Pierrot—she comes from Lisle, in France, and teaches French."

"Do you like the teachers?"

"Well enough."

"Do you like the little black-haired one, and the Madame—I cannot pronounce her name as you do."

"Miss Scatcherd is impatient—you must take care not to offend her; Madame Pierrot is not a bad sort of person."

"But Miss Temple is the best—isn't she?"

"Miss Temple is very good and very smart; she is above the rest, because she knows far more than they do."

"Have you been here long?"

"Two years."

"Are you an orphan?"

"My mother is dead."

"Are you happy here?"

"You ask rather too many questions. I have given you enough answers for now. I want to read."

But at that moment the bell sounded for dinner and everyone re-entered the house. The odor which now filled the dining room was hardly more appetizing than breakfast. The dinner was served in two huge bowls, which smelled of disgusting fat. I found the mess to consist of potatoes and strange pieces of rusty meat, mixed and cooked together. A large plateful

Jane Eyre

was given to each girl. I ate what I could, and wondered whether every meal would be like this.

After dinner, we immediately filed into the schoolroom; more lessons continued till five o'clock. During the afternoon, the girl with whom I had spoken was sent away in disgrace from a history class by Miss Scatcherd, and sent to stand in the middle of the large schoolroom. The punishment seemed humiliating to me, especially since the girl looked at least fourteen.

I expected her to be greatly distressed and shamed, but to my surprise she neither wept nor blushed. "How can she bear it so quietly, so firmly?" I asked of myself. "Were I in her place, it seems to me I would wish the earth to open and swallow me up. She looks as if she were daydreaming. I wonder what sort of a girl she is—whether good or naughty."

Soon after five o'clock we had another meal, consisting of a small mug of coffee and half a slice of brown bread. I devoured my bread and drank my coffee, but I would have been glad with much more—I was still hungry. Afterwards, we had half an hour of recreation, then study. Then the glass of water and the piece of oat cake, prayers, and bed. Such was my first day at Lowood.

Chapter 6

The next day began as before, getting up and dressing by candlelight; but this morning we were unable to wash—the water in the pitchers was frozen.

Before the hour and a half of prayers and Bible reading was over, I felt I would die from the cold. Breakfast time came at last, and this morning the porridge was not burnt—the quality was eatable, the quantity small. How small my portion seemed! I wished it had been doubled.

During the day I was enrolled a member of the fourth class and assigned regular tasks. At first, being unaccustomed to memorizing, the lessons seemed long and difficult. I was glad when, about three o'clock in the afternoon, Miss Smith put into my hands a border of cotton two yards long, together with a needle, thread and thimble, and sent me to sit in a quiet corner of the schoolroom, and ordered me to hem the cloth.

At that hour, most of the girls were also sewing; but one class still stood round Miss Scatcherd's chair, reading English history. Their lessons could be easily heard. Among the readers, I noticed my new friend from the veranda. At the beginning of the lesson, she had been placed at the head of the class, but for some error of pronunciation she was suddenly sent to the very bottom. Still, Miss Scatcherd continued to criticize her. She called her by her surname, as all the girls were:

"Burns, you are standing on the side of your shoe; turn your toes out immediately." And, "Burns, you poke your chin out most unpleasantly; draw it in." And, "Burns, I insist you hold your head up."

After the chapter had been read twice, the books were closed and the girls were tested. Most of the girls were unable to answer the questions, but Burns answered every question correctly. I kept expecting Miss Scatcherd to praise her, but instead, she suddenly cried out:

"You dirty, disagreeable girl! You never cleaned your nails this morning!"

Burns made no answer—I wondered at her silence. I thought, "Why does she not explain that the water was frozen?"

My attention was now turned to Miss Smith, who asked me to hold a spool of thread; while she was winding it, she talked to me from time to time, and so I could not observe Miss Schatcherd.

When Miss Smith left, I saw that Burns had walked into the book closet. She soon returned, carrying a bundle of twigs tied together. She presented it to Miss Scatcherd with a respectful curtsey. Then, without being told, she quietly loosened her pinafore from around her neck. The teacher instantly and sharply whipped her neck a dozen times with the bunch of twigs. Not a tear came to Burns' eye, nor did her face flinch.

"Hardened girl!" exclaimed Miss Scatcherd. "Nothing can correct you of your filthy habits. Carry the rod away."

Burns obeyed and, as she emerged from the book closet, she was just putting her handkerchief back into her pocket, and the trace of a tear glistened on her thin cheek.

The play hour in the evening was the pleasantest part of the day at Lowood; the bit of bread and the sip of coffee, swallowed at five o'clock, revived me a bit, even if it had not satisfied my hunger. And the schoolroom felt warmer than in the morning, its fires being allowed to burn a little more brightly.

That evening, I wandered about as usual without a friend, yet not feeling lonely. When I passed the windows, I lifted a blind and looked out; it snowed hard, and I heard the gloomy moan of the wind outside.

Probably, if I had left a good home and kind parents, the wind would have saddened my heart; as it was, I felt a strange, reckless excitement from it, and wished the wind to howl more wildly and the gloom to deepen to darkness.

I made my way to one of the fireplaces. There, I found Burns, reading silently by the dim glare of the embers.

"Is it still 'Rasselas'?" I asked, coming behind her.

"Yes," she said, "and I have just finished it." She closed her book. I was glad, for now perhaps I could get her to talk. I sat down beside her on the floor.

"What is your name besides Burns?"

"Helen."

"Do you live a long way from here?"

"I come from a place on the border of Scotland."

"Will you ever go back?"

"I hope so; but nobody can be sure of the future."

"You must wish to leave Lowood."

"No! Why should I? I was sent to Lowood to get an education, and it would be no use going away until I have."

"But that teacher, Miss Scatcherd, is so cruel to you."

"Cruel? Not at all! She is severe—she dislikes my faults."

"If I were in your place, I would dislike her—I would resist her. If she struck me with that rod, I would get it from her hand and break it under her nose."

"You would probably do nothing of the sort; but if you did, Mr. Brocklehurst would expel you from the school, and that would be a great grief to your relatives. It is far better to patiently endure a pain which nobody feels but yourself, than to do something whose consequences will affect everyone connected to you; and besides, the Bible asks us to return evil with good."

"But it seems disgraceful to be flogged, and to be sent to stand in the middle of a room full of people; you are such a great girl—I am far younger than you, and I could not bear it."

"Yet it would be your duty to bear it, if you could not avoid it. It is weak and silly to say that you cannot bear something, if you are required to."

I heard her with wonder. I could not understand her rule of accepting punishment, and still less could I understand or sympathize with her forgiveness toward her punisher. Still, I felt that Helen Burns saw things by a different light than I. I suspected that she might be right and I might be wrong; but I chose to put the matter off till another time.

"You say you have faults, Helen. What are they? To me you seem very good."

"Then learn from me and not judge by appearances. I am, as Miss Scatcherd said, filthy; I seldom keep things in order; I am careless; I forget rules; I read when I should learn my lessons; and sometimes, like you, I say I cannot bear to follow the rules. This is all very annoying to Miss Scatcherd, who is naturally neat, punctual, and particular."

"And cross and cruel," I added; but Helen Burns would not agree—she kept silent.

"Is Miss Temple as severe to you as Miss Scatcherd?"

At the mention of Miss Temple's name, a soft smile flitted over her grave face.

"Miss Temple is full of goodness; it pains her to be harsh to anyone, even the worst in the school. She sees my errors and tells me of them gently; and if I do anything worthy of praise, she praises me greatly. One strong proof of my wretchedness is that even Miss Temple's kindness has not cured me of my faults; and even her praise cannot make me be more careful."

Jane Eyre

"That is curious," said I, "for it is so easy to be careful."

"For you it is. I observed you in your class this morning, and saw that you paid close attention. Your thoughts never seemed to wander while Miss Miller explained the lesson and questioned you. Now, my thoughts continually drift away; when I should be listening to Miss Scatcherd, often I fall into sort of a dream. Then, when it is my turn to reply, I have to be awakened; and having heard nothing of what was read, I have no answer ready."

"Yet you replied so well this afternoon."

"The subject we had been reading about, King Charles I, interested me. I wondered how a man with such integrity as he, who wished to do right, could act so unwisely. Still, I like Charles; I respect him, I pity him—poor murdered king!"

Helen had forgotten that I was ignorant of the subject she discussed. I brought her back to my level.

"And when Miss Temple teaches you, do your thoughts wander?"

"No, not often, because Miss Temple generally teaches me something that I often wish to learn."

"Well, then, with Miss Temple you are well-behaved?"

"Yes, I am good when I feel like it. But there is no merit in such goodness."

"Yes, there is a great deal of merit—you are good to those who are good to you. It is all I ever desire to be. If people were always kind to those who are cruel, then the wicked people would have it all their own way. They would never feel afraid, so they would never change, but would grow worse and worse. When we are whipped without a reason, we should strike back again very hard. I am sure we should—so hard as to teach the person who struck us never to do it again."

"I hope you will change your mind when you grow older; now you are a little girl who has not yet learned."

"But I feel this, Helen—I must hate those who, no matter what I do to please them, continue to hate me; I must resist those who punish me unjustly. And it is just as natural that I should love those who show me affection, or accept punishment when I feel I deserve it."

"Heathens and savage tribes hold that belief; but Christians and civilized nations do not."

"How? I don't understand."

"Violence does not overcome hate, and revenge does not heal someone who has been hurt."

"What does, then?"

"Read the New Testament, and observe what Christ says, and how He acts; make His word your rule, and His conduct your example."

"What does He say?"

"Love your enemies; bless them that curse you; do good to them that hate you."

"Then I should love Mrs. Reed, which I cannot do; I should bless her son John, which is impossible."

Helen Burns asked me to explain, and I poured out my tale of suffering and resentment. I bitterly spoke what I felt, without any softening.

Helen heard me patiently to the end; I expected she would then make a remark, but she said nothing.

"Well," I asked impatiently, "is Mrs. Reed not a hard-hearted, bad woman?"

"She has been unkind to you, no doubt, because you see, she dislikes your type of person, as Miss Scatcherd does me. But you cling to every small thing she has done and said to you! I do not let every little hurt affect me. Would you not be happier if you tried to forget her every insult? To me, life is too short to be spent in nursing hatred. We are all burdened with faults in this world. But the time will soon come when we shall leave our earthly bodies, and only our spirits will remain."

She paused, then continued, "I hold a belief, which no one ever taught me, that makes Eternity a home, a place of rest. With this belief, I can forgive the punisher, though I hate the punishment. Revenge never worries my heart—I live in calm, looking to the end."

Helen lowered her head. I saw by her look she wished no longer to talk to me, but rather to be with her own thoughts.

But she was not allowed much time for meditation. A monitor, a large, rough girl, came up, exclaiming loudly:

"Helen Burns, if you don't go and put your drawers in order this minute, I'll tell Miss Scatcherd to come and look at it!"

Helen sighed as her reverie ended and, getting up, silently obeyed the monitor without delay.

Chapter 7

My first three months at Lowood seemed like an age—and not the golden age, either. It was a difficult struggle to adjust to new rules and unwanted tasks; and my fear of failure worried me more than the hardships themselves.

During January, February, and part of March, the deep snows prevented us from leaving the school, except to go to church; but still, we had an hour every day in the open air. Our clothing was too thin to protect us from the severe cold. We had no boots, and the snow got into our shoes and melted; without gloves, our hands became numb and swollen, as did our feet. I remember well the torture of thrusting my swelled, raw, stiff toes into my shoes in the morning.

The small supply of food was distressing, especially with the large appetites of growing children. And whenever the famished older girls had an opportunity, they would bully the little ones out of their portions. Many times I shared my precious morsel of brown bread with two others, and surrendered half my mug of coffee, swallowing the remainder with silent tears.

Sundays were dreary days in that wintry season—we had to walk two miles to Brocklebridge Church. We started out cold, we arrived at church colder; during the service we became almost paralyzed. It was too far to return to dinner and, between services, we received a small portion of cold meat and bread.

At the close of the afternoon service, we walked back on a hilly road where the bitter wind almost stripped the skin from our faces. I can remember Miss Temple walking lightly and rapidly along our drooping line, her plaid cloak gathered close around her, and encouraging us to keep up our spirits and march forward 'like brave soldiers'. The other teachers, poor things, were generally too unhappy to attempt any cheering up.

How we longed for the light and heat of a blazing fire when we got back! But, to the younger girls, this was denied; each fireplace in the schoolroom was immediately surrounded by a double row of older girls.

A little relief came at tea time, when we received a double ration of bread—a whole slice, instead of a half—with the delicious addition of a thin scrape of butter. It was the weekly treat to which we all looked forward on Sunday, although I generally had to give most of it to the older girls.

Sunday evening was spent in reciting, by heart, the Church Catechism, and the fifth, sixth, and seventh chapters of St. Matthew, and listening to a long sermon by Miss Miller, interrupted by yawns of weariness. Frequently, several little girls would fall asleep during the sermon, and they would be forced to stand in the center of the schoolroom until the sermon was finished.

I have not yet spoken of Mr. Brocklehurst. During my first three weeks at Lowood, he was away from home. His absence was a relief to me—I had my own reasons for dreading his coming. But at last, he did come.

One afternoon, as I was sitting with a chalkboard slate in my hand, puzzling over a sum in long division, my eyes raised to the window, and I caught sight of a tall, thin figure passing by. And when, two minutes later, the whole school stood as a group, it was not necessary for me to look up to know who had entered the room.

The stern black pillar who had frowned on me so ominously at Gateshead now stood beside Miss Temple. This piece of architecture, Mr. Brocklehurst, looked longer, narrower, and more rigid than ever. I remembered too well the deceitful hints Mrs. Reed gave him about my behavior, and Mr. Brocklehurst's promise to inform Miss Temple and the teachers of my vicious nature—all of which would brand me as a bad child forever. And now there he was.

He spoke to Miss Temple in a low voice; I was certain he was acquainting her with my villainy. Since I happened to be seated near the front of the room, I was able to listen and, to my relief, was spared immediate worry.

"I suppose, Miss Temple, the thread I bought at Lowton will do. You may tell Miss Smith that she is not to give out more than one needle at a time to each pupil, otherwise they will lose them. And, ma'am! The girls' woolen stockings drying on the line are in a very bad state of repair; the pupils need to mend them from time to time."

"Your instructions shall be attended to, sir," said Miss Temple.

"And, ma'am," he continued, "I find that a lunch, consisting of bread and cheese, has twice been served to the girls. How is this? I looked over the rules, and I find no such meal is mentioned. By what authority was this done?"

"I am responsible, sir," replied Miss Temple. "The breakfast was so ill-prepared that the pupils could not possibly eat it; and I dared not allow them to remain hungry till dinnertime."

"Madam you are aware that my plan in bringing up these girls is not to accustom them to habits of luxury, but to render them strong, patient, and self-denying. If there occurred a little accident in the food, a wise teacher would mention the sufferings of the primitive Christians, and the torments of martyrs and our blessed Lord Himself; His warnings that man shall not live by bread alone; His divine words, 'If ye suffer hunger or thirst for My sake, happy are ye.' Oh, madam, when you put bread and cheese, instead of burnt porridge, into these children's mouths, you may feed their vile bodies, but you starve their immortal souls!"

Miss Temple said not a word, but gazed straight ahead and her face became cold as marble, her mouth clenched, and her brow furrowed.

Meantime, Mr. Brocklehurst grandly inspected the whole school. Suddenly his eye gave a blink, as if it had met something that shocked him; turning, he said:

"Miss Temple, Miss Temple, what is that girl with curled hair? Red hair—curled all over?" With his cane, he pointed to the awful pupil, his hand shaking.

"It is Julia Severn," replied Miss Temple, very quietly.

"Julia Severn! And why does she have curled hair? Why, in defiance of every principle of this charitable establishment, is her hair a mass of curls?"

"Julia's hair is naturally curly," returned Miss Temple, still more quietly.

"Naturally, yes! But we are not here to conform to nature; I wish these girls to be the children of Grace. Miss Temple, that girl's hair must be cut off entirely; I will send a barber tomorrow. And I see others who have far too much hair—that tall girl, tell her to turn round. Tell all the girls to stand up and turn their faces to the wall."

The girls obeyed, and I leaned back a little, to see the frowns on my fellow students' faces. Mr. Brocklehurst studied the backs of the girls, then pronounced sentence. These words fell like the knell of doom:

"All those braids and topknots must be cut off."

Miss Temple quietly argued with him.

"Madam," he pursued, "my mission is to teach these girls to clothe themselves with shame, not with braided hair and costly dresses—"

Mr. Brocklehurst was interrupted—three ladies now entered the room. They ought to have come a little sooner to have heard his lecture on dress, for they were splendidly attired in velvet, silk, and furs. The younger two, fine girls of sixteen and seventeen, had grey beaver hats and elaborately curled hair; the elder lady was enveloped in a costly velvet shawl, trimmed with mink.

Mrs. Brocklehurst and her two daughters were politely greeted by Miss Temple and given seats of honour at the front of the room. They had come in the carriage with Mr. Brocklehurst, and had been inspecting the dormitory upstairs. They now proceeded to criticize Miss Smith about the care of the linen.

Meanwhile, in order to protect my personal safety, I had quietly moved to the back of the room and held my slate up to hide my face. I might have escaped notice, had not my slate somehow slipped from my hand and fallen with a loud crash, drawing every eye upon me. I knew it was all over now, and as I stooped to pick up the pieces, I prepared for the worst. It came.

"A careless girl!" said Mr. Brocklehurst.

And immediately after, "It is the new pupil, I see."

And before I could draw a breath, he said, "I must not forget—I have a word to say about her."

Then aloud—how loud it seemed to me! He exclaimed:

"Let the child who broke her slate come forward!"

I was paralyzed. I could not move, but two older girls, on each side of me, pushed me toward the dread judge, and then Miss Temple gently led me to him, and she whispered:

"Don't be afraid, Jane; I saw it was an accident; you shall not be punished."

The kind whisper went to my heart like a dagger. I was no Helen Burns. I felt a stab of fury against Reed, Brocklehurst, and Company.

"Fetch that stool," said Mr. Brocklehurst, pointing to a very high one, "and place the child upon it."

And I was placed there, by whom I don't know. I was hoisted up to the height of Mr. Brocklehurst's nose; he was within a yard of me.

"Ladies," said he, referring to his family, "and Miss Temple, teachers, and children, you all see this girl?"

Of course they did; for I felt their eyes directed like burning magnifying glasses against my scorched skin.

"You see she is still young; she possesses the ordinary form of childhood. Who would ever think that the Evil One had already found a servant in her? Yet such, I grieve to say, is the case."

A pause—in which I began to steady my nerves and prepare for the trial that must be endured.

"My dear children," continued the black marble clergyman, "this is a sad occasion, for it becomes my duty to warn you that this girl, who could have been one of God's own lambs, is a not a member of the true flock. You must be on your guard against her; you must shun her, if necessary— avoid her company, exclude her from your sports, and shut her out from your conversations. Teachers, you must watch her, keep your eyes on her movements, weigh her words, study her actions, punish her body to save her soul—if, indeed, such salvation is possible; because this girl, this child is—a liar!"

Now came a pause of ten minutes, during which I, by this time in perfect self-control, observed the female Brocklehursts dab their eyes with their handkerchiefs, the mother sway to and fro, and the two daughters whisper, "How shocking!"

Mr. Brocklehurst resumed. "This I learned from her benefactress; from the pious and charitable lady who adopted this orphan, raised her as her own daughter, and whose kindness and generosity the unhappy girl repaid so horribly, so dreadfully, that at last her excellent patroness had to separate this child from her own young ones, fearful that her vicious example would contaminate their purity. She has sent this child here to be healed; teachers, superintendent, I beg you to heal her."

With this sublime conclusion, Mr. Brocklehurst nodded to his family, who all rose and bowed to Miss Temple; then all the great Brocklehursts sailed from the room. Turning at the door, my judge said:

"Let her stand half an hour longer on that stool, and let no one speak to her for the remainder of the day."

There was I, then, mounted on the stool, exposed to general view on a pedestal of shame. As all the girls stood up, my throat closed and I could not breathe.

But then a girl passed by, lifted her eyes, and smiled at me. What an extraordinary feeling it was! Her smile gave me strength! I lifted up my head and mastered my fear!

Then Helen Burns smiled at me as she went by. What a smile! I remember it now, and I know it was a smile of true courage, for just an hour before, Miss Scatcherd had fastened the 'untidy badge' to her arm, and condemned her to a dinner of bread and water, because she had blotted her paper while copying it.

Chapter 8

efore the half-hour ended, five o'clock struck; school was dismissed, and all went into the dining hall for tea. It was dusk. I ventured down from my stool of shame, and sat down on the floor in a corner. I now began to react to what had taken place, and my grief was so overwhelming I sank to the floor and wept.

Helen Burns was not here and, left to myself, no one could help me. I had meant to be so good, and to do so much at Lowood; to make so many friends, to earn respect and win affection. Already I had made progress—that very morning I had reached the head of my class; Miss Miller had praised me warmly; Miss Temple had smiled her approval. I was well received by my fellow pupils; treated as an equal by those of my own age; and now, here I lay again, crushed and stepped on.

Could I ever rise again? "Never," I thought, and I sincerely wanted to die. While sobbing, someone approached and surprised me—it was Helen Burns, bringing me coffee and bread.

"Come, eat something," she said, but I could not. I tried hard to stop my feelings, but I could not, and continued to weep aloud. She sat down on the floor near me, wrapped her arms around her knees, and rested her head upon them. In that position she remained silent. I was the first who spoke:

"Helen, why do you sit here with a girl whom everybody believes to be a liar?"

"Everybody, Jane? Why, there are only eighty girls who heard you called one, and the world contains hundreds of millions."

"But what have I to do with millions? I know that the eighty despise me."

"Jane, you are mistaken; probably not a single one despises or dislikes you; many, I am sure, pity you very much."

"How can they pity me after what Mr. Brocklehurst said?"

"Mr. Brocklehurst is not a god; nor is he even a great and admired man. He is not liked here; he never took steps to make himself liked. Had he treated you as a special favourite, you would have found enemies all around you. Teachers and pupils may look coldly on you for a day or two, but friendly feelings are hidden in their hearts; and if you continue to do well, these feelings will soon appear evident. Besides, Jane—" She paused.

"Yes, Helen?" said I, putting my hand into hers.

"Even if all the world hated you, and believed you wicked, as long as your own heart knew you were innocent, you would not be without friends."

"I know I should think well of myself, but that is not enough: if others don't love me, I would rather die than live—I cannot bear to be alone and hated, Helen. To gain real affection from you, or Miss Temple, or any other whom I truly love, I would gladly have my arm broken, or stand behind a kicking horse—"

"Hush, Jane! You care too much for the love of other human beings; the One who created you gave you strength. There is an invisible kingdom of angels around us, and the spirits watch us and guard us; and if we are dying in pain and shame, and hatred crushes us, angels see our tortures and know our innocence, and God waits to crown our spirit with a full reward. Why, then, should we ever be overwhelmed with distress, when life is so soon over, and death is the beginning of happiness and glory?"

I was silent—Helen had calmed me—but in the peace she gave me, there was a hint of sadness in her voice. I felt it as she spoke, but I could not tell where it came from. She began to breathe a little fast, and coughed a short cough, and I momentarily forgot my own sorrows to feel concern for her.

Resting my head on Helen's shoulder, I put my arms around her waist, and we sat in silence. We had not sat long when another person came in. It was Miss Temple.

"I came to find you, Jane Eyre," said she. "I want you to come to my room; and since Helen Burns is with you, she may come too."

We went; her apartment contained a good fire and looked cheerful. Miss Temple told Helen Burns to be seated on one side of the fireplace and, taking another seat, she called me to her side.

"Is it all over?" she asked, looking at my face. "Have you cried your grief away?"

"I am afraid I never shall do that."

"Why?"

"Because I have been wrongly accused; and you, ma'am, and everybody else, will now think me wicked."

"We shall think of you whatever you prove yourself to be, my child. Continue to act as a good girl, and you will satisfy us."

"I will, Miss Temple?"

"You will," said she, putting her arm round me. "And now tell me—who is the lady whom Mr. Brocklehurst called your benefactress?"

"Mrs. Reed, my uncle's wife. My uncle is dead, and he left me to her care."

"She did not willingly adopt you?"

"No, ma'am; she was sorry to have to do it. My uncle got her to promise, before he died, that she would always keep me."

"Well now, Jane, when a criminal is accused, he is always allowed to tell his own story. You have been charged with lying; defend yourself to me as well as you can."

I told her the whole story of my sad childhood. I was exhausted, and my words were said quietly; and remembering Helen's advice, I left out the tone of hatred. As I went on, I felt that Miss Temple fully believed me.

During my tale, I mentioned that Mr. Lloyd had come to see me after I fainted in the red-room. After I finished, Miss Temple looked at me for a few minutes in silence; she then said:

"I know of Mr. Lloyd; I shall write to him; if his reply agrees with your statement, you shall be publicly cleared from every accusation. To me, Jane, you are clear now."

She kissed me, and still keeping me at her side, she addressed Helen Burns.

"How are you tonight, Helen? Have you coughed much today?"

"Not quite so much, I think, ma'am."

"And the pain in your chest?"

"It is a little better."

Miss Temple got up, took Helen's hand, and felt her pulse; then she returned to her own seat. As she sat down, I heard her sigh. She was quiet for a few minutes, then she said cheerfully: "But you two are my visitors tonight; I must treat you as such." She rang her bell.

"Barbara," she said to the servant who answered it, "I have not yet had tea; bring the tray, and cups for these two young ladies."

And a tray was soon brought. How pretty the china cups and bright teapot looked, placed on the little round table near the fire! How fragrant was the steam of the tea, and the scent of the toast! To my dismay, however, I saw only small portions. Miss Temple noticed it, too.

"Barbara," said she, "can you bring a little more bread and butter? There is not enough for three."

Barbara left, but soon returned. "Madam, Mrs. Harden says she has sent up the usual quantity."

Mrs. Harden was the housekeeper—a woman after Mr. Brocklehurst's own heart, made of equal parts of bone and iron.

"Oh, very well!" returned Miss Temple. "We must make it do, Barbara, I suppose." As the servant left, she added, smiling, "Fortunately, I can add to our supply."

Miss Temple gave each of us a cup of tea with one delicious but thin morsel of toast. Then she got up, unlocked a drawer, and brought out a large seed cake, wrapped in paper. She cut slices with a generous hand.

We feasted that evening not just on tea and cake, but on the smiles of our hostess.

With tea over and the tray removed, Miss Temple again summoned us to the fire; we sat on each side of her, and a conversation took place between her and Helen which was indeed a privilege to hear.

Miss Temple always had something of refinement, in her air and her language, which inspired awe. But something awoke that night in Helen Burns which struck me with wonder—a radiance glowed in her cheeks, the powers of her mind came alive, and she spoke with such eloquence as I thought no girl of fourteen was able. Her spirit seemed to be in a hurry to live its fullest in a very brief span of time.

They conversed about things I had never heard of—of nations and times past; of countries far away; of secrets of nature discovered. They spoke of books—how many they had read! What knowledge they possessed! They seemed so familiar with French names and authors. But my amazement peaked when Miss Temple asked Helen if she recalled the Latin her father had taught her and, taking a book from a shelf, asked her to read a page of Virgil, and Helen obeyed.

She had scarcely finished before the bell announced bedtime! Miss Temple embraced us both, saying, as she drew us to her heart, "God bless you, my children!"

Miss Temple held Helen a little longer than me, and she let her go more reluctantly; her eyes followed Helen to the door; it was for Helen that she breathed a sad sigh; and for Helen she wiped a tear from her cheek.

On reaching the bedroom, we heard the voice of Miss Scatcherd. She was examining the drawers and had just pulled out Helen's; and when we entered, Helen received a sharp reprimand, and was told that tomorrow she would have half a dozen untidy pieces of clothing pinned to her shoulder.

"My things were in shameful disorder," murmured Helen to me, in a low voice. "I intended to arrange them, but I forgot."

The next morning, Miss Scatcherd wrote the word 'Slut' in large letters on a piece of cardboard, wrapped it around Helen's intelligent, kind forehead, and fastened it like a headband. She wore it till evening—patient, with no anger, believing it to be a deserved punishment.

After school ended, the moment Miss Scatcherd left, I ran to Helen, tore it off, and threw it into the fire. Helen's lack of fury had been burning in my soul all day, and tears had burned my cheek.

About a week later, Miss Temple, who had written to Mr. Lloyd, received an answer—he agreed with my retelling of the events at Gateshead. Miss Temple assembled the whole school, announced that the charges against Jane Eyre had been investigated, and that she was most happy to pronounce me completely innocent of every charge. The teachers then shook hands with me and kissed me, and murmurs of pleasure ran through the ranks of my companions.

With great relief, from that hour, I set to work, determined to overcome every obstacle. I worked hard, and my success equaled my efforts. My memory improved with practice; exercise sharpened my wits; in a few weeks I was promoted to a higher class; in less than two months I was allowed to begin French and drawing.

At night, going to bed hungry, my mind feasted on the drawings which I saw in the dark—houses and trees, pretty rocks, sweet paintings of butterflies and roses and birds. I dreamed of translating a little French story which Madame Pierrot had shown me that day. And I fell sweetly asleep.

I would now not have exchanged Lowood, with all its hardships, for Gateshead and its daily luxuries.

Chapter 9

The hardships of Lowood lessened. Spring came and the frosts of winter ceased—its snows melted, its cutting winds improved. My wretched feet, swollen to lameness by the sharp air of January, began to heal under the gentler air of April; the nights and mornings no longer froze the very blood in our veins.

We could now endure our play hour in the garden; sometimes on a sunny day it began to be pleasant, and a greenness grew over those brown beds, freshening daily. Flowers peeped out amongst the leaves. On Thursday afternoons, during our half-holidays, we now took walks, and found still sweeter flowers opening by the wayside.

I discovered, too, that a great pleasure lay outside the high walls of our garden—purple mountains surrounding our valley, rich in colours and shadows. How different this scene looked beneath the iron sky of winter, covered with snow, when chilly mists rolled down and blended with the frozen fog of the river. That river in spring was now a torrent, sending a raging sound through the air.

April advanced to May, and a bright serene May it was; days of blue sky, peaceful sunshine, and soft breezes. And now Lowood became all green, all flowery; woodland plants sprang up and moss filled its hollows. All this I enjoyed often, fully, and free—and almost alone. There was a reason for this unusual pleasure, which I will now explain.

Have I not described a pleasant scene? Yes, pleasant enough—but whether healthy or not is another question. That valley where Lowood lay was the cradle of fog-bred disease which, quickening with spring, crept into Lowood, breathed typhus into its crowded schoolroom and dormitory and, before May arrived, turned the schoolroom into a hospital.

Near-starvation and neglected colds had caused most of the pupils to become infected—forty-five out of the eighty girls lay ill at one time. Classes were broken up, rules relaxed. The few girls who stayed well were allowed almost unlimited freedom, because the medical attendant insisted that they get frequent exercise to keep them healthy.

Miss Temple's attention was completely focused on the patients; she lived in the sick room, never leaving except to snatch a few hours' rest at night. The teachers were fully occupied with packing up and sending away those girls who had friends and relatives willing to take them. Many pupils, already sick, went home only to die; some died at the school, and were buried quietly and quickly.

Disease lived at Lowood, and death was its frequent visitor; outside, the bright May sun shone over the bold hills and beautiful woodlands. The garden glowed with flowers—lilies, tulips and roses—and the sweetbriars gave out their scent of spice and apples. But these fragrant treasures were all useless for most of the inmates of Lowood, except to provide a handful of flowers to put in a coffin.

But I, and the rest who continued well, fully enjoyed the beauties of the season. The school let us ramble in the woods; we did what we liked, went where we liked. We lived better, too. Mr. Brocklehurst and his family never came near Lowood now; the cruel housekeeper was gone, driven away by the fear of infection.

And there were fewer girls to feed—the sick could not eat—and so our breakfast bowls were filled and, at dinner, we ate a large piece of pie or a thick slice of bread and cheese, which we carried away to the woods, where we each chose the spot we liked best.

My favourite seat was a large, smooth stone, rising from the very middle of the river, and only to be reached by wading through the water, a feat I accomplished barefoot. The stone was just broad enough for two girls, and at that time my chosen friend was Mary Ann Wilson. She was a smart, clever girl whose company I took pleasure in, partly because she was witty and original, and partly because she had a calm manner. Older than I, she knew more of the world, and could tell me many things I liked to hear. She satisfied my curiosity, accepted my faults, and never criticized me. She had a knack for explaining, I for questioning, so we got on well together.

And where, meantime, was Helen Burns? Why did I not spend these sweet days of freedom with her? Had I forgotten her? Or was I so worthless as to have grown tired of her? Surely the Mary Ann Wilson I have mentioned was inferior to Helen—she could only tell me amusing stories, and exchange gossip; Helen could give me a taste of far higher things.

True, reader, and I knew and felt this; and though I am a flawed person with few good qualities, I never tired of Helen Burns, nor ever ceased to cherish my feelings for her—feelings as strong, tender, and respectful as any I ever felt. How could it be otherwise, when Helen always gave me quiet, faithful friendship?

But Helen was ill. For several weeks, she had been kept in a room upstairs, but I did not know where. She was not in the hospital portion of the house with the fever patients, for her disease was consumption—tuberculosis—not typhus; and in my ignorance, I did not know that consumption was the disease of wasting away; I thought it to be something mild, which time and care would be sure to cure.

In fact, I was convinced of this idea because once or twice she came downstairs on warm, sunny afternoons, taken by Miss Temple into the garden; but, on these occasions, I was not allowed to go and speak to her. I only saw her from the schoolroom window, and she was all wrapped up, and sat at a distance under the veranda.

One evening, in the beginning of June, I had stayed out very late with Mary Ann in the woods; we had, as usual, separated ourselves from the others, and had wandered far; so far that we lost our way, and had to ask for help at a lonely cottage. When we got back, it was by moonlight. The surgeon's pony was standing at the garden door. Mary Ann said that someone must be very ill for Mr. Bates to be summoned so late.

Mary Ann went into the house; I stayed behind a few minutes to plant in my garden a handful of roots I had dug up in the forest. This done, I lingered a little longer; the flowers smelled so sweet; it was such a pleasant evening, so serene, so warm. I was enjoying these things as a child might, when I suddenly thought:

"How sad to be lying in a sick bed, and to be in danger of dying! This world is pleasant—it would be dreary to leave it, and go to who knows where?"

And then my mind made its first true effort to understand heaven and hell; and for the first time, I felt an endless gulf around me—the place where I stood was real, and all the rest was formless cloud and vacant depth, and I shuddered at the thought of plunging into that depth of chaos.

While pondering this new idea, I heard the front door open. Mr. Bates came out, and with him was a nurse.

After he departed, I ran up to her.

"How is Helen Burns?"

"Very poorly," was the answer.

"Was Mr. Bates here to see her?"

"Yes."

"And what does he say about her?"

"He says she'll not be here long."

Had I heard this phrase yesterday, I might have thought she was about to be moved to her own home. But now, I knew instantly that she was dying!

I knew that Helen Burns was numbering her last days in this world, and that she was going to be taken to the realm of spirits, if there was such a realm. I felt a shock of horror, then a strong surge of grief, then a desire—a necessity—to see her. I asked in what room she lay.

"She is in Miss Temple's room," said the nurse.

"May I go up and speak to her?"

"Oh no, child! It is time for you to come in; you'll catch the fever if you stay out when the dew is falling."

I went into the schoolroom; I was just in time, for it was nine o'clock, and Miss Miller was calling the pupils to go to bed.

It might have been two hours later, probably near eleven when, not being able to fall asleep, I rose softly, put on my robe and, without shoes, crept from the dormitory, and set off for Miss Temple's room.

It was at the other end of the house, but I knew my way; and the light of the moon enabled me to find it without difficulty. When I passed the fever room, an odor of camphor and burnt vinegar warned me, and I passed its door quickly, fearful that the night nurse should hear me. I dreaded being discovered and sent back, for I must see Helen—I must embrace her before she died, I must give her one last kiss, one last word.

I reached Miss Temple's room. A light shone under the door; complete stillness prevailed. Coming near, I found the door slightly ajar, probably to let some fresh air into the place of sickness. My senses quivering, I opened the door and looked in. My eyes sought Helen, and feared to find death.

Near Miss Temple's bed, and half-covered with white curtains, stood a little crib. I saw Helen's body, but her face was hidden; the nurse sat in the chair, asleep; a candle burned dimly on the table. Miss Temple was not there—I learned afterwards that she had been called to help a delirious patient in the fever room.

I advanced, then paused by the side of the crib. My hand was on the curtain, but I spoke before I moved it. I still dreaded seeing a corpse.

"Helen!" I whispered softly, "are you awake?"

She stirred. I pulled back the curtain, and I saw her face—pale and wasted, but quite composed; she looked so little changed that my fear instantly faded.

"Can it be you, Jane?" she asked, in her gentle voice.

Oh! I thought, she is not going to die; they are mistaken; she could not speak and look so calm if she were going to die. I climbed onto her crib and kissed her. Her forehead was cold, and her cheek was cold and thin, and so was her hand; but she smiled the way she always she used to.

"Why did you come here, Jane? It is past eleven; I heard the clock strike some minutes ago."

"I came to see you, Helen. I heard you were very ill, and I could not sleep till I had spoken to you."

"You came to say goodbye, then; you are probably just in time."

"Are you going somewhere, Helen? Are you going home?"

"Yes—to my last home."

"No, no, Helen!" I said, distressed. While I tried to stop my tears, a fit of coughing seized Helen; it did not, however, wake the nurse; when it was over, she lay exhausted for several minutes; then she whispered:

"Jane, your little feet are bare; lie down and cover yourself with my quilt."

I did so; she put her arm over me, and I nestled close to her. After a long silence, she said, still whispering:

"I am very happy, Jane; and when you hear that I am dead, you must not grieve; there is nothing to grieve about. We all must die one day, and my illness is not painful; it is gentle and gradual; my mind is at rest. No one will miss me much—I have only a father, and he was recently married. By dying young, I shall escape great suffering. I did not have the qualities or talents to make my way very well in the world; I would have been always at fault."

"But where are you going to, Helen? Can you see? Do you know?"

"I believe; I have faith; I am going to God."

"Where is God? What is God?"

"My Maker and yours, who will never destroy what He created. I rely completely on His power and His goodness; I count the hours till the angel arrives who shall reveal Him to me."

"You are sure, Helen, that there is such a place as heaven, and that our souls can get there when we die?"

"I am sure there is a future place; I believe God is good; I can give my soul to Him without any misgiving. God is my father; God is my friend. I love Him; I believe He loves me."

"And shall I see you again, Helen, when I die?"

"You will come to the same place of happiness, be received by the same mighty, universal Parent, no doubt, dear Jane."

Again I thought, "Where is that place? Does it exist?" And I clasped my arms closer round Helen; she seemed dearer to me than ever; I felt as if I could not let her go; I lay with my face hidden in her neck. Soon she said, in the sweetest tone:

"How comfortable I am. That last fit of coughing has tired me a little; I feel as if I could sleep; but don't leave me, Jane; I like to have you near me."

"I'll stay with you, dear Helen; no one shall take me away."

"Are you warm, darling?"

"Yes."

"Goodnight, Jane."

"Goodnight, Helen."

She kissed me, and I her, and we both soon fell asleep.

When I awoke, it was day. I felt a strange movement; I was in the nurse's arms—she was carrying me through the passage back to the dormitory. I was not punished for leaving my bed.

No one answered my many questions, but a day or two later, I learned that Miss Temple, returning to her room at dawn, had found me in the little crib, my face against Helen's shoulder, my arms around her neck. I was asleep, and Helen was—dead.

Her grave is in Brocklebridge churchyard. For fifteen years after her death it was only covered by a grassy mound; but I have now placed a grey marble tablet marking the spot, inscribed with her name, and the word 'Resurgam'—Latin for 'I shall rise again'.

Chapter 10

I have recorded in detail the events of the first ten years of my insignificant existence. But this is not to be a regular autobiography. Therefore, I now pass a space of eight years almost in silence—only a few lines are necessary to connect the past with the present.

The devastation that the typhus fever caused at Lowood drew public attention to the school. Inquiries were made into the cause of the scourge, and various facts came out—the unhealthy location in the valley; the quantity and quality of the children's food; the diseased water used to prepare it; the pupils' wretched clothing and living conditions—all these things were discovered, which pointed to Mr. Brocklehurst.

Several wealthy and charitable individuals in the county paid for the building of a new school in a better location; new rules were made; improvements in diet and clothing introduced; and the school's funds were placed in the hands of a committee. Mr. Brocklehurst could no longer use the school's funds for his own personal luxury.

Mr. Brocklehurst still retained the post of treasurer, but he was assisted in his duties by more sympathetic gentlemen—who combined reason with strictness, and comfort and compassion with economy. Over time, the school improved to become a truly useful and noble institution.

I remained an inmate of the institution for eight years—six as pupil, and two as teacher. During these years, my life was happy because it was active. I had an excellent education, a desire to excel, and a great delight in pleasing my teachers, especially those I loved, and who urged me on. In time, I rose to be the first girl of the first class; then I was awarded the office of teacher, which I served with enthusiasm for two years, until something changed in me.

Miss Temple had continued as superintendent of the school. I owed the best part of my education to her instruction; her friendship and company were my constant source of comfort. She was like a mother, governess, and companion.

Then, in my second year of teaching, she married a clergyman—an excellent man, almost worthy of such a wife as Miss Temple—and they moved to a distant county.

From the day she left, I was no longer the same. Gone with her was everything that had made Lowood a home to me. I had absorbed, from her, some of her nature and many of her habits—calmer thoughts and feelings; loyalty, duty and order; I was content, not angry and resentful. I had become a disciplined and quiet person.

Shortly after the marriage ceremony, I saw the carriage bearing the former Miss Temple and Mr. Nasmyth disappear beyond the hill. Then I retired to my own room, and there I spent in solitude the remainder of the day.

By evening, I discovered that Miss Temple had taken with her the peace and calm that I had breathed from her—and now, left only with myself, I began to feel the stirring of old emotions. For years, my world had been the rules of Lowood; I remembered now that the real world was large, and that unlimited hopes, fears, and excitement awaited those who had the courage to go forth, to seek the real knowledge of life.

I went to my window, opened it, and looked out. My eyes saw beyond the building and garden of Lowood to the distant blue peaks—it was those I longed to climb. I traced the white road winding around and vanishing in a gorge—how I longed to follow it farther! I recalled the time when I had traveled that very road in a coach.

In one afternoon, I suddenly tired of the routine of eight years. I desired liberty; for liberty I gasped; for liberty I said a prayer. Then I cried, half-desperate, "Let me at least serve elsewhere!"

That night, in bed, my thoughts came alive again. I could not dare to truly dream words such as Liberty, Excitement, Enjoyment—those would never come my way. But Servitude! That was possible for me. I have served here eight years; now all I want is to serve elsewhere. Yes, that is possible. If my brain could only figure out the means of achieving it.

I sat up in bed to arouse my brain. It was a chilly night, I covered my shoulders with a shawl, and then I proceeded to think again with all my might.

What do I want? A new place, in a new house, among new faces; I want this because it is no use wanting anything better. How do people get to a new place? They speak to friends, I suppose; but I have no friends. I must look out for myself and be my own helper—but how?

I then ordered my brain to find an answer, and quickly. It worked hard and worked harder; I felt the pulses throb in my head; but for nearly an hour no answer came. I got up and walked around the room, opened the curtain, noted a star or two, shivered with cold, and again crept into bed.

Then, as I lay down on my pillow, the answer came quietly and naturally to my mind. Those who want new positions advertise! You must advertise in the newspaper. I felt satisfied, and fell asleep.

Early the next morning, I was up; I had my advertisement written and addressed before the bell rang to wake the school; it said:

"A young lady desires a position in a private family where the children are under fourteen. She is qualified to teach a good English education, together with French, Drawing, and Music."

The letter remained locked in my drawer all day. After tea, I asked permission from the new superintendent to go to into town to perform some small errands; it was readily granted. I went.

It was a walk of two miles, and the evening was wet. I visited a shop or two, slipped the letter into the post office, and came back through heavy rain, with dripping garments, but with a relieved heart.

The next week seemed long, but it came to an end at last. It was a pleasant autumn day and I found myself walking again to town. A beautiful walk it was, but I thought more of the letters that might or might not be awaiting me.

I first got measured for a pair of shoes and, when it was done, I stepped across the quiet little street from the shoemaker's to the post office. It was run by an old lady, who wore spectacles on her nose and black mittens on her hands.

"Are there any letters for me?" I asked.

She peered at me over her spectacles, and then she opened a drawer and fumbled among its contents for a long time, so long that my hopes began to fade. At last, peering at a letter for nearly five minutes, she presented it across the counter.

"Is there only one?" I demanded.

"There are no more," said she. I put it in my pocket and turned my face homeward—I could not open it then, for the rules required me to be back by eight, and it was already half past seven.

Various duties awaited me back at Lowood. I had to sit with the girls during their hour of study; then it was my turn to read prayers and see them to bed; afterwards I dined with the other teachers.

When we finally retired for the night, the candle in my room had only one inch remaining. I feared that my roommate, a talkative teacher named Miss Gryce, would converse till the light was all burnt out. Fortunately, however, due to the heavy supper she had eaten, she was already snoring before I had finished undressing.

I now took out my letter; the seal was an initial 'F', and the contents were brief.

"If the young lady possesses the qualifications mentioned, and if she is able to give satisfactory references as to character and ability, a position can be offered to her, where there is but one pupil, a little girl, under ten years of age; and where the salary is thirty pounds per year. She is requested to send references, name, address, and all particulars to the attention of: Mrs. Fairfax at Thornfield, Millcote."

I studied the document at length. The writing was old-fashioned and rather shaky, like that of an elderly lady. The position was satisfactory. A private fear had haunted me—that by acting on my own, I ran the risk of getting myself into a bad situation. But I now felt that an elderly lady was safe.

Mrs. Fairfax! I saw her in a black gown and widow's cap; frigid, perhaps, but polite; a model of elderly English respectability. Thornfield! That, certainly, was the name of her house—neat and orderly, I was sure. Millcote! I recalled the map of England and, yes, the town was seventy miles closer to London than the remote county where Lowood sat. That was appealing to me. I longed to go where there was life and movement; Millcote was a large manufacturing town on the banks of a river.

At that moment, the candle went out.

The next day, I requested a meeting with the superintendent during the noon play hour. I told her I had the prospect of getting a new position where the salary would be double what I now received. I requested that she speak to Mr. Brocklehurst, or some of the committee members, and ask whether I might mention them as references. She willingly consented.

When she laid the matter before Mr. Brocklehurst, he said that Mrs. Reed must be written to, as she was my natural guardian. A note was addressed to my aunt, who replied:

"She may do as she pleases, for she I have long ago given up meddling in her affairs."

This note went around the committee and, at last, a formal letter was given to me, stating with assurance that I had always conducted myself well at Lowood, both as teacher and pupil—a testimonial of character and ability, signed by the officers of the school.

I forwarded a copy of this recommendation to Mrs. Fairfax, and received her reply, stating that she was satisfied, and setting the day, a fortnight later, for me to begin my post as governess in her house.

I now busied myself in preparations—the two weeks passed rapidly. I had a small but adequate wardrobe, and on the last day I packed my trunk—the same trunk I had brought with me eight years ago from Gateshead.

I brushed off my black traveling dress, prepared my bonnet, gloves, and muff; searched my drawers to see that nothing was left behind; and now having nothing more to do, I sat down and tried to rest. I could not; though I had been on my feet all day, I could not now relax for an instant; I was too excited.

A phase of my life was closing tonight, a new one opening tomorrow—it was impossible to sleep in between the two.

Wandering around in the lobby of the school, like a troubled spirit, a servant approached. "Miss, a person downstairs wishes to see you."

The man is here to take my trunk, I thought, and ran downstairs. As I passed by the back parlour, someone ran out. It was a woman attired like a well-dressed servant, attractive, with black hair and eyes.

"You've not quite forgotten me, have you, Miss Jane?"

"Bessie! Bessie! Bessie!" and in another second I was embracing and kissing her rapturously, as she half-laughed, half-cried, and we both went into the parlour.

Near the fire stood a little fellow of three years old, in a plaid frock and trousers.

"That is my little boy," said Bessie.

"Then you are married, Bessie?"

"Yes, nearly five years to Robert Leaven, the coachman; and I've a little girl besides Bobby there, that I've named Jane."

"And you don't live at Gateshead?"

"I live at the old porter's lodge."

"Well, tell me everything, Bessie, but sit down first; and, Bobby, come and sit on my knee, will you?" But Bobby preferred to be near his mother.

"You have not grown very tall, Miss Jane, or so very heavy," continued Mrs. Leaven. "I dare say they have not kept you too well at school. Miss Eliza is head and shoulders taller than you are; and Miss Georgiana would make two of you in width."

"Georgiana is handsome, I suppose, Bessie?"

"Very. She went up to London last winter with her Mama, and a young lord fell in love with her. But his relatives were against the match and—what do you think?—he and Miss Georgiana eloped; but they were found out and stopped. It was Miss Eliza who found them out—I believe she was envious—and now she and Georgiana fight like cats and dogs; they are always quarrelling."

"And what of John Reed?"

"Oh, he is not doing so well as his Mama would wish. He went to college, but was caught cheating and was expelled. Then his uncles wanted him to be a barrister, and study the law; but he is always so drunk that he will never amount to much, I think."

"What does he look like?"

"He is very tall; some people call him a fine-looking young man; but he has such thick lips."

"And Mrs. Reed?"

"She is heavy, and looks well enough in the face, but I her mind is worried; Mr. John's conduct does not please her—he spends a great deal of his Mama's money."

"Did she send you here, Bessie?"

"No, indeed: but I have long wanted to see you, and when I heard about the letter from you, and that you were going to another part of the country, I thought I'd just set off and get a look at you, before you were out of reach."

"I am afraid you are disappointed in me, Bessie." I said this laughing.

"No, Miss Jane, not exactly. You are genteel enough, you look like a lady, and it is all I expected of you—you were no beauty as a child."

I smiled at Bessie's frank answer. I felt that it was correct, but I confess I was disappointed. At eighteen, most young women wish to be beautiful, and the belief that they are not, is not pleasing.

"I dare say you are clever, though," continued Bessie, by way of comfort. "What can you do? Can you play the piano?"

"A little."

There was a piano in the room; Bessie went and opened it, and asked me to sit down and give her a tune. I played a waltz or two, and she was charmed.

"The Miss Reeds could not play as well," said she with triumph. "I always said you would surpass them in learning; and can you draw?"

"That is one of my paintings over the fireplace." It was a landscape in watercolours, which I had made as a gift to the superintendent as thanks for her help with the committee.

"Well, that is beautiful, Miss Jane! It is as fine a picture as any Miss Eliza's drawing teacher could paint, let alone the young ladies themselves; and have you learnt French?"

"Yes, Bessie, I can both read it and speak it."

"Oh, you are quite a lady, Miss Jane! I knew you would be— you will succeed whether your relatives notice you or not. There was something I wanted to ask you. Have you ever heard anything from your father's family, the Eyres?"

"Never in my life."

"Well, you know, Mrs. Reed always said they were poor and quite despicable; and they may be poor, but I believe they are equal in social class to the Reeds; for one day, nearly seven years ago, a Mr. Eyre came to Gateshead and wanted to see you. Mrs. Reed said you were at school fifty miles away; he seemed so disappointed, for he could not stay. He was going on a voyage to a foreign country, and the ship was to sail from London in a day or two. He looked quite like a gentleman, and I believe he was your father's brother."

"What foreign country was he going to, Bessie?"

"An island thousands of miles off, where they make wine—the butler did tell me—"

"Madeira?" I suggested.

"Yes, that is it—that is the very place."

"So he left?"

"Yes; he did not stay long in the house. Mrs. Reed was very snooty with him—afterwards, she called him a 'sneaking tradesman'. My Robert believes he was a wine merchant."

"Very likely," I replied, "or perhaps a clerk or an agent to a wine merchant."

Bessie and I talked about old times an hour longer, and she then had to leave. I saw her again for a few minutes the next morning in Lowton, while I was waiting for the coach. We parted finally at the door of the Brocklehurst Arms there—each went our separate way. She set off for the coach to take her back to Gateshead; I mounted the coach which was to take me to new duties and a new life in the unknown place called Thornfield.

Chapter 11

A new chapter in a novel is something like a new scene in a play; and when I draw up the curtain this time, reader, you must fancy you see a room at the George Inn in Millcote. It has wallpapering, as inns have, and carpet, furniture, and ornaments on the mantelpiece; and prints, including a portrait of King George the Third, and another of the Prince of Wales.

I sit near an excellent fire in my cloak and bonnet. I am warming away the numbness and chill from sixteen hours of travel in the rawness of an October day—I left Lowton at four in the morning and the Millcote town clock is now just striking eight p.m.

Reader, though I look comfortable, my mind is not at peace. I thought that when the coach stopped here, there would be someone to meet me; I looked anxiously round, expecting to hear my name pronounced, and to see a carriage waiting to convey me to Thornfield. Nothing of the sort was visible; and when I asked a waiter if anyone had inquired after a Miss Eyre, he said 'no'. So I requested a private room, and here I am waiting, while all sorts of doubts and fears are troubling my thoughts.

It is a very strange feeling for an inexperienced young woman to feel herself quite alone in the world, cut off from every connection, uncertain where she is going, but unable to return to the place she has left. When half an hour passed and I was still alone, my fear surfaced. I decided to ring the bell.

"Is there a place in this neighbourhood called Thornfield?" I asked of the waiter who came.

"Thornfield? I don't know, ma'am; I'll inquire at the bar." He vanished, but reappeared instantly. "Is your name Eyre, Miss?"

"Yes."

"There is a person here, waiting for you."

I jumped up and hurried into the lobby. A man was standing by the open door, and in the lamp-lit street I saw a one-horse carriage.

"This will be your luggage, I suppose?" said the man rather abruptly when he saw me, pointing to my trunk.

"Yes."

He hoisted it onto the carriage, and then I got in; I asked him how far it was to Thornfield.

"Six miles."

"How long before we get there?"

"About an hour and a half."

He fastened the door, climbed in to his own seat outside, and we set off. Our progress was leisurely, and gave me ample time to reflect; I was content to be near the end of my journey; I leaned back in the comfortable, though not elegant, carriage, and began to think.

I suppose, thought I, judging from the plainness of the servant and carriage, that Mrs. Fairfax is not a very dashing person. So much the better—I once lived amongst fine people and was very miserable with them. I wonder if she lives alone except for this little girl? If she is friendly, I shall surely be able to get along with her; I will do my best. I remember that with Mrs. Reed, my best was always spurned with scorn. I pray God Mrs. Fairfax may not turn out to be a second Mrs. Reed; but if she does, I am not obligated to stay with her! I can advertise again.

The roads were heavy, the night misty; my driver let his horse walk the whole way, and the hour and a half extended to two hours. At last, he turned in his seat and said, "You're not so far from Thornfield now."

Again I looked out; we were passing a church. I saw lights on a hillside, marking a village or hamlet. About ten minutes later, the driver got down and opened a pair of iron gates. We passed through, and they clashed closed behind us.

We now slowly ascended a drive and came upon the long front of a house; candlelight gleamed from one curtained window—all the rest were dark. The carriage stopped in front of the house.

The front door was opened by a maid. I stepped from the carriage and went in.

"Will you walk this way, ma'am?" said the girl, and I followed her across a square hall with high doors all around. She led me into a small, cozy room, bright with candles and a fireplace.

In a high-backed armchair sat an elderly little lady in a black silk gown, widow's cap, and white linen apron—exactly like I had imagined Mrs. Fairfax, only plainer and milder looking. She was knitting, and a large cat sat at her feet. It was a comforting introduction for a new governess—no grandeur to overwhelm and embarrass me. As I entered, the old lady got up and promptly and kindly came forward to meet me.

"How do you do, my dear? I am afraid you have had a tedious ride; John drives so slowly. You must be cold; come to the fire."

"Mrs. Fairfax, I suppose?" said I.

"Yes, you are right; do sit down."

She led me to her own chair, and then began to remove my shawl and untie my bonnet; I begged her not to go to so much trouble.

"Oh, it is no trouble; I daresay your hands are almost numb with cold. Leah, bring us a little warm sherry and cut a sandwich or two; here are the keys to the storeroom."

From her pocket, she produced a bunch of keys and handed them to the servant.

"Now, then, draw nearer to the fire," she continued. "You brought your luggage with you, haven't you, my dear?"

"Yes, ma'am."

"I'll have it carried into your room," she said, and hurried out.

She treats me like a visitor, I thought. I did not expect such a reception; I anticipated only coldness and stiffness. This is not how I have heard governesses are treated; but I should not be too happy just yet.

She returned with Leah, who placed the tray on the table. Mrs. Fairfax herself handed me the refreshments. I felt rather confused at receiving more attention than ever before—and from my employer! But she did not seem awkward, and so I thought it better to accept her politeness quietly.

"Shall I have the pleasure of seeing Miss Fairfax tonight?" I asked.

"What did you say, my dear? I am a little deaf," returned the good lady. I repeated the question more distinctly.

"Oh, you mean Miss Varens! Varens is the name of your future pupil."

"Indeed! Then she is not your daughter?"

"No—I have no family."

I would have asked how Miss Varens was related to her, but I remembered it was not polite to ask too many questions; I was sure to find out in due time.

"I am so glad you have come," she continued, as she sat down and took the cat on her knee. "It will be quite pleasant living here now with a companion. Thornfield is a fine old hall, rather neglected lately perhaps, but still it is a respectable place. In winter one feels quite alone even in the best quarters. Leah is a nice girl, and John and his wife are very decent people, but you see, they are only servants, and one can't converse with them on terms of equality—one must keep them at a distance, for fear of losing one's authority.

"Last winter, not a creature but the butcher and postman came to the house from November till February, and I got quite melancholy sitting night after night alone. In the spring and summer, it got better; sunshine and long days make such a difference; and then, little Adela Varens and her nurse came. A child makes a house alive all at once; and now that you are here, I shall be quite gay."

My heart really warmed to the worthy lady as I heard her talk; and I drew my chair a little nearer to her, and expressed my sincere wish that she might find my company as agreeable as she hoped.

"I'll not keep you sitting up late tonight," said she. "It is midnight now, and you have been traveling all day; you must feel tired. I had the room next to mine prepared for you as your bedroom. It is only a small apartment, but I thought you would like it better than one of the large front chambers."

I thanked her and, being quite fatigued, said I was ready to retire. She took her candle, and I followed her from the room. First she locked the front door, then she led the way upstairs. The steps and banisters were of beautiful polished oak; the staircase window was high and latticed; both it and the long gallery into which the bedroom doors opened looked more like a church than a house. Very chilly air filled the stairs and gallery, and I was glad, when finally reaching my chamber, to find it small, and furnished in ordinary, modern style.

When Mrs. Fairfax bid me a kind goodnight, and I had fastened my door, I gazed leisurely round and was grateful to be in a safe haven at last. I knelt down at the bedside and offered up thanks where thanks were due, not forgetting to beg for help on my further path, and to earn the kindness that had been shown me.

Weary and contented, I slept soon and soundly; when I awoke, it was broad daylight. My spirits rose at seeing my bedroom in the sunshine—a bright little place with blue chintz curtains, papered walls and a carpeted floor, so unlike the bare planks and stained plaster of Lowood. Externals have a great effect on the young—I was hoping that a pleasanter stage of life was beginning for me, and now my senses were awakened by this hope.

I rose, and dressed myself with care, so that I would appear neat in my simple clothes. I always cared about the impression I made, and wished to look as well as I could, and to please as much as my lack of beauty would permit. I sometimes regretted that I was not handsomer; I sometimes wished to have rosy cheeks, a straight nose, and a small cherry mouth; I desired to be tall, stately, and finely developed in figure; I felt it a misfortune that I was so little, so pale, and had features so irregular.

And why did I have these regrets? It would be difficult to say. However, when I brushed my hair very smooth, and put on my black dress, which fit nicely, I thought I looked respectable enough to appear before Mrs. Fairfax, and that my new pupil would not at least react with horror.

I walked down the long gallery, descended the slippery steps of oak, and reached the hall. I stopped there a minute and looked at some pictures on the walls. One portrait was of a grim man in armor, and one was a lady with powdered hair and a pearl necklace. I gazed upon a bronze lamp hanging from the ceiling, a great clock whose oak case was curiously carved and ebony black from polishing. Everything appeared very stately and imposing to me, but then I was so little accustomed to grandeur. The hall door, which was half-glass, stood open; I stepped over the threshold and went outside.

It was a fine autumn morning; the early sun shone serenely on green fields. Advancing onto the lawn, I looked up and surveyed the front of the mansion. It was three stories high, of considerable size but not vast—a gentleman's manor house, not a nobleman's estate. Mighty old thorn trees, strong, knotty, and broad as oaks, explained the source of the mansion's name—Thornfield.

Farther off were hills—quiet and lonely hills that seemed to embrace Thornfield with a seclusion I had not expected to find so near town. A little hamlet crept up the side of one of these hills; the church stood near.

I was enjoying the calmness and the pleasant fresh air, and thinking what a great place it was for a lonely little dame like Mrs. Fairfax to live, when she appeared at the door.

"What! Out already?" said she. "I see you are an early riser."

I went up to her and she gave me a friendly kiss and shake of the hand.

"How do you like Thornfield?" she asked.

I told her I liked it very much.

"Yes," she said, "it is a pretty place, but I fear it will get out of order unless Mr. Rochester lives here permanently, or at least, visits more often; great houses and fine grounds require constant attention."

"Mr. Rochester!" I exclaimed. "Who is he?"

"The owner of Thornfield," she responded quietly. "Did you not know he was called Rochester?"

Of course I did not—I had never heard of him before; but the old lady seemed to regard his existence as a universally known fact.

"I thought," I continued, "Thornfield belonged to you."

"To me? Bless you, child, what an idea! To me! I am only the house-keeper—the manager. To be sure, I am distantly related to the Rochesters—his mother was a Fairfax, and second cousin to my late husband. But the relation is nothing to me; I consider myself quite an ordinary housekeeper. My employer is always polite, and I expect nothing more."

"And the little girl? My pupil?"

"She is Mr. Rochester's ward. He instructed me to find a governess for her. Here she comes, with her 'bonne', as she calls her nurse."

The puzzle was explained—this kind and friendly little widow was no great dame, but an employee like myself. I did not think less of her—on the contrary, I felt more pleased than ever. The equality between us was real; so much the better—my position was all the freer.

As I was thinking about this, a little girl, followed by her nurse, came running up the lawn. I looked at my pupil, who did not at first appear to notice me. She was a child, perhaps seven or eight years old, slightly built, with a pale, small-featured face, and an abundance of hair falling in curls to her waist.

"Good morning, Miss Adela," said Mrs. Fairfax. "Come and speak to the lady who is to teach you and make you a clever woman someday." She approached.

"Is it my governess?" said she in French, pointing to me.

Her nurse answered in French, "Yes, that is right."

"Are they foreigners?" I inquired, amazed at hearing the French language.

"The nurse is a foreigner, and Adela was born in France and, I believe, came here only six months ago. When she first arrived, she could speak no English; now she can manage to say a few words. I don't understand her, she mixes it so with French, but you will understand her meaning very well, I dare say."

Having been taught French by a French lady, and since I conversed with Madame Pierrot as often as I could, and had, during the last seven years, learned a bit of French daily, I felt comfortable with Mademoiselle Adela.

When she learned I was her governess, she came and shook my hand; and as I led her in to breakfast, I addressed her in French. She replied briefly at first, but after we were seated at the table, and she had examined me for ten minutes with her large hazel eyes, she suddenly began chatter-ing fluently.

"Ah!" cried she, in French, "you speak my language as well as Mr. Rochester does; I can talk to you as I can to him, and so can my nurse Sophie. She will be glad; nobody here understands her; Madame Fairfax is all English. Sophie came with me over the sea in a great ship with a chimney that smoked—how it did smoke! And I was sick, and so was Sophie, and so was Mr. Rochester. He lay down on a sofa in a pretty room called the salon, and Sophie and I had little beds in another place. I nearly fell out of mine; it was like a shelf. And Mademoiselle—what is your name?"

"Eyre—Jane Eyre."

"Aire? Bah! I cannot say it. Well, our ship stopped in the morning at a great city with very dark houses, and Mr. Rochester carried me in his arms and we all got into a coach, which took us to a beautiful large house, larger than this and finer, called a hotel. We stayed there nearly a week; Sophie and I used to walk every day in a great green place full of trees, called the Park; and there were many children there besides me, and a pond with beautiful birds in it, that I fed with crumbs."

"Can you understand her when she runs on so fast?" asked Mrs. Fairfax.

I understood her very well.

"I wish," continued the good lady, "you would ask her a question or two about her parents; I wonder if she remembers them?"

"Adele," I inquired, "with whom did you live when in that pretty town?"

"I lived long ago with Mama; but she is gone to the Holy Virgin. Mama used to teach me to dance and sing, and to say verses. Many gentlemen and ladies came to see Mama, and I used to dance before them, or sit on their knees and sing to them; I liked it. Shall I let you hear me sing now?"

She had finished her breakfast, so I permitted her to give a song. She left her chair and sat on my knee; then, folding her little hands, shaking back her curls, and lifting her eyes to the ceiling, she began singing a song from an opera. She sang the passage well enough for her age. Then, she jumped from my knee and said, "Now, Mademoiselle, I will say some poetry."

She began "The League of the Rats: a fable by La Fontaine". She recited the little piece with great attention to punctuation and emphasis, and with gestures very unusual for her age, proving she had been carefully trained.

"Was it your Mama who taught you that piece?" I asked.

"Yes, and she used to make me lift my hand, to remind me to raise my voice when one of the rats asked a question. Now shall I dance for you?"

"No, that will do, but after your Mama went to the Holy Virgin, with whom did you live?"

"With Madame Frederic and her husband; she took care of me, but she is not related to me. I think she is poor, for she had not so fine a house as Mama. I was not long there. Mr. Rochester asked me if I would like to go and live with him in England, and I said yes; for I knew Mr. Rochester before I knew Madame Frederic, and he was always kind to me and gave me pretty dresses and toys. But you see, he has not kept his word, for he has brought me to England, and now he is gone, and I never see him."

After breakfast, Adele and I went to the library, which Mr. Rochester had selected as the schoolroom. Most of the books were locked up behind glass doors; but there was one bookcase left open, containing everything that could be needed in the way of elementary works, and several volumes of light literature, poetry, biography, travels, and a few romances. They were ample for the present, compared to the spare pickings at Lowood. There was also a piano, an easel for painting, and a pair of globes.

I found Adele to be easy, though not disciplined to apply herself; she had not been used to regular schooling. I felt it would be wrong to confine her too much at first; so, after we talked, and I got her to learn a little, and it became noon, I allowed her to return to her nurse.

As I was going upstairs, Mrs. Fairfax called to me. "Your morning school hours are over now, I suppose," said she. She was in a large, stately room with purple chairs and curtains, an oriental rug, walnut paneled walls, and a lofty, beautifully moulded ceiling. Mrs. Fairfax was dusting some fine purple vases which stood on a sideboard.

"What a beautiful room!" I exclaimed, as I looked round; for I had never before seen any room so imposing.

"Yes, this is the dining room. I have just opened the window to let in a little air and sunshine; for everything gets so damp in rooms that are little used; the drawing room feels like a vault."

She pointed to a wide arch near the window. It led to a very pretty drawing room, and within it a bedroom, both with white carpets, and crimson couches—like snow and fire.

"You keep these rooms in such fine order, Mrs. Fairfax!" said I. "Except for the chilly air, one would think they were inhabited daily."

"Why, Miss Eyre, though Mr. Rochester's visits here are rare, they are always sudden and unexpected; and since it annoyed him to have everything closed up, then to have a bustle of activity when he arrived, I thought it best to keep the rooms always ready."

"Is Mr. Rochester a demanding sort of man?"

"Not particularly; but he has a gentleman's tastes and habits, and he expects to have things managed accordingly."

"Do you like him? Is he generally liked?"

"Oh, yes; the family has always been respected here. Almost all the land in this neighbourhood, as far as you can see, has belonged to the Rochesters forever."

"Well, but do you like him for himself, and not because of his land?"

"Yes, and he is considered a kind and fair landlord by his tenants, though he has never lived among them."

"But has he no peculiarities? What is his character?"

"Oh! His character is unquestionable, I suppose. He is rather peculiar, perhaps; he has traveled a great deal in the world. I daresay he is clever, but I never had much conversation with him."

"In what way is he peculiar?"

"I don't know—it is not easy to describe—nothing striking, but you can feel it when he speaks to you. You cannot be always sure whether he is joking or earnest, whether he is pleased or angry. One cannot thoroughly understand him—at least, I don't. But it is of no consequence; he is a very good master."

This was all I got from Mrs. Fairfax about Mr. Rochester. There are people who seem unable to observe and describe a character—my questions did not draw her out. Mr. Rochester was simply Mr. Rochester in her eyes; a gentleman, a landed proprietor—nothing more; she inquired no further, and perhaps wondered at my wish to know more about his personality.

When we left the dining room, she offered to show me the rest of the house; and I followed her upstairs and downstairs, admiring as I went; for all was well-arranged and handsome. The large front rooms I thought were especially grand; and some of the third story rooms, though dark, were interesting with their antique furniture—bedsteads a hundred years old, walnut chests carved with cherubs' heads, rows of high-backed chairs. All these relics gave the third story the sense of a shrine of memory. I liked the quaintness of these rooms by day, but I did not desire a night's sleep in any of them—they would have looked strange, indeed, by the pale gleam of moonlight.

"Do the servants sleep in these rooms?" I asked.

"No, they occupy smaller rooms in back; no one ever sleeps here—one would almost say that, if there were a ghost at Thornfield Hall, this would be its haunt."

"I agree—you have no ghost, then?"

"None that I ever heard of," returned Mrs. Fairfax, smiling.

"No legends or ghost stories?"

"I believe not. And yet, it is said the Rochesters have been rather a violent family in their time; perhaps that is the reason they rest peacefully in their graves now."

I recalled the line from Macbeth. "After life's fitful fever they sleep well," I muttered.

"Where are you going now, Mrs. Fairfax?" for she was moving away.

"Onto the roof; will you come and see the view?"

I followed her up a very narrow staircase to the attic, and then by a ladder, through a trap door, to the roof of the mansion. I surveyed the grounds laid out like a map—the bright velvet lawn around the grey base of the mansion; the fields and woods; the church, the road, the peaceful hills. All was pleasing.

When I left the roof and passed through the trap door, I could scarcely see my way down the ladder; the attic seemed black as a vault. Mrs. Fairfax stayed behind a moment to fasten the trap door. Groping, I found the door from the attic and descended the narrow staircase back to the third floor.

Then I heard a laugh—certainly the last sound I expected to hear in so still a space. It was a curious laugh—distinct, formal, sad. I stopped; the sound ceased, only for an instant. Then it began again, louder. It ended in a loud noise that seemed to echo through every room.

"Mrs. Fairfax!" I called out. "Did you hear that loud laugh? Who is it?"

"Some of the servants, very likely," she answered. "Perhaps Grace Poole."

"Did you hear it?"

"Yes, plainly. I often hear her; she sews in one of these rooms. Sometimes Leah is with her; they are frequently noisy together."

The laugh repeated in its low voice and ended in an odd murmur.

"Grace!" exclaimed Mrs. Fairfax.

I really did not expect any Grace to answer; for the laugh was as tragic, as unnatural a laugh as any I ever heard. Then, however, I realized I was a fool for being concerned and surprised, for the door nearest me opened, and a servant came out—a woman of between thirty and forty; a square figure, red-haired, with a hard, plain face. One could not imagine anything less ghostly.

"Too much noise, Grace," said Mrs. Fairfax. "Remember directions!"

Grace curtseyed silently and went back into the room.

"She is a person who sews, and assists Leah in her housemaid's work," continued Mrs. Fairfax. "Not always pleasing in some points, but she does well enough. By-the-bye, how did you get along with your new pupil this morning?"

The conversation thus turned to Adele and continued till we reached the light and the cheerful floor below. Adele came running to meet us in the hall, exclaiming in French:

"Ladies, dinner is served!" She added, "I am really hungry!"

We found dinner ready and waiting for us in Mrs. Fairfax's room.

Chapter 12

My hope for a smooth career at Thornfield was encouraged the longer I stayed. Mrs. Fairfax turned out to be what she appeared—a calm, kind woman of average intelligence. Adele was a lively child who had been spoiled, but under my guidance soon became obedient and teachable. She had no great talents which raised her above the ordinary level of childhood. She made reasonable progress, was affectionate, and tried to please; and so we were comfortable with each other.

Some might criticize me for not becoming devoted to my pupil or idolizing her, but I am merely telling the truth. I felt a careful concern for Adele's welfare and progress, and a quiet liking for her, just as I was thankful for Mrs. Fairfax's kindness, and enjoyment of her company.

I may also be blamed when I add that, now and then, I took walks by myself on the grounds; when I went down to the gates and looked down the road; or when, while Adele played with her nurse and Mrs. Fairfax made jellies in the storeroom, I climbed the three staircases, raised the trap door of the attic, and having reached the roof, looked out over the fields and hills.

Gazing at the horizon, I longed for the power to see further—to the busy world, to towns full of life that I had heard of but had never seen. I wished for more interaction with different kinds of people than I had here.

Who could blame me? Many, no doubt, and they would call me discontented. I could not help it; I was restless by nature; it caused me pain sometimes. My relief was to walk along the gallery of the third story, backwards and forwards, safe and alone in the silence there, and allow my imagination to see bright visions and vivid stories of life, fire and feelings that I desired but had never lived.

It is useless to say that human beings ought to be satisfied with peacefulness—they must have action; and they will make it if they cannot find it. Millions are condemned to a stiller doom than mine, and millions are in silent revolt against their lot.

Women are supposed to be very calm generally. But women feel just as men feel; they need exercise for their abilities, and an outlet for their efforts, as much as their brothers do. They suffer from being too rigidly held back, from stagnating, exactly as men would suffer; and it is narrow-minded for men to say that women ought to limit themselves to making puddings and knitting stockings, to playing on the piano and embroidering bags. It is unkind to condemn them, or laugh at them, if women seek to do more, or learn more, than society has decided is necessary for them.

Pacing the gallery alone, I often heard Grace Poole's laugh—the same low, slow, "Ha! Ha!" and her murmurs, stranger than her laugh. There were days when she was silent. Sometimes I saw her; she would come out of her room with a tray in her hand, go down to the kitchen and shortly return, generally—forgive me for telling the plain truth!—bearing a pot of beer. I made some attempts to speak to her, but she was a person of few words—a brief reply cut short every effort to converse.

The other members of the household—John and his wife, Leah the housemaid, and Sophie the French nurse—were decent people, but not special. I used to talk French with Sophie, and ask questions about France, but she seemed to have no interest in conversation.

October, November, and December passed. One afternoon in January, Adele had a cold, and Mrs. Fairfax requested that she have a holiday from schooling. I agreed; it was a fine, calm day, though very cold. I was tired of sitting still in the library through a long morning.

Mrs. Fairfax had just written a letter which needed posting, so I put on my bonnet and cloak and volunteered to carry it to the hamlet, Hay. The distance, two miles, would be a pleasant winter afternoon walk. Adele was comfortably seated in her little chair by Mrs. Fairfax's fireside, with her favorite wax doll to play with, and a storybook.

"Come back soon, my good friend, my dear Miss Jeannie," said Adele in French; I gave her a kiss and set out.

The ground was hard, the air was still, my road was lonely; I walked fast till I got warm, and then I walked slowly to enjoy the countryside. It was three o'clock, and the church bell tolled as I passed; the charm of the hour lay in the low lying sun with its pale beams.

I was a mile from Thornfield, in a lane noted for wild roses in summer, for nuts and blackberries in autumn. But now, no breath of air stirred, and on each side were barren fields.

This lane was uphill all the way to Hay; having reached the middle, I sat down on the steps of a fence. Gathering my cloak about me, and sheltering my hands in my muff, I did not feel the cold. From my seat I could look down on Thornfield, grey and imposing in the valley. I sat till the sun went down amongst the trees, then I looked east at the rising moon—pale, and looking over Hay, a mile away.

A rude noise broke the silence, far away and yet so clear; a metallic clatter—a horse was coming. As it approached, and as I watched for it to appear through the dusk, I remembered Bessie's tale of an evil spirit called a 'Gytrash' which, in the form of a horse or large dog, haunted lonely roads and came upon travelers late at night.

I heard a rush in the trees and saw great black-and-white dog. It was exactly like one of Bessie's Gytrash—a lion-like creature with long hair and a huge head; it passed me quietly, however, and the horse followed, with a rider.

The man broke the spell at once. No Gytrash was this—only a traveler taking the short cut to Millcote.

He passed, and I stood up to continue my walk. But then I heard a sliding sound and I turned back. The man exclaimed "What the deuce is to do now?" followed by a loud tumble—the horse had slipped on a sheet of ice. The dog, seeing his master fallen, and hearing the horse groan, barked till the hills echoed the sound.

The dog sniffed around, and then he ran up to me; it was all he could do—there was no other help at hand. I obeyed him and walked over to the traveler, who by this time had struggled free of his horse.

"Are you injured, sir?"

I think he was swearing, but am not certain; however, he did not reply to me directly.

"Can I do anything?" I asked again.

"You must just stand to one side," he answered as he rose, first to his knees, and then to his feet. I did; whereupon he righted his horse after a process of heaving, stamping, and clattering.

The dog was barking and baying, then was silenced with a command of "Down, Pilot!" The traveler, now stooping, felt his foot and leg. Apparently he was hurt, for he limped to the fence steps and sat down.

I was in the mood for being useful; I drew near him again.

"If you are hurt and want help, sir, I can fetch someone either from Thornfield Hall or from Hay."

"Thank you; I have no broken bones, only a sprain," and again he stood up and tried his foot, but the result produced an "Ugh!"

I looked at him now, in the bright moon, and could see him plainly. He was wrapped in a fur-collared riding cloak. He was of average height and broad chest. He had a dark face, with stern features and a heavy brow; his eyes looked angry and frustrated just now; he was past youth, but had not reached middle-age; perhaps he might be thirty-five.

I felt no fear of him, and little shyness. Had he been a handsome, heroic-looking young gentleman, I would never have dared to stand there, offering my services against his will. I had hardly ever seen a handsome man, and never in my life spoken to one. If I ever did see a gallant, elegant man, I would know instinctively that he would see nothing in me, and I would avoid him like lightning or fire.

If this stranger had even smiled or been good-humoured to me when I addressed him, if he had thanked me for my offer of assistance, I would have gone on my way. But his frown, his roughness, set me curiously at ease. When he waved to me to go away, I stayed, and announced:

"I cannot think of leaving you, sir, at so late an hour, on this secluded lane, till I see that you are able to mount your horse."

Having barely looked at me before, he now turned his eyes in my direction.

"I should think you ought to be at home yourself," said he, "if you have a home in this neighbourhood; where do you come from?"

"From just down the lane; and I am not at all afraid of being out late when it is moonlight. I will run to Hay for you with pleasure, if you wish it; indeed, I am going there to post a letter."

"You mean you live at that grey house?" pointing to Thornfield Hall.

"Yes, sir."

"Whose house is it?"

"Mr. Rochester's."

"Do you know Mr. Rochester?"

"No, I have never seen him."

"He is not at home, then?"

"No."

"Can you tell me where he is?"

"I cannot."

"You are not a servant, of course. You are—" He stopped, ran his eye over my dress, which was not fine enough for a lady's maid. He seemed puzzled to decide what I was; I helped him.

"I am the governess."

"Ah, the governess!" he repeated. "Deuce take me, if I had not forgotten! The governess!" and again he studied my clothing. Two minutes later, he rose, but his face expressed pain when he tried to move.

"I cannot ask you to fetch help," he said, "but you may help me a little yourself, if you will be so kind."

"Yessir."

"Do you have an umbrella that I can use as a walking stick?"

"No."

"Try to get hold of my horse's bridle and bring him to me—you are not afraid?"

I would have been afraid to touch a horse when alone, but when told to do it, I was inclined to obey. I put down my muff on the fence, and went up to the tall steed. I tried to catch the bridle, but it was a spirited animal and would not let me come near its head. I made effort after effort, though in vain. Meantime, I was mortally afraid of being trampled. The traveler waited and watched for some time, and at last he laughed.

"I see," he said, "the mountain will never be brought to Mohammed, so all you can do is to help Mohammed go to the mountain; I must beg you to come here."

I came. "Excuse me," he continued, "but necessity compels me to make you useful." He laid a heavy hand on my shoulder and, leaning on me with some stress, limped to his horse. Having caught the bridle, he mastered it and sprang to his saddle—grimacing as he did, for it wrenched his ankle.

"Now," said he, "just hand me my whip; it lies there under the hedge."

I found it and gave it to him.

"Thank you; now hurry with the letter to Hay, and return as fast as you can."

His heel touched the horse, and they bounded away, the dog rushing behind him. All vanished "Like heath that, in the wilderness, the wild wind whirls away."

I took up my muff and walked on. In a sense, the incident was of no importance, no romance, no interest—yet it marked a change in my monotonous life. My help had been needed, and I had given it; I was pleased to have done something active, weary of a life so passive.

His face, too, was like a new picture in my gallery of memory—different from all the others because it was masculine, and because it was dark, strong, and stern. His face was still before me when I entered Hay, and slipped the letter into the post office, and as I walked fast downhill all the way home.

When I came to the fence, I stopped a minute, and looked round and listened. I heard only the faintest waft of wind among the trees round Thornfield, a mile away; and when I glanced down at the house, my eye caught a light in a window—it reminded me that I was late, and I hurried on.

I did not like returning to Thornfield. To cross its threshold was to return to stagnation; to cross the silent hall, to climb the dark staircase, to find my lonely little room, and then to meet the tranquil Mrs. Fairfax, and spend the long winter evening with only her, was to kill the excitement awakened by my walk.

I was becoming ungrateful for my privileges of security and ease. It would have done me good to be tossed around in the storms of an uncertain, struggling life, to be taught by rough and bitter experience to long for the calm which I now complained about!

I lingered at the gates; I lingered on the lawn; I paced forwards and backwards on the pavement; the shutters of the glass door were closed; I could not see into the interior; and both my eyes and spirit seemed drawn from the gloomy house to the sky above me, to the moon and the trembling stars—they made my heart tremble and my veins glow.

Little things bring us back to earth—the clock struck in the hall. That was enough; I turned from the moon and stars, opened a side door, and went in.

The hall glowed with light from the great dining room, whose door stood open, and showed a genial fire, and a group near the mantle place. I heard cheerful voices, among them the distinct tones of Adele, when the door closed.

I hurried to Mrs. Fairfax's room. There was a fire there too, but no candle, and no Mrs. Fairfax. Instead, all alone, sitting upright on the rug, and staring at the blaze, I beheld a great black and white long-haired dog, just like the Gytrash of the lane.

It was so like the dog I saw, that I went forward and said, "Pilot." He got up, came to me, and sniffed me. I caressed him, and he wagged his great tail; but he looked an eerie creature to be alone with, and I did not know where he came from.

I rang the bell, for I wanted a candle; and I wanted, too, to learn about this visitor. Leah entered.

"What dog is this?"

"He came with master."

"With whom?"

"With master—Mr. Rochester—he has just arrived."

"Indeed! And is Mrs. Fairfax with him?"

"Yes, and Miss Adele; they are in the dining room, and John has gone for a surgeon; for Master had an accident; his horse fell and his ankle is sprained."

"Did the horse fall in Hay Lane?"

"Yes, coming down the hill; it slipped on some ice."

"Ah! Bring me a candle, will you Leah?"

Leah brought it; she entered, followed by Mrs. Fairfax, who repeated the news, adding that Mr. Carter the surgeon had come, and was now with Mr. Rochester; then she hurried out to give orders about tea, and I went upstairs to take off my things.

Chapter 13

Mr. Rochester, by the surgeon's orders, went to bed early that night; nor did he rise soon the next morning. When he did come down, it was to attend to business; his agent and some of his tenants had arrived and waited to speak to him.

Adele and I had to leave the library—it would be used as a reception room for callers. A fire was lit in a room upstairs, and there I carried our books and arranged it for the schoolroom. During the morning, I sensed that Thornfield Hall was a changed place. No longer silent as a church, it echoed every hour or two with a knock at the door, or a clang of the bell; steps crossed the hall, and new voices spoke; a stream from the outside world was flowing through it; it had a master. For my part, I liked it better.

Adele was not easy to teach that day; she could not concentrate. She kept running to the door and looking over the banister to see if she could catch a glimpse of Mr. Rochester. Then she invented reasons to go downstairs to visit the library, where I knew she was not wanted. Then, when I got a little angry and made her sit still, she continued to talk of her "friend, Mr. Edward Fairfax de Rochester", and to guess what presents he had brought her—for he had hinted the night before that, when his luggage came from Millcote, there would be a little box.

"And that must mean," said she in French, "that there will be a present for me in there, and perhaps for you too, miss. Monsieur has talked about you; he asked me the name of my governess, and whether she wasn't a small person, quite thin and rather pale. I said yes; for it is true, isn't it, miss?"

My pupil and I had lunch as usual in Mrs. Fairfax's parlour; the afternoon was wild and snowy, and we spent it in the schoolroom. At dark, I allowed Adele to put away her books, and to run downstairs—from the silence below, I guessed that Mr. Rochester was now free.

Left alone, I walked to the window; but nothing could be seen—twilight and snowflakes thickened the air. I let down the curtain and went back to the fireside. In the fire I imagined a picture I remembered, of the castle of Heidelberg in Germany, when Mrs. Fairfax came in, breaking up some unhappy thoughts that were beginning to form.

"Mr. Rochester would be glad if you and Adele would take tea with him in the drawing room this evening," said she. "He has been so engaged all day that he could not ask to see you before."

"When is his tea time?" I inquired.

"Oh, at six o'clock; he keeps early hours in the country. You had better change your frock now; I will go with you and bring a candle."

"Is it necessary to change my frock?"

"Yes, you had better; I always dress for the evening when Mr. Rochester is here."

This seemed a bit stately; however, I went to my room and, with Mrs. Fairfax's aid, replaced my black dress with one of black silk—the best and only other dress I had.

"You need a brooch," said Mrs. Fairfax. I had a little pearl ornament which Miss Temple gave me as a parting keepsake; I put it on, and then we went downstairs.

As I was unused to strangers, it was rather trying to appear formally in Mr. Rochester's presence. I let Mrs. Fairfax precede me into the dining room, and stayed in her shadow as we crossed the room.

Two wax candles stood on the table, and two on the mantel place; Pilot lay basking in the light and heat of a superb fire; Adele knelt near him. Half-reclined on a couch was Mr. Rochester, his foot supported by the cushion; he was looking at Adele and the dog—the fire shone full on his face.

I knew my traveler by his broad, black eyebrows; his square forehead, made squarer by the sweep of his black hair. I recognized his strong nose, more remarkable for character than beauty; his full nostrils; his grim mouth, chin, and jaw—yes, all three were very grim. I saw his figure, now without a cloak, was athletic, though neither tall nor graceful.

Mr. Rochester must have been aware of our entrance, but he seemed not to be in the mood to notice us, for he never lifted his head as we approached.

"Here is Miss Eyre, sir," said Mrs. Fairfax, in her quiet way. He bowed, still not taking his eyes off the dog and child.

"Let Miss Eyre be seated," said he, and there was something in the forced, stiff bow of his head, and his formal tone, which seemed to say, "What the deuce is it to me whether Miss Eyre is there or not?"

I sat down quite embarrassed. Had he been polite, I probably would not have had the elegance and grace to respond. But his harshness gave me the advantage. I was interested to see what he would do next.

He behaved like a statue—neither spoke nor moved. Mrs. Fairfax seemed to think it necessary that someone should be friendly, and so she began to talk—about the pressure of his business, his painful sprain, and his patience to endure it all. "Madam, I should like some tea," was all she got. She hurriedly rang the bell; and when the tray came, she quickly arranged the cups and spoons. Adele and I went to the table, but the master did not leave his couch.

"Will you hand Mr. Rochester his cup?" Mrs. Fairfax said to me. "Adele might perhaps spill it."

I did as she requested. As he took the cup from my hand, Adele, thinking the moment right for making a request on my behalf, cried out in French:

"There's a present for Miss, isn't there, sir, in your little chest?"

"Who talks of presents?" said he gruffly. "Did you expect a 'cadeau', Miss Eyre? Are you fond of presents?" And he searched my face with eyes that I saw were dark, angry, and piercing.

"I hardly know, sir; I have little experience with them; they are generally thought to be pleasant things."

"Generally thought? But what do you think?"

"I should need some time, sir, before I could give you an answer worthy of your acceptance; a present has many faces to it, has it not? And one should consider them all, before expressing an opinion about them."

"Miss Eyre, you are more sophisticated than Adele—she demands a 'cadeau', loudly, the moment she sees me; you beat around the bush."

"That is because I have less confidence in my rewards than Adele has. She is accustomed to presents, for she says you always give her things; but I am a stranger and have done nothing to deserve one."

"Oh, don't be so modest! I find you have taken great pains with Adele—she is not bright, she has no talents; yet in a short time, she has made much improvement."

"Sir, you have now given me my 'cadeau'; it is what teachers most covet—praise of their pupils' progress."

"Humph!" said Mr. Rochester, and he took his tea in silence.

When the tray was taken away, and Mrs. Fairfax had settled into a corner with her knitting, Adele led me by the hand round the room, showing me the beautiful books and ornaments.

"Come to the fire," said the master. We obeyed; Adele wanted to take a seat on my knee, but she was ordered to amuse herself with Pilot.

"You have been resident in my house three months?" he said.

"Yes, sir."

"And you came from—?"

"From Lowood School."

"Ah! A charitable concern. How long were you there?"

"Eight years."

"Eight years! You must be persistent. Half the time in such a place would have ruined anyone! No wonder you have the look of another world. I marveled where you got that sort of face. When you came upon me in Hay Lane last night, I thought of fairy tales, and almost demanded whether you had bewitched my horse—I am still not sure. Who are your parents?"

"I have none."

"Nor ever had, I suppose; do you remember them?"

"No."

"I thought not. And you were waiting for your family when you sat on that fence?"

"For whom, sir?"

"For the men in green—the elves—it was a proper moonlit evening for them. Did I break through one of your rings, that you spread that damned ice on the road?"

I shook my head. "The men in green all left England a hundred years ago," said I, speaking as seriously as he had done. "And not even in Hay Lane, or the fields about it, could you find a trace of them. I don't think either summer or harvest or winter moon will ever shine on their revels again."

Mrs. Fairfax dropped her knitting and, with raised eyebrows, wondered what sort of talk this was.

"Well," resumed Mr. Rochester, "if you have no parents, you must have some sort of kin—uncles and aunts?"

"No; none that I ever saw."

"And your home?"

"I have none."

"Where do your brothers and sisters live?"

"I have no brothers or sisters."

"Who recommended you to come here?"

"I advertised, and Mrs. Fairfax answered my advertisement."

"Yes," said the good lady, "and I am thankful daily for the choice Providence led me to make. Miss Eyre has been an invaluable companion to me, and a kind and careful teacher to Adele."

"Don't trouble yourself to give her a character reference," returned Mr. Rochester. "Praise will not sway me; I shall judge for myself. She began by causing my horse to fall."

"Sir?" said Mrs. Fairfax.

"I have her to thank for this sprain."

The widow looked bewildered.

"Miss Eyre, have you ever lived in a town?"

"No, sir."

"Have you seen much society?"

"Only the pupils and teachers of Lowood, and now the inmates of Thornfield."

"Have you read much?"

"Only books that came my way; and there have not been many, or very learned."

"You have lived the life of a nun: no doubt you are well drilled in religious ways—Brocklehurst, who I understand directs Lowood, is a parson, is he not?"

"Yes, sir."

"And you girls probably worshipped him."

"Oh, no."

"No! What! You are very cool! A novice not worship her priest! That sounds blasphemous."

"I disliked Mr. Brocklehurst, and I was not alone. He is a harsh man—pompous and meddling; he cut off our hair; and bought us bad needles and thread, with which we could hardly sew."

"That was a very poor way to save money," remarked Mrs. Fairfax, who now again caught the drift of the conversation.

"And was that the extent of his offenses?" demanded Mr. Rochester.

"He starved us when he was in charge of the food; he bored us with long lectures once a week, and with evening readings from books about sudden death and judgment, which made us afraid to go to bed."

"What age were you when you went to Lowood?"

"About ten."

"And you stayed there eight years—you are now eighteen?"

I agreed.

"Arithmetic, you see, is useful; without it, I should hardly have guessed your age. It is difficult when the features and face make it difficult to tell, as in your case. What did you learn at Lowood? Can you play the piano?"

"A little."

"Of course; that is the standard answer. Go into the library—I mean, if you please; excuse my tone of command; I am used to saying 'do this' and it is done; I cannot change my habits for one new inmate. Go, then, into the library, take a candle with you, leave the door open, sit down to the piano, and play a tune."

I departed, obeying his directions.

"Enough!" he called out in a few minutes. "You play a little, I see, like any other English schoolgirl; perhaps better than some, but not well."

I closed the piano and returned. Mr. Rochester continued, "Adele showed me some sketches this morning, which she said were yours. I don't know whether they were entirely of your doing—probably a master helped you?"

"No, indeed," I interjected.

"Ah! I prick your pride. Well, fetch me your portfolio, if you can vouch for it being original; but don't give your word unless you are certain."

"Then I will say nothing, and you shall judge for yourself, sir."

I brought the portfolio from the library.

"Bring the table nearer," said he; and I wheeled it to his couch. Adele and Mrs. Fairfax drew near to see the pictures.

"No crowding," said Mr. Rochester. "Take the drawings from my hand as I finish with them, but don't push your faces up to mine."

He studied each sketch and painting. Three he laid aside; the others he swept away.

"Take them to the other table, Mrs. Fairfax," said he, "and look at them with Adele. You—" he said, glancing at me, "take your seat and answer my questions. I perceive those pictures were done by one hand—was that hand yours?"

"Yes."

"And when did you find time to do them? They have taken much time, and some thought."

"I did them on the last two vacations I spent at Lowood, when I had nothing else to do."

"Where did you get your subjects to paint?"

"Out of my head."

"That head I see now on your shoulders?"

"Yes, sir."

"Your head has in it other subjects of the same kind within it?"

"I think it may have; I hope—better subjects."

He spread the pictures before him, and again surveyed them.

I believed the pictures were nothing wonderful. The subjects had risen vividly in my mind—they were striking, though my hand produced pale versions of my visions.

These pictures were in watercolours. The first was of low clouds, rolling over a swollen sea; a gleam of light shone on the mast of a boat, on which sat a large, dark bird; its beak held a gold bracelet with jewels; sinking below the mast, a drowned corpse floated in the green water, the arm only visible, where the bracelet was once worn.

The second picture showed the peak of a hill; above was an expanse of dark blue sky; rising into the sky was a woman's form in soft tints; a star crowned the forehead; the eyes shone dark and wild; the hair streamed shadowy; on the neck was a pale reflection like moonlight.

The third showed the peak of an iceberg piercing a winter sky; in the foreground rose a colossal head, resting against the iceberg; two thin hands supported the head; a sable veil covered the face, except for a white fore-head and a hollow eye, glassy with despair; above the temples, amidst black turban folds, a ring of white flame gleamed with sparkling gems; this pale crescent was the likeness of a kingly crown.

"Were you happy when you painted these pictures?" asked Mr. Rochester presently.

"I was absorbed, sir; yes, and I was happy. To paint them was to enjoy one of the greatest pleasures I have ever known."

"That is not saying much. Your pleasures, you admit, have been few; but I daresay you existed in a kind of artist's dreamland while you painted them. Did you spend long at them each day?"

"I had nothing else to do, because it was the vacation, and I sat at them from morning till noon, and from noon till night."

"And you felt satisfied with the result of your labours?"

"Far from it. I was tormented by the difference between my vision and my work—in each case I imagined something which I could not realize."

"I wouldn't say that. Yes, you did not have enough of the artist's skill to fully realize it, yet the drawings are unique for a schoolgirl. As to the thoughts, they are full of mischief. You must have seen these eyes in a dream. How could you make them look so clear, and yet not brilliant? And what is the meaning in their solemn depth? And who taught you to paint wind? There! Put the drawings away!"

I had just tied the strings of the portfolio when, looking at his watch, he said abruptly:

"It is nine o'clock. What are you doing, Miss Eyre, to let Adele sit up so long? Take her to bed."

Adele went to kiss him before leaving the room—he endured it, but barely seemed to enjoy it more than Pilot would have.

"I wish you all goodnight, now," said he, waving toward the door, to indicate that he was tired of our company, and wished us to leave. Mrs. Fairfax folded up her knitting; I took my portfolio; we curtseyed to him, he bowed frigidly in return, and so we left.

When I joined Mrs. Fairfax in her room, after putting Adele to bed, I observed, "You said Mr. Rochester was not peculiar."

"Well, is he?"

"I think so; he is very changeable and abrupt."

"True; no doubt he may appear that way to a stranger, but I am so accustomed to his manner, I never think about it; but if his temper is peculiar, one should make allowances."

"Why?"

"Partly because it is his nature—and none of us can help our nature—and partly because he has painful thoughts that torture him."

"What about?"

"Family troubles, for one thing."

"But he has no family."

"Not now, but he did—or, at least, relatives. He lost his older brother a few years ago."

"His older brother?"

"Yes. Mr. Rochester has not owned Thornfield Hall for very long—only about nine years."

"Nine years is a long time. Was he so fond of his brother that he is still distressed at his loss?"

"Why, no—perhaps not. There were some misunderstandings between them. His brother, Mr. Rowland Rochester, was not quite fair to Mr. Edward; and perhaps Rowland turned his father against him. The old gentleman was fond of money, and anxious to keep the family estate together. He did not want to divide the property, and yet he wanted Mr. Edward to have wealth, too, to keep up the family name. Steps were taken that were not quite fair. Old Mr. Rochester and Mr. Rowland combined to put Mr. Edward into a painful position, for the sake of making his fortune.

"I never knew what that position was, but Mr. Edward could not tolerate what he had to suffer. He is not very forgiving—he broke with his family, and for many years he has led an unsettled life. I don't think he has ever stayed at Thornfield for longer than fortnight, ever since his brother's death left him master of the estate; and, indeed, no wonder he shuns the old place."

"Why should he shun it?"

"Perhaps he thinks it gloomy."

The answer was evasive. I would have liked something clearer, but Mrs. Fairfax either could not, or would not, give me clearer information about Mr. Rochester's trials. She claimed they were a mystery to her, and that what she knew was mainly guesswork. It was evident that she wished me to drop the subject, which I did accordingly.

Chapter 14

For the next several days, I saw little of Mr. Rochester. In the mornings he was engaged with business and, in the afternoon, gentlemen from Millcote or the neighbourhood called, and sometimes stayed to dine with him. When his sprain was well enough, he rode a good deal—probably to return his callers' visits, as he generally did not come back till late at night.

During this time, even Adele saw little of him, and I saw him only occasionally in the hall, on the stairs, or in the gallery. At times he would pass me coldly, just acknowledging my presence with a distant nod or a cool glance, and other times he would bow and smile with gentlemanlike friendliness. His changes of mood did not offend me, because I saw that I had nothing to do with them.

One day he had company for dinner, and had sent for my portfolio—probably to show it to his guests. Soon after they left, he rang the bell; a message came that Adele and I were to go downstairs. I brushed Adele's hair and made her neat, and descended down the stairs. Adele wondered whether her little box had come, for it had been delayed.

She was happy—a little carton sat on the table when we entered the dining room. She appeared to know it by instinct.

"My box! My box!" exclaimed she in French, running toward it.

"Yes," said the deep, sarcastic voice of Mr. Rochester from his easy chair, "there is your 'boite' at last. Take it into the corner, you genuine daughter of Paris, and amuse yourself with disemboweling it; and don't bother me with any details of the anatomical process or the condition of the entrails; let your operation be conducted in silence." Then, in French, he added, "Keep quiet, child; do you understand?"

Adele had already sat on a sofa with her treasure, and was busy unwrapping the box. Upon seeing the present, she exclaimed in French, "Oh heavens! How lovely!" then remained there, ecstatic.

"Is Miss Eyre there?" now demanded the master, half-rising from his seat to look round to the door, where I stood.

"Ah! Well, come forward; be seated here." He pulled a chair near his own.

"I am not fond of the prattle of children," he continued, "for, old bachelor as I am, I could not bear to spend a whole evening with a brat. Don't move that chair away, Miss Eyre, sit down exactly where I placed it—if you please, that is. I hate polite behavior! I continually forget it. Nor do I particularly impress simple-minded old ladies. By-the-bye, I must be thinking of mine; it won't do to neglect her—she is a Fairfax, or wed to one, and blood is said to be thicker than water."

He rang, and Mrs. Fairfax soon arrived, knitting basket in hand.

"Good evening, madam; I have forbidden Adele to talk to me about her presents, and she is bursting with excitement; have the goodness to listen to her; it will be one of the kindest acts you ever performed."

Adele saw Mrs. Fairfax and summoned her to the sofa, and quickly filled her lap with the porcelain, the ivory, all the contents of her 'boite', pouring out raptures in broken English. "Now that I have been a good host," pursued Mr. Rochester, "I can attend to my own pleasure. Miss Eyre, draw your chair still closer; I cannot see you without moving from my comfortable chair."

I did as I was bid; Mr. Rochester had such a direct way of giving orders, it seemed natural to obey him.

Mr. Rochester looked different—not quite so stern, much less gloomy. There was a smile on his lips, and his eyes sparkled—whether from wine or not, I am not sure, but I think it very probable.

Still, he looked grim, with the light of the fire on his granite-like features, and in his great, dark eyes. He had been looking at the fire, and I had been looking at him when, turning suddenly, he caught my gaze.

"You examine me, Miss Eyre," said he. "Do you think I am handsome?"

If I had thought about it, I would have replied with something polite; but the answer somehow slipped from my tongue before I was aware:

"No, sir."

"Ah! By my word! There is something unique about you," said he. "You have the air of a little nun—quaint, quiet, grave, and simple—as you sit with your hands folded, and your eyes looking down; but then, when you are asked a question, you rap out a blunt reply. What do you mean by it?"

"Sir, I beg your pardon. I ought to have said that it was not easy to give a quick answer to a question about appearances; tastes differ, and beauty is of little consequence."

"Beauty of little consequence, indeed! And so, pretending to soften the insult, you stick a knife under my ear! Go on—what fault do you find with me? Do I not have all my limbs and all my features like any other man?"

"Mr. Rochester, allow me to disown my first answer; it was a blunder."

"Yes, I think so, and you will answer for it. Go ahead, criticize me—does my forehead not please you?"

He lifted up the hair which lay over his brow, and showed a solid enough head, but a lack of kindness.

"Now, ma'am, do you think I am a fool?"

"Far from it, sir. Would you think me rude, perhaps, if I asked whether you are a philanthropist?"

"There again! Another stick of the knife, when she pretended to pat my head, and all because I said I did not like the company of children and old women. No, young lady, I am not a general philanthropist; but I have a conscience." He pointed to the prominences on his head which are thought to indicate a conscience.

"And besides," he said, "I once had a tender heart. When I was your age, I had sympathy for the young, unloved, and unlucky; but Fortune has knocked me about since, and now I am hard and tough as an India rubber ball; though I still have feeling somewhere. Does that leave hope for me?"

"Hope for what, sir?"

"Of transforming me from India rubber back to flesh?"

Clearly he has had too much wine, I thought; I did not know how to answer his queer question—how could I tell whether he was capable of being transformed?

"You look very puzzled, Miss Eyre; and though you are not pretty, any-more than I am handsome, a puzzled look is quite attractive on you; besides, it keeps your eyes away from me and focused on the rug—so, puzzle on. I am inclined to be talkative tonight."

He rose from his chair and stood, leaning his arm on the marble mantel; the unusual width of his chest was now visible. I am sure most people would think him ugly; yet there was so much pride, so much ease, as if he did not care about his appearance. He depended so much on his other qualities to make up for it, that it gave me faith in his confidence.

"I feel like being talkative tonight," he repeated, "and that is why I sent for you. The fire and the chandelier were not good company for me, nor is Pilot, for none of them can talk. Adele is a bit better, Mrs. Fairfax ditto. You, I believe, can please me, if you choose. You puzzled me the first evening I invited you down here. I have almost forgotten you since, but tonight I will be at ease. It would please me now to draw you out—to learn more of you—therefore, speak."

Instead of speaking, I smiled; and not a very eager smile, either.

"Speak," he urged.

"What about, sir?"

"Whatever you like. I leave the choice of subject entirely to you."

I sat and said nothing. If he expects me to talk for the sake of talking, I thought, he will find he has addressed the wrong person.

"You are silent, Miss Eyre."

I remained silent. He bent his head a little toward me, and with a glance seemed to dive into my eyes.

"Stubborn?" he said. "And annoyed. Ah! I was disrespectful in my request. Miss Eyre, I beg your pardon. The fact is, I don't wish to treat you like an inferior; I am only superior in my twenty years' difference in age and a century more of experience. And now I desire you to have the goodness to talk to me a little."

"I am willing to amuse you, if I can, sir—quite willing; but how do I know what will interest you? Ask me questions, and I will do my best to answer them."

"Then do you agree that I have a right to be a little masterful since I am old enough to be your father, and that I have roamed over half the globe, while you have lived quietly with one set of people in one house?"

"Do as you please, sir."

"That is a very irritating answer, because it is vague. Reply clearly."

"I don't think, sir, that you have a right to command me, merely because you are older than I, or because you have seen more of the world. Your superiority only depends on how well you used your time and experience."

"Humph! Promptly spoken. That doesn't count, since I have not made careful use of my time or experience. But still, you must agree to obey my orders now and then, without being hurt by my tone of command. Will you?"

I smiled. I thought to myself, Mr. Rochester is peculiar; he seems to forget that he pays me thirty pounds a year to obey his orders.

"The smile is very good," said he, "but speak, too."

"I was thinking, sir, that very few masters bother asking their paid employees whether they were hurt by their orders."

"What! Oh yes, I had forgotten the salary! Well then, on that basis, will you agree to let me intimidate you a little?"

"No, sir."

"Will you agree to talk informally, without thinking it comes from rudeness?"

"I am sure, sir, that I would never confuse informality with rudeness—the first I like, the second no free-born person would submit to, even for a salary."

"Humbug! Most people will submit to anything for a salary. However, your response was frank and sincere. Not three in three thousand governesses would have answered me as you have just done. But I don't mean to flatter you; if you are different than most women, it is no merit of yours—nature did it. But then, you may have hideous defects to offset your few good points."

And so may you, I thought. My eyes met his, and he seemed to read my mind; he answered as if I had spoken.

"Yes, yes, you are right," said he. "I have plenty of faults of my own, and I don't wish to excuse them, I assure you. I started off on the wrong tack at the age of twenty-one, and have never recovered the right course since. But I might have been very different; I might have been as good as you. I envy your peace of mind, your clean conscience, your unpolluted memory. Little girl, a memory without blot must be an exquisite treasure, is it not?"

"How was your memory when you were eighteen, sir?"

"All right—clear, healthy—I was your equal at eighteen. Nature meant me to be a good man, Miss Eyre. One of the better kind—and you see I am not so. You might say you don't see it—then take my word for it. I am not a villain; but I truly believe, that due more to circumstance than my natural bent, I am a boring, commonplace sinner. Do you wonder why I reveal this to you? You have a kind of natural sympathy; you will find that people will often confide in you, as I have done. They will feel, as I have, that you listen without judgment. It is not your forte to tell much of yourself, but to listen while others talk."

"How do you know? How can you guess all this, sir?"

"I know it well. I should have held myself above my circumstances, but you see, I did not. When fate wronged me, I had not the wisdom to remain cool—I turned desperate; then I turned to sin. I wish I had stood firm—God knows I do! When you are tempted to do wrong, Miss Eyre, always fear the regret that will come; regret is the poison of life."

"Repentance is said to be its cure, sir."

"It is not the cure. Change may be its cure; and I could change—I have strength for that—but what is the use of thinking about it, cursed as I am? Besides, since happiness will always be denied me, I have a right to get pleasure out of life, whatever the cost."

"Then you will degenerate still more, sir."

"Not if I can get sweet, fresh pleasure."

"It will sting—it will taste bitter, sir."

"How do you know? You never tried it. How very serious you look; you are ignorant of the matter. You have no right to preach to me; you are completely ignorant of life's mysteries."

"I only remind you of your own words, sir. You said sin brought regret, and said that regret is the poison of existence."

"And who talks of sin now? My thoughts of temptation are very agreeable and soothing."

"Distrust them, sir."

"Once more, how do you know?"

"I judged by your face, sir, which looked troubled when you said the thoughts had come. I feel sure they will cause you more misery if you listen to them."

"Not at all—they give me the most pleasing thoughts in the world. You are not my conscience-keeper, so don't worry yourself."

"To speak the truth, sir, I don't understand you at all. I cannot keep up this conversation, because it has gotten out of my depth. The only thing I know is this—you said you were not as good as you would like to be, you regretted your imperfections, and your dirty memory is a constant misery. It seems to me that if you tried hard, you could become what you yourself would approve, and store up pleasant new memories."

"Rightly said, Miss Eyre; and, at this moment, I am vigorously paving hell."

"Sir?"

"I am laying down good intentions, and my pursuits shall be different than they have been."

"And better?"

"And better—so much better. You seem to doubt me—I don't doubt myself. I know what my aim is, what my motives are; and both are right."

"May they be right, then," I said, as I rose, deeming it useless to continue a conversation which was all darkness to me.

"Where are you going?"

"To put Adele to bed; it is past her bedtime."

"You are afraid of me."

"Though I am confused, I am certainly not afraid. I have no wish to talk nonsense."

"If you did, it would be in such a quiet, serious manner, that I would mistake nonsense for sense. Do you never laugh, Miss Eyre? Don't bother to answer—I see you laugh rarely. But I know you are able to laugh very

Jane Eyre

merrily; believe me, you are not naturally serious, anymore than I am naturally vicious. The Lowood influence still clings to you—controlling your expressions, muffling your voice—and you are afraid, in the presence of a man, to smile too gaily, speak too freely, or move too quickly.

"But, in time, I think you will learn to be natural with me, as I find it impossible to be normal with you; and then, your looks and movements will have more energy and variety than they dare offer now. At times, I see in you a sort of restless, captive bird who, if it were free, would soar to the clouds. You are still set on leaving?"

"It has struck nine, sir."

"Adele is not ready to go to bed yet. From where I stand, I can see that she pulled out of her box, about ten minutes ago, a little pink silk frock; rapture lit her face, and she said in French 'I've got to try it on! This very instant!' and she rushed out of the room. In a few minutes she will enter, and I know what I shall see—a miniature of Celine Varens—but never mind that. However, my tenderest feelings are about to receive a shock; stay now, to see whether it will be realized."

Before long, Adele's little feet were heard tripping across the hall. She entered, transformed, in a dress of rose satin, a wreath of rosebuds around her forehead, and her feet were dressed in silk stockings and small white satin sandals.

"Does my dress suit me?" she cried in French. "And my shoes? And my stockings? Look, I think I'm about to dance!" Spreading out her dress, she sashayed across the room and, in front of Mr. Rochester, turned on tip-toe and dropped on one knee, exclaiming in French:

"Sir, thank you a thousand times for your generosity." Then rising, she added, "That's how Mother used to do it, isn't it, sir?"

"Pre-cise-ly!" he answered. "And, just like that, your mother charmed the English gold out of my British pocket." Then to Jane, he said, "My Spring is gone, but it has left me this little French flower. I keep her and raise her—atoning for many sins by one good work. I'll explain all of this some day, Miss Eyre. Goodnight."

Chapter 15

 r. Rochester did, on a future occasion, explain it. It was one afternoon, when he happened to meet me and Adele on the grounds of the estate; and while she played with Pilot and her badminton shuttlecock, he asked me to stroll with him, within sight of her.

He then said that Adele was the daughter of a French opera dancer, Celine Varens, with whom he had once cherished a 'grande passion'. He thought he was her idol, ugly as he was; he believed that she preferred his athletic build to that of a classical Greek statue.

"And, Miss Eyre, I was so flattered, that I put her up in a hotel, with servants, a carriage, cashmeres and diamonds. In short, I began the process of ruining myself like any other amorous fool. I did not have the originality to pave a new road to shame and destruction, but fell victim to the fate of all other fools, as I deserved.

"One evening, I came unannounced to visit Celine; she was not there. I waited in her apartment, breathing her cheap perfume, then stepped out onto the balcony for some air. I sat on a chair, lit a cigar, watched the moonlight, and waited for her to return."

Here Mr. Rochester paused, begged my forgiveness, and pulled out a cigar, which he lit and breathed a trail of smoke, then continued:

"An elegant carriage—the one I had given Celine—pulled up to the hotel door. She was returning; of course my heart thumped with impatience; my flame alighted from the carriage. Bending over the balcony, I was about to murmur, "My angel," when another figure jumped from the carriage after her; he was also cloaked, and wore a hat.

"You never felt jealousy, did you, Miss Eyre? Of course not—I need not ask you, because you never felt love. You think life is as quiet as a flowing stream. You do not see the rocks or hear the breakers. But mark my words—someday you will come to a craggy pass in the channel, where life's stream will be broken up into whirl and tumult, foam and noise; either you will be dashed to atoms, or lifted up into a calmer current—as I am now. I like this day; I like the grey sky, the grimness and stillness of the winter world under this frost. I like Thornfield—its oldness, its quiet, its thorn trees, its grey facade, and lines of dark windows; and I long hated the very thought of it, shunned it like a great plague. And I do still hate—"

He ground his teeth and was silent; he stopped and struck his boot against the hard ground. A hateful thought gripped him and held him tightly.

We walked up the road and he paused—Thornfield Hall was before us. Lifting his eye to its roof, he gave it a glare which I have never seen before, or since. Pain, shame, anger, impatience, disgust, hatred, all seemed to wage a battle in his eyes. But then, another feeling triumphed—something hard, cynical, and determined. It settled him. He went on:

"During this moment I was silent, Miss Eyre, I was arranging a date with my destiny. 'She' stood there, by that tree—a hag like one who appeared to Macbeth. 'You like Thornfield?' she said, lifting her finger; and then she wrote a message in the air, all across the house: 'Like it if you can! Like it if you dare!' I said to her, 'I will like it. I dare like it,' and I will keep my word; I will break the barriers to happiness and goodness. I wish to be a better man than I have been, than I am."

Then Adele ran up to him. "Away!" he cried harshly. "Keep at a distance, child, or go in to Sophie!"

Continuing his walk in silence, I ventured to bring him back to his story.

"Did you leave the balcony, sir," I asked, "when Mademoiselle Varens entered?"

He turned his eyes toward me, and the darkness seemed to clear from his brow.

"Oh, I had forgotten Celine! Well, to resume. When I saw her come in, accompanied by a gentleman, I felt the green snake of jealousy eating into my heart."

Suddenly Mr. Rochester said to me, "Strange that I should choose you as my confidant, young lady; and strange that you should listen to me quietly, as if it were the most usual thing in the world for a man like me to tell the story of his opera mistress to a quaint, inexperienced girl like you! But as I mentioned before, you were made to listen to secrets. The more you and I converse, the better; for while I cannot harm you, you may refresh me."

Then he proceeded. "I remained on the balcony and hid behind the curtain to prepare an ambush, leaving an opening for me to observe them. The pair came in. Both removed their cloaks. There she was, shining in satin and jewels—my gifts of course—and there was her companion in an officer's uniform. I knew him—the young son of a viscount, a brainless, vicious youth whom I had met in society, and had never thought of hating because I already despised him.

"At that moment, the snake of jealousy died, as did my love for Celine. A woman who could betray me for such a rival was not worth competing for. She deserved only scorn—less scorn than I deserved, however, for being duped by her. They began to talk, and my name was mentioned. They insulted me coarsely, especially Celine, who spoke brilliantly of my personal defects—deformities she called them—"

Adele came running up again. "Monsieur, John says that your agent has called and wishes to see you."

"Ah! In that case I must cut my story short. Opening the curtain, I walked in on them; ordered Celine to leave the hotel; offered her money for her immediate needs; ignored hysterics and prayers; and made an appointment with the viscount to meet me for a duel. The next morning I had the pleasure of leaving a bullet in one of his poor weak arms, feeble as a chicken wing, and thought I was done with the whole matter.

"But unluckily, 'the Varens' had given me this girl Adele, who she claimed was my daughter; and perhaps she may be, though I see no similarity in her face—Pilot is more like me than she. Some years later, Celine abandoned her child and ran away to Italy with a musician or singer. I admitted no responsibility for her support, nor do I now, for I am not her father.

"But hearing that Adele was quite destitute, I took the poor thing out of the slime and mud of Paris, and moved it here, to grow up in an English country garden. Mrs. Fairfax found you to train it; but now you know it is the illegitimate offspring of a French opera girl, you will perhaps think differently of your pupil; you will be coming to me someday with notice that you have found another position—eh?"

"No. Adele is not responsible for her mother's faults or yours. I like her; and now that I know she is like an orphan—abandoned by her mother and disowned by you, sir—I shall cling to her closer than before. How could I possibly prefer the spoiled pet of a wealthy family, who hates her governess as a nuisance, to a lonely little orphan, who leans toward her as a friend?"

"Oh, so that is how you see it! Well, I must go in now, and you should too; it darkens."

But I stayed out a few minutes longer with Adele and Pilot—ran a race with her, and played a game of badminton. When we went in, I removed her bonnet and coat, and sat her on my knee. I kept her there an hour, letting her chatter as she liked; I wanted to appreciate all that was good in her to the utmost. I searched her face for a likeness to Mr. Rochester, but found none. It was a pity—if she could have been proved to resemble him, he would have thought more of her.

After I went to my chamber for the night, I reviewed the tale Mr. Rochester had told me. As he had said, there was probably nothing unusual in a wealthy Englishman's passion for a French dancer, and her treachery to him—these were probably everyday matters in society.

But there was something strange in the sudden outburst of emotion which seized him when he was gazing at Thornfield Hall. I couldn't explain it, so I turned my thoughts to his recent behaviour toward me.

His attitude toward me for some weeks had been more steady—I never seemed in his way; he did not act haughty; when he saw me, he always had a word or a smile for me; evening fireside meetings with him were cordial and pleasurable.

I would talk little; he talked with relish. He liked to open my mind—which was unacquainted with the world—to new ideas, and draw new pictures for my imagination.

The ease of his manner freed me; the friendly frankness, with which he treated me, drew me to him. I felt at times as if he were my relative rather than my master. Though he was sometimes still haughty, I did not mind that—I saw it was his way.

So happy, so grateful did I become with this new interest in my life, that I ceased to yearn for my own family. My world seemed to enlarge; the blanks in my life were filled up; my physical health improved; my body added flesh and strength.

And was Mr. Rochester now ugly in my eyes? No, reader—his face became my favorite object to see; his presence in a room was more cheering than the brightest fire.

Yet I had not forgotten his faults—how could I? They were frequently before me. He was proud and harsh to those inferior to him. I knew that his great kindness to me was balanced by unfair severity to many others. He was moody, too; more than once I found him sitting alone in his library, his head bent on his folded arms; and, when he looked up, a gloomy frown blackened his face.

But I believed that his moodiness, his harshness, and his former sins were caused by some cruel hand of fate. I believed he was, by nature, a man of better intentions, higher principles, and purer tastes. I grieved for his grief, whatever that was, and would have given much to relieve it.

After I snuffed out my candle and lay in bed, I could not sleep, thinking about Mr. Rochester's look when he paused in the road, and said how his destiny had risen up and dared him to be happy at Thornfield.

Why? I asked myself. What alienates him from the house? Will he leave it again soon? Mrs. Fairfax said he seldom stayed here longer than a fortnight at a time; and he has now been here eight weeks. If he does go, the change will be sad. Suppose he is absent spring, summer, and autumn—how joyless the sunshine and fine days will seem!

I must have drifted off to sleep, for I jolted wide awake on hearing a strange, sad murmur, which sounded just above me. I wished I had kept my candle burning—the night was drearily dark and my spirits were depressed. I rose and sat up in bed, listening. The sound was hushed.

I tried again to sleep, but my heart beat anxiously—my inner peace was broken. The clock, far down in the hall, struck two. Just then I heard a noise outside my bedroom door, as if fingers had brushed it, groping along the dark gallery outside.

I said, "Who is there?" Nothing answered. I was chilled with fear.

All at once I remembered that it might be Pilot, who sometimes made his way up to the door of Mr. Rochester's chamber. The idea calmed me somewhat; I lay down. Silence settles the nerves and, as an unbroken hush now settled again through the whole house, I began to feel the return of sleep. But it was not fated that I should sleep that night, for a bone-freezing incident occurred.

It was a demonic laugh—low and deep; it seemed to come from the very keyhole of my chamber door. The head of my bed was near the door, and I thought at first the goblin stood at my bedside—or worse, crouched by my pillow; but I rose, looked round, and could see nothing; as I still gazed, the unnatural sound was repeated, and I knew it came from outside the door. My first impulse was to rise and fasten the bolt; my next, to cry out, "Who is there?"

Something gurgled and moaned. Before long, I heard steps up the gallery toward the third-story stair; I heard the staircase door open and close, and all was still.

Was that Grace Poole? And is she possessed with a devil?. It was impossible now to remain alone—I must go to Mrs. Fairfax. I hurriedly put on my frock and a shawl; I slid the bolt and opened the door with a trembling hand. There was a candle burning just outside, and on the matting in the gallery. I was surprised at this—but still more amazed to sense that the air was quite dim, as if filled with smoke; and, while looking to the right and left, I became more aware of a strong smell of burning.

Something creaked—a door was ajar—and that door was Mr. Rochester's, and the smoke rushed out in a cloud. I thought no more of Mrs. Fairfax, or Grace Poole, or the laugh. In an instant, I was inside his chamber. Tongues of flames darted round the bed—the curtains were on fire! In the midst of the blaze and smoke, Mr. Rochester lay motionless on his bed, in deep sleep.

"Wake! Wake!" I cried. I shook him, but he only murmured and turned— the smoke had overcome him. Not a moment could be lost; I rushed to his basin and pitcher; fortunately, both were filled with water. I heaved them up, soaked the bed and Mr. Rochester, flew back to my own room, brought my own water jug, baptized the bed again and, by God's aid, succeeded in dousing the flames.

The hiss of the quenched fire, the sound of the pitcher crashing to the floor after I emptied it, and the splash of water, awakened Mr. Rochester at last. Though it was now dark, I knew he was awake, because I heard him cursing at finding himself lying in a pool of water.

"Is there a flood?" he cried.

"No, sir," I answered, "but there has been a fire. Get up, it is quenched now; I will fetch you a candle."

"In the name of all the elves in Christendom, is that Jane Eyre?" he demanded. "What have you done with me, witch, sorceress? Who is in the room besides you? Have you plotted to drown me?"

"I will fetch you a candle, sir; and, in Heaven's name, get up. Somebody has plotted against you; you must find out who and what it is."

"There! I am up now; you fetch a candle at your peril—wait two minutes till I get into some dry garments, if there are any—yes, here is my dressing gown. Now run!"

I did run; I brought the candle which still remained in the gallery. He took it from my hand, held it up, and surveyed the bed, all blackened and scorched, the sheets drenched, the carpet swimming in water.

"What is it? And who did it?" he asked. I briefly stated all that had transpired.

He listened very gravely; his face expressed more concern than surprise; he did not immediately speak when I had finished.

"Shall I call Mrs. Fairfax?" I asked.

"Mrs. Fairfax? No—what the deuce would you call her for? What can she do? Let her sleep undisturbed."

"Then I will fetch Leah, and wake John and his wife."

"Not at all; just be still. If you are not warm enough, you may take my cloak and wrap it about you. Sit down in the armchair and place your feet on the stool, to keep them out of the wet. I am going to leave you for a few minutes. I shall take the candle. Remain where you are till I return; be as still as a mouse. I must pay a visit to the third story. Remember—don't move or call anyone."

He went; I watched the light fade out. He moved up the gallery very softly, opened the staircase door with as little noise as possible, shut it after him, and the last ray of light vanished. I was left in total darkness. I listened for some noise, but heard nothing. A very long time elapsed. I grew weary—it was cold, in spite of the cloak. And then, I did not see the use of staying. I was about to leave, when the light gleamed dimly on the gallery wall, and I heard his bare feet. I hope it is he, thought I, and not something worse.

He entered, pale and very gloomy.

"I have found out everything," said he, setting his candle down on the washstand. "It is just as I thought."

"What, sir?"

He made no reply, but stood with his arms folded, looking at the ground. After few minutes, he inquired in rather a peculiar tone:

"I forget whether you said you saw anything when you opened your chamber door."

"No, sir, only the candlestick on the ground."

"But you heard an odd laugh? You have heard that laugh before, I should think, or something like it?"

"Yes, sir. There is a woman who sews here, called Grace Poole—she laughs in that way. She is an unusual person."

"Yes—Grace Poole—you have guessed it. She is, as you say, unusual—very. Well, I shall reflect on the subject. Meanwhile, I am glad that you are the only person, besides myself, who knows the details of tonight's incident. You are no talking fool—say nothing about it. And now, return to your own room. I shall do very well on the sofa in the library for the rest of the night. It is near four—in two hours the servants will be up."

"Goodnight, then, sir," said I, departing.

He seemed surprised, though he had just told me to go.

"What!" he exclaimed. "Are you leaving me already, and in that way?"

"You said I might go, sir."

"But you have just saved my life! Snatched me from a horrible and excruciating death! And you walk past me as if we were mutual strangers!

At least shake hands."

He held out his hand; I gave him mine; he took it first in one, then in both of his own.

"You have saved my life—it is my pleasure to owe you so immense a debt. I could not bear to owe anyone else such a debt; but with you, it is different—I feel no burden from your kindness, Jane."

He paused and gazed at me—words trembled on his lips—but he could not speak them.

"Goodnight again, sir. You owe me no debt or obligation."

"I knew," he continued, "that you would do me good in some way, at some time—I saw it in your eyes when I first saw you. Their expression and your smile—" he stopped, then said quickly, "gave delight to my very inmost heart. My cherished protector, goodnight!"

Strange energy was in his voice, strange fire in his look.

"I am glad I happened to be awake," I said, and then I was going.

"What! You will go?"

"I am cold, sir."

"Cold? Yes, and standing in a pool! Go then, Jane, go!" But he still held my hand, and I could not free it. I thought of an excuse.

"I think I hear Mrs. Fairfax, sir," said I.

"Well, leave me." He relaxed his fingers, and I was gone.

I returned to my bed, but never thought of sleep. Till morning dawned, I felt I was tossed on an unquiet sea, where clouds of trouble rolled under surges of joy. I thought sometimes I saw, beyond the wild waters, a sweet shore; and a fresh wind, awakened by hope, took my spirit triumphantly toward the shore—but I could not reach it; an opposing breeze from the land drove me back. Sense would resist emotion, judgment would warn passion. Too restless to rest, I rose as soon as day dawned.

Chapter 16

I both wished and feared to see Mr. Rochester the day after this sleepless night—I wanted to hear his voice again, yet feared to meet his eye. During the morning, I expected to see him, but the hours passed with no interruption of Adele's studies in the schoolroom.

Soon after breakfast, I heard some noise near Mr. Rochester's chamber—the voices of Mrs. Fairfax, Leah, John, and his wife. There were exclamations of "What a mercy he was not burnt in his bed!" and "It is always dangerous to keep a candle lit at night!" and "How lucky he had presence of mind to think of the water jug!" and "I wonder why he waked nobody!" and "I hope he will not take cold sleeping on the library sofa."

When I passed the room, going downstairs to dinner, I saw through the open door that all was again restored to complete order; only the bed was stripped. Leah stood in the window seat, rubbing the panes of glass dimmed with smoke. I was about to ask her what she had been told about the incident, but upon entering, I saw a second person in the chamber—a woman sitting on a chair by the bed, sewing rings to new curtains. That woman was none other than Grace Poole.

There she sat, quiet and settled as usual in her brown dress, checked apron, white handkerchief, and cap. She was absorbed in her work—her face had none of the paleness or desperation of a woman who had attempted murder or had been accused of it last night by her intended victim, Mr. Rochester.

I was amazed and confused. She looked up while I still gazed at her—and there was no reaction, no blushing, emotion or fear, consciousness of guilt, or fear of detection.

She said "Good morning, Miss," in her usual manner.

I will put her to a test, thought I.

"Good morning, Grace," I said. "Has anything happened here? I thought I heard the servants all talking together a while ago."

"Master had been reading in his bed last night; he fell asleep with his candle lit, and the curtains got on fire. But fortunately, he awoke before the bedclothes or the woodwork caught, and quenched the flames with the water in the jug."

"A strange affair!" I said, in a low voice; then, looking directly at her, "Did Mr. Rochester wake anybody? Did anyone hear him move?"

She again raised her eyes to me, and this time with some awareness. She looked at me warily, then she answered:

"The servants sleep so far away, you know, Miss, they would not be likely to hear. Mrs. Fairfax's room and yours are the nearest to master's—but Mrs. Fairfax said she heard nothing. When people get elderly, they often sleep heavy."

She paused, and then added, with an observing eye, "But you are young, Miss; and I should say a light sleeper; perhaps you may have heard a noise?"

"I did," said I, dropping my voice, so that Leah, who was still polishing the panes, could not hear me, "and at first I thought it was Pilot—but Pilot cannot laugh; and I am certain I heard a laugh, and a strange one."

Grace took a new needle, threaded it with a steady hand, and then observed, with perfect composure:

"It is hardly likely master would laugh, I should think, Miss, when he was in such danger. You must have been dreaming."

"I was not dreaming," I said, with some warmth, for her bold coolness provoked me.

Again she looked at me with searching eyes and asked, "Have you told master that you heard a laugh?"

"I have not seen him this morning."

"You did not think of opening your door and looking out into the gallery?" she further asked.

She appeared to be cross-examining me, trying to gather information from me. The idea struck me that, if she discovered I suspected her, she might play of some of her evil pranks on me; I thought it wise to be on my guard.

"On the contrary," said I. "I bolted my door."

"You do not bolt your door every night before you get into bed?"

Fiend! I thought. She wants to know my habits, so she can lay her plans! Anger again prevailed over caution. I replied sharply:

"Till now, I have often neglected to fasten the bolt—I did not think it necessary. I was not aware any danger lay at Thornfield Hall. But in the future, I shall take care to make everything secure before I venture to lie down."

"It will be wise so to do," was her answer. "This neighbourhood is as quiet as any I know, and I never heard of the hall being attempted by robbers, though there are hundreds of pounds' worth of silverplate in the closet, as is well known. And you see, for such a large house, there are very few servants, because master has never lived here much. And when he does come, being a bachelor, he needs little waiting on. But I always think it best to err on the safe side—a door is well to have a bolt drawn against any mischief that may be about." And she closed her speech—a long one for her.

I still stood absolutely dumbfounded, when the cook entered.

"Mrs. Poole," said she, "the servants' dinner will soon be ready; will you come down?"

"No; just put my pint of beer and a bit of pudding on a tray, and I'll carry it upstairs."

"You'll have some meat?"

"Just a morsel, and a taste of cheese, that's all."

The cook turned to me, saying that Mrs. Fairfax was waiting for me; so I departed.

I barely heard Mrs. Fairfax's retelling of the curtain fire during dinner, I was so occupied in puzzling over the bizarre character of Grace Poole, her position at Thornfield, and why she had not been arrested that morning or, at the very least, dismissed.

Mr. Rochester had as much as declared his certainty of her guilt last night—why did he not accuse her? And why had he pledged me to secrecy? It was strange—a bold, vengeful, and haughty gentleman seemed to be under the power of his lowest servant—so much in her power that, even when she tried to murder him, he dared not openly charge her, much less punish her for it.

Had Grace been young and handsome, I should have suspected that tender feelings were involved. Yet, I reflected, she was young once—her age would be similar to her master's; and Mrs. Fairfax said that she had lived here many years.

But at this point in my guessing, I recalled Mrs. Poole's square, flat figure, and dry, coarse face, and I thought, "No, impossible! And yet," suggested the secret voice inside my heart, "I am not beautiful either, and perhaps Mr. Rochester approves of me."

That afternoon, I was in the schoolroom; Adele was drawing; I bent over her and directed her pencil. She looked up with a sort of start.

"What's wrong, miss?" she said in French. "Your fingers are trembling like leaves, and your cheeks are red; they're red as cherries!"

"I am hot from bending over, Adele!" She went on sketching; I went on thinking.

I tried to rid my mind of the hateful thoughts about Grace Poole. I compared myself with her, and found we were different. Bessie had said I was quite a lady, and she spoke the truth—I was a lady. And now I looked much better than I did when Bessie saw me—I had more colour and more flesh, more life, more vivacity, because I had brighter hopes and more enjoyment.

"Evening approaches," said I, as I looked toward the window. "I have not heard Mr. Rochester's voice in the house today, but surely I shall see him before night."

When dusk came, and Adele left me to play in the nursery with Sophie, I listened for the bell to ring below; I listened for Leah coming up with a message. Still, it was not late; he often sent for me at seven or eight o'clock, and it was only six. Surely I would see him tonight, when I had so many things to say to him! I wanted again to mention Grace Poole, and to hear what he would answer; I wanted to ask him plainly if he really believed she had made last night's hideous attempt; and if so, why he kept her wickedness a secret.

The stairs creaked at last, and Leah made her appearance; but it was only to announce that tea was ready in Mrs. Fairfax's room. I went downstairs, for that brought me at least closer to Mr. Rochester's presence.

"You must want your tea," said the good lady, as I joined her. "You ate so little at dinner. I am afraid you are not well today; you look flushed and feverish."

"Oh, quite well! I never felt better."

"Then you must prove it with a good appetite." She rose to draw down the blind. "It is fair tonight," said she, as she looked through the panes. "Mr. Rochester has had a favourable day for his journey."

"Journey! Is Mr. Rochester gone? I did not know he was out."

"Oh, he set off just after breakfast! He is gone to the Leas—Mr. Eshton's place, ten miles on the other side of Millcote. I believe there is quite a party assembled there; Lord Ingram, Sir George Lynn, Colonel Dent, and others."

"Do you expect him back tonight?"

"No—nor tomorrow either; he is very likely to stay a week or more; when these fine, fashionable people get together, they are so surrounded by elegance and gaiety, they are in no hurry to separate. Mr. Rochester is so talented and so lively in society—the ladies are very fond of him, though you would not think so from his appearance; but I suppose his accomplishments, and perhaps his wealth and good blood, make up for any fault of look."

"Are there ladies at the Leas?"

"There are Mrs. Eshton and her three daughters—very elegant young ladies indeed; and there are the Honourable Blanche and Mary Ingram, most beautiful women. Indeed, I have seen Blanche, six or seven years ago, when she was a girl of eighteen. She came here to a Christmas ball that Mr. Rochester gave. You should have seen the dining room that day—how richly it was decorated, how brilliantly lit up! I should think there were fifty ladies and gentlemen present—all of the first county families—and Miss Ingram was considered the belle of the evening."

"What was she like?"

"Yes, I saw her. I never saw a more splendid scene; the ladies were magnificently dressed; but Miss Ingram was certainly the queen."

"And what was she like?"

"Tall, fine bust, sloping shoulders; long, graceful neck: olive complexion, dark and clear; noble features; eyes rather like Mr. Rochester's—large and black, and as brilliant as her jewels. And then she had such a fine head of hair; raven black and so attractively arranged—a crown of thick braids behind, and in front the longest, glossiest curls I ever saw. She was dressed in pure white; an amber-coloured scarf over her shoulder and across her breast, tied at the side, and descending in long, fringed ends below her knee. She wore an amber-coloured flower, too, in her hair."

"She was greatly admired, of course?"

"Yes, indeed, and not only for her beauty, but for her accomplishments. She was one of the ladies who sang—a gentleman accompanied her on the piano. She and Mr. Rochester sang a duet."

"Mr. Rochester? I was not aware he could sing."

"Oh! He has a fine bass voice, and an excellent taste for music."

"And Miss Ingram—what sort of a voice had she?"

"A very rich and powerful one; she sang delightfully; it was a treat to listen to her; and she played afterwards. I am no judge of music, but Mr. Rochester is, and I heard him say she was remarkably good."

"And this beautiful, accomplished lady, she is not yet married?"

"It appears not; neither she nor her sister have very large fortunes. Old Lord Ingram's estate went to the eldest son."

"But I wonder why no wealthy nobleman or gentleman has taken a fancy to her—Mr. Rochester, for instance. He is rich, is he not?"

"Oh! Yes. But you see, there is a considerable difference in age; Mr. Rochester is nearly forty; she is but twenty-five."

"What of that? More unequal matches are made every day."

"True, yet I should not think Mr. Rochester would entertain an idea of the sort. But you eat nothing—you have scarcely tasted since you began tea."

"No, I am too thirsty to eat. Will you let me have another cup?"

I was about to ask her about the probability of marriage between Mr. Rochester and the beautiful Blanche, but Adele came in, and the conversation was turned.

When once more alone, I looked into my heart, examined my thoughts and feelings, and tried to bring my imagination back to common sense. I came to this conclusion:

That a greater fool never breathed than Jane Eyre. You? I thought to myself. A favourite with Mr. Rochester? You—gifted with the power of pleasing him? You are important to him in any way? Your foolishness sickens me! You have received a little attention, given from a gentleman of the world to a servant. How dare you? Poor stupid fool!

He said a few words of praise, did he? Blind puppy! Open your eyes! It does a woman no good to be flattered by her superior if he does not possibly intend to marry her; and it is madness for any woman to let a secret love burn within her which, if unreturned, will devour her.

Listen, then, Jane Eyre. Tomorrow, draw your own picture, faithfully, without softening one defect. Leave out no harsh line, smooth away no displeasing irregularity. Under it, write: 'Portrait of a Governess, disconnected, poor, and plain.' Afterwards, take a piece of miniature ivory; mix your freshest, finest, clearest oils; carefully paint the loveliest face you can imagine; paint it in your softest shades and sweetest lines, according to the description given by Mrs. Fairfax of Blanche Ingram—remember the raven ringlets, the oriental eyes; remember the Grecian neck and bust; omit neither the diamond ring nor gold bracelet; portray faithfully the lace and glistening satin, graceful scarf and golden rose; call it: 'Blanche, an accomplished lady of rank.'

In the future, whenever you imagine that Mr. Rochester thinks well of you, take out these two pictures and compare them—say, "Mr. Rochester would probably win that noble lady's love if he chose to strive for it. Is it likely that he would waste a serious thought on this poor, insignificant commoner?"

I'll do it, I resolved, and then I grew calm and fell asleep.

I kept my word. An hour or two was enough to sketch my own portrait in crayons; and in less than two weeks I had completed an ivory miniature of an imaginary Blanche Ingram. When the two were compared, the contrast was as great as could be. I received a great benefit from the task—it had kept my head and hands busy, and had fixed the images I wished to stamp indelibly on my heart.

Before long, I congratulated myself on having disciplined my feelings. Thanks to it, I was able to have future encounters with Mr. Rochester with a sense of calm which, had I been unprepared, I should probably have been unable to maintain.

Chapter 17

A week passed, and no news arrived of Mr. Rochester; ten days, and still he did not come. Mrs. Fairfax said she would not be surprised if he were to go straight from the Leas to London, and then to the Continent, and not show his face again at Thornfield for a year; he had often left in such an abrupt and unexpected manner.

When I heard this, I began to feel a strange chill and a failing heart; but regrouping, I reined in my feelings. I just said to myself:

"You have nothing to do with the master of Thornfield, other than to receive the salary he gives you for teaching his ward, and to be grateful for the respectful and kind treatment you receive. That is the only tie he seriously acknowledges between you and him, so don't make him the object of your feelings, raptures, and agonies. He is not of your rank—keep to your class, and do not give over your heart, soul, and strength where it is not wanted."

I went on with my day's business peacefully, but I kept thinking of reasons why I should quit Thornfield; and I wrote imaginary advertisements and pondered about new positions.

Mr. Rochester had been absent about a fortnight when, during breakfast, the post brought Mrs. Fairfax a letter.

"It is from the master," said she. "Now I suppose we shall know whether he will return or not."

And while she broke the seal and read the letter, I continued taking my coffee—it was hot, giving my face a fiery glow. Why my hand shook, and why I spilled half my cup into my saucer, I did not choose to consider.

"Well, we may be busy now, for a little while at least," said Mrs. Fairfax, still holding the note before her spectacles.

I tied the string of Adele's pinafore, which happened to be loose, and said nonchalantly:

"Mr. Rochester is not likely to return soon, I suppose?"

"Indeed he is—in three days—and not alone either. I don't know how many of the fine people at the Leas are coming with him; he wants all the best bedrooms to be prepared, and the library and drawing rooms cleaned out. I am to get more kitchen help from the George Inn at Millcote. The ladies will bring their maids and the gentlemen their valets, so we shall have a full house." Mrs. Fairfax swallowed her breakfast and hurried away to begin preparations.

The next three days were busy, as she had predicted. I thought all the rooms at Thornfield were beautifully clean, but it appears I was mistaken. Three additional women were brought in to help; and such scrubbing and washing of paint, beating carpets, taking down and putting up pictures, polishing mirrors and silver, lighting fires in bedrooms, airing sheets and feather beds, I have never seen before or since.

Adele ran wild in the midst of it—the preparations threw her into ecstasies. She asked Sophie to look over all her dresses and mend any that were worn. Meanwhile, Adele did nothing but run around the front chambers and jump on and off the beds. She was dismissed from school because Mrs. Fairfax had pressed me into service, and I was all day in the storeroom, helping—or hindering—her and the cook, learning to make custards and cheesecakes and French pastry, and decorate desserts.

I was so busy, I had no time to nurse unrealistic ideas about Mr. Rochester. Still, now and then, I was thrown into dark thoughts. This happened when I saw the third story staircase door slowly open, and I watched Grace Poole glide along the gallery; when I saw her look into the bustling bedrooms to suggest to the cleaning woman the proper way to clean a marble mantelpiece or take stains from papered walls, and then pass on.

She would enter the kitchen once a day, eat her dinner, smoke a pipe, and carry her pot of beer back to her own private, gloomy, upper haunt. There she sat and sewed—and probably laughed drearily to herself—like a prisoner in a dungeon.

The strangest thing of all was that not a soul in the house, except me, noticed her habits, or seemed to wonder at them; no one discussed her position or employment; no one pitied her solitude or isolation. I once overheard part of a conversation between Leah and one of the cleaning women, mentioning Grace:

"She gets good wages, I guess?"

"Yes," said Leah, "I wish mine were as good—not that I am complaining; there's no stinginess at Thornfield; but they're not one fifth of the sum Mrs. Poole receives. And she is saving it all—she goes every few months to the bank at Millcote. I should imagine she has saved enough be independent if she wanted to leave; but I suppose she's gotten used to the place; she's not forty yet, and strong and able. It is too soon for her to retire."

"She is a good hand, I daresay," said the woman.

"Ah! She understands what she has to do—nobody better," rejoined Leah, "and it is not just anyone who could fill her shoes—not for all the money she gets."

"That is certainly true!" was the reply. "I wonder whether the master—"

The cleaning woman was going on, but Leah turned and noticed me, and she instantly gave her companion a nudge.

"Doesn't she know?" I heard the woman whisper.

Leah shook her head, and the conversation was dropped. All I had gathered from it was this—that there was a mystery at Thornfield Hall from which I was purposely excluded.

Thursday came. All the work had been completed the previous evening—carpets were laid down, beds made, tables arranged, furniture rubbed, flowers piled in vases—the chambers and parlours looked as fresh and bright as could be.

The hall, too, was scoured; and the great carved clock, as well as the steps and banisters of the staircase, were polished to the brightness of glass; in the dining room, the sideboard flashed with silver.

Afternoon arrived. Mrs. Fairfax wore her best black satin gown, her gloves, and her gold watch—for it was her duty to receive the company and to conduct the ladies to their rooms. Adele, too, was dressed in a full muslin frock.

For myself, I had no need to make any change; I would not be called upon to leave my sanctum of the schoolroom, for a sanctum it had now become—"a very pleasant refuge in time of trouble."

It had been a mild spring day—one of those days which, toward the beginning of April, shine over the earth as a herald of summer. It was near dusk now, but the evening was warm, and I sat at work in the schoolroom with the window open.

"It is getting late," said Mrs. Fairfax, bustling into the room. "I am glad I ordered dinner for seven, for it is past six now. I sent John down to the gates to see if there is anything on the road."

She went to the window. "Here he is!" said she. Leaning out, she called, "Well, John, any news?"

"They're coming, ma'am," was the answer. "They'll be here in ten minutes."

Adele flew to the window. I followed, taking care to stand to one side, to avoid being seen.

The ten minutes seemed very long to me but, at last, wheels were heard; four horses galloped up the drive, followed by two open carriages. Fluttering veils and waving plumes filled the carriages. Two of the horse-men were young, dashing-looking gentlemen; the third was Mr. Rochester, on his black horse; Pilot bounding beside; and at his side rode a lady. Her purple riding habit almost swept the ground, her long veil streaming in the breeze; and gleaming through them, shone rich black ringlets.

"Miss Ingram!" exclaimed Mrs. Fairfax, and away she hurried to her post downstairs. Adele asked to go, too, but I took her on my knee and said she must wait until Mr. Rochester requested her presence. A few tears were shed, but at last she wiped them.

Joyous voices were now heard in the hall—gentlemen's deep tones and ladies' silvery accents blended harmoniously together, and above all, though not loud, was the rich voice of the master of Thornfield Hall, wel-coming his fair and gallant guests. Then light steps climbed the stairs, then through the gallery, and soft cheerful laughs, and opening and closing of doors, and then quiet.

"They are changing their clothes," said Adele in French; listening care-fully, she had followed every movement; then she sighed, and again in French, said:

"At my mother's, when there were guests, I used to follow them every-where, from the drawing rooms to their bedrooms; often I used to watch the maids arrange the ladies' hair and dress them, and that was so interest-ing; you can learn from that."

"Don't you feel hungry, Adele?"

"Oh, yes, miss; it's been five or six hours since we've eaten."

"Well now, while the ladies are in their rooms, I will venture down and get you something to eat."

Leaving the room with caution, I descended a back stair that connected directly to the kitchen. There, all was fire and commotion. The soup and fish were in the last stage of preparation; in the servants' hall, two coach-men and three valets stood round the fire; the new servants from Millcote were bustling about everywhere. I finally reached the storeroom and took some cold chicken, a roll of bread, some tarts, two plates and a knife and fork, then made a hasty exit.

I had just reached the gallery, when the ladies began to leave their chambers. I stood quietly at the dark end of the hall, so as not to be seen.

The ladies came out gaily and airily, with dresses that gleamed with luster. For a moment they stood, grouped together, at the other end of the gallery, then descended the staircase as quietly as mist rolling down a hill. Their appearance had left me with an impression of high-born elegance such as I had never before seen.

Upon returning, I found Adele peeping through the schoolroom door. "What beautiful ladies!" cried she. "Oh, I wish I might go to them! Do you think Mr. Rochester will send for us after dinner?"

"No, indeed I don't. Mr. Rochester has something else to think about. Never mind the ladies tonight; perhaps you will see them tomorrow. Here is your dinner."

She was really hungry, so the chicken and tarts were well received. Both Sophie and I shared them as well—it was our dinner, for everyone downstairs was too busy to think of us.

The dessert was not served till after nine, and at ten footmen were still running to and fro with trays and coffee cups. I allowed Adele to sit up much later than usual because, she said, a message might come from Mr. Rochester when she was undressed, and exclaimed in French, "and then what a shame!"

I told her stories for a time, and then I took her out into the gallery. Music wafted from the drawing room, and Adele and I sat down on the top step of the stairs to listen. Presently a lady sang, and very sweet her notes were. After the solo was over, a duet followed.

The clock struck eleven. I looked at Adele, whose head leaned against my shoulder; her eyes were heavy, so I took her up in my arms and carried her off to bed. It was near one before the gentlemen and ladies retired to their chambers.

The next day was just as fine, devoted to an outing. They set out before noon, some on horseback, the rest in carriages; I witnessed both the departure and the return. Miss Ingram, as before, was the only lady equestrian and Mr. Rochester galloped at her side; the two rode a little apart from the rest.

I pointed this out to Mrs. Fairfax, who was standing at the window with me:

"You said it was not likely they would think of getting married," said I, "but you see that Mr. Rochester prefers her to any of the other ladies."

"Yes, I daresay; no doubt he admires her."

"And she, him," I added. "Look how she leans her head toward him as if they were talking intimately; I wish I could see her face; I have never had a glimpse of it yet."

"You will see her this evening," answered Mrs. Fairfax. "I remarked to

Mr. Rochester how much Adele wished to be introduced to the ladies, and he said, 'Oh! Let her come into the drawing room after dinner, and request Miss Eyre to accompany her.'"

"He said that from mere politeness; I am sure I need not go," I answered.

"Well, I mentioned that you were unused to company and I did not think you would like appearing before so gay a party of all strangers, and he replied, in his quick way, 'Nonsense! If she objects, tell her it is my particular wish; and if she resists, say I shall come and fetch her.'"

"I will not give him that trouble," I answered. "I will go, but I don't like it. Will you be there, Mrs. Fairfax?"

"No, I begged off, and he accepted my plea. I'll tell you how to avoid the embarrassment of making a formal entrance. You must go into the drawing room while it is empty, before the ladies leave the dinner table; choose your seat in any quiet nook you like; you need not stay long after the gentlemen come in; just let Mr. Rochester see you are there and then slip away—nobody will notice you."

"Will these people remain long, do you think?"

"Perhaps two or three weeks, certainly not more. After the Easter recess, Sir George Lynn, who was lately elected a member of Parliament for Millcote, will have to go to London and take his seat; I daresay Mr. Rochester will accompany him."

It was with some anxiety that the hour approached when I was to appear with Adele in the drawing room. Adele had been in a state of ecstasy all day; the operation of getting dressed calmed her down. By the time her curls were arranged, her pink satin frock put on, her long sash tied, and her lace mittens adjusted, she looked as grave as a judge.

After Adele was dressed, she sat down in her little chair till I was ready. This I quickly was—my best dress, the silver-grey one, purchased for Miss Temple's wedding, and never worn since, was soon put on; my hair was soon smoothed; my sole ornament, the pearl brooch, soon pinned. I picked up my netting needles and we descended.

Fortunately, there was another entrance to the drawing room besides the dining room where they were all seated. We found the room empty—a large fire burned in the marble hearth, and wax candles shone brightly amid the exquisite flowers.

Adele sat down, without a word, on the footstool near the window seat where I sat. I took a book from a table and tried to read. Soon Adele touched my knee.

"What is it, Adele?"

In French, she asked, "May I take one of these glorious flowers, miss? Just to complete my outfit?"

"You think too much of your outfit, Adele, but you may have a flower." And I took a rose from a vase and fastened it in her sash. She sighed with happiness; I concealed a smile at the little Parisienne's earnest devotion to matters of dress.

The sounds began to rise, and a group of eight ladies flocked into the room. Some of them were very tall; many were dressed in white; and all had sweeping gestures that seemed to magnify themselves. I rose and curt-seyed to them—one or two bent their heads in return, the others only stared at me.

They scattered around the room, reminding me, by the lightness of their movements, of a flock of white plumy birds. Some of them sat in half-reclining positions on the sofas and ottomans; some examined the flowers and books; the rest gathered in a group round the fire. I knew their names afterwards, and may as well mention them now.

First, there was Mrs. Eshton and two of her daughters. She had been a handsome woman, and was well-preserved. Of her daughters, the eldest, Amy, was rather little—childlike in face and manner, attractive in her white muslin dress and blue sash. The second, Louisa, was taller and more elegant, with a very pretty face; both sisters were fair as lilies.

Lady Lynn was large and stout, about forty, very erect and haughty-looking, richly dressed in a satin robe; her dark hair shone glossily under blue feathers, tied with a band of gems.

Mrs. Colonel Dent was less showy but more ladylike. She had a slight figure, a pale, gentle face, and fair hair. Her black satin dress, her scarf of rich foreign lace, and her pearl ornaments pleased me better than the flash of Lady Lynn.

But the three most distinguished ladies—partly, perhaps, because they were the tallest—were the Dowager Lady Ingram and her daughters, Blanche and Mary. The Dowager might be between forty and fifty; her shape was still fine, her hair still black, her teeth still perfect. Though splendid for her age, she wore an air of haughtiness. She had Roman features and a double chin, jutted out with pride. Her fierce, hard eyes reminded me of Mrs. Reed's; her words were deep, pompous, and com-manding. Her red velvet robe and gold turban gave her an imperial dignity.

Blanche and Mary were straight and tall as poplars. Mary was too slim for her height, but Blanche was molded like a Greek statue of Diana. I studied her, of course, with special interest. First, I wished to see whether her appearance met Mrs. Fairfax's description; secondly, whether it resembled the miniature I had painted of her; and thirdly—whether I thought she would suit Mr. Rochester's taste.

She matched, point for point, my picture and Mrs. Fairfax's description. The noble bust, the sloping shoulders, the graceful neck, the dark eyes and black ringlets were all there.

But her face? Her face was a youthful likeness of her mother's—dark as a Spaniard, the same low brow, the same high features, the same pride. She laughed continually—her laugh was sarcastic, and so was the fixed expression of her haughty lip.

Genius is said to be self-conscious. I cannot tell whether Miss Ingram was a genius, but she was self-conscious—remarkably self-conscious indeed. She began a conversation on botany with the gentle Mrs. Dent. It seemed Mrs. Dent had not studied the science of plants, though she liked flowers. Miss Ingram had studied botany, and she spouted its vocabulary with a haughty air. I saw that she was playing on Mrs. Dent's ignorance—it was clever, but not good-natured. Blanche also played the piano, and her performance was brilliant; she sang, and her voice was fine; she talked French, and talked it well.

Mary had a milder and more open face than Blanche; softer features and fairer skin—but Mary's face lacked expression, her eyes lacked luster; she had nothing to say and, having once taken her seat, remained fixed like a statue. The sisters were both dressed in spotless white.

And did I now think Miss Ingram was a choice that Mr. Rochester was likely to make? I could not tell—I did not know his taste in female beauty. If he liked the majestic, she was the very type of majesty; and she was accomplished. Most gentlemen would admire her, I thought; and I already seemed to have proof that he did admire her. What remained? To see them together.

You are not to suppose, reader, that Adele has been sitting motionless all this time on the stool at my feet; no, when the ladies entered, she rose, advanced to meet them, made a stately curtsey, and said, "Bonjour, madams."

Miss Ingram looked down at her with a mocking air, and exclaimed, "Oh, what a little puppet!"

Lady Lynn remarked, "It is Mr. Rochester's ward, I suppose—the little French girl he was speaking of."

Mrs. Dent kindly took Adele's hand and gave her a kiss.

Amy and Louisa Eshton cried out together, "What a love of a child!"

They called Adele over to a sofa, where she now sat between the ladies, chattering in French and broken English, and getting spoiled to her heart's content.

At last coffee is brought in, and the gentlemen are summoned. I sit in the shade, half-hidden by the window curtain. The gentlemen are very imposing, all dressed in black; most of them are tall, some young. Henry and Frederick Lynn are very dashing indeed, and Colonel Dent is a fine soldierly man. Mr. Eshton, the magistrate of the district, is gentleman-like; his hair is quite white, his eyebrows and whiskers still dark. Lord Ingram, like his sisters, is very tall and handsome, but he shares Mary's sad and listless look.

And where is Mr. Rochester?

He comes in last—I am not looking at him, yet I see him enter. I try to concentrate on the netting needles that are in my lap. Now I distinctly behold his figure, and remember the last time I saw it—just after I had saved his life, and he, holding my hand, and looking down on my face, looked at me with eyes that revealed a heart full and eager to overflow, in whose emotions I had a part.

How close I had been to him at that moment! What had occurred since, that changed our situations? And now, how distant, how far apart we were! So far apart, that I did not expect him to come and speak to me. I did not wonder, when, without looking at me, he took a seat at the other side of the room, and began conversing with some of the ladies.

As soon as I saw that his attention was fixed on them, and that I might look without being seen, my eyes were drawn to his face—I could not keep them under control. I looked, and had pleasure in looking—a precious yet agonizing pleasure.

So true it is that 'beauty is in the eye of the beholder'. My master's colourless olive face, massive brow, broad black eyebrows, deep eyes, strong features, grim mouth—all energy, decision, and will—were not beautiful, according to the rules of beauty, but they were more than beautiful to me. They were full of an influence that quite mastered me, that took my feelings from my own power and tied them to his.

I had not intended to love him; the reader knows I had tried hard to wrench from my soul the seeds of love that began; and now, at the sight of him again, they grew all at once, green and strong! He made me love him without even looking at me.

I compared him with his guests. What was the gallant grace of the Lynns, the elegance of Lord Ingram, even the military distinction of Colonel Dent, contrasted with Mr. Rochester's look of natural energy and genuine power? Most observers would call the other gentlemen attractive, handsome, and imposing, while they would pronounce Mr. Rochester as harsh-featured and melancholy looking. I saw them smile, laugh—it was nothing. I saw Mr. Rochester smile—his stern features softened; his eyes grew brilliant and gentle.

He was talking at the moment to Louisa and Amy Eshton. I looked to see if their eyes fell, their colour blushed; and I was relieved when they were not moved with emotion. He is not to them what he is to me, I thought. He is not of their kind. I believe he is of mine—I am sure he is—I feel akin to him; I understand the language of his face and movements. Though rank and wealth separate us widely, I have something in my brain and heart, in my blood and nerves, that cements me to him.

Did I say, a few days ago, that I had nothing to do with him but to receive my salary? Did I forbid myself to think of him in any other light than as a paymaster? Every good, true, vigorous feeling I have centers round him. I know I must conceal my feelings; I must smother hope; I must remember that he cannot care much for me. For when I say that I am of his kind, I only mean that we have certain tastes and feelings in common. I must, then, continually repeat that we are forever apart—and yet, while I breathe and think, I must love him.

Coffee is handed out. Since the gentlemen entered, the ladies have become lively as larks; conversation is animated. Colonel Dent and Mr. Eshton argue about politics; their wives listen. The two proud dowagers, Lady Lynn and Lady Ingram, talk together. Sir George—whom I have forgotten to describe—a very big and fresh-looking country gentleman, stands before their sofa and occasionally puts in a word. Mr. Frederick Lynn has taken a seat beside Mary Ingram, and is showing her a splendid book. The tall and boring Lord Ingram leans on the back of the chair where lively Amy Eshton sits; she glances up at him, and chatters like a wren. Henry Lynn sits on an ottoman at the feet of Louisa—Adele shares it with him; he is trying to talk French with her, and Louisa laughs at his blunders.

With whom will Blanche Ingram converse? She is standing alone at the table, bending gracefully over an album. She seems to be waiting for someone, but she does not wait too long—she herself selects a mate.

Mr. Rochester, having left the Eshtons, stands on the hearth as solitary as Blanche stands by the table. She confronts him, standing on the opposite side of the mantelpiece.

"Mr. Rochester, I thought you were not fond of children?"

"I am not."

"Then what induced you to take charge of such a little doll as that?" she said, pointing to Adele. "Where did you pick her up?"

"I did not pick her up; she was left on my hands."

"You should have sent her to school."

"I could not afford it; schools are so expensive."

"Why, I suppose you have a governess for her. I saw a person with her just now—is she gone? Oh, no! There she is, behind the window curtain. You pay her, of course; I should think it would be just as expensive—more so, for you have them both to keep."

I feared—or should I say, hoped?—that the mention of me would make Mr. Rochester glance my way; and I shrank further into the shade, but he never turned his eyes.

"I have not considered the subject," said he, looking straight ahead.

"No, you men never do consider economy and common sense. You should hear Mama on the subject of governesses; Mary and I have had, I should think, at least a dozen; half of them detestable and the rest ridiculous, and all demons—were they not, Mama?"

"Did you speak, my dear?"

The young lady repeated her question.

"My dearest, don't mention governesses; the word makes me nervous. I have suffered like a martyr from their incompetence. I thank Heaven I am now done with them!"

Mrs. Dent bent over to Lady Ingram and whispered something in her ear; I suppose it was a reminder that one of the detested creatures was present.

"Too bad!" said her Ladyship in French. "I hope it may do her good!" Then, in a lower voice, but still loud enough for me to hear, "I noticed her; I am a judge of appearances, and in hers I see all the faults of her class."

"What are they, madam?" inquired Mr. Rochester aloud.

"I will tell you in private," replied she, wagging her turban three times with importance.

"But my curiosity will be past its appetite; it craves food now."

"Ask Blanche; she is nearer to you than I."

"Oh, don't pass him to me, Mama! I have just one word to say of the whole tribe of governesses—they are a nuisance. Not that I ever suffered much from them; I took care to turn the tables. What tricks Theodore and I used to play on our Miss Wilsons, and Mrs. Greys, and Madame Jouberts!

Theodore, do you remember those merry days?"

"Yaas, to be sure I do," drawled Lord Ingram.

"And Teddo, you know, I helped you in tormenting your tutor, the sickly Mr. Vining. He and Miss Wilson fell in love with each other, and I promise you that dear Mama soon learned about their immoral business. Did you not, my lady-mother?"

"Certainly, my dearest. Depend on that; there are a thousand reasons why liaisons between governesses and tutors should never be tolerated in any well-run house; firstly—"

"Oh, gracious, Mama!" said Blanche. "Spare us the list! We all know them—danger of a bad example to innocent children; neglect of duty on the part of the employees—am I right, Baroness Ingram, of Ingram Park?"

"My lily flower, you are right, as always."

"Then no more need be said—change the subject."

Amy Eshton, not hearing this order, joined in with her soft, childlike tone, "Louisa and I used to quiz our governess too; but she was such a good creature, she would bear anything. She was never cross with us; was she, Louisa?"

"No, never; we did what we pleased—ransacked her desk and her work-box, and turned her drawers inside out."

"I suppose, now," said Blanche, curling her lip sarcastically, "we shall hear the memoirs of all the governesses existing. In order to avoid such a pleasure, I again propose a new topic. Mr. Rochester, do you second my motion?

"Madam, I support you on this point, as on every other."

"Then, Signor Eduardo, are you 'in voice' tonight?"

"Donna Bianca, if you command it, I will be."

"Then, signor, I summon your vocal organs to my royal service."

Miss Ingram seated herself proudly at the piano, spreading out her snowy robes like a queen, and began a brilliant prelude, while talking. She was on her high horse tonight; her words and her air were intended to excite and amaze her listeners and appear very dashing and daring.

"Oh, I am so sick of the young men today!" exclaimed she, rattling away at the piano. "Poor, puny things, not fit to go far without mama's per-mission! Creatures so absorbed about their pretty faces, as if a man had anything to do with beauty! As if loveliness were not the special right of women! I grant an ugly woman is a blot on the fair face of creation; but as to the gentlemen, let them possess only strength and valour; let their motto be—hunt, shoot, and fight."

Jane Eyre

"Whenever I marry," she continued after a pause, "my husband shall not be a rival; I will suffer no competitor near the throne; his devotion shall not be shared with his reflection in the mirror. Mr. Rochester, now sing, and I will play for you."

"I am all obedience," was the response.

Now is my time to slip away, thought I, but Mr. Rochester's mellow, powerful bass, into which he threw his own feeling, his own force, found a way to my heart. I waited till the last deep, full note ended, then left my sheltered corner and made my exit by the nearby side door.

In the gallery, I felt my sandal coming loose; I stopped to tie it, kneeling down. I heard the dining room door open; a gentleman came out; rising hastily, I stood face to face with Mr. Rochester.

"How do you do?" he asked.

"I am very well, sir."

"Why did you not come and speak to me in the room?"

I considered a sharp answer to the question, but instead I said, "I did not wish to disturb you, as you seemed engaged, sir."

"What have you been doing during my absence?"

"Nothing in particular; teaching Adele as usual."

"And getting a good deal paler than you were. What is the matter?"

"Nothing at all, sir."

"Did you get a cold that night you half-drowned me?"

"Not in the least."

"Return to the drawing room; you are leaving too early."

"I am tired, sir."

He looked at me for a minute. "And a little depressed," he said. "What about? Tell me."

"Nothing—nothing, sir. I am not depressed."

"But I say that you are; so depressed, that a few more words would bring tears to your eyes. Indeed, they are there now—shining. If I had time, and did not fear some gossipy servant appearing, I would find out what all this means. Well, tonight I excuse you; but understand that so long as my visitors stay, I expect you to appear in the drawing room every evening; it is my wish; don't neglect it. Now go."

Then he looked at me and said, "Goodnight, my—" He stopped, bit his lip, and abruptly left me.

Chapter 18

These were merry days at Thornfield Hall, and busy days too; how different from the first three months of stillness, monotony, and solitude! All sad feelings were gone from the house; there was life everywhere, movement all day long. You could not go anywhere in the house without seeing a smart lady's maid or a dandy valet.

The house was only quiet when the blue sky and peaceful sunshine of spring called their occupants out into the grounds. Even when continuous rain set in for some days, the enjoyment was not dampened; indoor amusements were lively and varied.

One evening they spoke of 'playing charades'. I wondered what that meant. The dining room tables were wheeled away and the chairs placed in a semicircle. The ladies were running around gathering shawls, dresses, draperies, petticoats, and other clothing.

Mr. Rochester gathered the ladies round him and selected certain ones for his group. "Miss Ingram is mine, of course," then named the two Misses Eshton and Mrs. Dent.

He looked at me. "Will you play?" he asked. I shook my head. He did not insist, and allowed me to return quietly to my usual seat.

He and his aides now withdrew behind a curtain; the other group, headed by Colonel Dent, sat down on the chairs.

Mr. Eshton, observing me, proposed that I should join them; but Lady Ingram instantly negated the idea.

"No," I heard her say, "she looks too stupid for any game of the sort."

A bell tinkled. Then appeared the magnificent figure of Miss Ingram, clad in white, a long veil on her head, and a wreath of roses round her brow; by her side walked Mr. Rochester, and together they drew near the table. They knelt; a silent ceremony followed, in which it was easy to recognize the pantomime of a wedding.

Colonel Dent and his party consulted in whispers for two minutes, then the Colonel called out, "Bride!" and Mr. Rochester bowed to acknowledge their correct answer, and the curtain fell.

In the second charade, Mr. Rochester, a shawl and turban on his head, sat beside a large bowl. Blanche appeared, dressed in Biblical fashion as well, supporting a pitcher on her head. She bent over, as if to fill her pitcher from the bowl.

Colonel Dent's party could not agree on the word that described the scene, and requested another hint.

In the third charade, Mr. Rochester sat at a card table on a kitchen chair. His face was grimy, his clothes tattered, and his face desperate and frowning. His wrists were chained together.

"Bridewell!" exclaimed Colonel Dent, recognizing the common name for a prison, and the charade was solved.

After the performers changed their clothes, they re-entered the dining room. Mr. Rochester led in Miss Ingram; she was complimenting him on his acting.

"Do you know," said she, "that, of the three characters, I liked you in the last best? Oh, what a gallant gentleman highwayman you would have made!"

"Is all the soot washed from my face?" he asked, turning it towards her.

"Alas! Yes; nothing could be more attractive to your face than that ruffian's rouge."

"You would like a hero of the road then?"

"An English hero of the road would be the next best thing to an Italian bandit, only to be surpassed by a Mediterranean pirate."

"Well, whatever I am, remember you are my wife; we were married an hour ago, in the presence of all these witnesses."

Blanche giggled, and her colour rose as she blushed.

"Now, Colonel Dent," continued Mr. Rochester, "it is your turn." And as the other party withdrew, Mr. Rochester and his group took the seats. Miss Ingram placed herself beside him.

I no longer cared to watch the next charade. My attention was fixed on the spectators. I saw Mr. Rochester turn to Miss Ingram, and Miss Ingram to him; I saw her incline her head toward him, till her black curls almost touched his shoulder and waved against his cheek; I heard their whisperings, their exchanged glances.

I have told you, reader, that I had learned to love Mr. Rochester—I could not unlove him now, merely because I found that he ceased to notice me, because I might spend hours in his presence and he would never once turn his eyes in my direction, because I saw all his attentions directed toward a great lady, who wouldn't touch me even with the hem of her robes as she passed by; whose dark, haughty eyes could never look upon such an insignificant creature as I.

I could not unlove him, though I felt sure he would soon marry this very lady—because I saw that she was proudly secure of his intentions, and his style of courtship was captivating and, in its very pride, irresistible.

Though you will think, reader, there was much to cause jealousy, I was not jealous. Miss Ingram was a mark beneath jealousy—she was too inferior to excite the feeling. She was very showy, but she was not genuine; she had many brilliant talents, but her mind was poor, her heart empty; she was not original—she repeated phrases from books and never had an opinion of her own.

She had no sympathy, pity, tenderness, or truth. She betrayed this by her treatment of little Adele—pushing her away if she approached her; always treating her with coldness. Mr. Rochester himself kept a steady eye on her defects, and it was his lack of passion toward her that caused my tortured pain.

I saw he was only going to marry her for family or political reasons, because of her social rank and connections. I felt that he was not in love. This was the point—this was where the nerve was touched and teased—she could not charm him.

If he had laid his heart at her feet, I would have covered my face, turned to the wall, and gone away. If Miss Ingram had been a good and noble woman, with kindness and sense, I would have felt jealousy and despair; then, with my heart torn out, I would have acknowledged her excellence, and been quiet for the rest of my days.

But as matters really stood, to watch the repeated failure of Miss Ingram's efforts to fascinate Mr. Rochester—and she unaware that they failed—and with her pride and self-satisfaction further repulsing him, to witness this, was almost unbearable.

Surely she cannot like him with true affection! If she did, she need not make her smiles so lavish, nor flash her glances so constantly. It seems to me that by merely sitting quietly at his side, saying little and staring less, she would get closer to his heart.

How will she manage to please him when they are married? I do not think she will, and yet she might, and she might be the very happiest woman the sun shines on.

I have not yet condemned Mr. Rochester's marrying for social position. It surprised me at first—I had thought him a man unlikely to be influenced by such motives; but the longer I considered it, the less I could blame him for conforming to ideas and principles instilled from childhood—all members of his social class held these principles of marriage.

Meanwhile, I found I was forgetting all his faults, for which I had once kept a sharp lookout. I had formerly tried to study all sides of his character, to take the bad with the good, and form a fair judgment. Now I saw no bad. The sarcasm, the harshness that had startled and repelled me, did no more.

One day, Mr. Rochester was summoned to Millcote on business, and was not likely to return till late. The afternoon was wet, and his guests delayed a proposed walk to see a gypsy camp which had been set up in a field beyond Hay. Some of the gentlemen went to the stables; the younger ones, together with the younger ladies, were playing billiards. The dowagers Ingram and Lynn played a quiet game at cards. Blanche Ingram flung herself on a sofa with a book to pass the tedious hours without Mr. Rochester.

It was nearly dusk, when little Adele, who knelt by me in the drawing room window seat, suddenly exclaimed in French, "Here's Mr. Rochester coming home!"

I turned, and Miss Ingram darted forward from her sofa, and the others looked up from their activities. A carriage drawn by horses was approaching.

"What can possess him to come home in that style?" said Miss Ingram. "He rode the black horse, did he not, when he left? And Pilot was with him."

The carriage stopped; the driver rang the doorbell; and a gentleman got out, dressed in traveling clothes; but it was not Mr. Rochester—it was a tall, fashionable-looking man, a stranger.

"How provoking!" exclaimed Miss Ingram to Adele. "You tiresome monkey! Perched up in the window to give false information?" and she cast me an angry glance, as if I were at fault.

Soon the newcomer entered the room. He bowed to Lady Ingram, deeming her the oldest lady present.

"It appears I come at an inconvenient time, madam," said he, "when my friend, Mr. Rochester, is away from home; but I have journeyed very long, and I think I may impose on such an old and intimate acquaintance to stay here till he returns."

His manner was polite; his accent was not foreign, but not altogether English; his age might be about Mr. Rochester's, between thirty and forty; his face was singularly pale, otherwise he was a fine-looking man. Looking closer, something was displeasing. His features were too relaxed—his eyes were vacant.

It was not till after dinner that I saw him again—and I liked him even less. His face seemed lifeless. For a handsome man, he repelled me; there was no power in the smooth oval face, no thoughts emanating from the low forehead.

As I sat in my usual nook, I compared him with Mr. Rochester. I think the contrast could not be much greater between a sleek goose and a fierce falcon. He had spoken of Mr. Rochester as an old friend. A curious friendship it must have been—a pointed example of the old adage that 'opposites attract'.

Louisa Eshton and Mary Ingram, who sat near me, called him "a beautiful man." Louisa said she "adored him", and Mary was fond of his "pretty little mouth, and nice nose."

"And what a sweet-tempered forehead he has!" cried Louisa, "so smooth—none of those frowning lines I dislike; and such a calm eye and smile!"

I presently learned that the newcomer was called Mr. Mason; he had just arrived in England from Kingston, Jamaica, and that the West Indies was his home. I was surprised to gather, before long, that there he had first met Mr. Rochester. He spoke of his friend's dislike of the burning heat, the hurricanes, and rainy seasons of that region.

I knew Mr. Rochester had been a traveler—Mrs. Fairfax had said so; but I thought his wanderings had been confined to Europe; till now I had never heard of visits to more distant shores.

I was pondering these things when an unexpected incident occurred. The footman stopped near Mr. Eshton's chair and said something to him in a low voice, to which Mr. Eshton replied:

"Tell her if she does not leave, she shall be put in the stocks."

"No—stop!" interrupted Colonel Dent. "Don't send her away, Eshton; better consult the ladies." And speaking aloud, he continued:

"Ladies, you talked of going to Hay Common to visit the gypsy camp; Sam here says that an old gypsy woman is here, at this moment, and insists upon being brought in to tell your fortunes. Would you like to see her?"

"Surely, colonel," cried Lady Ingram, "you would not encourage such a vulgar impostor? Dismiss her, by all means, at once!"

"But I cannot persuade her to go away, my lady," said the footman. "Nor can any of the servants. Mrs. Fairfax is with her just now, begging her to be gone; but she has sat down in a chair and says nothing shall stir her, till she comes in here."

"What does she want?" asked Mrs. Eshton.

Jane Eyre

"To tell the gentry their fortunes, she says, ma'am; and she swears she must and will do it."

"What is she like?" inquired the Misses Eshton, in a breath.

"A shockingly ugly old creature, miss; almost as black as a smudge."

"Why, she's a real sorceress!" cried Frederick Lynn. "Let us have her in, of course."

"To be sure," rejoined his brother. "It would be a thousand pities to throw away such a chance of fun."

"My dear boys, what are you thinking about?" exclaimed Mrs. Lynn.

"I cannot possibly permit any such proceeding," chimed in the Dowager Ingram.

"Indeed, mama, but you can—and will," pronounced the haughty voice of Blanche. "I have a curiosity to hear my fortune told; therefore, Sam, order the witch forward."

"My darling Blanche! Remember—"

"I do—I remember, and I must have my will—quick, Sam!"

"Yes—yes—yes!" cried all the young ladies and gentlemen. "Let her come—it will be excellent sport!"

The footman still lingered. "She looks like such a rough one," said he.

"Go!" spurted Miss Ingram, and the man went.

Excitement instantly seized the whole party; then Sam returned.

"She won't come now," said he. "She says it's not her mission to appear before the 'vulgar herd', as she says. I must show her into a room by herself, and then those who wish to consult her must go in one by one."

"You see now, my queenly Blanche," began Lady Ingram, "she intrudes. Be advised, my angel girl, and—"

"Show her into the library, of course," said Blanche. "It is not my mission to listen to her before the vulgar herd, either; I will have her all to myself. Is there a fire in the library?"

"Yes, ma'am—but she looks naughty."

"Cease that chatter, blockhead! And do my bidding."

Again Sam vanished; and mystery and expectation rose to full flow once more.

"She's ready now," said the footman, as he reappeared. "She wishes to know who will be her first visitor."

"I think I had better look in upon her before any of the ladies go," said Colonel Dent.

"Tell her, Sam, a gentleman is coming."

Sam went and returned.

"She says, sir, that she'll have no gentlemen; they need not trouble themselves to come near her—nor, any ladies either, except the young and single."

"By Jove, she has taste!" exclaimed Henry Lynn.

Miss Ingram rose solemnly. "I go first," she said, in a tone which might have befitted a captain leading his men into a hopeless battle.

"Oh, my best! Oh, my dearest! Pause—reflect!" was her mama's cry; but she swept past her in stately silence, passed through the door which Colonel Dent held open, and we heard her enter the library.

A silence ensued. Lady Ingram sat wringing her hands. Amy and Louisa Eshton tittered under their breath and looked a little frightened.

The minutes passed very slowly—fifteen were counted before the library door again opened and Miss Ingram returned.

Would she laugh? Would she take it as a joke? All eyes met her with a glance of eager curiosity, and she met all eyes with one of coldness; she walked stiffly to her seat, and sat in silence.

"Well, Blanche?" said Lord Ingram.

"What did she say, sister?" asked Mary.

"What did you think? How do you feel? Is she a real fortune teller?" demanded the Misses Eshton.

"Now, now, good people," returned Miss Ingram, "don't press upon me. You seem to believe we have a genuine witch in the house. She is a gypsy vagabond; she has practiced tired old palmistry and told me what such people usually tell. My whim is gratified; and now I think Mr. Eshton should put the hag in the stocks tomorrow morning, as he threatened."

Miss Ingram took a book, leaned back in her chair, and declined further conversation. I watched her for nearly half an hour; during all that time she never turned a page, and her face grew darker and more disappointed. She had obviously not heard anything to her advantage; and it seemed that she attached a great deal of importance to the revelations.

Meantime, Mary Ingram, Amy and Louisa Eshton, dared not go in alone. A negotiation was opened through the ambassador, Sam; and after much pacing to and fro, permission was at last granted for the three young ladies to enter together.

Their visit was not so quiet as Miss Ingram's had been; we heard hysterical giggling and little shrieks from the library; and after twenty minutes they burst the door open, and came running across the hall, as if they were half-scared out of their wits.

"I am sure she is something evil!" they cried, one and all. "She told us such things! She knows all about us!" and they sank breathless into their various seats.

Pressed for details, they declared she had told them of things they had said and done when they were mere children; described books and ornaments they had at home; keepsakes that different relatives had presented to them. They said that she even read their thoughts, and had whispered in the ear of each young lady, the name of the person she liked best in the world, and revealed what they most wished for.

Here the gentlemen asked to know what the gypsy told them on these last two points, but were met with blushes and titters, despite earnest requests.

During the commotion, Sam approached me and said, "If you please, miss, the gypsy declares that there is another young single lady in the room who has not been to her yet, and she swears she will not leave till she has seen everyone. I thought it must be you—there is no one else. What shall I tell her?"

"Oh, I will go by all means," I answered; and I was glad of the unexpected opportunity to satisfy my curiosity. I slipped out of the room, unseen by any eye, and I closed the door quietly behind me.

"If you like, miss," said Sam, "I'll wait in the hall for you; and if she frightens you, just call and I'll come in."

"No, Sam, return to the kitchen. I am not in the least afraid." Nor was I; but I was a good deal interested and excited.

Chapter 19

The library looked peaceful enough as I entered it, and the gypsy was seated snugly in an easy chair by the fireplace. She had on a red cloak and a black bonnet. She was bending over the fire, and seemed to be reading a little black book; she muttered the words to herself, as most old women do, while she read.

I stood on the rug and warmed my hands. The gypsy shut her book and slowly looked up; her hat brim partially shaded her face, yet I could see that it was a strange one. It looked all brown and black; her eyes confronted me at once, with a bold and direct gaze.

"Well, and you want your fortune told?" she said, in a voice as harsh as her features.

"I don't care about it, mother; you may please yourself; but I ought to warn you, I have no faith."

"I expected that from you; I heard rudeness in your step as you crossed the threshold."

"Did you? You've a quick ear."

"I have; and a quick eye and a quick brain."

"You need them all in your trade."

"I do; especially when I've customers like you to deal with. Why don't you tremble?"

"I'm not cold."

"Why don't you turn pale?"

"I am not sick."

"Why did you not consult my advice?"

"I'm not silly."

The old crone uttered a laugh; she then drew out a short black pipe and, lighting it, began to smoke. Then she raised her bent body, took the pipe from her lips, and while gazing steadily at the fire, said very deliberately:

"You are cold; you are sick; and you are silly."

"Prove it," I rejoined.

"I will, in few words. You are cold, because you are alone; you are sick, because love stays far away from you; you are silly, because, suffer as you may, you will not beckon love to approach, nor will you take one step to meet it where it waits for you."

"You could say that to almost anyone who lived as a single servant in a great house."

"I might say it to almost anyone; but would it be true of almost anyone?"

"In my circumstances, yes," I said.

"Yes, in your circumstances; but find me another lady precisely placed as you are."

"It would be easy to find you thousands."

"You could scarcely find me one," said the gypsy. "You are very near happiness—within reach of it. The materials are all prepared; there only needs movement to combine them. Chance laid them somewhat apart; let them be brought together, and bliss results."

"I don't understand riddles—I never could."

"If you wish me to speak more plainly, show me your palm."

"And it must contain some silver, I suppose?"

"To be sure."

I gave her a shilling; she put it into an old stocking which she took out of her pocket; she told me to hold out my hand. I did. She pored over my palm without touching it.

"It is too fine," said she. "I can make nothing of such a hand as that—almost without lines. Besides, what is in a palm? Destiny is not written there."

"I believe you," said I.

"It is in the face," she continued, "on the forehead, about the eyes, in the lines of the mouth. Kneel, and lift up your head."

"Ah! Now you are coming back to reality," I said, as I obeyed her. "I shall begin to put some faith in you soon."

I knelt. She stirred the fire, so that a ripple of light illuminated my face.

"I wonder with what feelings you came to me tonight," she said, when she had examined me a while. "I wonder what thoughts are busy in your heart during all the hours you sit in that room, with the fine people flitting before you like shapes in a magic lantern."

"I often feel tired, sleepy sometimes, but seldom sad."

"Then you have some secret hope for the future to buoy you up?"

"Not I. My utmost hope is to save money enough out of my earnings to set up a school someday in a little house."

"A small hope for the spirit to exist on, and sitting in that window seat—you see, I know your habits—"

"You have learned them from the servants."

"Ah! You think yourself sharp. Well, perhaps you are right; to speak the truth, I have an acquaintance with one of them—Mrs. Poole."

I started to my feet when I heard the name.

Oh, you have—have you? thought I; there is black art in the business after all, then!

"Don't be alarmed," continued the strange being. "She's a safe servant—private and quiet. But as I was saying, sitting in that window seat, do you think of nothing but your future school? Have you no interest in any of the company who occupy the sofas and chairs before you? Is there not one face you study? One figure whose movements you follow with at least curiosity?"

"I like to observe all the faces and all the figures."

"But do you ever single one out from the rest—or two?"

"I do, when a pair seems to tell a tale; it amuses me to watch them."

"What tale do you like best to hear?"

"Oh, I have not much choice! They generally run on the same theme—courtship; and promise to end in the same catastrophe—marriage."

"And do you like that monotonous theme?"

"I don't care about it; it is nothing to me."

"Nothing to you? When a lady, young and full of life and health, charming with beauty and endowed with the gifts of rank and fortune, sits and smiles in the eyes of a gentleman you—"

"I what?"

"You know—and perhaps think well of."

"I don't know the gentlemen here. I have scarcely exchanged a word with any of them. They are free to receive any smiles they please, without meaning anything to me."

"You don't know the gentlemen here? You have not exchanged a syllable with any one of them? Even the master of the house?"

"He is not home."

"A clever remark! He went to Millcote this morning, and will be back here tonight or tomorrow; does that exclude him from the list of your acquaintance—blot him out of existence?"

"No, but I can scarcely see what Mr. Rochester has to do with the topic."

"I was talking of ladies smiling in the eyes of gentlemen; and lately, so many smiles have been shed into Mr. Rochester's eyes that they overflow."

"Mr. Rochester has a right to enjoy the society of his guests."

"But have you never observed that, of all the tales told here about matrimony, most have included Mr. Rochester?"

"The eagerness of a listener quickens the tongue of a narrator."

The gypsy's strange talk, voice, and manner had wrapped me in a kind of dream. One unexpected sentence came from her lips after another, till I wondered what unseen spirit had been watching my heart for weeks, and recording every pulse.

"Eagerness of a listener!" repeated she. "Yes, Mr. Rochester has sat by the hour, listening to the lips that loved to talk. He looked so grateful for the pleasure—you have noticed this?"

"Grateful! I cannot remember seeing that on his face."

"And what did you see, if not gratitude?"

I said nothing.

"You have seen love, have you not? And looking into the future, you have seen him married, and seen his bride happy?"

"Humph! Not exactly. Your witch's skill is rather at fault sometimes."

"What the devil have you seen, then?"

"Never mind—I came here to inquire, not to confess. Is it known that Mr. Rochester is to be married?"

"Yes; and to the beautiful Miss Ingram."

"Soon?"

"It would appear so; and, no doubt, they will be a supremely happy pair. He must love such a handsome, noble, witty, accomplished lady; and probably she loves him, or at least his money. I know she considers the Rochester estate to be vast, though, God pardon me, I told her something about an hour ago that made the corners of her mouth fall half an inch. I would advise Mr. Rochester to beware; if another, wealthier gentleman comes along, he's dished—"

"I did not come to hear Mr. Rochester's fortune; I came to hear my own; and you have told me nothing of it."

"Your fortune is doubtful. Chance has given you a measure of happiness, that I know. She has laid it carefully on one side for you—I saw her do it. It depends on you to stretch out your hand and take it; but whether you will do so, is the problem I study. Kneel again on the rug."

"Don't keep me long; the fire scorches me."

I knelt. She gazed at me, leaning back in her chair. She began muttering:

"The eyes look soft and full of feeling; the lids are weary—loneliness makes them sad; the eyes turn from me, denying the truth of what I have said. The eyes are favourable.

"As to the mouth, it delights in laughter at times; it was never intended to be silent in loneliness; it is a mouth which should speak much and smile often, and have human affection. The mouth is favourable.

"I see no enemy to happiness except in the brow; and that brow wants to say, 'I can live alone, if I must. I need not sell my soul to buy happiness.'

"The forehead declares, 'Judgment and reason sit firm and shall have the last word in every decision. I will not let feelings carry her away. Passions may rage, but I shall follow my conscience.'

"That will do," said the gypsy. "I think I rave in a kind of exquisite delirium. I wish to stretch this moment out to infinity, but I dare not. Any more might try me beyond my strength. Rise, Miss Eyre, leave me; the play is played out."

Where was I? Had I been dreaming? The old woman's voice had changed—her accent, her gesture, all were familiar to me. I got up, but did not go. I looked, and at once I noticed that hand. It was no longer withered; it had smooth fingers; a ring flashed on the little finger, with a gem I had seen a hundred times before. Again I looked at the face; the bonnet was gone, the bandage removed.

"Well, Jane, do you know me?" asked the familiar voice—and Mr. Rochester was out of his disguise.

"Now, sir, what a strange idea!"

"But well carried out, eh? Don't you think so?"

"With the ladies, you must have managed well."

"But not with you?"

"You did not act the character of a gypsy with me."

"What character did I act? My own?"

"No; I believe you have been trying to draw me out—or in; it was hardly fair, sir."

"Do you forgive me, Jane?"

"I cannot tell till I have thought it all over. I shall try to forgive you; but it was not right."

"Oh, you have been very correct—very careful, very sensible."

I reflected, and thought that, on the whole, I had. I had been on my guard almost from the beginning. I suspected a masquerade. I knew gypsies and fortune tellers did not express themselves as this seeming old woman had; besides, I had noted her disguised voice. But my mind had turned to

Jane Eyre

Grace Poole—that living enigma, that mystery of mysteries. I had never thought of Mr. Rochester.

"Well," said he, "what are you thinking about?"

"Wonder and self-congratulation, sir. I have your permission to retire now, I suppose?"

"No, stay a moment, and tell me what the people in the drawing room are doing."

"Discussing the gypsy, I daresay."

"Sit down! Let me hear what they said about me." He took my hand, as if to lead me to a chair.

"I had better not stay long, sir; it must be near eleven o'clock. Oh, are you aware, Mr. Rochester, that a stranger has arrived here since you left this morning?"

"A stranger! No—who can it be? I expected no one; is he gone?"

"No, he said he had known you long, and that he could take the liberty of staying here till you returned."

"The devil he did! Did he give his name?"

"His name is Mason, sir; and he comes from the West Indies."

As I spoke, he gave my wrist a convulsive grip; the smile on his lips froze.

"Mason!—the West Indies!" he said three times, growing whiter than ashes; he hardly seemed to know what he was doing.

"Do you feel ill, sir?" I inquired.

"Jane, I've had a blow; I've had a blow, Jane!" He staggered.

"Oh, lean on me, sir."

"Jane, you offered me your shoulder once before; let me have it now."

"Yes, sir, yes; and my arm."

He sat down, and made me sit beside him. Holding my hand in both his own, he rubbed it; gazing on me, at the same time, with the most troubled and dreary look.

"My little friend," said he, "I wish I were in a quiet island with only you; and trouble, and danger, and hideous memories removed from me."

"Can I help you, sir? I'd give my life to serve you."

"Jane, if I need help, I'll get it from you; I promise you that."

"Thank you, sir. Tell me what to do. I'll try, at least, to do it."

"Fetch me now, Jane, a glass of wine from the dining room. They will be at supper there, and tell me if Mason is with them, and what he is doing."

I went. I found all the party in the dining room at supper, which was arranged on the sideboard; each had taken what he chose, and they stood about here and there in groups, their plates and glasses in their hands. Everyone seemed in high glee; laughter and conversation were animated.

Mr. Mason stood near the fire, talking to Colonel and Mrs. Dent, and appeared as merry as any of them. I filled a wine glass—Miss Ingram watch me frowningly as I did so—and I returned to the library.

Mr. Rochester's extreme pallor had disappeared, and he looked once more firm and stern. He took the glass from my hand.

"Here is to your health!" he said. He swallowed the contents and returned it to me. "What are they doing, Jane?"

"Laughing and talking, sir."

"They don't look grave and mysterious, as if they had heard something strange?"

"Not at all; they are full of jests and gaiety."

"And Mason?"

"He was laughing, too."

"If all these people came in and spat at me, what would you do, Jane?"

"Turn them out of the room, sir, if I could."

He half-smiled. "But if I were to go to them, and they only looked at me coldly, and whispered sneeringly amongst each other, and then dropped off and left me one by one, what then? Would you go with them?"

"I think not, sir; I would have more pleasure in staying with you."

"To comfort me?"

"Yes, sir, to comfort you, as well as I could."

"And if they banned you for staying with me?"

"I would probably know nothing about their ban; and if I did, I would care nothing about it."

"Then you would risk being condemned for my sake?"

"I would risk it for the sake of any friend who deserved my comfort; as I am sure you do."

"Go back now into the room; step quietly up to Mason, and whisper in his ear that Mr. Rochester has come and wishes to see him; show him in here and then leave me."

I obeyed his request. The company all stared at me as I passed straight among them. I sought Mr. Mason, delivered the message, ushered him into the library, and then I went upstairs.

At a late hour, after I had been in bed some time, I heard the visitors retire to their chambers. I heard Mr. Rochester's voice say, "This way, Mason; this is your room."

He spoke cheerfully, and my heart was at ease. I was soon asleep.

Chapter 20

I had forgotten to draw my curtain and let down my window blind. And so the moon, which was full and bright, looked in and roused me. Awaking in the dead of night, I opened my eyes and half rose to draw the curtain. And then:

Good God! What a scream! The silence of the night was torn in half by a savage, sharp, shrill sound that ran from end to end of Thornfield Hall.

My pulse stopped; my heart stood still. The fearful shriek died, and was not repeated.

It came from the third story, in the room just above my chamber. I now heard a struggle—a deadly one it seemed, from the noise; and a half-smothered voice shouted:

"Help! Help! Help!" three times rapidly. "Will no one come?" it cried.

And then, during wild staggering and stamping of feet, I heard, "Rochester! Rochester! For God's sake, come!"

A bedroom door opened; someone rushed past my chamber. Another foot stamped on the floor above, and something fell; and then, there was silence.

I put on some clothes, though horror shook all my limbs. I slipped out of my room. The sleepers were all aroused—terrified murmurs came from every room; door after door opened; the gallery soon filled with people.

Gentlemen and ladies, confused, running to and fro, crowding together, some sobbing, and "Oh! What has happened?"—"Who is hurt?"—"Fetch a light!"—"Is it a fire?"—"Are there robbers?"—"Where shall we run?" was demanded all around.

"Where the devil is Rochester?" cried Colonel Dent. "I cannot find him in his bed."

"Here! Here!" he shouted in return. "Be composed, all of you; I'm coming."

The door at the end of the gallery opened, and Mr. Rochester advanced with a candle—he had just descended from the third story. One of the ladies ran to him and seized his arm—it was Miss Ingram.

"What awful event has taken place?" said she. "Speak! Let us know the worst at once!"

"Don't pull me down or strangle me," he replied, for the Misses Eshton were clinging to him now; and the two dowagers, in vast white robes, were bearing down upon him.

"All is right! All is right!" he cried. "It's a mere rehearsal of 'Much Ado About Nothing'. Ladies, keep off, or I shall become dangerous."

And dangerous he looked—his black eyes darted sparks. With effort, and calming himself, he added:

"A servant has had a nightmare, that is all. She's an excitable, nervous person. Now then, I must see you all back into your rooms. She cannot be looked after, till the house is settled. Gentlemen, have the goodness to set an example for the ladies. Miss Ingram, I am sure you will not fail to rise above idle terror. Amy and Louisa, return to your nests like a pair of doves. Mesdames," addressing the dowagers, "you will certainly catch cold if you stay in this chilly gallery any longer."

And so, by coaxing and commanding, Mr. Rochester managed to get them all once more enclosed in their separate chambers. I did not wait to be ordered back to mine, but retreated unnoticed.

Not, however, to go to bed; on the contrary, I dressed myself carefully. The sounds and words I had heard after the scream had probably been heard only by me, for they came from the room above mine. They convinced me it was not a servant's dream, and the explanation Mr. Rochester had given was merely invented to calm his guests.

I dressed, then, to be ready for emergencies, and sat a long time by the window looking out over the silent grounds, waiting for I knew not what. It seemed to me that something must follow the strange cry and struggle.

But, no—stillness returned. Each murmur and movement gradually ceased, and in about an hour Thornfield Hall was again as quiet as a desert. It seemed that sleep and night had resumed their reign.

I decided to lie down on my bed, dressed as I was. I left the window, and moved across the carpet. As I stooped to take off my shoes, a cautious hand tapped quietly at the door.

"Am I wanted?" I asked.

"Are you up?" asked the voice I expected to hear—my master's.

"Yes, sir."

"And dressed?"

"Yes."

"Come out, then, quietly."

I obeyed. Mr. Rochester stood in the gallery holding a light.

"I want you," he said. "Come this way. Take your time, and make no noise."

My slippers were thin—I could walk as softly as a cat. He glided along the gallery and up the stairs, and stopped in the dark corridor of the fateful third story; I followed and stood at his side.

"Have you a sponge and smelling salts in your room?" he asked in a whisper.

"Yes, sir."

"Go back and fetch both."

I left, retrieved the items, and returned to him. He still waited, with a key in his hand. Approaching one of the doors, he paused, and addressed me again.

"You don't turn sick at the sight of blood?"

"I think I shall not, but I have never seen it." I trembled as I answered him, but no coldness, and no faintness.

"Just give me your hand," he said. "It will not do to risk a fainting fit."

I put my fingers into his. "Warm and steady" was his remark; he turned the key and opened the door.

I remembered the room from the day Mrs. Fairfax first showed me the house; a tapestry hung on one wall, but now it was drawn back, revealing another door, leading to an inner room which had been concealed. This door was open, and a light shone from it.

I then heard a snarling, snatching sound, almost like a dog barking. Mr. Rochester, putting down his candle, said to me:

"Wait a minute," and he went forward to the inner room.

A shout of laughter greeted him, noisy at first, then ending with Grace Poole's own goblin "Ha! Ha!" She was in there. After some quiet words were exchanged, Mr. Rochester then came out and closed the door behind him.

The room in which we stood contained a large bed, concealed by drawn curtains. "Here, Jane!" said Mr. Rochester, and I walked round to the other side. A man sat in an easy chair near the headboard; he was dressed; he was still; his head leaned back; his eyes were closed.

Mr. Rochester held the candle over him; I recognized his pale, life-less face—Mason. I saw, too, that his shirt on one side, and one arm, was almost soaked in blood.

"Hold the candle," said Mr. Rochester, and I took it. He fetched a bowl of water from the washstand.

"Hold that," said he, and I obeyed. He took the sponge, dipped it in, and moistened the corpse-like face; he asked for my bottle of smelling salts and held it to Mason's nostrils.

Mr. Mason soon opened his eyes; he groaned. Mr. Rochester opened the shirt of the wounded man, whose arm and shoulder were bandaged; he sponged away blood, trickling down fast.

"Is there immediate danger?" murmured Mr. Mason.

"Pooh! No—a mere scratch. Don't be so overcome, man, bear up! I'll fetch a surgeon for you now, myself; you'll be able to leave by morning, I hope." Mr. Rochester looked at me.

"Jane?" he continued.

"Sir?"

"I shall have to leave you in this room with this gentleman, for an hour, perhaps two. You will sponge the blood when it returns; if he feels faint, you will give him some water, and put your salts to his nose. You will not speak to him under any condition—and Richard, it will be at the peril of your life if you speak to her. Open your lips—and I'll not answer for the consequences."

Again the poor man groaned; he looked as if he dared not move. Fear—either of death or something else, almost paralyzed him. Mr. Rochester put the bloody sponge into my hand, and I proceeded to use it as he had done. He watched me a second, then said, "Remember! No conversation." He left the room.

I experienced a strange feeling as the key turned in the lock, and the sound of his footsteps ceased to be heard.

Here then, I was in the third story, in one of its mystic cells; night around me; a pale and bloody spectacle of a man on my hands; a murderess, barely separated from me by a single door—yes, that was appalling. The rest I could bear, but I shuddered at the thought of Grace Poole bursting out upon me.

I must keep to my post, however. I must watch this ghastly face—these blue, still lips forbidden to speak; these eyes opening, closing, wandering through the room, fixing on me, glazed with the dullness of horror. I must dip my hand again and again in the basin of blood and water, and wipe away the trickling gore.

I must see the shadows on the antique tapestry, the bed hangings, and the doors of a great cabinet in the room—whose front, divided into twelve panels, bore the carved heads of the twelve disciples, while above them at the top rose an ebony crucifix and a dying Christ.

Amidst all this, I had to listen as well as watch—to listen for the movements of the wild beast in the next room. But since Mr. Rochester's visit, it had seemed subdued; during his absence, I heard only three sounds—a step creaking, a momentary snarling noise, and a deep human groan.

What evil was trapped in this mansion, and could neither be expelled nor subdued by the owner? What mystery, that broke out in fire and now in blood, at the deadest hours of night? What creature was it, disguised as an ordinary woman, uttered the voice of a mocking demon or a bird of prey?

And this quiet stranger I bent over—how had he become involved in the web of horror? And why had Grace Poole attacked him? What was he doing in this part of the house? I had heard Mr. Rochester assign him a room below—what brought him here? And why, now, was he so tame after the violence done to him?

Why did Mr. Mason so quietly submit to the silence Mr. Rochester ordered, and why did he order it? His guest had been attacked, and he smothered it in secrecy.

Lastly, why was Mr. Rochester so upset at the arrival of so passive a friend as Mr. Mason? I could not forget the master's paleness when he whispered, "Jane, I have had a blow." I could not forget how his arm had trembled when he rested it on my shoulder—something significant must have happened to shake the vigorous frame of Fairfax Rochester.

"When will he come? When will he come?" I cried inwardly, as the night lingered and lingered; my bleeding patient drooped, moaned, sickened; and neither daylight nor help arrived. I had, again and again, held the water to Mason's white lips; again and again offered him the smelling salts.

My efforts seemed helpless—bodily and mental suffering, and loss of blood, were fast sapping his strength. He moaned so, and looked so weak, wild, and lost, that I feared he was dying—and I couldn't even speak to him.

The candle, spent at last, went out; as it did, I saw through the window that dawn was approaching. Soon I heard Pilot bark below—hope revived. Five minutes later, the key turned in the lock.

Mr. Rochester entered, and with him the surgeon he had fetched.

"Now, Carter," he said to the doctor, "I give you half an hour for dressing the wound, fastening the bandages, and getting the patient downstairs."

"But is he fit to move, sir?"

"Yes, it is nothing serious; he is nervous; his spirits must be kept up. Come, set to work."

Mr. Rochester drew back the curtain and let in the daylight. Then he approached Mason, whom the surgeon was already caring for.

"Now, my good fellow, how are you?" he asked.

"I'm done for, I fear," was the faint reply.

"Nonsense! Courage! In a fortnight you'll hardly be the worse for it—you've just lost a little blood. Right, Carter? Assure him there's no danger."

"I can do that," said Carter, who had now undone the bandages. "I only I wish I could have gotten here sooner—he would not have bled so much. But what is this? The flesh on the shoulder is torn, as well as cut. This wound was not done with a knife—there have been teeth here!"

"She bit me like a tigress," he murmured, "when Rochester got the knife from her."

"You should not have given in—you should have grappled with her at once," said Mr. Rochester.

"But under the circumstances, what could I do?" returned Mason. "Oh, it was frightful!" he added, shuddering. "And I did not expect it—she looked so quiet at first."

"I warned you," was his friend's answer. "I said—be on your guard when you go near her. Besides, you might have waited till tomorrow, and had me with you. It was mere folly to attempt the interview tonight, and alone."

"I thought I could have done some good."

"You thought! You thought! It makes me impatient to hear you; but you have suffered enough for not taking my advice, so I'll say no more. Carter—hurry! Hurry! The sun will soon rise, and I must have him off."

"Right away, sir; the shoulder is just bandaged. I must look at this other wound in the arm—she has had her teeth here too, I think."

"She sucked my blood; she said she'd drain my heart," said Mason.

I saw Mr. Rochester shudder—an expression of disgust, horror, and hatred distorted his face; but he only said:

"Come, be silent, Richard, never mind her gibberish—and don't repeat it."

"I wish I could forget it," was Mason's answer.

"You will when you are out of the country. When you get back to Jamaica, you may think of her as dead and buried—or rather, you need not think of her at all."

"Impossible to forget this night!"

"It is not impossible; have some energy, man. You thought you were as dead as a herring two hours ago, and you are all alive and talking now. There! Carter is nearly done—I'll make you decent. Jane, take this key. Go down into my bedroom, and open the top drawer of the wardrobe; take out a clean shirt and neck-handkerchief, and bring them here."

I went, found the clothing, and returned.

"Was anybody stirring below when you went down, Jane?" inquired Mr. Rochester.

"No, sir; all was very still."

"We shall get you off cleverly, Richard; and it will be better, both for your sake, and for that poor creature in the next room. I have tried hard to avoid exposure, and I should not like it to come now. Here, Carter, help him on with his vest. Jane, run down to Mr. Mason's room, the one next to mine, and fetch his cloak."

Again I ran, and again returned, bearing an immense cloak lined and edged with fur.

"Now, I've another errand for you, Jane," said my untiring master. "In my room, open the middle drawer of my toilet table and take out a little vial and a little glass—quick!"

I flew there and back, bringing the desired vessels.

"That's well! Now, doctor, I shall take the responsibility of administering this dose myself. I got this cordial in Rome, from an Italian quack—a fellow you would have kicked, Carter. It is not something to be used carelessly, but it is good on certain occasions—like now, for instance. Jane, a little water."

He held out the tiny glass, and I half-filled it from the water bottle on the washstand. He measured twelve drops of the crimson liquid, and presented it to Mason.

"Drink, Richard; it will give you the heart you lack, for an hour or so."

"But will it hurt me?"

"Drink! Drink! Drink!"

Mr. Mason obeyed, because it was useless to resist. He was dressed now; he still looked pale, but he was no longer gory. Mr. Rochester let him sit three minutes, then took his arm.

"Now I am sure you can get on your feet," he said. "Try—try."

The patient rose.

"Carter, take him under the other shoulder. Be of good cheer, Richard. Step out—that's it!"

"I do feel better," remarked Mr. Mason.

"I am sure you do. Now, Jane, go down the back stairs ahead of us; unbolt the side door, and tell the driver of the carriage to be ready; we are coming—and Jane, if anyone is around, come to the foot of the stairs and cough."

It was half-past five, and the sun was on the point of rising; but the kitchen was still dark and silent. I opened the side door, and there was the carriage. I approached the driver and said the gentlemen were coming; he nodded.

The gentlemen now appeared. Mason, supported by Mr. Rochester and the surgeon, seemed to walk with tolerable ease; they assisted him into the carriage; the surgeon followed.

"Take care of him, Carter," said Mr. Rochester, "and keep him at your house till he is quite well. I shall ride over in a day or two to see how he gets on. Richard, how are you?"

"The fresh air revives me, Fairfax."

"Leave the window open on his side, Carter. Goodbye, Dick."

"Fairfax—"

"Well, what is it?"

"Take care of her. Let her be treated as tenderly as possible. Let her—" he stopped, and burst into tears.

"I do my best—have done, and will continue to do," was the answer. He closed the carriage door, and it drove away.

"I pray to God there was an end to all this!" added Mr. Rochester, as he closed the yard gates.

This done, he moved slowly toward the door leading to the orchard.

"Jane, come where there is some freshness, for a few moments," he said. "That house is a dungeon; don't you feel it?"

"It seems to me a splendid mansion, sir."

"The glamour of inexperience is over your eyes," he answered. "You cannot see that the gilt is slime and the silk draperies cobwebs; the marble is sordid rock, and the polished wood is scaly bark. Now here," he said, pointing to the leafy orchard, "all is real, sweet, and pure."

He strolled down a walkway edged with apple trees, pear trees, and cherry trees on one side, and on the other side, flowers—primroses, pansies, and sweet William. They were fresh now, after April showers and a lovely spring morning.

"Jane, will you have a flower?"

He gathered a rose, the first on the bush, and offered it to me.

"Thank you, sir."

"Do you like this sunrise, Jane? This placid and balmy air?"

"I do, very much."

"You have had a strange night, Jane."

"Yes, sir."

"And it has made you look pale—were you afraid when I left you alone with Mason?"

"I was afraid of Grace Poole coming out of the inner room."

"But I had locked the door. I would have been a careless shepherd if I had left my pet lamb so near a wolf's den, unguarded; you were safe."

"Will she still live here, sir?"

"Oh yes! Don't trouble your head about her—put the thing out of your thoughts."

"Yet it seems to me your life is hardly secure while she stays."

"Never fear—I will take care of myself."

"Is the danger you feared last night gone now, sir?"

"I cannot vouch for that till Mason is out of England—nor even then. For me, Jane, to live is to stand on the crust of a crater which may crack and spew fire any day."

"But Mr. Mason seems to be a man who is easily led. He would never willingly injure you."

"No, Mason will not defy me or knowingly hurt me—but unintention- ally, he might, by one careless word, deprive me of happiness forever."

"Tell him to be cautious, sir; let him know what you fear, and show him how to avoid danger."

He laughed cynically. "If I could do that, simpleton, where would the danger be? Ever since I have known Mason, I have only had to say to him "Do this," and it is done. But I cannot give him orders in this case—I must not let him know that he could harm me. Now you look puzzled—and I will puzzle you further. You are my little friend, are you not?"

"I like to serve you, sir, and to obey you in all that is right."

"Precisely—I see you do. I see genuine happiness in your eyes and face when you are helping me, pleasing me, working for me and with me. Well, you too have power over me, and can injure me; yet, faithful and friendly as you are, I dare not show you where I am vulnerable."

"If you have no more to fear from Mr. Mason than you have from me, sir, you are very safe."

"God grant it may be so! Here is an arbor, Jane; sit down."

The arbor was a shady arch in the wall, lined with ivy, and a bench. Mr. Rochester sat, leaving room for me—but I stood before him.

"Sit," he said. "The bench is long enough for two. You don't hesitate to take a place at my side, do you? Is that wrong, Jane?"

I answered him by sitting; to refuse would have been unwise.

"Now, my little friend, I'll tell you an imagined story; but first, look at me, and tell me you are at ease."

"Yes, sir; I am content."

"Well then, Jane, suppose you were a wild boy, spoiled from childhood; imagine yourself in a remote foreign land, and there you commit a capital error—it doesn't matter what kind—but one whose consequences must follow you through life and spoil your whole existence. Mind you, I don't say a crime—I am not speaking of shedding of blood or any act which would break the law—I am speaking of an error.

"In time, the results of your act become unbearable; you take extreme measures to relieve the pain; but still you are miserable, for hope has left you; your sun darkens at noon; your memories are bitter and immoral; you wander here and there, in exile, seeking happiness in heartless, sensual pleasure.

"With your heart weary and your soul withered, you come home after years of voluntary exile. You make a new acquaintance—how or where does not matter—and you find in this stranger much of the good and bright qualities which you have sought for twenty years, but never before encountered.

"This acquaintance revives and renews you; better days come back—higher wishes, purer feelings; you desire to begin your life anew, and to spend what remains of your days in a way more worthy of someone immortal.

"Now the question: In order to achieve this goal, is it acceptable for you to ignore an obstacle put there by society? An obstacle that neither your conscience or your judgment approves?"

He paused for an answer—what was I to say? Oh, for some good spirit to suggest a wise and satisfactory response!

Again Mr. Rochester proposed his query:

"Is the man justified in daring the world's disapproval, in order to attach himself forever to this gentle, gracious stranger, and securing his own peace of mind and renewal of life?"

"Sir," I answered, "a sinner's renewal should never depend on another person. Men and women die; let him look to God for the strength to heal."

"But God has appointed the person who will heal me. I tell you now, I am the one who has been a worldly, dissipated, restless man; and I believe I have found the person who will heal me. And that person is—"

He paused; the birds went on singing—I almost wondered why they did not stop their songs to hear the name of Mr. Rochester's chosen acquaintance. But they would have to wait many minutes—so long was his silence. At last, I looked up at him; he was looking eagerly at me.

"Little friend," said he, in a changed voice and a changed face—losing

all its softness, and becoming harsh and sarcastic—"you have n
tender preference for Miss Ingram; don't you think if I marrie
would renew me?"

He got up instantly, went to the other end of the walk an
came back, he was humming a tune.

"Jane, Jane," said he, stopping before me, "you are quite pale; don't you
curse me for disturbing your peace?"

"Curse you? No, sir."

"Shake hands to confirm it." We shook hands. "What cold fingers! They
were warmer last night when I touched them at the door of the mysterious
room. Jane, when will you sit with me again?"

"Whenever I can be useful, sir."

"For instance, the night before I am married! I am sure I shall not be
able to sleep. Will you promise to sit up with me and keep me company? I
can talk to you about my lovely Blanche; for you have seen her and know
her."

"Yes, sir."

"She's a rare one, is she not, Jane?"

"Yes, sir."

"A strapper, a real strapper, Jane—big, brown, and buxom."

Mr. Rochester then caught sight of Colonel Dent and Frederick Lynn.

"Bless me! There's Dent and Lynn in the stables! Jane, go inside through
that gate, by the shrubbery."

As I went one way, he went another, and I heard him in the yard, saying
cheerfully to his friends:

"Mason got started ahead of you all this morning; he was gone before
sunrise; I rose at four to see him off."

Chapter 21

*P*remonitions are strange things. I never laughed at premonitions, because I have had strange ones of my own. One night when I was six years old, I heard Bessie tell Miss Abbot that she had been dreaming about a little child—and there was an old saying that dreams of children were a sure sign of trouble. The next day Bessie was sent home to the deathbed of her little sister.

Lately I recalled this saying, for every night during the past week I had dreams of an infant—hushed in my arms, bouncing on my knee, playing with daisies on a lawn, or dabbling its hands in running water. One night it was wailing, the next night laughing, or nestling close, or running away from me.

On the seventh morning after this dream, I was summoned downstairs—I had a visitor. A gentleman's servant was waiting for me; he was dressed in mourning, with a black crepe band around his hat.

"I daresay you hardly remember me, Miss," he said, rising as I entered, "but my name is Robert Leaven; I was the coachman for Mrs. Reed when you were at Gateshead, eight or nine years ago, and I live there still."

"Oh, Robert! How do you do? I remember you very well; you are married to Bessie—how is she?"

"My wife is very hearty, thank you. She gave me another little child about two months ago—we have three now—and both mother and child are thriving."

"And is the family well at the house, Robert?"

"I am sorry I can't give you better news of them, Miss. They are very badly at present—in great trouble."

"I hope no one is dead," I said, glancing at his black clothing. He too looked down at his hat and replied:

"Mr. John died a week ago yesterday, at his chambers in London."

"Mr. John?"

"Yes."

"And how does his mother bear it?"

"Why, you see, Miss Eyre, his life has been very wild. These last three years he gave himself up to strange ways, and his death was shocking."

"I heard from Bessie he was not doing well."

"Doing well! He could not do worse; he ruined his health and his fortune. He got into debt and into jail—his mother helped him out twice, but as soon as he was free he returned to his old companions and habits. He came down to Gateshead about three weeks ago and wanted Mrs. Reed to give him all her fortune. She refused—her wealth had long been much reduced by his extravagance. So he went back to London again, and then the news was that he was dead—they say he killed himself."

I was silent; these things were frightful. Robert resumed:

"Mrs. Reed had been in ill health herself for some time; she had gotten very heavy, and the loss of money and fear of poverty was quite breaking her down. The information about Mr. John's death brought on a stroke. She was three days without speaking; but last Tuesday she seemed rather better. She appeared as if she wanted to say something, and kept making signs to my wife, and mumbling.

"It was yesterday morning that Bessie understood that Mrs. Reed was pronouncing your name; and at last she made out the words, 'Bring Jane—fetch Jane Eyre; I want to speak to her.' Bessie told Miss Eliza and Miss Georgiana, and advised them to send for you. The young ladies put it off at first; but their mother grew so restless, and said, 'Jane, Jane,' so many times, that at last they consented. I left Gateshead yesterday; and if you can get ready, Miss, I should like to take you back with me early tomorrow morning."

"Yes, Robert, I shall be ready; it seems to me that I ought to go."

"I think so too, Miss Jane. Bessie said she was sure you would not refuse; but I suppose you will have to ask leave before you can get off?"

"Yes, and I will do it now." And after directing him to the servants' hall, and giving him over to the care of John, I went in search of Mr. Rochester.

He was not in any of the lower rooms, the yard, the stables, or the grounds. I asked Mrs. Fairfax if she had seen him. Yes, she believed he was playing billiards with Miss Ingram. To the billiard room I hurried.

There, Mr. Rochester, Miss Ingram, the two Misses Eshton, and their gentlemen admirers, were all busied in the game. With a bit of courage, I approached the master where he stood, at Miss Ingram's side. She turned as I came near, and looked at me haughtily, as if to say, "What can the creeping creature want now?"

I said, in a low voice, "Mr. Rochester."

He turned with a curious frown, threw down his cue, and followed me from the room.

"Well, Jane?" he said.

"If you please, sir, I want a leave of absence for a week or two."

"What to do? Where to go?"

"To see a sick lady who has sent for me."

"What sick lady? Where does she live?"

"At Gateshead."

"That is a hundred miles off! Who is she that sends for people to come all that distance?"

"Her name is Reed, sir—Mrs. Reed."

"Reed of Gateshead? There was a Reed of Gateshead, a magistrate."

"It is his widow, sir."

"And how do you know her?"

"Mr. Reed was my uncle—my mother's brother."

"The deuce he was! You never told me that before—you always said you had no relatives."

"None that would own me, sir. Mr. Reed is dead, and Mrs. Reed sent me away."

"Why?"

"Because I was poor, and burdensome, and she disliked me."

"But Reed left children! You must have cousins! Sir George Lynn was talking of a Reed of Gateshead yesterday, who, he said, was one of the worst rascals in London; and Ingram was mentioning a Georgiana Reed, who was much admired for her beauty a season or two ago in London."

"John Reed is dead, sir; he ruined himself and half-ruined his family, and committed suicide. The news so shocked his mother that it brought on a stroke."

"And what good can you do her? Nonsense, Jane! I would never think of running a hundred miles to see an old lady who will, perhaps, be dead before you reach her—besides, you say she sent you away."

"Yes, sir, but that was long ago, when her circumstances were very different. I could not easily neglect her wishes now."

"How long will you stay?"

"As short a time as possible, sir."

"Promise me only to stay a week—"

"I had better not give my word—I might have to break it."

"In any event, you will come back—you will not be persuaded under any circumstance to move back there?"

"Oh, no! I shall certainly return if all is well."

"And who will go with you? You don't travel a hundred miles alone."

"No, sir; she has sent her coachman."

"A person to be trusted?"

"Yes, sir, he has lived ten years in the family."

Mr. Rochester meditated. "When do you wish to go?"

"Early tomorrow morning, sir."

"Well, you need some money; you can't travel without money, and I daresay you have not much—I have given you no salary yet. How much have you in the world, Jane?" he asked, smiling.

I drew out my purse; a meager thing it was. "Five shillings, sir."

He took the purse, poured the vast hoard into his palm, and chuckled over it. Soon he produced his pocket-book.

"Here," said he, offering me a note—it was fifty pounds, and he owed me only fifteen. I told him I had no change.

"I don't want change; you know that. Take your wages."

I declined to accept more than was my due. He scowled at first; then, as if recollecting something, he said:

"Right, right! Better not give you all of it now; you would, perhaps, stay away three months if you had fifty pounds. Here are ten—is it not plenty?"

"Yes, sir, but now you owe me five."

"Come back for it, then; I am your banker for forty pounds."

"Mr. Rochester, I may as well mention another matter of business, while I have the opportunity."

"A matter of business? I am curious to hear it."

"You have as much as told me, sir, that you are shortly going to be married?"

"Yes; what then?"

"In that case, sir, Adele ought to go to school; I am sure you perceive the necessity for it."

"Yes; to get her out of my bride's way, who might otherwise walk over her? There's good sense in the suggestion. Adele, as you say, must go to school; and you, of course, without a pupil, would go straight to—the devil?"

"I hope not, sir; but I must seek another governess position somewhere."

"In due course!" he exclaimed, distorting his face as he said it. He looked at me several minutes. Then he added:

"And you will ask old Mrs. Reed, or her daughters, to find you something, I suppose?"

"No, sir; I am not on such terms with my relatives to ask favours of them—but I shall advertise."

"You will advertise at your peril!" he growled. "I wish I had only offered you a sovereign instead of ten pounds. Give me back nine pounds, Jane; I've a need for it."

"And so have I, sir," I returned, putting my hands and my purse behind me. "I could not spare the money on any account."

"Little miser!" said he. "Refusing me a financial request! Give me five pounds, Jane."

"Not five shillings, sir; nor five pence."

"Just let me look at the cash."

"No, sir; you are not to be trusted."

"Jane!"

"Sir?"

"Promise me one thing."

"I'll promise you anything, sir, that I think I can honor."

"Promise not to advertise, and to trust the search for a new position to me. I'll find you one in time."

"I shall be glad so to do, sir, if you, in turn, will promise that Adele and I shall both be safe out of the house before your bride enters it."

"Very well! Very well! I'll pledge my word on it. You leave tomorrow, then?"

"Yes, sir; early."

"Will you come down to the drawing room after dinner?"

"No, sir, I must prepare for the journey."

"Then you and I must bid goodbye for a little while?"

"I suppose so, sir."

"And how do people perform that ceremony of parting, Jane? Teach me—I'm not quite up to it."

"They say farewell, or any other form they prefer."

"Then say it."

"Farewell, Mr. Rochester, for the present."

"What must I say?"

"The same, if you like, sir."

"Farewell, Miss Eyre, for the present; is that all?"

"Yes."

"It seems stingy, dry, and unfriendly. I should like something else—a little addition to the ceremony. If one shook hands, for instance; but no—that would not content me either. So you'll do no more than say farewell, Jane?"

"It is enough, sir; just as much goodwill may be expressed in one hearty word as in many."

"Very likely; but 'farewell' is blank and cool."

How long is he going to stand there? I asked myself. I want to commence my packing.

The dinner bell rang, and suddenly away he bolted, without another syllable—I saw him no more that day.

The next morning, I was off before Mr. Rochester had risen.

I reached the porter's lodge at Gateshead about five o'clock that afternoon; I stopped there before going up to the hall. It was very clean and neat; the windows had little white curtains; and the fire burnt clear.

Bessie sat on the hearth, nursing her new baby, and Robert and their daughter played quietly in a corner.

"Bless you! I knew you would come!" exclaimed Mrs. Leaven, as I entered.

"Yes, Bessie," said I, kissing her, "and I trust I am not too late. How is Mrs. Reed? Still alive, I hope."

"Yes, she is alive; and more sensible and collected than she was. The doctor says she may linger a week or two yet; but he hardly thinks she will recover."

"Has she mentioned me lately?"

"She was talking about you only this morning, and wishing you would come; but she is sleeping now. She sleeps all afternoon, and wakes up about six or seven. Will you rest here an hour, Miss, and then I will go up with you?"

Robert entered, and Bessie laid her sleeping child in the cradle and went to welcome him. I took off my bonnet and had some tea; she said I looked pale and tired. I remembered old times as she bustled about, preparing the tea and cake. I was going to approach the table, but she commanded me to sit still, so she could serve me at the fireside. I smiled and obeyed her, as in bygone days.

She wanted to know if I was happy at Thornfield Hall. I told her my master was rather an ugly man, but a gentleman; he treated me kindly, and I was content. Then I described the gay company that had been staying at the house; Bessie listened with interest—these were just the kinds of details she relished.

An hour later, I accompanied Bessie up to Gateshead Hall. Nine years ago, on a dark, raw January morning, we had walked down the same path when I left Gateshead, with a doubtful future and an aching heart, to travel to Lowood.

Now, again, the hostile Gateshead Hall rose before me. I still had a doubtful future and an aching heart. I still felt like a wanderer on the face of the earth; but I had greater trust in myself and my own powers. I no longer felt wounded by my wrongs, and my resentment was gone.

"You shall go into the breakfast room first," said Bessie, as she preceded me through the hall. "The young ladies will be there."

In the breakfast room, everything looked just as it did on the morning I was first introduced to Mr. Brocklehurst—the very rug he had stood upon still covered the hearth. Glancing at the bookcases, I saw Bewick's British Birds, Gulliver's Travels and the Arabian Nights. The objects had not changed—but the living things had changed beyond recognition.

My cousins Emily and Georgiana appeared before me. Emily was very tall and very thin, with a sallow face and a severe air. There was something puritanical in her look, with her plain black skirt, starched linen collar, hair combed back, and the nun-like necklace of black beads and a crucifix. She had very little resemblance to her former self.

Georgiana was certainly not the slim, fairy-like girl of eleven that I remembered. This full-blown, very plump damsel was pale as wax, with a handsome face, blue eyes, and yellow hair in ringlets. Her dress was black, too, but stylish and becoming.

Both ladies rose to welcome me, and both addressed me as 'Miss Eyre'. Eliza's greeting was in a short and abrupt voice, without a smile. Georgiana asked me about my journey, the weather, and so on, accompanied by side glances that measured me from head to toe.

Young ladies have a remarkable way of letting you know that they think you are ridiculous without actually saying the words. A certain look, a coolness of manner, an indifferent tone—fully express their feelings without any actual rudeness on their part.

However, a sneer no longer had the power over me it once possessed. As I sat between my cousins, I was surprised to find how easy I felt with them—Eliza did not mortify me, nor did Georgiana ruffle me.

The fact was, I had other things to think about. Within the last few months, pains and pleasures had been stirred in me that were so much more powerful than any they could raise; their airs no longer gave me concern.

"How is Mrs. Reed?" I asked, looking calmly at Georgiana, who bristled at my directness.

"Mrs. Reed? Ah! Mama, you mean. She is extremely poorly; I doubt if you can see her tonight."

"If you would just step upstairs and tell her I am here," I said, "I would be much obliged to you."

Georgiana opened her blue eyes wild and wide.

I added, "I know she had a particular wish to see me, and I would not wish to delay seeing her any longer than necessary."

"Mama dislikes being disturbed in the evening," remarked Eliza.

I rose, quietly took off my bonnet and gloves, uninvited, and said I would just step out to the kitchen, to ask Bessie whether Mrs. Reed was able to see me tonight or not. I found Bessie and sent her to inquire for me.

A year ago, I would have withered from the arrogance of my cousins—I would have left Gateshead the next morning. Now, however, having traveled a hundred miles to see my aunt, I knew I must stay with her until she was better—or dead. I must put my cousins' pride or folly to one side.

So I asked the housekeeper to show me to a room, told her I would probably be a visitor here for a week or two, and had my trunk brought to my chamber.

I met Bessie on the landing. "Mrs. Reed is awake," said she. "I have told her you are here; come, and let us see if she will know you."

I knew my way to her room, to which I had so often been summoned for punishment in former days. I softly opened the door; a shaded light stood on the table. There was the great four-poster bed, the armchair, and the footstool—where, a hundred times, I had been sentenced to kneel, to ask pardon for offenses I did not commit. I approached the bed, opened the curtains and leaned over the high-piled pillows.

I remembered Mrs. Reed's face well, and I eagerly sought the familiar image. It is a happy thing when time heals rage and vengeance. I had left this woman in bitterness and hate, and I came back to her now with sorrow for her great sufferings, and a strong desire to forgive and forget all injuries—to be reconciled and to clasp hands in friendship.

The well-known face was there—stern, relentless as ever. There were those peculiar eyes that nothing could melt, and the raised, haughty eyebrows. How often they had cast upon me menace and hate! And how the memory of childhood terrors and sorrows were renewed as I looked upon her! And yet, I stooped down and kissed her; she looked at me.

"Is this Jane Eyre?" she said.

"Yes, Aunt Reed. How are you, dear aunt?"

I had once vowed to never call her 'aunt' again, but I thought it was not a sin to forget and break that vow. My fingers took her hand—and had she pressed my hand kindly, I would, at that moment, have experienced true pleasure. But hard behaviours are not soon softened—Mrs. Reed took her hand away and, turning her face away from me, remarked that the night was warm.

She had once again treated me so icily, I felt at once that her opinion of me was unchanged. I knew by her stony eye that she was resolved to consider me bad to the last—because to believe that I was good would give her no pleasure.

I felt pain, then anger; and then I became determined to control her—in spite of her nature and her will. My tears had risen, just as in childhood; I ordered them back to their source. I brought a chair to the head of the bed, sat down, and leaned over the pillow.

"You sent for me," I said, "and I am here; and it is my intention to stay here till I see how you get on."

"Oh, of course! You have seen my daughters?"

"Yes."

"Well, you may tell them I wish you to stay till I can talk some things over with you that I have on my mind. Tonight, it is too late, and I have difficulty recalling them. But there was something I wished to say—let me see—"

Her wandering look and changed voice told me what damage had taken place in her once vigorous body. Turning restlessly, she drew the quilt round her; my elbow, resting on a corner of the quilt, held it down—she was immediately irritated.

"Sit up!" said she. "Don't annoy me by holding the covers down. Are you Jane Eyre?"

"I am Jane Eyre."

"I have had more trouble with that child than anyone would believe. Such a burden to be left on my hands—and so much annoyance she caused me, daily and hourly, with her impossible personality, and her sudden starts of temper, and her constant, unnatural staring at everyone's movements! I declare she talked to me once like something mad—no child ever spoke or looked as she did. I was glad to get her away from the house. What did they do with her at Lowood? The typhus fever broke out there, and many of the pupils died. She, however, did not die—I wish she had died!"

"A strange wish, Mrs. Reed; why do you hate her so?" I said.

"I always disliked her mother, for she was my husband's only sister. He favored her. He opposed the family's disowning her when she made her low marriage to that clergyman; and when news came of her death, he wept like a simpleton. He sent for baby Jane, though I begged him to pay a nurse to take it. I hated it the first time I set my eyes on it—a sickly, whiny thing! It would wail in its cradle all night long—not scream heartily like any other child, but whimper and moan.

"Mr. Reed pitied it; and he used to nurse it like it was his own—more than he ever noticed his own children. He would try to make my children friendly to the little beggar. My darlings could not bear it, and he was angry with them when they showed their dislike. In his last illness, he had it brought continually to his bedside; and an hour before he died, he made me promise to keep the creature.

"John does not resemble his father at all, and I am glad of it; John is like me and like my brothers—he is quite a Gibson. Oh, I wish he would stop tormenting me with letters for money. I have no more money to give him—we are getting poor. I must send away half the servants and shut up part of the house. How are we to get on? Two-thirds of my income goes to pay the mortgages. John gambles dreadfully, and always loses—poor boy! He is sunk and degraded; his appearance is frightful; I feel ashamed for him when I see him."

She was getting very excited.

"I think I had better leave her now," I said to Bessie, who stood on the other side of the bed.

"Perhaps you should, Miss; but she often talks in this way toward night—in the morning she is calmer."

I rose.

"Stop!" exclaimed Mrs. Reed. "There is another thing I wished to say. John threatens me—he continually threatens me with his own death, or mine; and I sometimes dream that he is dead, or with a swollen and blackened face. What is to be done? How is the money to be had?"

Bessie now persuaded Mrs. Reed to take a drink of sedative. Soon after, she grew quieter, and sank into sleep. I then left her.

More than ten days passed before I had another conversation with her. She continued either delirious or sleepy, and the doctor forbid everything that could excite her.

Meantime, I got on as well as I could with Georgiana and Eliza. They were very cold, indeed, at first. Eliza would sit half the day sewing, reading, or writing, and scarcely utter a word either to me or her sister. Georgiana would chatter nonsense to her canary bird by the hour, and take no notice of me.

But I was determined not to seem bored; I had brought my drawing materials with me. With my case of pencils and some sheets of paper, I would take a seat near the window and sketch fancy pictures, whatever entered my imagination.

One morning I began sketching a face—what sort of face it was to be, I did not care or know. I drew a broad, prominent forehead; square jaw; strong black eyebrows; well-defined nose; flexible mouth; firm chin with a cleft; black hair; and large eyes.

Good! But not quite the thing, I thought—the eyes need more force and spirit; and I made them flash more brilliantly. There, I had a friend's face under my gaze. I looked at it; I smiled at the likeness; I was absorbed and content.

"Is that a portrait of someone you know?" asked Eliza, who had crept up unnoticed. I responded that it was merely a fancy head, and hid it beneath the other sheets. Of course, I lied—it was, in fact, a very faithful likeness of Mr. Rochester.

But what was that to her, or to anyone but myself? Georgiana also stole a look. She called it "an ugly man". They both seemed surprised at my skill. I offered to sketch their portraits; each, in turn, sat for a pencil outline. Then I promised to draw Georgiana's watercolour portrait—this put her at once into a good humour.

Georgiana proposed that we take a walk on the grounds. Before we had been out two hours, we were deep in a confidential conversation. She described the exciting winter she had spent in London two seasons ago— all the attention she had received, and even her romantic involvement with an English nobleman.

Day after day, Georgiana reminisced about her past gaieties and fashionable life. It was strange that she never once mentioned either her mother's illness or her brother's death, or the present gloomy state of the family finances. She spent about five minutes each day in her mother's sick room, and no more.

Eliza spoke little; she had evidently no time to talk. I never saw a busier person. She awoke early; I do not know what she did before breakfast, but afterward she divided her time into regular portions. Three times a day she studied the Book of Common Prayer. For three hours, she stitched, with gold thread, the border of a crimson cloth—an altar covering for a new church near Gateshead. Two hours she devoted to her diary; two to working by herself in the garden; and one to her account book. She wanted no company, no conversation. Nothing annoyed her so much as any deviation from her clockwork day.

One evening, when she felt like conversing, Eliza told me that John's conduct, and the threatened ruin of the family, had been a source of profound pain for her—but she had now settled her mind. She had taken care to protect her own fortune and, when her mother died, she would seek a life that was safe from the frivolous world. I asked if Georgiana would accompany her.

Of course not, replied Eliza. Georgiana and she had nothing in common—they never had. Georgiana should follow her own path, and Eliza would take hers.

Georgiana, when not unburdening her heart to me, spent most of her time lying on the sofa, whining about the dullness of the house, and wishing that her Aunt Gibson would invite her to London. It would be so much better, she said, to get out of the way for a month or two, till all was over. I suppose she was referring to the expected death of her mother and the gloomy funeral.

Eliza generally ignored her sister's laziness and complaints. One day, however, she suddenly took her on:

"Georgiana, a more vain and absurd animal than you, never lived on this earth. You had no right to be born, for you make no use of life. You seek only to latch your fat, weak, puffy, useless self onto some other person; and if you cannot find someone, you cry that you are ill-treated, neglected, and miserable. You require that your life must have continual excitement, or else the world is a dungeon; you must be admired, courted, and flattered—you must have music, dancing, and society—or you die away.

"Have you no sense to find a way to become independent of others? Divide your day into sections, and find a task for each; your day will end before you know it, and you will be indebted to no one. Take this advice—it is all I shall offer you. Ignore it—continue craving, whining, and idling—and you will suffer the results.

"After my mother's death, I wash my hands of you; from the day her coffin is carried to the vault in Gateshead Church, you and I will be as separate as if we had never known each other. If the whole human race were swept away, except for us, I would leave you in the old world, and take myself to the new."

She closed her lips.

"Eliza, you might have saved yourself the trouble of delivering that tirade," answered Georgiana. "Everybody knows you are the most selfish, heartless creature in existence, and I know of your spiteful hatred toward me. I had a taste of it before, when you could not bear that I should marry

Lord Edwin Vere, to have a title, to be raised above you socially, to be received into circles where you dare not show your face—and so you became a spy and informer, told our mother, and ruined my prospects for happiness forever."

Georgiana took out her handkerchief and blew her nose for an hour afterwards; Eliza sat cold, unmoved, and busy with her stitching. Feeling, without judgment, is a watery drink indeed; but judgment, without feeling, is too bitter to drink at all.

It was a wet and windy afternoon. Georgiana had fallen asleep on the sofa; Eliza was gone to church. I thought I would go upstairs and visit the dying woman who lay there almost ignored—the servants paid her little attention; the hired nurse would slip out of the room whenever she could; Bessie was faithful, but she had her own family to mind.

I found the sick room unwatched, as I had expected. The patient lay still, sleeping, her pale face sunk into the pillows. The fire was dying in the grate. I renewed the flame, rearranged the quilt, and gazed on her awhile, and then I moved away to the window.

The rain beat strongly against the panes; the wind blew fiercely. A woman lies there, I thought, who will soon be beyond the earth elements. Where will that spirit go when released at last?

In pondering the great mystery, I thought of Helen Burns, and recalled her dying words, and her faith. I was still thinking of her voice, still picturing her pale, wasted face and sublime gaze, as she lay on her deathbed, whispering her desire to become one with her divine Father's bosom—when a feeble voice murmured from the bed:

"Who is that?"

I knew Mrs. Reed had not spoken for days—was she reviving? I went up to her.

"It is I, Aunt Reed."

"Who?" was her answer. "Who are you?" She looked at me with surprise and a sort of alarm. "You are quite a stranger to me—where is Bessie?"

"She is at her lodge, aunt."

"Aunt?" she repeated. "Who calls me aunt? You are not one of the Gibsons; and yet I know you—that face, and the eyes and forehead, are quiet familiar to me. You are like—why, you are like Jane Eyre!"

I said nothing; I was afraid of causing a shock by declaring my identity.

"Yet," said she, "I am afraid my thoughts deceive me. I wished to see Jane Eyre, and I see a likeness where none exists; besides, in eight years she must be so changed."

I now gently assured her that I was Jane Eyre. I explained how Bessie had sent her husband to fetch me from Thornfield.

"I am very ill, I know," she said before long. "It is just as well that I should ease my mind before I die—what we think little about in health, burdens us at such an hour as this. Is the nurse here? Or is there no one in the room but you?"

I assured her we were alone.

"Well, I have twice done you a wrong which I regret now. One was breaking the promise which I gave my husband to bring you up as my own child. The other—" she stopped. "Well, it is of no great importance, perhaps," she murmured to herself, "and I may get better, so to humble myself before you is painful."

Then her face changed—she seemed to feel some inward sensation—the precursor, perhaps, of her last breath.

"Well, I must get it over with. Eternity is before me—I had better tell you. Go to my dressing case, open it, and take out a letter you will see there."

I obeyed her directions.

"Read the letter," she said.

It was short—it was from my uncle, and thus I read:

"Madam, will you have the goodness to send me the address of my niece, Jane Eyre, and to tell me how she is? It is my intention to write to her shortly, and desire her to come to Madeira to be with me. God has blessed my efforts to secure a fortune; and as I am unmarried and childless, I wish to adopt her during my life, and leave all I have, to her, at my death. I am, JOHN EYRE. Madeira."

It was dated three years ago.

"Why did I never hear of this?" I asked.

"Because I disliked you too thoroughly to ever help you to prosperity. I could not forget your conduct to me, Jane—the fury with which you once turned on me; the look and tone in your voice with which you declared you hated me the worst of anybody in the world, that the thought of me made you sick, and said I had treated you with miserable cruelty. Bring me some water! Oh, hurry!"

"Dear Mrs. Reed," said I, as I offered her a drink of water, "think no more of all this; let it pass from your mind. Forgive me for my passionate language—I was a child then. Nine years have passed since that day."

She ignored all that I said, and then continued:

"I could not forget it, and I took my revenge. I could not endure you to be adopted by your uncle and placed in a state of ease and comfort. I wrote to him and said I was sorry for his disappointment, but you were dead—you had died of typhus fever at Lowood. Now, Jane act as you please; write and contradict me—expose my lie. You were born, I think, to be my torment; my last hour is tortured by the memory of a deed which, but for you, I would never have been tempted to commit."

"Can you think no more of it, aunt, and regard me with kindness and forgiveness?"

"You have a very bad behaviour," said she, "and one that, to this day, I cannot understand—how you could be patient and passive for the first nine years of your life, and in the tenth break out all fire and violence."

"My behaviour is not so bad as you think—I am passionate, but not vindictive. Many times, as a little child, I would have been glad to love you if you had let me; and I sincerely desire to be reconciled with you now; kiss me, aunt."

I brought my cheek to her lips—but she would not touch it. She said I bothered her by leaning over the bed, and again demanded water.

As I gave her water, I laid my hand on her ice-cold, clammy fingers. She shrank from my touch and the glazing eyes shunned my gaze.

"Love me, then, or hate me, as you will," I said at last. "You have my full and free forgiveness; ask now for God's forgiveness, and be at peace."

Poor, suffering woman! It was now too late for her to change her frame of mind. Living, she had always hated me—dying, she must hate me still.

The nurse now entered, and Bessie followed. I lingered half an hour longer, hoping to see some sign of friendship—but she gave none. She was fast relapsing into a stupor; her mind never again recovered. At midnight she died.

I was not present at the end, nor were her daughters. They came to tell us the next morning that all was over. Eliza and I went to look at her; Georgiana, who had burst into tears, could not go.

Lying before us was Mrs. Sarah Reed's once robust and active frame—rigid and still; her eyes of steel were shut; her strong brow and face still reflected her stubborn soul. I gazed on her corpse with gloom and pain—nothing soft, nothing sweet, nothing pitying or hopeful did it inspire; only pain for her woes—not my loss.

Eliza surveyed her mother calmly. After a silence of some minutes, she observed:

"With her strength, she should have lived to a good old age; her life was shortened by trouble." Her mouth tightened for an instant, then we both turned and left the room. Neither of us had shed a tear.

Chapter 22

Mr. Rochester had given me one week's leave of absence—yet a month passed before I left Gateshead. I wished to leave immediately after the funeral, but Georgiana begged me to stay till she could get off to London, where she had finally been invited by her uncle, Mr. Gibson. Georgiana said she dreaded being left alone with Eliza; and Georgiana received no help from her sister in the preparations for her journey. So I put up with Georgiana's feeble-minded whining as well as I could, and did my best to pack her dresses. While I worked, she sat idle, of course.

At last I saw Georgiana off; but now it was Eliza's turn to request that I stay another week. She was about to depart for some unknown place—all day long she stayed in her own room, her door bolted, filling trunks, emptying drawers, and burning papers. Meanwhile, she asked me to look after the house, to see callers, and answer notes of condolence.

One morning she told me I was free to leave. "And," she added, "I thank you for your valuable service! Tomorrow I set out for France; I shall live in a nunnery near Lisle—there I shall be quiet and alone. I shall devote myself for a time to a careful study of the Roman Catholic religion and, if I find it suits me, I shall probably take the veil."

I neither expressed surprise at this decision, nor attempted to discourage her from it. This vocation will fit you perfectly, I thought, and it may do you much good!

When we parted, she said, "Goodbye, cousin Jane Eyre; I wish you well; you have some sense."

I then returned, "You are not without sense, cousin Eliza; but in another year, I suppose, what you have will be walled up alive in a French convent. However, it is not my business, and so if it suits you, I don't much care."

"You are correct," said she; and with these words, we each went our separate way. As I shall not have occasion to refer to Eliza or Georgiana again, I may as well mention here, that Georgiana made an advantageous match with a wealthy worn-out man of society, and Eliza actually took the veil, and is now Mother Superior of the convent, to which she donated her fortune.

I did not know how people feel when they are returning home from an absence, long or short—I had never experienced it. As a child, I knew what it was like to come back to Gateshead after a long walk, to be scolded for looking cold or gloomy; and later, what it was like to come back to Lowood from church, to long for a good meal and a good fire, and to receive neither. My return to Thornfield was yet to be tried.

My journey seemed tedious—very tedious; fifty miles one day, a night spent at an inn, fifty miles the next day. During the first day, I thought of Mrs. Reed in her last moments; I saw her pale, disfigured face, and heard her strange voice. I mused on the funeral day, the coffin, the hearse, the black train of few mourners, the gaping vault, the silent church, the solemn service. Then I thought of Georgiana and Eliza—one the center of attention in a ballroom, the other the inmate of a convent cell.

The next day of my journey, I left memories behind and dwelt on anticipation. I was going back to Thornfield—but how long would I stay there? Not long, I was sure.

I had heard from Mrs. Fairfax while at Gateshead. The guests had all departed; Mr. Rochester had left for London three weeks ago, but he was then expected to return in a fortnight. Mrs. Fairfax assumed that he was making arrangements for his wedding, and he talked of purchasing a new carriage. She said the idea of his marrying Miss Ingram still seemed strange to her; but from what everybody said, and from what she had seen, there was no doubt the event would shortly take place. I certainly did not doubt it.

The question followed, "Where was I to go?" During my overnight at the inn, I dreamt of Miss Ingram. In a vivid dream I saw her closing the gates of Thornfield against me and pointing me toward another road; and Mr. Rochester looked on with his arms folded—smiling cynically at both her and me.

I had not notified Mrs. Fairfax of the exact day of my return, for I did not wish anyone to meet me at Millcote. I planned to walk the distance quietly by myself.

And so, arriving at Millcote about six o'clock on a June evening, I directed the host of the George Inn to send my trunk to Thornfield, and quietly took the old road to the Hall—a road which ran through fields and was now little traveled.

It was not a bright or splendid summer evening, though fair; the haymakers were at work all along the road. I felt glad as the end of my journey was near; so glad, that I stopped once to ask myself what that joy meant,

Jane Eyre

and to remind myself I was not going home, or to a place where fond friends looked out for me and waited my arrival. Mrs. Fairfax will smile a calm welcome, to be sure, thought I, and little Adele will clap her hands and jump to see you; but you know very well that you are thinking of someone else, and he is not thinking of you.

I then realized that it was pleasure enough to have the privilege of again looking at Mr. Rochester, whether he looked at me or not; and I thought, Hurry! Hurry! Be with him while you may, for in a few more days or weeks, you will be parted from him forever! And then I ran on.

I have only a field or two left to cross, then I shall reach the gates of Thornfield. How full the hedges are of roses! But I have no time to gather any; I want to be at the house. I see a fence across the road, and the narrow stone steps to cross over; and I see—Mr. Rochester sitting on the steps, a book and a pencil in his hand; he is writing.

Well, he is not a ghost; yet every nerve I have is snapped. What does it mean? I did not think I would tremble like this when I saw him, or lose my voice. I need not make an absolute fool of myself—I know another way to the house. But it does not matter if I knew twenty ways—for he has seen me.

"Hello!" he cries, and he puts up his book and his pencil. "There you are! Come on, if you please."

I went, but can scarcely remember walking; I tried to make my face appear calm, but can scarcely hide my joy. But I have a veil over my face—I may yet be able to appear composed.

"And is this Jane Eyre? Are you coming from Millcote, and on foot? Yes—just one of your tricks, not to send for a carriage, but to quietly steal into the vicinity of your home in twilight, as if you were a dream. What the deuce have you done with yourself this last month?"

"I have been with my aunt, sir, who is dead."

"A true 'Janeian' reply! Good angels protect me! She comes from the other world—from the house of people who are dead; and tells me so when she meets me alone here in the twilight! If I dared, I'd touch you to see if you are real or shadow, you elf!" He paused an instant, then added, "Truant! Truant! Absent from me a whole month, and quite forgetting me, I'd swear!"

I knew there would be pleasure in meeting my master again, though I was broken by the fear that he would soon not be my master, and by the knowledge that I was nothing to him. But Mr. Rochester had such a power to communicate happiness! His last words seemed to imply that I was important to him, whether I forgot him or not. And he had spoken of Thornfield as my home—would that it were my home!

He did not leave the steps, and I did not want to ask him to let me pass. I inquired if he had been to London.

"Yes; I suppose you found that out secondhand."

"Mrs. Fairfax told me in a letter."

"And did she inform you what I went to do?"

"Oh, yes, sir! Everybody knew your errand."

"You must see the carriage, Jane, and tell me if you don't think it will suit Mrs. Rochester perfectly; and whether she won't look like a queen, leaning back against those purple cushions. I wish, Jane, that I were more handsome, to match her. Tell me now, fairy as you are—can't you give me a charm to make me a handsome man?"

"It would be more than magic could do, sir." Then I thought, a loving eye is all the charm one needs; you are handsome enough; or rather, your sternness has a power beyond beauty.

Mr. Rochester sometimes had an uncanny ability to read my thoughts; now, he ignored my words, but he smiled at me with his own certain smile, which he used on rare occasions.

"Pass Janet," said he, making room for me to cross the fence. "Go home and rest your weary little wandering feet at a friend's house."

All I had to do now was obey him in silence—no need for me to speak further. I got over the fence, and meant to leave him calmly. But an impulse held me fast—a force turned me round. I said—or something in me said:

"Thank you, Mr. Rochester, for your great kindness. I am strangely glad to get back again to you; and wherever you are, is my home—my only home."

I walked on so fast that even he could not have overtaken me had he tried. Little Adele was half wild with delight when she saw me. Mrs. Fairfax received me with her usual plain friendliness. Leah smiled, and even Sophie bid me "bonsoir" with glee. This was very pleasant; there is no happiness like that of being loved by your fellow creatures, and feeling that your presence is an addition to their comfort.

That evening I resolved to not think about the future. When tea was over, and Mrs. Fairfax had taken her knitting, and I had taken a seat near her, and Adele, kneeling on the carpet, had nestled up close to me, and a sense of mutual affection and golden peace seemed to surround us, I uttered a silent prayer that we might not be parted soon or far.

When Mr. Rochester entered unannounced and, looking at us, seemed to take pleasure in seeing a group so amicable—when he said he supposed Mrs. Reed was all right now that she had gotten her adopted daughter back again, and added that he saw Adele was "ready to crush her little English mother" with affection, I half ventured to hope that he would, even after his marriage, keep us together somewhere under the shelter of his protection, and not exile us from the sunshine of his presence.

A fortnight of uncertain calm followed my return to Thornfield Hall. Nothing was said of the master's marriage, and I saw no preparation going on for such an event. Almost every day I asked Mrs. Fairfax if she had heard anything—her answer was always in the negative. Once she said she had actually asked Mr. Rochester when he was going to bring his bride home; but he had answered her only by a joke and one of his queer looks, and she could not tell what to make of him.

One thing specially surprised me—there were no visits back and forth to Ingram Park. Granted, it was twenty miles away, but what was that distance to an ardent lover? To a horseman like Mr. Rochester, it would be just a morning's ride.

I began to cherish hopes I had no right to hope for—that the marriage was broken off. I used to look at my master's face to see if it were sad or angry, but it was completely clear of clouds or evil feelings. If, in his presence, I sank into low spirits, he even became happy. He had never called me into his presence more frequently, never been kinder to me—and, alas! never had I loved him so much.

Chapter 23

A splendid midsummer shone over England—skies so pure, suns so radiant. The hay was all gathered in; the fields round Thornfield were green; the roads white and baked; the woods, full-leaved.

Adele, weary with gathering wild strawberries in Hay Lane half the day, had gone to bed at dusk. I watched her drop asleep, and when I left her, I sought the garden.

It was now the sweetest hour of the twenty-four; the sun had gone down, burning with the light of flames, and the sky was a solemn purple and, to the east, a fine deep blue.

I walked a while on the pavement; but a subtle, familiar scent—that of a cigar—came from a library window. I knew I might be watched, so I went into the orchard. There was no place on the grounds more sheltered—it was full of trees, it bloomed with flowers; a very high wall ensured privacy. It had a winding walk that led to a giant chestnut tree, circled by a bench.

Here, one could wander unseen. While silence reigned, I now felt as if I could haunt this shade forever, with the light of the rising moon to guide me.

But my steps are halted—not by sound or sight, but once more by a warning fragrance. It is not a flower; I know it well—it is Mr. Rochester's cigar. I look round and I listen. I see no movement, but the perfume increases. I must flee. I walk toward the fence, and I see Mr. Rochester entering. I step aside into an ivy recess; he will not stay long; he will soon return to the house, and if I sit still he will never see me.

But no—the evening is as pleasant to him as to me, and this antique garden as attractive; and he strolls on, taking a ripe cherry from the wall, and stooping to inhale the fragrance of a batch of flowers.

Now his back is toward me, thought I, and he is occupied; perhaps if I walk softly, I can slip away unnoticed.

I walked on grass to avoid the pebbly gravel; he was standing a yard or two away from me; a moth had landed on his foot and he leaned down to observe it. I shall get by very well, I thought.

As I crossed his shadow, he said quietly, without turning:

"Jane, come and look at this fellow."

I had made no noise; I started at first, and then I approached him.

"Look at his wings," said he. "He reminds me of a West Indian insect; one does not often see so large and gay a night rover in England. There! He is flown."

I was sheepishly leaving also; but Mr. Rochester followed me, and when we reached the fence, he said:

"Come back, Jane; it is a shame, on so lovely a night, to sit in the house; and surely no one can wish to go to bed while the sunset meets the moonrise."

It is one of my faults that, though my tongue is sometimes quick with an answer, there are times when it sadly fails me. I did not like to walk at this hour alone with Mr. Rochester in the shadowy orchard; but I could not find a reason to leave him.

I lagged behind him, and my thoughts were busy to find a means to leave; but he looked so calm, and also quite serious, that I was ashamed of my feelings.

"Jane," he said, as we entered the laurel walk, and slowly strolled down toward the chestnut tree, "Thornfield is a pleasant place in summer, is it not?"

"Yes, sir."

"You must have become somewhat attached to the house—you, who have an eye for natural beauty?"

"I am attached to it, indeed."

"And though I don't understand why, I sense that you have grown fond of that foolish little child Adele, too; and even for simple dame Fairfax?"

"Yes, sir. In different ways, I have an affection for both."

"And would be sorry to part with them?"

"Yes."

"Pity!" he said, and sighed and paused. "It is always the way of events in this life," he continued, "that no sooner have you gotten settled in a pleasant place, than a voice calls out to you to rise and move on, for your time has expired."

"Must I move on, sir?" I asked. "Must I leave Thornfield?"

"I believe you must, Jane. I am sorry, Janet, but I believe indeed you must."

This was a blow; but I did not let it paralyze me.

"Well, sir, I shall be ready when the order to march comes."

"It is now—I must give the order tonight."

"Then you are going to be married, sir?"

"Ex-act-ly. Pre-cise-ly. With your usual sharpness, you have hit the nail straight on the head."

"Soon, sir?"

"Very soon, my—that is, Miss Eyre. And you'll remember, Jane, the first time I—or rumour—hinted to you that I intended to put my old bachelor's neck into the sacred noose, to enter into the holy estate of matrimony, to take Miss Ingram to my bosom. In short—she's an extensive armful, but that's not the point—one can't have too much of a very excellent thing as my beautiful Blanche—well, as I was saying—listen to me, Jane! You're not turning your head to look after more moths, are you? I wish to remind you that it was you who first said to me, with that foresight, prudence, and humility which befit your position—that in case I married Miss Ingram, both you and little Adele had better leave forthwith. Adele must go to school; and you, Miss Eyre, must get a new situation."

"Yes, sir, I will advertise immediately; and meantime, I suppose—" I stopped. I was going to say "till I find another place to go" but my voice was not quite under command.

"In about a month I hope to be a bridegroom," continued Mr. Rochester, "and meanwhile, I shall look for employment and a residence for you."

"Thank you, sir; I am sorry to give—"

"Oh, no need to apologize! I consider that when an employee does her duty as well as you have, she can expect assistance from her employer. Indeed, through my future mother-in-law, I have already heard of a place that I think will suit you. It is governess to the five daughters of Mrs. Dionysius O'Gall of Bitternutt Lodge, Connaught, Ireland. You'll like Ireland, I think—they're such warm-hearted people there, they say."

"It is a long way off, sir."

"No matter—a girl of your sense will not object to the voyage or the distance."

"Not the voyage, but the distance; the sea is a barrier—"

"From what, Jane?"

"From England and from Thornfield, and—"

"Well?"

"From you, sir."

As I said this, my tears gushed out. I did not cry so as to be heard, however; I avoided sobbing. The thought of Mrs. O'Gall and Bitternutt Lodge gave a chill to my heart; and colder was the thought of all the brine and foam destined to rush between me and the master at whose side I now walked; and coldest was the memory of the wider ocean—wealth, caste, and custom—between me and what I loved.

"It is a long way," I again said.

"It is, to be sure; and when you get to Bitternutt Lodge, Connaught, Ireland, I shall never see you again, Jane—that's certain. I never go over to Ireland, not having much of a fancy for the country. We have been good friends, Jane, have we not?"

"Yes, sir."

"And when friends are on the eve of separation, they like to spend the little time that remains, close to each other. Come! We'll quietly talk over the voyage, and our parting, for half an hour or so. Here is the chestnut tree and the bench. Come, we will sit here in peace tonight, though we should never again be destined to sit here together."

We sat down.

"It is a long way to Ireland, Janet, and I am sorry to send my little friend on such weary travels; but how is it to be helped? Are you related to me, do you think, Jane?"

My heart was still. By this time, I could not answer.

"Because," he said, "I sometimes have a queer feeling with regard to you—especially when you are near me, as now. It is as if I had a string somewhere under my left ribs, connected to a similar string in your little frame. And if the English Channel and two hundred miles of land come between us, I am afraid that cord of communion will be snapped; and then I've got a nervous feeling that I would begin bleeding inside. As for you— you'd forget me."

"That I never would, sir; you know—"

It was impossible to proceed.

"Jane, do you hear that nightingale singing? Listen!"

I listened, and I sobbed convulsively, for I could no longer suppress what I was enduring; I was shaken from head to toe. When I did speak, it was only to say that I wished I had never been born, or never come to Thornfield.

"Because you are sorry to leave it?"

The strength of emotion, stirred by grief and love within me, was overwhelming.

"I grieve to leave Thornfield. I love Thornfield. I love it because I have lived a full and delightful life here. I have not been trampled on. I have not been terrified. I have not been excluded from what is bright, and energetic, and good. I have talked, face to face, with what I treasure and delight in—an original, vigorous, expanded mind. I have known you, Mr. Rochester. And I am filled with terror and anguish that I absolutely must be torn from you forever. I see the necessity of leaving, and it is like looking at death."

"Where do you see the necessity?" he asked suddenly.

"Where? You, sir, have placed it before me."

"In what shape?"

"In the shape of Miss Ingram, a noble and beautiful woman—your bride."

"My bride! What bride? I have no bride!"

"But you will have."

"Yes—I will! I will!" He clenched his teeth.

"Then I must go; you have said it yourself."

"No, you must stay! I swear it."

"I tell you I must go!" I retorted. "Do you think I can stay and become nothing to you? Do you think I am a machine without feelings, and can bear to have my morsel of bread snatched from my lips, and my drop of living water dashed from my cup? Do you think because I am poor, obscure, plain, and little, I am soulless and heartless? You think wrong! I have as much soul as you, and as much heart! And if God had given me some beauty and much wealth, I would have made it as hard for you to leave me, as it is now for me to leave you. I am not talking to you now as one human to another. It is my spirit that addresses your spirit, just as if both of us had passed through death and stood at God's feet—equal—as we are!"

"As we are!" repeated Mr. Rochester.

Then he held me in his arms, gathered me to his breast, and pressed his lips against my lips. "So, Jane!"

"Yes, so, sir," I replied, "and yet not so. For you are a married man, or as good as married; and you are wed to a woman inferior to you, one with whom you have no sympathy, whom I do not believe you truly love. For I have seen and heard you sneer at her. I would reject such a marriage. Therefore, I am better than you—let me go!"

"To where, Jane? Ireland?"

"Yes—to Ireland. I have spoken my mind, and I can go anywhere now."

"Jane, be still—don't struggle so, like a wild frantic bird."

"I am no bird. I am a free human being with an independent will, which I now exert to leave you."

Another effort set me free from his arms, and I stood erect before him.

"And your will shall decide your destiny," he said. "Jane Eyre, I offer you my hand, my heart, and a share of all my possessions."

"You play a game, which I merely laugh at."

"I ask you to pass through life by my side—to be my second self, and my best earthly companion."

"For that fate, you have already made your choice, and must abide by it."

"Jane, be still a few moments. You are over-excited. I will be still too."

A breeze came sweeping down the walk and trembled through the branches of the chestnut tree. The nightingale's song was then the only voice. I listened to it, and again I wept.

Mr. Rochester sat quietly, looking at me gently and seriously. Some time passed before he spoke. At last he said:

"Come to my side, Jane, and let us understand one another."

"I will never again come to your side. I am torn away now, and cannot return."

"But, Jane, I summon you as my wife. It is only you I intend to marry."

I was silent. I thought he mocked me.

"Come, Jane—come here."

"Your bride stands between us."

He rose, took a step, and reached me.

"My bride is here," he said, again drawing me to him, "because my equal is here, and my likeness. Jane, will you marry me?"

Still I did not answer, and still I pulled myself from his grasp, for still I could not believe it.

"Do you doubt me, Jane?"

"Entirely."

"You have no faith in me?"

"None."

"Am I a liar in your eyes?" he asked passionately. "Little skeptic, you shall be convinced. What love do I have for Miss Ingram? None. And that you know. What love has she for me? None—as I have taken pains to prove. I started a rumour to reach her that my fortune was not a third of what she supposed, and after that I waited to see the result. It was coldness from both her and her mother. I would not—I could not—marry Miss Ingram. You—you strange, almost unearthly thing! I love you as my own flesh. You—poor and obscure, small and plain as you are—I beg you to accept me as your husband."

"What, me?" I spouted, beginning to believe his sincerity. "Me, who has not a friend in the world but you, if you are my friend, and not a shilling, but what you have given me?"

"You, Jane, I must have you for my own—entirely my own. Will you be mine? Say yes, quickly."

"Mr. Rochester, let me look at your face. Turn to the moonlight."

"Why?"

"Because I want to read your face—turn!"

"There! You will find my face scarcely more readable than a crumpled, scratched page. Read on—only hurry, for I suffer."

His face was very anxious and flushed, and there were strong movements in the features, and strange gleams in the eyes.

"Oh, Jane, you torture me!" he exclaimed. "With that searching, yet faithful and generous look, you torture me!"

"How can I do that? If you are true, and your offer is real, my only feelings to you must be gratitude and devotion—they cannot torture you."

"Gratitude!" he shouted wildly, and added, "Jane, accept me quickly. Say 'Edward, I will marry you.'"

"Are you in earnest? Do you truly love me? Do you sincerely wish me to be your wife?"

"I do. And if an oath is necessary to satisfy you, I swear it."

"Then, sir—I will marry you."

"—Edward. My little wife!"

"Dear Edward!"

"Come to me—come to me entirely now," said he; and added, in his deepest tone, speaking in my ear as his cheek was against mine, "Make my happiness—I will make yours."

Then he added, "God pardon me, let man not meddle with me—I have her, and will hold her."

"There is no one to meddle, sir. I have no family to interfere."

"No—that is the best of it," he said.

Sitting beside him, spared from the nightmare of having to leave Thornfield, united in paradise with him, I thought only of the overflow of happiness given to me.

Again and again he said, "Are you happy, Jane?"

And again and again I answered, "Yes."

He then murmured, "This will atone for the past—it will atone. Did I not find Jane friendless, cold, and comfortless? Will I not guard, and cherish, and comfort her? Is there not love in my heart, and firmness in my decision? This will atone on God's judgment day. I know my Maker approves of what I do. And the world's judgment? I wash my hands of it. And man's opinion? I defy it."

But what had now happened to the evening? The moon was out, yet we were in shadows—I could scarcely see my master's face, near as I was. The wind roared in the orchard, sweeping over us, and the chestnut tree twisted and groaned.

"We must go in," said Mr. Rochester. "The weather changes. I could have sat with you till morning, Jane."

And so could I with you, thought I. Perhaps I should have said so, but a vivid flash of lightning leaped out of a cloud, and there was a crack and a crash; and I thought only of hiding my eyes on Mr. Rochester's shoulder.

The rain rushed down. He hurried me up the walk, through the grounds, and into the house; but we were already quite wet. He was taking off my shawl in the hall, and shaking the water out of my loosened hair, when Mrs. Fairfax emerged from her room. I did not observe her at first, nor did Mr. Rochester. The clock was on the stroke of midnight.

"Hurry to take off your wet things," said he, "and before you go, good-night—goodnight, my darling!"

He kissed me repeatedly. When I looked up, after leaving his arms, there stood Mrs. Fairfax—pale, stern, and amazed. I only smiled at her and ran upstairs. Explanation can wait for another time, thought I.

Still, when I reached my chamber, I felt distressed that she should misunderstand what she had seen. But joy soon surpassed every other feeling; and as loud as the wind blew, as near and deep as the thunder crashed and the lightning gleamed, as blinding as the rain fell for two hours, I experienced no fear and little awe.

Mr. Rochester came to my door three times during the storm, to ask if I was safe and peaceful—and that was comfort enough, strength enough for anything.

The next morning, before I left my chamber, Adele came running in to tell me that the great chestnut tree at the bottom of the orchard had been struck by lightning in the night, and was split in half.

Chapter 24

As I rose and dressed, I thought over what had happened, and wondered if it were a dream. I could not be certain of the reality till I had seen Mr. Rochester again, and heard him renew his words of love and promise.

While arranging my hair, I looked at my face in the mirror, and felt that it was no longer plain—there was hope in its appearance, and life in its colour, and my eyes beamed. I had often been unwilling to look at Mr. Rochester, because I feared he would not be pleased with my face; but now I was sure I could gaze upon him, and not cool his affection.

I took a plain, but light, summer dress from my drawer and put it on; it seemed no clothing had ever flattered me so well, because I had never worn any in such a blissful mood.

When I ran down into the hall, I saw a brilliant June morning and, through the open glass door, I felt a fresh and fragrant breeze. Nature must be glad when I was so happy.

A beggar woman and her little boy—both pale and ragged—were coming up the walk, and I ran down and gave them all the money in my purse—three or four shillings. I must share my happiness with them. The crows cawed and birds sang; but nothing was so merry or so musical as my own rejoicing heart.

Mrs. Fairfax surprised me by looking out of the window with a sad face, and saying gravely, "Miss Eyre, will you come to breakfast?"

During the meal she was quiet and cool—but I could not explain to her what had happened; I must wait for my master to do that, and so must she. I ate what I could, and then I hastened upstairs. I met Adele leaving the schoolroom.

"Where are you going?" I asked. "It is time for lessons."

"Mr. Rochester has sent me to the nursery."

"Where is he?"

"In there," pointing to the room she had left; and I went in, and there he stood.

"Come and bid me good morning," said he. I gladly entered, and it was not a cold word now, or even a shake of the hand that I received, but an embrace and a kiss. It seemed natural to be so well loved, so caressed by him.

"Jane, you look blooming, and smiling, and pretty," said he. "Truly pretty this morning. Is this my pale, little elf? This little sunny-faced girl with the dimpled cheek and rosy lips, the satin-smooth hair, and the radiant hazel eyes?"

I had green eyes, reader, but you must excuse the mistake—I suppose, for him, they were newly dyed.

"It is Jane Eyre, sir."

"Soon to be Jane Rochester," he added. "In four weeks, Janet, not a day more. Do you hear that?"

I did, and I could not quite comprehend it—it made me giddy. The feeling was something stronger than joy—it stunned me. The feeling was, I think, almost fear.

"You blushed, and now you are white, Jane; what is that for?"

"Because you gave me a new name—Jane Rochester; and it seems so strange."

"Yes, Mrs. Rochester," said he. "Young Mrs. Rochester—Fairfax Rochester's girl bride."

"It can never be, sir; it does not sound possible. Human beings never enjoy complete happiness in this world. I was not born for a different destiny from the rest of women. To imagine such a destiny is a fairy tale—a daydream."

"Which I can and will realize. I shall begin today. This morning I wrote to my banker in London to send me certain jewels he has in his keeping—heirlooms for the ladies of Thornfield. In a day or two, I will pour them into your lap. Every privilege, every attention that I would accord a nobleman's daughter whom I was about to marry, shall be yours."

"Oh, sir! Never rain jewels! I don't like to hear them spoken of. Jewels for Jane Eyre sounds unnatural and strange—I would rather not have them."

"I will put the diamond chain round your neck myself, and place the circlet on your forehead. Nature has stamped 'nobility' on your brow, Jane. I will clasp bracelets on these fine wrists, and place rings on these fairy-like fingers."

"No, no, sir! Speak of other things; don't address me as if I were a beauty; I am your plain, Quakerish governess."

"You are a beauty in my eyes, and a beauty after my heart—light and delicate."

"Puny and insignificant, you mean. You are dreaming, sir—or you are sneering."

"I will also make the world recognize that you are a beauty," he went on, while I really became uneasy, because I felt he was either deluding himself or trying to delude me. "I will dress my Jane in satin and lace, and she shall have roses in her hair; and I will cover the head I love best with a priceless veil."

"And then you won't know me, sir; and I shall not be your Jane Eyre any longer. I don't call you handsome, sir, though I love you most dearly, far too dearly to flatter you. Don't flatter me."

He continued his theme, however. "Today I shall take you in the carriage to Millcote, and you must choose some dresses for yourself. I told you we shall be married in four weeks. The wedding is to take place quietly, in the church down below; and then I shall sweep you away to London. After a brief stay, I shall take you to French vineyards and Italian plains, to see whatever is famous, old and new; and taste the life of cities, and learn to value yourself by fair comparison to others."

"I shall travel with you, sir?"

"Paris, Rome, and Naples; Florence, Venice, and Vienna; all the places I have wandered shall be revisited by you. Ten years ago, I flew through Europe half-mad with disgust, hate, and rage as my companions; now I shall revisit it healed and cleansed, with a very angel as my comforter."

I laughed at him as he said this. "I am not an angel, and I will not be one till I die—I will be myself. Mr. Rochester, you must neither expect nor obtain anything heavenly from me—for you will not get it, any more than I shall get it from you, which I don't expect."

"What do you expect of me?'

"For a little while, you will perhaps be the same; and then you will turn cool; and then you will suddenly change, and be stern, and I will have to do much to please you. But when you get used to me, you will perhaps like me again—like me, I say, not love me. I suppose your love will boil over in six months—or less. I have read in books written by men, that half a year is the longest that a husband's love lasts. Yet, as a friend and companion, I hope never to become distasteful to my dear master."

"Distasteful? I think I shall like you again and again—and I will make you confess that I not only like you, but love you—truthfully, passionately, and constantly."

"You are not likely to change, sir?"

"To women who please me only by their faces, I am the very devil when

I find out they have neither souls nor hearts, and are trivial, coarse, stupid and ill-tempered. But to the woman with a clear eye and eloquent tongue, with a soul made of fire, and a character that bends but does not break, I am ever tender and true."

"Did you ever know someone of such character, sir? Did you ever love such a woman?"

"I love her now."

"Any woman before you knew me?"

"I never met anyone like you. Jane, you please me, and you master me—you seem to submit, and while I am turning you around my finger, it sends a thrill to my heart. I am influenced and conquered—the influence is sweet and the conquest is witchery."

"I wonder how you will answer me a year from now, if I should ask a favour that does not suit you."

"Ask me something now, Jane—the least little thing."

"I will, sir; I have my request all ready."

"Speak! But if you look up and smile with that face, I will consent before I know what I am agreeing to, and that will make a fool out of me."

"Not at all, sir. I ask only this—don't send for the jewels, and don't crown me with roses."

"Your request is granted—for the time being. I will withdraw my order to my banker. But you have not yet asked for anything—you have only had a gift withdrawn; try again."

"Well then, sir, satisfy my curiosity about something."

He looked disturbed. "What? What?" he said hastily.

"Why did you take such pains to make me believe you wished to marry Miss Ingram?"

"Is that all? Thank God it is no worse!" He looked down, smiling at me, and stroked my hair, as if well-pleased at seeing a danger averted. "Well, Janet, I pretended to court Miss Ingram because I wished to make you as madly in love with me as I was with you; and I knew jealousy would be my best ally."

"Excellent! Now you are small. It was a burning shame and a scandalous disgrace to act in that way. Did you think nothing of Miss Ingram's feelings, sir?"

"She has one feeling—pride—and that needs humbling. Were you jealous, Jane?"

"Never mind, Mr. Rochester; it is not interesting for you to know that. Answer me truly once more. Do you not think Miss Ingram will feel abandoned?"

"Impossible. I told you how she deserted me—the idea of my being poor cooled her flame in a moment."

"You have a curious, scheming mind, Mr. Rochester. I am afraid your principles can be eccentric."

"My principles were never trained, Jane; they may have gone a little astray for lack of attention."

"But seriously, may I enjoy my great happiness without fearing that anyone else is suffering because of it?"

"That you may, my good little girl. There is no one in the world who loves me as purely as you."

I turned my lips to the hand that lay on my shoulder. I loved him very much—more than I could say, more than words could express.

"Ask something more," he said. "It is my delight to be asked, and to give."

I was again ready with my request. "Talk to Mrs. Fairfax, sir; she saw me with you last night in the hall, and she was shocked. Give her some explanation before I see her again. It pains me to be misjudged by so good a woman."

"Go put on your bonnet," he replied. "I want you to accompany me to Millcote this morning; and while you prepare for the drive, I will enlighten the old lady's understanding. What did she think, Janet?"

"I believe she thought I had forgotten my station—and yours, sir."

"Your place, your status, your station! Your station is in my heart, and on the backs of those who would insult you, now and forever. Go."

I was soon dressed, and when I heard Mr. Rochester leave Mrs. Fairfax's parlour, I hurried down to it. The old lady had been reading her morning Bible, and her spectacles were upon it. Her eyes were fixed on the blank wall. Seeing me, she made a sort of effort to smile, and said a few words of congratulation; but then the smile faded.

"I feel so astonished," she began, "I hardly know what to say, Miss Eyre. I have surely not been dreaming, have I? Mr. Rochester came in here five minutes ago and said that in a month you would be his wife."

"He said the same thing to me," I replied.

"He has! Do you believe him? Have you accepted him?"

"Yes."

She looked at me, bewildered. "I would never have thought it. He is a proud man—all the Rochesters were proud; and his father, at least, liked money. The master has always been called careful. He means to marry you?"

"He tells me so."

She studied me closely. In her eyes I read that they could not under-stand it. "It is beyond me!" she continued. "How it will turn out, I really don't know. Equality of position and fortune is often advisable in marriage, and there are twenty years of difference in your ages. He could almost be your father."

"No, indeed, Mrs. Fairfax!" exclaimed I, annoyed. "No one who saw us together would suppose that for an instant. Mr. Rochester looks as young, and is as young, as some men at twenty-five."

"Is it really for love that he is going to marry you?" she asked.

I was so hurt by her coldness and doubt that the tears rose to my eyes.

"I am sorry to grieve you," pursued the widow, "but you are so young, and so little acquainted with men, I wish to put you on your guard. It is an old saying that 'All is not gold that glitters,' and in this case I fear that something will be found to be different from what either you or I expect."

"Why? Am I a monster?" I said. "Is it impossible that Mr. Rochester should have a sincere affection for me?"

"No, you are much improved lately; and Mr. Rochester, I daresay, is fond of you. I have always noticed that you were a sort of pet of his. There are times when I have been concerned, and wished to put you on your guard; but I knew that would perhaps offend you; and you were so modest and sensible, I hoped you might be trusted to protect yourself. And then, last night at midnight, I saw you come in with him."

"Well, never mind that now," I interrupted impatiently.

"I hope all will be right in the end," she said, "but you cannot be too careful. Try and keep Mr. Rochester at a distance—distrust yourself as well as him. Gentlemen of his station do not usually marry their governesses."

I was growing truly irritated. Happily, Adele ran in.

"Let me go to Millcote too!" she cried. "Mr. Rochester won't let me—beg him to let me go, mademoiselle."

"That I will, Adele," and I hurried away with her, glad to leave the gloomy widow.

The carriage was ready; they were bringing it round to the front, and my master was waiting, Pilot bounding around.

"Adele may accompany us, may she not, sir?"

"I told her no. I'll have no brats! I'll have only you."

"Do let her go, Mr. Rochester, if you please; it would be better."

"Not it; she will hold us back."

He was quite abrupt, both in look and voice. The chill of Mrs. Fairfax's warnings were upon me. I felt a loss of power over him. I was about to mechanically obey him, but as he helped me into the carriage, he looked at my face.

"What is the matter?" he asked. "All the sunshine is gone. Do you really wish the child to come? Will it annoy you if she is left behind?"

"I would much rather she came, sir."

"Then off with your bonnet, and get inside like a flash of lightning!" cried he to Adele.

She obeyed him with all her speed.

"After all, a single morning's interruption will not matter much," said he, "when I will shortly claim you for life."

Adele kissed me with gratitude; Mr. Rochester put her in a corner of the carriage.

"Let her sit with me," I begged, "so she does not trouble you."

He handed her over like a lapdog. "I'll send her to school yet," he said, but now he was smiling.

Adele heard him and asked, "Without mademoiselle?"

"Yes," he replied, "for I am taking mademoiselle to the moon, and there she shall live with me in a cave."

"She will have nothing to eat; you will starve her," observed Adele.

"I shall gather sugar for her—the moon is filled with sugar, Adele."

"She will want to warm herself; what will she do for a fire?"

"Fire rises out of the lunar mountains; when she is cold, I'll carry her up to a peak, and lay her down on the edge of a crater."

"Her clothes will wear out; how can she get new ones?"

Mr. Rochester was puzzled. "How would a pink cloud do for a gown? And I could cut a pretty scarf out of a rainbow."

"She is far better as she is," concluded Adele. "Besides, she would get tired of living with only you on the moon. If I were mademoiselle, I would never agree to go with you."

"She has already consented; she has pledged her word."

We were now outside Thornfield gates, on the road to Millcote.

"Adele, look at that field," he said. "In that field, I was walking late one evening about a fortnight ago, and I sat down to rest on the steps of the fence. There I took out a little book and a pencil, and began to write about a misfortune that happened to me long ago, and a wish for happy days to come, when something came up the path and stopped. I looked at it. It was a little thing with a veil on its head. It drew nearer; we never spoke, but we read each other's eyes.

"It was a fairy, and came from Elf-land to make me happy. She said I must leave the ordinary world and go with her to a special place. She gave me a pretty gold ring for my fourth finger of my left hand, and said, 'I am yours, and you are mine; and we shall leave the earth, and make our own heaven.'

"The ring, Adele, is in my pants pocket, disguised as a gold coin, but I will soon change it to a ring again."

The hour we spent at Millcote was somewhat bothersome to me. Mr. Rochester took me to a silk warehouse; there I was ordered to choose half a dozen dresses. I hated the whole business and begged him to defer it, but no—it should be done now. Whispering, I begged him to reduce the number of dresses to two—he insisted on selecting them himself.

With anxiety, I watched as his eyes fixed on a rich silk of the most brilliant purple color, and a superb pink satin. I told him that he might as well have chosen a gold gown and a silver bonnet, for I would certainly never wear his chosen dresses.

With great difficulty, for he was stubborn as a stone, I persuaded him to exchange purple and pink in favour of sober black satin and pearl grey silk.

"It might pass for the present," he said, "but I will yet see you glittering."

I was glad to get him out of the silk warehouse, and then out of a jeweler's shop; the more he bought me, the more I felt annoyed and degraded.

As we re-entered the carriage, and I sat back, hot and exhausted, I remembered that, in the hurry of all the events, I had wholly forgotten about the letter from my uncle, John Eyre, to Mrs. Reed, and his intention to adopt me and bequeath me his fortune.

It would indeed be a relief, I thought, if I had even a small inheritance. I can never bear being dressed like a doll by Mr. Rochester. I will write to Madeira the moment I get home, and tell my uncle John that I am going to be married, and to whom. If I had a hope of one day bringing a fortune to the marriage, I could better tolerate being kept by him now.

Somewhat relieved by this idea, I was able, during the rest of the carriage ride home, to meet my master's and lover's eyes, though I avoided looking at both his face and gaze. He smiled, and it reminded me of the smile that a sultan might bestow on a slave to whom he had given his gold and jewels. When his hand found mine, I squeezed it and thrust it back at him, red with pressure.

"Mr. Rochester," I said, "if you look at me that way, I'll wear nothing but my old Lowood frocks, and I'll be married in this lilac cotton dress. And then you can make a robe for yourself out of the pearl grey silk, and vests out of the black satin."

He chuckled and rubbed his hands. "Oh, it is rich to see and hear her!" he exclaimed. "Is she original? Is she spicy? I would not exchange this one little English girl for the Grand Turk's entire harem!"

"Sir, do not equate me with them. If that is what you want, then take your cash to Istanbul and purchase all the flesh you desire."

"Oh," he said, "and what will you do then, Janet?"

"I shall become a missionary and preach freedom to the poor women enslaved in those harems."

He paused a moment, then asked, "Jane, what is it you really want?"

"I want not to feel that I owe you anything, sir. Do you remember what you said about Celine Varens? The diamonds, the cashmeres you gave her? I will not be your English Celine Varens. I shall continue to be Adele's governess, and earn my room, my board, and thirty pounds a year. I'll furnish my own wardrobe out of that money, and you shall give me nothing but—"

"Well, what?"

"Your respect. And if I give you mine in return, then we shall be even."

"Well, for cool rudeness and pure pride, there is no one equal to you," said he.

We were now approaching Thornfield.

"Will you dine with me tonight?" he asked, as we entered the gates.

"No thank you, sir."

"And why, if I may inquire?"

"I have never dined with you, sir, and I see no reason why I should now, till—"

"Till what?"

"Till I can't help it."

"Do you suppose I eat like an ogre or a ghoul, that you dread being my dinner companion?"

"I have no idea, sir; but I want to go on as usual for another month."

"You will give up your governess slavery at once."

"I beg your pardon, sir; I shall not. I shall go on with it as usual. I shall keep out of your way all day, as usual; you may send for me in the evening, when you wish to see me, and I'll come then; but at no other time."

"Listen, Jane. It is your time now, little tyrant, but it will soon be mine; and once I have you, to have and to hold, I'll just—figuratively speaking—chain you to me, like my watch guard."

He said this as he helped me step from the carriage and, while he lifted Adele out, I entered the house and went upstairs.

That evening, I went downstairs at his request. I was determined not to spend the whole time in private conversation; I remembered his fine voice, and knew he liked to sing. And so I rose from my chair, opened the piano, and begged him, for the love of heaven, to give me a song. He said he would rather sing another time; but I replied that there was no time like the present.

"Do you like my voice?" he asked.

"Very much." I was not fond of pampering his vanity, but in order to achieve my goal, I did.

"Then, Jane, you must accompany me on the piano."

"Very well, sir, I will try."

I did try, but soon he pushed me to one side—which is precisely what I wanted—and proceeded to accompany himself, for he could play as well as he could sing.

I went to the window seat, and while I looked out at the still trees, he sung in mellow tones:

"My love has placed her little hand
With noble faith in mine,
And vowed that wedlock's sacred band
Our nature shall entwine.
My love has sworn, with sealing kiss,
With me to live—to die;
I have at last my nameless bliss.
As I love—loved am I!"

He rose and came toward me, and I saw tenderness and passion in his face.

As he reached me, I asked with harshness, "Whom are you going to marry now?"

"That is a strange question from my darling Jane. Any other woman would have melted at hearing such lines sung in her praise."

I assured him I was naturally hard—very flinty—and that he would often find me so; and that I was determined to show him the sharp points in my character before our marriage day, so that he would know exactly what sort of a bargain he had made, while there was still time to undo it.

"Will you be quiet and talk rationally?"

"I will be quiet, if you wish, and as to talking rationally, I was doing that just now."

He fretted and fumed and fidgeted.

Very good, I thought, you may fume and fidget all you please, but this is the best plan for me. I like you more than I can say, but I'll not sink into deep sentiment. I'll keep a distance between us that will be to our mutual advantage.

I worked him up to considerable irritation; then, after he had moved to the other end of the room, I got up and said, "I wish you goodnight, sir," in my natural and respectful manner and slipped out the side door.

I continued this behavior during the whole four weeks before our marriage, with the best success. It made him rather cross and crusty; but on the whole, I could see he was excellently entertained and, had I given him lamb-like submission, while it would have fed his ego, would have not satisfied his common sense.

In other people's presence I was quiet and submissive, as before. It was only in the evening that I afflicted him. He continued to send for me at seven o'clock, though when I appeared before him now, he no longer called me "love" and "darling", but words such as "provoking puppet" and "malicious elf".

Instead of embraces, I now got scowls; for a squeeze of the hand, I got a pinch on the arm; for a kiss on the cheek, I received a tweak of the ear. It was all right; for now, I preferred these fierce favours to anything more tender.

Meanwhile, I saw that Mrs. Fairfax had approved of me—her anxiety for me vanished. Mr. Rochester declared that I was wearing him down to skin and bone, and threatened awful revenge after our marriage. I laughed in my sleeve at his threats. I can keep you in check now, I reflected, and I am sure I will be able to do so afterwards—if one scheme fails, I'll think of another.

After all, my task was not easy; often I would rather have pleased than teased him. My future husband was becoming my whole world to me; more than the world—almost my hope of heaven. He stood between me and every thought of God—I had made him my idol.

Chapter 25

The month of courtship was down to its very last hours. There was no putting off the bridal day, and all preparations were complete. I had nothing more to do—there were my trunks, packed, locked, and arranged in a row along the wall of my little chamber; tomorrow at this time, they would be on the road to London, and so would I—or rather, Jane Rochester, a person whom I did not yet know.

The address cards were ready to attach to the trunks. Mr. Rochester had written the words "Mrs. Rochester" and the name of the hotel on the cards, but I could not make myself attach them. Mrs. Rochester! She did not exist—she would not be born till tomorrow.

It was enough that, in the closet, my wedding dress had already replaced my black Lowood frock and straw bonnet. I shut the closet to hide the pearl-colored robe and veil. "I will leave you by yourself," I said. "I am overheated; I hear the wind blowing—I will go outdoors and feel it."

It was not only the rush of preparation and the anticipation of my new life that made me restless and anxious. A third reason had me hurrying outside onto the darkened grounds of the estate—something had happened the previous night which I could not understand; no one else knew of the event but me.

The previous night, Mr. Rochester was away from home, on business. I now waited for his return, eager for him to solve the mystery that upset me.

I ran to the orchard. The wind had blown all day, strong and full, but without any rain. Running down the laurel walk, I faced the wreck of the chestnut tree; the trunk, split down the centre, gasped ghastly. The great boughs on each side were dead, but they still formed one tree—a ruin, but an entire ruin.

I addressed each half of the tree. "You did right to hold fast to each other; you will never again have green leaves, but you are not desolate— each of you has the other half in your decay."

As I looked up, the moon appeared for a moment between the two halves of the tree—she was blood red, and shone a dreary beam on me. The wind fell for a second, then it made a wild, sad wail, and I ran off again.

I entered the house, then went into the library to be certain the fire burned brightly, for I knew that Mr. Rochester would like to see a cheerful hearth when he returned home. I placed his armchair by the chimney corner.

More restless than ever, I could not sit still, as the old clock in the hall struck ten. "How late it grows!" I said. "I will run down to the gates. He may be coming now, and to meet him will save a few minutes of suspense."

The wind roared high in the trees, but the road, as far as I could see, was bare. A tear of disappointment and impatience blurred my eye. I lingered; the night grew dark; rain came driving fast.

"I wish he would come!" I exclaimed, seized with worry. What could keep him? Had an accident happened? I again remembered the event from last night—it seemed to be a warning of disaster. I feared my hopes for the future were too bright to be realized. I had enjoyed so much bliss lately, that I imagined my fortune had peaked and must now decline.

Well, I cannot return to the house, I thought, and sit by the fireside while he is out in this weather. I will go forward and meet him.

I set out; I walked fast, but not far. Before long, I heard the tramp of hoofs; a horseman came up, and a dog ran by his side. It was Mr. Rochester, followed by Pilot. He saw me, took his hat off, and waved. I ran to meet him.

"There!" he exclaimed, as he stretched out his hand and bent from the saddle, "you can't do without me, that is evident. Step on my boot, give me both hands, and mount!"

I obeyed, then sprang up. I got a hearty kiss as a welcome. "Is there anything the matter, Janet, that you come to meet me at such an hour? Is there anything wrong?"

"No, but I thought you would never come. I could not bear to wait in the house for you, especially with this rain and wind."

"Rain and wind, indeed! Yes, you are dripping like a mermaid; pull my cloak round you; but I think you are feverish, Jane; both your cheek and hand are burning hot. I ask again, is there anything the matter?"

"Nothing now; I am neither afraid nor unhappy."

"Then you have been both?"

"Rather, but I'll tell you all about it later, sir, and I daresay you will only laugh at me for my pains."

Jane Eyre

"I'll laugh at you heartily after tomorrow—but till then, I dare not. This is you, who have been thorny as a briar rose? And now I seem to have gathered up a stray lamb in my arms. You wandered out of the fold to seek your shepherd, did you, Jane?"

"Yes, I wanted you—but don't boast. Here we are at Thornfield; now let me get down."

He let me down. As John took his horse, and he followed me into the hall, he told me to hurry and put something dry on, and then return to him in the library.

In five minutes, I rejoined him. I found him at supper.

"Take a seat and give me company, Jane."

I sat down near him, but told him I could not eat.

"Is it because you have the honeymoon journey before you, Jane? Is it the thought of going to London that takes away your appetite?"

"I hardly know what thoughts I have in my head. Everything in life seems unreal."

"Except me; I am substantial enough—touch me."

"You, sir, are the most phantom-like of all—you are a mere dream."

He held out his hand, laughing. "Is that a dream?" said he, placing it close to my eyes. He had a strong, muscular hand, as well as a long, strong arm.

"Yes, though I touch it, it is a dream," said I, as I put his hand down from my face. "Sir, have you finished supper?"

"Yes, Jane."

I rang the bell and ordered away the tray. When we were again alone, I stirred the fire, and then took a low seat at my master's knee.

"It is near midnight," I said.

"Yes, but remember, Jane, you promised to stay awake with me the night before our wedding."

"I did, and I will keep my promise for an hour or two at least—I have no wish to go to bed."

"Are all your arrangements complete?"

"All, sir."

"And mine likewise," he returned. "We shall leave Thornfield tomorrow, half an hour after our return from church."

"Very well, sir."

"Your cheeks are flushed! And how strangely your eyes glitter! Are you well?"

"I believe I am."

"Believe? What is the matter? Tell me what you feel."

"I could not, sir, tell you what I feel. I wish this moment would never end—who knows what lies ahead?"

"Take me into your confidence, Jane," he said. "Relieve your mind. What do you fear? That I shall not prove to be a good husband?"

"That is the idea farthest from my thoughts."

"Are you anxious of the new life into which you are passing?"

"No."

"You puzzle me, Jane; I want an explanation."

"Then, sir, listen. You were away from home last night?"

"I was, and you hinted a while ago at something which had happened in my absence; nothing, probably, of consequence, but it has disturbed you. Let me hear it."

I began. "All day yesterday I was very busy, and very happy, in my preparations; for I am not, as you seem to think, troubled by any haunting fears about my marriage; I think it is a glorious thing to have the hope of living with you, because I love you. At sunset, Sophie called me upstairs to look at my wedding dress, which they had just brought; and under it, in the box, I found your present—the veil which, in your princely extravagance, you sent for from London. I smiled as I unfolded it, and devised how I would tease you about your aristocratic tastes, and your efforts to dress your common bride as a noble lady."

"How well you read me, you witch!" interrupted Mr. Rochester. "But what did you find in the veil that you look so mournful now? Poison? A dagger?"

"No, no, sir; besides the beauty of the fabric, I found nothing except Fairfax Rochester's pride; and that did not scare me, because I am used to the sight of that demon. But, sir, as it grew dark, the wind blew with a sad, moaning sound. I wished you were here. After I went to bed, I was anxious and could not sleep. At last I did, but in my dreams, the dark and gusty night continued.

"I dreamed that I was walking on a strange, winding road, with the rain pelting me; I carried a little child that shivered in my cold arms. I thought you were on the road far ahead of me, and I made every effort to reach you, but you gained more and more distance from me.

"Then I dreamt another dream, sir, that Thornfield Hall was a dreary ruin; nothing remained of the stately front but a shell-like wall. Still carrying the child, I wandered through the ruins. Then I heard the gallop of a horse in the distance; I was sure it was you. I frantically climbed the wall to catch a glimpse—you were a speck on the road, leaving for some distant country. The wind blew so strong I could not stand. I sat down on the narrow ledge, then the wall crumbled, and the child rolled from my knee. I then also fell, and awoke from my dream."

"Now, Jane, is that all?"

"All of the dream, sir; the tale is yet to come."

"Proceed, then, with haste."

"On waking, it was still night. A lighted candle shone from the dressing table. I thought Sophie had come in. The door of the closet, where my wedding dress and veil hung, stood open. I heard a rustling noise. I asked, 'Sophie, what are you doing?' but no one answered.

"Then someone emerged from the closet, took the candle, held it up, and surveyed the wedding veil. 'Sophie! Sophie!' I cried again, and still it was silent. I rose up in bed and bent forward—surprise and bewilderment came over me; and then my blood ran cold through my veins.

"Mr. Rochester, it was not Sophie, nor Leah, nor Mrs. Fairfax. It was not—and I am sure of this—it was not even that strange woman, Grace Poole."

"It must have been one of them," interrupted my master.

"No, sir, I solemnly swear to the contrary. I had never before seen, at Thornfield Hall, the shape standing before me; the height and the figure were new to me."

"Describe it, Jane."

"It seemed, sir, like a woman, tall and large, with thick dark hair hanging long down her back. Her dress was white and straight—but whether it was a gown, sheet, or shroud, I cannot tell."

"Did you see her face?"

"Not at first. But then she took my wedding veil in her hands, held it up, gazed at it long, and then placed it on her own head, and turned to the mirror. At that moment I saw her face quite distinctly in the looking glass."

"And how was it?"

"Fearful and ghastly—oh, sir, I never saw a face like it! It was discoloured—it was a savage face. I wish I could forget the rolling red eyes and the fearful swollen face!"

"Ghosts are usually pale, Jane."

"This, sir, was purple; the lips were swelled and dark; the brow furrowed; the black eyebrows raised widely over the bloodshot eyes. Shall I tell you of what it reminded me?"

"You may."

"Of—a vampire."

"Ah! What did it do?"

"Sir, it removed my veil from its head, ripped it in half, flung it on the floor, and trampled on it."

"Afterwards?"

"It opened the window curtain and looked out; perhaps it saw dawn approaching; taking the candle, it stopped at my bedside. The fiery eyes glared upon me; she thrust her candle close to my face and snuffed the flame before my eyes. I fainted—for the second time in my life—only the second time—I fainted from terror."

"Who was with you, when you revived?"

"No one, sir, but the broad daylight. I rose, bathed my head and face in water, took a long drink; felt that, though weak, I was not ill; and determined that I would reveal this vision to no one but you. Now, sir, tell me who and what that woman was?"

"The creature of an over-stimulated brain, that is certain. I must be careful of you, my treasure—nerves like yours were not made for rough handling."

"Sir, depend on it, my nerves were not at fault—the thing was real; the event actually took place."

"And your previous dreams, were they real too? Is Thornfield Hall a ruin? Am I leaving you without a kiss—without a word?"

"Not yet."

"Am I about to do it? Why, the wedding day has already begun; and when we are united, there shall be no repeat of these mental terrors—I guarantee that."

"Mental terrors, sir! I wish I could believe that; I wish it more now than ever, since even you cannot explain to me the mystery of that awful visitor."

"And since I cannot do it, Jane, it must have been unreal."

"But, sir, when I rose this morning, and looked round the room to gather courage and comfort in full daylight, there—on the carpet—I saw the veil, torn from top to bottom in two halves!"

I felt Mr. Rochester start and shudder; he quickly flung his arms round me. "Thank God!" he exclaimed, "that if anything evil did come near you last night, it was only the veil that was harmed. Oh, to think what might have happened!"

He drew his breath short, and squeezed me so close to him, I could scarcely breathe. After some minutes of silence, he continued, cheerily:

"Now, Janet, I'll explain to you all about it. It was half dream, half reality. A woman, no doubt, did enter your room; and that woman was—must have been—Grace Poole. You call her a strange being yourself; and for good reason—remember what she did to me? And to Mason? In a state between sleeping and waking, as delirious as you were, you imagined a goblin appearance different from her own—the long disheveled hair and the swelled black face were figments of your imagination, results of your nightmare.

"The spiteful tearing of the veil was real—and it is just like her to do that. I understand that you would ask me why I keep such a woman in my house. When we have been married a year and a day, I will tell you; but not now. Are you satisfied, Jane? Do you accept my solution of the mystery?"

I reflected, and in truth it appeared to me the only possible one. I was not satisfied, but to please him I tried to appear so. I certainly did feel relieved, so I answered him with a contented smile. And now I prepared to leave, as it was past one o'clock in the morning.

"Does Sophie sleep with Adele in the nursery?" he asked.

"Yes, sir."

"There is room enough in Adele's little bed for you. You must share it with her tonight, Jane. It is no wonder that the incident you have related should make you nervous, and I would rather you did not sleep alone—promise me to go to the nursery."

"I shall be very glad to do so, sir."

"And lock the door securely on the inside. Wake Sophie when you go upstairs, and ask her to wake you early tomorrow; for you must dress and have breakfast before eight. And now, no more somber thoughts; chase your cares away, Janet. The wind blows softly, and the moon shines peacefully."

Mr. Rochester gazed into my eyes, "Well, how is my Janet now?"

"The night is serene, sir; and so am I."

"And you will not dream of separation and sorrow tonight, but of happy love and blissful marriage tomorrow."

His prediction was half correct. I did not dream of sorrow, but I also did not dream of joy—for I never slept at all. With little Adele in my arms, I watched the slumber of childhood—so calm, so innocent—and waited for the coming day.

As soon as the sun rose, I rose too. Adele clung to me as I left her; I kissed her as I loosened her little hands from my neck. I cried over her with strange emotion, and left her so that my sobs would not wake her.

Adele seemed to represent a symbol of my past life; I was now to prepare myself for Mr. Rochester, the dreaded, but adored, symbol of my unknown future.

Chapter 26

Sophie came at seven to dress me. She took so long that Mr. Rochester, grown impatient, sent word up to ask why I did not come. She was just fastening my veil—a plain, blond square—to my hair with a brooch; I hurried to leave the room.

"Stop!" she cried in French. "Look at yourself in the mirror; you have not taken one peep."

I turned around and saw a robed and veiled figure, so unlike my usual self, that it almost seemed like the image of a stranger.

"Jane!" called a voice, and I hastened downstairs. I was met at the foot of the stairs by Mr. Rochester.

"My brain is on fire with impatience," he said, "and you linger so long!"

He took me into the dining room, surveyed me carefully all over, pronounced me "fair as a lily, and not only the pride of his life, but the desire of his eyes," and then, telling me he would give me only ten minutes to eat breakfast, he rang the bell. A servant answered it.

"Is John getting the carriage ready?"

"Yes, sir."

"Is the luggage brought down?"

"They are bringing it down, sir."

"Go to the church; see if the clergyman, Mr. Wood, and the clerk are there; return and tell me."

The church was just beyond the gates; the footman soon returned.

"Mr. Wood is in the vestry, sir, putting on his garments."

"And the carriage?"

"The horses are harnessing."

"It must be ready the moment we return from church—all the boxes and luggage arranged and strapped on, and the coachman in his seat."

"Yes, sir."

"Jane, are you ready?"

I rose. There were no groomsmen, no bridesmaids, no relatives to wait for—none but Mr. Rochester and I. Mrs. Fairfax stood in the hall as we passed. I would have spoken to her, but Mr. Rochester held my hand in a grip of iron; he hurried me along in a stride I could hardly follow; and to look at Mr. Rochester's face was to feel that he would not tolerate a second of delay. I wonder what other bridegroom ever looked as he did—so grimly determined, with such flaming and flashing eyes.

I do not know whether the day was fair or foul. As we walked quickly to the church, I saw neither the sky nor the earth—my eyes were fixed on Mr. Rochester.

At the churchyard fence, he stopped and discovered I was quite out of breath. "Is my love cruel?" he said. "Wait an instant; lean on me, Jane."

And now I can recall the picture of the grey old house of God rising calm before me. I remember, too, the green gravestones; and I have not forgotten, either, two strangers walking in the cemetery and reading the headstones. I noticed them because, as they saw us, they walked round to the back of the church; and I had no doubt they were going to enter by the side door and witness the ceremony.

Mr. Rochester did not see them; he was earnestly looking at my face, from which the blood had drained—my forehead was sweating, and my cheeks and lips were cold. When I rallied, which I soon did, he walked gently with me up the path to the church door.

We entered the quiet and humble temple; the priest waited at the lowly altar, the clerk beside him. All was still—two shadows moved in a remote corner. My guess had been correct—the strangers had slipped in before us, and they now stood by the Rochester family vault, their backs towards us.

We took our places at the communion rails. Hearing a cautious step behind me, I glanced over my shoulder. One of the strangers—a gentleman—was advancing up the aisle. The service began. The clergyman explained the purpose of matrimony, then he stepped forward and, bending slightly toward Mr. Rochester, went on.

"I require and charge you both, that if either of you know any impediment why you may not lawfully be joined together in matrimony, you now confess it; for be well assured that those coupled together other than God's Word allows, neither is their matrimony lawful."

He paused, as is the custom. When is the pause ever broken by a reply? Not, perhaps, once in a hundred years. And the clergyman, who had not lifted his eyes from his book, and had held his breath for just a moment, was continuing.

His hand was already stretched toward Mr. Rochester, as his lips opened to ask, "Will thou have this woman for thy wedded wife?"—when a clear voice said:

"The marriage cannot go on—I declare that an impediment exists."

The clergyman looked up at the stranger and stood silent; the clerk did the same. Mr. Rochester moved slightly, as if an earthquake had rolled under his feet. Taking a firmer footing, and not turning his head or eyes, he said to the clergyman: "Proceed."

When he spoke that word, in a deep but low voice, profound silence fell upon the church. Then Mr. Wood said:

"I cannot proceed without investigation of what has been stated, and evidence of its truth or falsehood."

"The ceremony is quite broken off," added the stranger behind us. "I am able to prove my allegation—there exists an impediment to this marriage that is impossible to overcome."

Mr. Rochester heard, but he did not obey; he stood stubborn and rigid, making no movement but to hold my hand. What a hot and strong grasp he had! And how like marble was his pale, firm, massive face at this moment! How his eyes shone—watchful, yet wild!

Mr. Wood seemed at a loss.

"What is the nature of the impediment?" he asked. "Perhaps it may be explained away?"

"Hardly," was the answer. "I have said it was impossible, and I speak after careful consideration."

The speaker came forward and leaned on the rails. He continued, speaking each word distinctly, calmly, and steadily, but not loudly:

"It is simply that a previous marriage exists. Mr. Rochester has a wife now living."

My nerves vibrated to those words as they had never vibrated to thunder—my blood felt their violence as it had never felt frost or fire; but I was collected, and in no danger of fainting. I looked at Mr. Rochester—and I made him look at me. His whole face was colourless, his eyes were sparks. He denied nothing; he seemed as if he would defy all things. Without speaking, without smiling, without seeming to recognize me as a human being, he only put his arm around my waist and held me to his side.

"Who are you?" Mr. Rochester asked of the stranger.

"My name is Briggs, a lawyer, of London."

"And you would force a wife upon me?"

"I would remind you of your wife's existence, sir, which the law recognizes, even if you do not."

"Please tell me her name, her parents, her home."

"Certainly." Mr. Briggs calmly took a paper from his pocket and read out in a sort of official, nasal voice:

"I affirm and can prove that on the 20th of October, 1832 (fifteen years ago), Edward Fairfax Rochester, of Thornfield Hall, Millcote, England, was married to my sister, Bertha Antoinetta Mason, daughter of Jonas Mason, merchant, and of Antoinetta his wife, a Creole, in Spanish Town, Jamaica. The record of the marriage will be found in the register of the church—a copy of it is now in my possession. Signed, Richard Mason."

"That," declared Mr. Rochester, "if it is a genuine document, may prove I have been married, but it does not prove that the woman mentioned as my wife is still living."

"She was living three months ago," returned the lawyer.

"How do you know?"

"I have a witness, sir, whose testimony even you cannot dispute."

"Produce him—or go to hell."

"I will produce him—he is here. Mr. Mason, have the goodness to step forward."

Mr. Rochester, on hearing the name, gritted his teeth, and had a strong convulsive quiver. Near to him as I was, I felt the spasm of fury or despair run through his body.

The second stranger, who had lingered in the background, now drew near. His pale face looked over the lawyer's shoulder—yes, it was Mason himself.

Mr. Rochester turned and glared at him. His eyes looked bloody in their gloom, and his face flushed. He lifted his strong arm, as if he could have struck Mason and dashed him on the church floor, but Mason shrank away, and cried faintly, "Good God!"

Mr. Rochester's anger died. He only asked, "What have you to say?"

Mason' white lips spoke, but it could not be heard.

"The devil if you cannot answer distinctly. I again demand, what have you to say?"

"Sir—sir," interrupted the clergyman, "do not forget, you are in a sacred place." Then addressing Mason, he inquired gently, "Are you aware, sir, whether or not this gentleman's wife is still living?"

"Courage," the lawyer urged Mason. "Speak out."

"She is now living at Thornfield Hall," said Mason, in a more articulate voice. "I saw her there last April. I am her brother."

"At Thornfield Hall!" shouted the clergyman. "Impossible! I am an old resident in this neighbourhood, sir, and I never heard of a Mrs. Rochester at Thornfield Hall."

I saw a grim smile appear on Mr. Rochester's lips, and he muttered, "No, by God! I took care that no one should hear of her under that name."

For ten minutes Mr. Rochester pondered, then made his decision, and announced it:

"Enough! We shall all bolt out of the church at once. Clergyman Wood, close your book and take off your garment; clerk, leave the church; there will be no wedding today." The clerk obeyed and left.

Mr. Rochester continued recklessly, "Bigamy is an ugly word! I meant, however, to be a bigamist, but fate has out-maneuvered me, or God has checked me—perhaps the last. I am little more than a devil at this moment and, as my pastor there would tell me, deserve the sternest judgment of God.

"Gentlemen, my plan has been ruined. What this lawyer and his client say is true—I have been married, she is alive! You say you never heard of a Mrs. Rochester at Thornfield Hall, Mr. Wood, but I daresay you have heard gossip about the mysterious lunatic kept there under lock and key.

"Some have whispered to you that she is my bastard half-sister; some, my cast-off mistress. I now inform you that she is my wife, whom I married fifteen years ago—Bertha Mason by name—sister of this man, who is now, with his quivering limbs and white cheeks, showing you what a strong heart men can have. Cheer up, Dick! Never fear me! I'd almost as soon strike a woman as you.

"Bertha Mason is mad; she came from a mad family—idiots and maniacs through three generations. Her mother, the Creole, was both a madwoman and a drunkard, as I found out after I had wed Bertha, for they were silent on family secrets before the wedding.

"But I owe you no further explanation. Briggs, Wood, Mason, I invite you all to come up to the house and visit Mrs. Poole's patient, and my wife! You shall see what sort of being I was cheated into marrying, and judge whether or not I had a right to break the vows and seek sympathy with something at least human. This girl," he said, looking at me, "knew nothing about the disgusting secret. She thought all was fair and legal, and never dreamed she was going to be trapped into a false union with a man who was already married to a bad, mad, beast! Come, all of you—follow!"

Still holding me fast, we all left the church and walked to the house.

Upon entering Thornfield Hall, Mrs. Fairfax, Adele, Sophie, and Leah all came to meet and greet us.

"Turn around, everyone!" cried the master. "Away with your congratulations! Who wants them? Not I! They are fifteen years too late!"

He ascended the stairs, still holding my hand, and still inviting the gentlemen to follow him, which they did. We mounted the first staircase, passed up the gallery, and proceeded to the third story.

Mr. Rochester's master key opened the low, black door, admitting us to the room with the tapestry hanging on the wall.

"You know this place, Mason," said our guide. "She bit and stabbed you here."

He lifted the tapestry from the wall, uncovering the second door; this, too, he opened. In a room without a window, there burnt a fire, and a lamp hung from the ceiling. Grace Poole bent over the fire, cooking something in a saucepan. In the deep shade at the far end of the room, a figure ran backwards and forwards. What it was, whether beast or human being, one could not tell. It crawled on all fours; it snatched and growled like some strange wild animal; but it was covered with clothing—and dark, grizzled hair, wild as a mane, hid its head and face.

"Good morning, Mrs. Poole!" said Mr. Rochester. "How are you? And how is your charge today?"

"We're tolerable, sir, I thank you," replied Grace, stirring the boiling mess. "Rather snappish, but not outrageous."

Shrieking out a fierce cry, the clothed hyena rose up, and stood tall on its hind feet.

"Ah! Sir, she sees you!" exclaimed Grace. "You'd better not stay."

"A few moments, Grace; you must allow me a few moments."

"Take care then, sir! For God's sake, take care!"

The maniac shouted; she parted her shaggy locks from her face, and gazed wildly at her visitors. I recognized that purple face, those bloated features. Mrs. Poole stepped forward.

"Keep out of the way," said Mr. Rochester, pushing her aside. "She has no knife now, I suppose, and I'm on my guard."

"One never knows what she has, sir; she is so cunning."

"We had better leave her," whispered Mason.

"Go to the devil!" was his brother-in-law's recommendation.

"Beware!" cried Grace. The three gentlemen sprang back; Mr. Rochester flung me behind him.

The lunatic sprang and grappled Mr. Rochester's throat viciously, and laid her teeth to his cheek. They struggled—she was a big woman, almost equal to her husband. She showed great force—more than once she almost throttled him, athletic as he was.

Mr. Rochester could have ended it with a well-planted blow, but he would not strike—he would only wrestle. At last he gained control of her arms. Grace Poole gave him a rope, and he tied her arms behind her. With more rope, he bound her to a chair, amidst fierce yelling. He then turned to the spectators, and looked at them with a smile both bitter and empty.

"That is my wife," said he. "This is the only marital embrace I will ever know! And this is what I wished to have—" He laid his hand on my shoulder. "This young girl, who stands so grave and quiet at the mouth of hell. Wood and Briggs, look at the difference! Compare these clear eyes with the red eyeballs there—this face with that mask—this form with that bulk. Then judge me, priest of the gospel and man of the law, and remember—judge not, lest ye be judged! Off with you now. I must shut up my prize."

We all left the room. Mr. Rochester stayed a moment behind, to give some further orders to Grace Poole. The lawyer addressed me as he descended the stairs.

"You, madam," said he, "are cleared from all blame. Your uncle will be glad to hear it—if, indeed, he is still alive—when Mr. Mason returns to Madeira."

"My uncle! What about him? Do you know him?"

"Mr. Mason does. Mr. Eyre has been a business associate of his for some years. When your uncle received your letter about your coming marriage, he mentioned the news to Mr. Mason, who was visiting Mr. Eyre in Madeira on his way back to Jamaica. He knew that Mr. Mason was acquainted with Mr. Rochester. Mr. Mason, astonished and distressed as you may suppose, revealed the truth about the matter.

"Your uncle, I am sorry to say, is now on a sick bed, from which, considering the nature of his disease, he is unlikely to ever rise. He could not travel to England himself, but he begged Mr. Mason to save you from a false marriage. I am thankful I was not too late. I do not advise that you accompany Mr. Mason back to Madeira, for I am certain your uncle will be dead when you arrive."

Mr. Briggs turned to Mr. Mason. "Have we anything else to stay for?" he asked.

"No, no—let us be gone," was the anxious reply; and without speaking to Mr. Rochester, they left by the hall door. The clergyman also departed.

I had withdrawn to my own room. Once the house cleared, I shut myself in and locked the bolt so no one might intrude. I then proceeded—not to weep, not to mourn, I was yet too calm for that—but to mechanically take off the wedding dress and put on my old dress.

I then sat down; I felt weak and tired. I put my arms on a table, and my head dropped on them. And now I began to think. Till now, I had only heard, seen, moved, followed, been led or dragged. But now, I thought.

I thought about all that had occurred that morning. Now I was in my own room as usual—just myself, without an obvious change. Nothing had struck me, or damaged me, or wounded me. And yet, where was the Jane Eyre of yesterday? Where was her life? What were her prospects for the future?

Jane Eyre, who had been a passionate, expectant woman—almost a bride—was a cold, solitary girl again; her life was pale; her prospects were desolate. A Christmas frost had come at midsummer; a white December storm had whirled over June; ice glazed the ripe apples, snowdrifts crushed the roses; a frozen shroud lay over the fields; lanes which last night blushed full of flowers, today were covered with snow; and the leafy woods were as white as wintry Norway.

My hopes were all dead. I looked at my cherished wishes, yesterday so blooming and glowing; they were now stark, chilly corpses that could never revive. I looked at my love, that feeling which my master had created—it shivered in my heart, like a suffering child in a cold cradle. Sickness and anguish had seized my love—it could not seek Mr. Rochester's arms or receive warmth from his breast.

Never more could my love turn to him—faith and confidence were destroyed! Mr. Rochester was not to me what he had been, for he was not what I had thought he was. I would not say he had betrayed me; but truth was gone—and from his presence I must go; that I well knew.

When—how—where I should go, I could not yet decide; but I was certain that he would hurry me away from Thornfield. It seemed he could not have real affection for me; it had only been bursts of passion. With that gone, he would want me no more. I would be afraid even to cross his path now—he must hate the sight of me. Oh, how blind I had been!

My eyes were covered and closed; darkness seemed to swim round me. I had no will to rise, no strength to flee. I lay faint, wishing to be dead. Only one idea still throbbed within me—a remembrance of God. I said a silent prayer:

"Be not far from me, for trouble is near: there is no one to help me."

Then it came—the torrent poured over me. The whole awareness of my life forsaken, my love lost, my hope gone, my faith struck dead—that bitter hour cannot be described; in truth, "the waters came into my soul; I sank into deep waters; the floods overflowed me."

Chapter 27

Sometime that afternoon I raised my head and, looking round and seeing the sun beginning to set, I asked myself, "What am I to do?" But the answer my mind gave—"Leave Thornfield at once"—was so prompt, so dreadful, that I held my ears. I could not bear such words now.

That I was not Edward Rochester's bride was the least of my woes, I thought. That I have awakened from a most glorious dream and found it all gone, was a horror I could bear; but that I must leave him, instantly and entirely, was intolerable. I could not do it.

But, then, a voice within me said that I could do it, and predicted that I would do it. I wrestled with my decision—I wanted to be weak, so I might avoid further suffering, but my conscience told me that my life would be agony if I stayed.

You must tear yourself away, I thought; no one will help you. I stood up suddenly, and felt weak, for I had eaten no food that day. I then realized that, while I had been shut up in my room, no one had been sent to ask how I was, or to invite me to come down; not even little Adele had tapped at the door; not even Mrs. Fairfax had sought me.

"Friends always forget those whom fortune forsakes," I murmured, as I opened the door and fainted.

I fell, but not onto the ground—an outstretched arm caught me. I looked up; I was caught by Mr. Rochester, who sat in a chair outside my door. He sat me down gently on the floor.

"You come out at last," he said. "Well, I have been waiting for you long, and listening—yet not one movement have I heard, nor one sob. So you shut yourself up and grieve alone! I would rather you had come down and screamed at me. You are angry. I expected a scene of some kind. I was prepared for a rain of tears. But now I see that you have not wept at all!

"Well, Jane? Not a bitter or stinging word? You sit quietly where I have placed you, and give me a weary, passive look. Jane, I never meant to hurt you this way. Will you ever forgive me?"

Reader, I forgave him on the spot. There was such deep remorse in his eyes, such true pity in his voice, such manly energy in his manner, that I forgave him all—not in words, but in my heart.

"You know I am a scoundrel, Jane?" he asked, wondering at my continued silence—which was more the result of weakness than of will.

"Yes, sir."

"Then tell me so, sharply—don't spare me."

"I cannot. I am tired and sick. I want some water."

He heaved a shuddering sigh and, taking me in his arms, carried me downstairs. Soon I felt the warmth of a fire; for, though it was summer, I had become icy cold in my chamber. He put wine to my lips; I tasted it and revived; then I ate something he offered me, and was soon myself.

I was in the library—sitting in his chair—he was quite near. If I could die now, without too much pain, it would be well for me, I thought; then I would not have to break my heart when I tear it away from Mr. Rochester's.

I must leave him. But I do not want to leave him—I cannot leave him.

"How are you now, Jane?"

"Much better, sir; I shall be well soon."

"Taste the wine again, Jane."

He stooped down to kiss me, but kisses were now forbidden. I turned my face away.

"What! How is this?" he exclaimed. "Oh, I know! You won't kiss the husband of Bertha Mason. You consider my arms filled and my embraces taken?"

"There is no room for me, sir."

"Why, Jane? Because I have a wife already?"

"Yes."

"If you think so, you must have a strange opinion of me; you must regard me as an immoral pleasure seeker who plotted to draw you in, and rob you of your honor and self-respect. I see that you cannot speak, or your tears would rush out, and you do not wish to make a scene. You are thinking how to act—talking is of no use. I know you."

"Sir, I do not wish to act against you," I said.

"No, but since I am a married man, you will shun me, and keep out of my way, just as you have now refused to kiss me. You intend to make yourself a complete stranger to me—to live under this roof only as Adele's governess. If I ever say a friendly word to you, you will say, 'That man nearly made me his mistress; I must be ice to him.' And so, in that sense, you are scheming to destroy me."

I steadied my voice to reply, "Everything has changed around me, sir; I must change too—there is no doubt of that. And there is only one way to avoid conflict. Adele must have a new governess, sir."

"Oh, Adele will go to school—I have settled that already; and you and I will not remain at Thornfield Hall, this accursed place. I was wrong to ever to bring you to here, knowing as I did how it was haunted. Before I ever saw you, I instructed my servants to conceal all knowledge of its curse, because I feared no governess would stay if she knew about the inmate that was here—and I could not move the maniac elsewhere.

"Though I own another old house, Ferndean Manor, even more secluded than this, where I could have kept her, my conscience could not place her in Ferndean's damp walls deep in the woods; the place is unhealthy, and she would have slowly died.

"But concealing the madwoman from you was wrong. I'll shut Thornfield Hall. I'll nail up the front door and board the lower windows. I'll give Mrs. Poole money to live here with my wife, as you call that fearful hag."

"Sir," I interrupted him, "you have no pity for that unfortunate lady; you speak of her with hate; it is cruel—she cannot help being mad."

"Jane, my little darling, you don't know what you are talking about; you misjudge me again. It is not because she is mad that I hate her. If you were mad, do you think I would hate you?"

"I do indeed, sir."

"Then you are mistaken, and you know nothing about me, and nothing about the love of which I am capable. Every atom of your flesh is as dear to me as my own—in pain and sickness it would still be dear. If you raved, my arms would embrace you; in your quiet moments, you would have no nurse but me; and I could never grow weary of gazing into your eyes, though they might no longer recognize me.

"But why do I follow that train of thought? I was talking of leaving Thornfield. Everything is ready; tomorrow we shall go. I only ask you to endure one more night under this roof, Jane; and then, farewell to its miseries and terrors forever! I have a place to go to, which will be a sanctuary from all this."

"Take Adele with you, sir," I interrupted. "She will be a companion for you."

"What do you mean, Jane? I told you I would send Adele to school. What do I want with a child for a companion? And not even my own child—a French dancer's bastard. Why do you give me Adele for a companion?"

"You said solitude is too dull for you."

"Solitude! Solitude!" he repeated with irritation. "You, Jane, are to share my solitude. Do you understand?"

I shook my head—it required a degree of courage, excited as he was becoming. He looked at me long and hard; I turned my eyes from him and looked at the fire.

"Now for the hitch in Jane's character," he said at last, speaking calmly. "Everything has run smoothly so far, but I always knew there would come an obstacle. Jane! Will you hear reason?"

He stooped down and put his lips to my ear. "Because, if you won't, I'll try violence."

His voice was hoarse; he had a wild look in his eyes. I saw that, in another moment, I would be able to do nothing with him. But I was not afraid—not in the least. I felt an inward power, a sense of influence, which supported me. The crisis was perilous, but not without its excitement. I took his clenched hand, loosened his fingers, and said to him, soothingly:

"Sit down. I'll talk to you as long as you like, and hear all you have to say, whether reasonable or unreasonable."

He sat down; but I did not allow him to speak right away. I had been struggling with tears for some time; I had taken great pains to suppress them, because I knew he would not like to see me weep. Now, however, I decided to let my tears flow as freely and as long as they liked. If that annoyed him, so much the better. So I let go, and cried heartily.

Soon he begged me to stop. I said I could not, as long as he was so angry.

"But I am not angry, Jane; I only love you too much. Hush, now, and wipe your eyes."

His softened voice let me know he was calm; so I, in turn, became calm. He tried to rest his head on my shoulder, but I would not permit it. Then he tried to draw me near to him—no.

"Jane! Jane!" he said, in such bitter sadness that it pierced me, "you don't love me, then? It was only my social position that you valued? Now that you think I am disqualified to be your husband, you pull back from my touch as if I were some toad or ape."

These words cut me—yet what could I do or say? I probably should have said nothing; but I was so tortured by the thought of hurting his feelings, I could not help but comfort him.

"I do love you," I said, "more than ever. But I must not give in to the feeling; and this is the last time I can say it."

"The last time, Jane! What! Do you think you can live with me, and see me daily, and yet be cold and distant?"

"No, sir, I am certain I could not; and therefore I see there is only one way—but you will be furious if I mention it."

"Oh, mention it! If I rage, you can always weep."

"Mr. Rochester, I must leave you."

"For how long, Jane? A few minutes, while you smooth your hair, which is somewhat disheveled—and bathe your face, which is flushed?"

"I must leave Adele and Thornfield. I must part with you for my whole life. I must begin a new existence among strange faces and strange places."

"Of course; I said you should. You shall virtually be my wife—like Mrs. Rochester. You shall go to a place I have in the south of France—a villa on the shores of the Mediterranean. There you shall live a happy, safe, and most innocent life." He paused, then said, "Why do you shake your head? Jane, you must be reasonable, or I shall again become frantic."

His voice and hand quivered; his large nostrils dilated; his eyes blazed; still, I dared to speak.

"Sir, your wife is living. That is a fact you admitted yourself this morning. If I lived with you as you desire, I would then be your mistress; to say otherwise is false."

"Jane, I am not a gentle-tempered man; I am not cool and dispassionate. Out of pity to me and yourself, put your finger on my pulse, feel how it throbs, and—beware!"

He bared his wrist, and offered it to me; the blood was leaving his cheek and lips; he was becoming distressed. To resist him was cruel. But to yield to him was out of the question. I did what human beings do when they need help from one higher than they—the words "God help me!" burst from my lips.

"I am a fool!" cried Mr. Rochester suddenly. "I keep telling you I am not married, but do not explain why. I forget you know nothing of the character of that woman, or of the circumstances of my marriage to her. Oh, Jane, I am certain you will agree with me when you know the whole story! Just put your hand in mine, Janet, to prove you are near me—and I will state my real case in a few words. Can you listen to me?"

"Yes, sir; for hours if you wish."

"I ask only minutes."

He paused, then spoke.

"Jane, did you know that I was not the eldest son of my father? That I once had a brother older than I?"

"I remember Mrs. Fairfax told me so once."

"And did you ever hear that my father was a greedy man?"

"I heard something to that effect."

"Well, Jane, he resolved to keep his estate together; he could not bear to see it divided in two upon his death. And so, he left it all to my brother, Rowland. Yet he could not bear that I should be a poor man. I must be provided for—by making a wealthy marriage. An old friend, Mr. Mason, a West Indies merchant with vast wealth, had a son, Richard, and a daughter, Bertha.

"When I left college, I was sent to Jamaica to marry a bride already selected for me. My father said nothing about her money, but he told me Miss Mason was the pride of Jamaica for her beauty—and this was no lie. I found her a fine woman, in the style of Blanche Ingram—tall, dark, and majestic. She and her family wished to ally with me because I was from a good background. They introduced her to me at parties, splendidly dressed. I seldom saw her alone, and had very little private conversation with her. She flattered me, and lavished me with her charms and accomplishments. All the men in her circle seemed to admire her and envy me. I was dazzled and aroused; my senses were excited; and being young and inexperienced, I thought I loved her.

"There is no folly worse than the rashness of youth. Her family encouraged me; her competitors were jealous of me; she allured me. And we were married almost before I knew where I was. Oh, I have no respect for myself when I think of that! I never loved her, I never valued her, I did not even know her. I was not sure she had a single virtue—I had not seen modesty, kindness, candor, or refinement—and yet, I married her. Gross, groveling blockhead that I was!

"I had never seen my bride's mother—I thought she was dead. The honeymoon over, I learned my mistake. Her mother was mad, and shut up in a lunatic asylum. She had a younger brother, too—a complete dumb idiot. The elder brother, Mr. Richard Mason, whom you have seen, and whom I cannot hate, will probably also go mad one day. My father and my brother Rowland knew all this—but they thought only of her fortune, and joined in the plot against me.

"These were vile discoveries, but I did not blame my wife—even when I found her to be obnoxious, common, and narrow-minded; even when I found I could not spend a single hour with her in comfort; even when conversation with her became crude, twisted and stupid; even when no servants would stay employed, because of her violent temper and absurd orders. Even then, I restrained my anger and criticism, and swallowed my disgust and hatred.

"Jane, I will not trouble you with horrible details. I lived with that woman upstairs for four years in Jamaica, during which time she developed perverse sexual excesses, violated the vows of marriage, had sexual partners with many vulgar men. What a pygmy intellect she had, and what giant sexual appetites! Only cruelty could stop them, and I would not use cruelty. Bertha Mason, the true daughter of a mad mother, dragged me through all the hideous and degrading agonies that come to a man who is married to an unchaste wife.

"Meanwhile, my brother died, and four years later, my father died too. I was rich now, from inheriting their estates, yet poor because I was tied by law and society to the most impure, depraved woman I ever saw. And I could not rid myself of her by any legal proceedings—because the doctors now discovered that my wife was mad. They ruled that her sexual excesses were the result of insanity. I could not rid myself of her by any means.

"Jane, you don't like my story—you look almost sick. Shall I defer the rest to another day?"

"No, sir, finish it now. I pity you—I do earnestly pity you."

"For some people, Jane, pity is an insult which should be hurled back at those who offer it. But I know that is not your kind of pity, Jane. Your eyes are almost overflowing with tears; your heart is heaving; your hand is trembling in mine. Your pity, my darling, is the suffering mother of love. I accept your pity, Jane."

"Now, sir, proceed. What did you do when you found she was mad?"

"Jane, I was on the verge of despair. I disowned any connection to her behaviour, yet society still connected my name with hers. I knew that while she lived, I could never be the husband of another wife—and she was likely to live as long as I. Thus, at the age of twenty-six, I was hopeless.

"One night I was awakened by her yells; it was a fiery West Indian night, just before a hurricane. I got up and opened a window; the air was like steam; mosquitoes surrounded me; the sea rumbled like an earthquake; the clouds were black and the moon was red; the maniac shrieked curses at my name with demonic hate.

"This life," said I at last, "is hell. I have a right to end this if I can. I have no fear of burning in eternity—no future state is worse than this. Let me break away, and go home to God!

"I knelt down and unlocked a trunk which contained loaded pistols. Only for a second did I consider shooting myself. Then it passed. A fresh wind rushed into the window; the storm broke. I then made a resolution.

And now listen, Jane, for it was true Wisdom that showed me the right path to follow.

"My heart, which had been dried up, swelled and filled with life; my soul thirsted for drink. I saw hope, and felt renewal was possible.

"Hope said to me, 'That woman—who has so abused you, tarnished your name, ruined your youth, insulted your honor—she is not your wife, nor are you her husband. Take the maniac to England and confine her to Thornfield; see that she is cared for, and do all that God and humanity require of you. Then leave her and go to Europe; no one will know you there, or what a filthy burden you bear; travel through Europe, and form whatever new friendships you like.'

"To England, then, I conveyed her; at Thornfield, I safely lodged her in that third-story room, whose secret inner chamber she has, for ten years now, made into a wild beast's den. I had to find an attendant on whom I could depend. At last I hired Grace Poole from the Grimsby Retreat. She and the surgeon, Carter, are the only two people I have ever confided in. Mrs. Fairfax may have suspected something, but has no knowledge of the facts.

"Grace has proved to be a good keeper; though, at times, she has lapsed. The lunatic is both cunning and evil. She has never failed to take advantage of Grace's temporary lapses—once to steal the knife with which she stabbed her brother; and twice to steal the key to her room and leave in the nighttime—when she attempted to burn me in my bed, and then that ghastly visit to you. I thank God that she lashed out her fury only on your wedding veil—it perhaps reminded her of her own bridal day."

"And what, sir," I asked, while he paused, "did you do in Europe after you had settled her here?"

"What did I do, Jane? I transformed myself. Where did I go? I traveled Europe to find a good and intelligent woman, whom I could love—"

"But you could not marry, sir."

"I had decided, and was convinced, that I could and ought. It was not my original intention to deceive anyone, as I have deceived you. I meant to tell my tale plainly, and make my proposals openly; and it seemed so logical that I should be free to love and be loved, that I always believed some woman might be willing and able to understand my case and accept me, in spite of the curse with which I was burdened."

"What happened? Did you find anyone you liked?"

"For ten long years I roved about, living first in one capital, then another—St. Petersburg, Paris, Rome, Naples, and Florence. With plenty of money and an old name, no circles of society were closed to me. I sought my ideal of a woman amongst English ladies, French countesses, and Italian signoras—but I could not find her. I did not desire perfection, only what suited me—the opposite of the Creole—and I searched in vain. I found no one whom I would have asked to marry me.

"Disappointment made me reckless. I engaged in excess—but never immoral behavior—that I hated, and hate. Yet I could not live alone, so I tried the company of mistresses. The first I chose was Celine Varens. After her, an Italian, Giacinta, and a German, Clara—both were considered beauties. But after a few weeks, what did beauty matter? Giacinta was immoral and violent; Clara was honest and quiet, but mindless, not my taste. But, Jane, I see by your face you are not forming a very favourable opinion of me just now. You think me an unfeeling, immoral seeker of pleasure, don't you?"

"I don't like you as well as I did before, indeed, sir. Did it not seem to you the least bit wrong to live in that way, first with one mistress and then another? You talk of it as a mere matter of course."

"It was with me, and I did not like it. It was a groveling existence; I would never like to return to it. Hiring a mistress is the next worse thing to buying a slave—both are often inferior by nature, and always by position; and to live with inferiors is degrading. I now hate the memory of the time I passed with Celine, Giacinta, and Clara."

I felt the truth of these words; and I drew from them the certain feeling that, if I were ever to become the next in line after these poor girls, he would one day regard me with the same disrespect that he now held for them. I impressed this feeling on my heart, so that it might remain there to serve me as an aid in time of trial.

"And so, last January, rid of all mistresses—in a harsh, bitter frame of mind, the result of a useless, roving, lonely life, gnawed with disappointment, sour against all men and all women, I came back to England. On a frosty winter afternoon, I rode to Thornfield Hall on my horse. I expected no peace, no pleasure there. On the steps of a fence in Hay Lane, I saw a quiet little figure sitting by itself.

"I passed by, with no thought that the person who would have the greatest influence in my life, waited there in humble disguise. I did not know it even when, after my horse fell, she came up and offered me help. Childish and slender creature! I was surly, but she would not leave—she stood by me with strange determination, and looked and spoke with authority. I must be aided, and aided I was.

"I heard you come home that night, Jane, though you probably were not aware that I watched for you. The next day I observed you, unseen, for half an hour, while you played with Adele in the gallery. You were very patient with her, my little Jane. You talked to her and amused her a long time. Now and then, you glanced out at the snow; your look revealed sweet thoughts of youth when its spirit is full of hope.

"Impatiently I waited for evening, when I might summon you to my presence. I desired to know you better. You entered the room with a look and air that were both shy and independent. You were quaintly dressed—much as you are now—yet you had sharp, daring eyes; there was power in each glance. Very soon you seemed to get used to me. Snarl as I would, you showed no surprise, fear, or displeasure. I was both content and stimulated with what I saw. I liked what I had seen, and wished to see more. Yet, for a long time, I treated you distantly, and sought your company rarely. I wanted to prolong the pleasure of getting acquainted.

"Moreover, I wished to see whether you would seek me out if I shunned you—but you did not, out of respect. I wondered what you thought of me, or if you ever thought of me, and resolved to find this out. I resumed my notice of you. There was something happy in your eyes, and friendly in your manner. I saw you had a social heart; I permitted myself the delight of being kind to you; kindness soon stirred emotion. Your face became soft in expression, your tones gentle. I used to enjoy a chance meeting with you, Jane, at this time; you glanced at me with a slight worry—you did not know whether I was going to be the stern master or the kind friend. I knew I could no longer act like the former. When I stretched my hand out to you, your young face had such happiness and light."

"Don't talk anymore of those days, sir," I interrupted, wiping away some tears from my eyes; his language was torture to me; for I knew what I must do—and do soon—and all these memories, his revealing these feelings, only made my work more difficult.

"You are right, Jane," he returned. "Why dwell on the Past, when the Present is so much surer—the Future so much brighter? After a youth and manhood half-spent in pure misery and half in dreary solitude, I have for the first time found what I can truly love—I have found you. You are my better self—my good angel. It was because I felt and knew this, that I resolved to marry you. To tell me that I already have a wife is empty mockery—you know now that I have a hideous demon. I was wrong to deceive you, but I wanted you safe before taking the risk of revealing the secret. This was cowardly—I should have opened up to you. Then I should have asked you to accept my pledge of fidelity and to give me yours. Jane—give it to me now."

A pause.

"Why are you silent, Jane?"

I was experiencing a fiery ordeal, a terrible moment full of struggle, blackness, and burning! No human being that ever lived could wish to be loved better than I was loved. I absolutely worshipped the man who loved me—and now I must renounce love. One word defined my unbearable duty: Depart!

"Jane, you understand what I want of you? Just make this promise: 'I will be yours, Mr. Rochester.'"

"Mr. Rochester, I will not be yours."

Another long silence.

"Jane!" he began again, with a gentleness that broke me down with grief, and turned me stone-cold with terror—for his quiet voice was beginning to rise in anger.

"Jane, do you mean to go one way in the world, and to let me go another?"

"I do."

He bent toward me and gently embraced me.

"Jane, do you mean it now?"

"I do."

"And now?" as he softly kissed my forehead and cheek.

"I do," pulling myself away completely.

"Oh, Jane, this is bitter! This—this is wicked. It would not be wicked to love me."

"It would be wicked to obey you."

A wild look crossed his face. He rose. I laid my hand on the back of a chair for support. I shook, I feared—but I resolved.

"Jane, my life will be horrible when you are gone. All happiness will be torn away. What is left? For a wife, I have only the maniac upstairs. What shall I do, Jane? Where do I turn for a companion and for some hope?"

"Do as I do—trust in God and yourself. Believe in heaven. Hope that we will meet again there."

"Then you will not give in?"

"No."

His voice rose. "Then you condemn me to live a wretched life and to die cursed?"

"I advise you to live sinless, and I wish that you die in peace. We were born to strive and survive—you as well as I. Do so. You will forget me before I forget you."

"Is it better that you leave me and drive me to despair, than to disobey the human law of my marriage to Bertha? No one will be hurt by our loving each other. You have no relatives or friends whom you will offend by living with me."

This was true. My conscience and reason shouted wildly, "Give in! Think of his misery; think of the danger—consider how reckless he can be when left alone with despair. Soothe him, save him, tell him you love him and that you will be his. Who in the world cares for you? Who will be hurt by what you do?"

My answer was unchanged—I care for myself. The more alone, the more friendless, the more unsatisfied I am, the more I will respect myself. I will obey God's law—as man obeys it. Laws and principles are made for moments of temptation such as this—they must not be violated. If I break them at my convenience, then what are they worth? These are all I have to stand by at this hour.

Mr. Rochester read my face and saw that I had made my stand. His fury raged; he crossed the floor and seized my arm and grasped my waist. He seemed to devour me with his flaming eyes. Physically, I felt powerless at the moment; mentally, I still possessed my soul, and he saw it in my eyes. I looked in his fierce face and gave a sigh. His grip was painful, and I was exhausted.

"Never," said he, as he gritted his teeth, "never was anyone so frail and yet so strong." He shook me forcefully. "I could crush you, but what good would it do? Your eyes defy me with courage. If I break your body, I cannot capture your soul. And it is your spirit—its will and energy, its virtue and purity—that I want. Oh! Come, Jane, come!"

As he said this, he released me from his grasp and just looked at me. His look was far harder to resist than his frantic hold—only an idiot, however, would give in now. I had dared his anger; I now must avoid his sorrow. I walked to the door.

"You are going, Jane?"

"I am going, sir."

"You are leaving me?"

"Yes."

"You will not be my comforter, my rescuer? My deep love, my wild despair, my frantic prayers are all nothing to you?"

What unspeakable sadness was in his voice! How hard it was to repeat firmly:

"I am going."

"Jane!"

"Mr. Rochester!"

"Leave, then—I consent; but remember, you leave me here in anguish. Go up to your room; think over all I have said, and Jane, take a look at my sufferings—think of me."

He turned away; he threw himself on the sofa.

"Oh, Jane! My hope—my love—my life!" broke in anguish from his lips. Then came a deep, strong sob.

I had already reached the door; but, reader, I walked back—walked back as determinedly as I had left. I knelt down by him; I turned his face from the cushion to me; I kissed his cheek; I smoothed his hair with my hand.

"God bless you, my dear master!" I said. "God keep you from harm and wrong—direct you, comfort you, reward you well for your past kindness to me."

"Little Jane's love would have been my best reward," he answered. "Without it, my heart is broken. But Jane will give me her love; yes—nobly, generously."

The blood rushed to his face; the fire flashed in his eyes; he sprang from the sofa and held his arms out; but I evaded the embrace and at once left the room.

"Farewell!" was the cry of my heart as I left him. Despair added, "Farewell, forever!"

That night, sleep fell on me as soon as I lay down in bed. I dreamt I lay in the red-room at Gateshead; the night was dark, and I was fearful. The ceiling became clouds, and the moon shone in. But it was not the moon—a white human form shone down. It gazed and gazed on me. It whispered to my heart:

"My daughter, flee temptation."

"Mother, I will."

I woke from the trance-like dream. It was still night, but July nights are short—soon after midnight, dawn comes. It is not too early to begin the task I have to fulfill, thought I.

I rose. I was still dressed, for I had taken off nothing but my shoes. In my drawers I found some linen, a locket, a ring. I came across the pearl necklace Mr. Rochester had forced me to accept a few days ago. I left that; it was not mine—it belonged to the vision of the bride that was no longer.

I tied the other articles in a parcel. I put my purse, with twenty shillings, in my pocket. I tied on my straw bonnet, pinned my shawl, took the parcel, and quietly left my room.

"Farewell, kind Mrs. Fairfax!" I whispered, as I glided past her door. "Farewell, my darling Adele!" I said, as I glanced toward the nursery. I could not enter to embrace her.

I would have gotten past Mr. Rochester's chamber without a pause, but my heart momentarily stopped beating at his door, and I stopped. He was walking restlessly from wall to wall; and again and again he sighed while I listened. There was a heaven—a temporary heaven—in this room for me, if I chose. I only needed to go in and say, "Mr. Rochester, I will love you and live with you till death," and a fountain of rapture would spring to my lips. I thought about this.

My kind master was waiting with impatience for daylight. He would send for me in the morning; I would be gone. He would search for me—in vain. He would feel himself forsaken; his love rejected; he would suffer; perhaps grow desperate. I thought of this, too. My hand moved toward the lock on his door—I caught myself, pulled back, and glided on.

Drearily I went downstairs—I knew what I had to do, and I did it mechanically. In the kitchen, I got some bread and water, for perhaps I would have to walk far, and my strength must not break down. All this I did without one sound. I opened the door, walked out, and shut it softly.

Dim dawn glimmered in the yard. The great gates were closed and locked; but a door in one of them was only latched. Through that I departed; I shut it, too; and now I was out of Thornfield.

A mile away, beyond the fields, lay a road which stretched in the opposite direction from Millcote, a road I had never traveled. I took it.

I allowed myself no reflection—not one glance was to be cast back, not even one forward. Not one thought was to be given either to the past or the future. The past was so heavenly sweet—so deadly sad—that to think of it would dissolve my courage and break down my energy. The future was an awful blank.

I walked the fields, and hedges, and lanes till after sunrise. It was a lovely summer morning—my shoes were wet with dew. But I did not look at the rising sun, the smiling sky, or wakening nature. I thought only of dreary flight and homeless wandering, and—oh! with agony—I thought of what I left. I could not help it.

I thought of him now, in his room, watching the sunrise, hoping I would soon come to his chamber and say that I would stay with him and be his.

Jane Eyre

I longed to be his; I panted to return. It was not too late; I was sure my departure had not yet been discovered. I could go back and be his comforter, his pride, his redeemer from misery, perhaps from ruin. What had I done? I had injured—wounded—abandoned—my master. I was hateful in my own eyes.

Still, I could not turn back or retrace one step. God must have led me on. I was weeping wildly as I walked along my solitary way—fast, fast I went, almost delirious. My legs were seized with weakness, and I fell. I lay on the ground some minutes, pressing my face to the wet grass. I feared—hoped—that here I should die. But I was soon up, crawling forward on my hands and knees, and then again back on my feet—as eager and as determined as ever to reach the road.

When I got to the road, I sat down to rest; soon I heard wheels, and saw a coach coming. I stood up and lifted my hand; it stopped. I asked where it was going: the driver named a place a long way off, where I was sure Mr. Rochester had no connections. I asked how much he wanted to take me there; he said thirty shillings; I answered I had but twenty; well, he would try to make it do. I got inside the empty coach, and it rolled on its way.

Gentle reader, may you never feel what I felt then! May your eyes never shed such stormy, heartfelt tears as poured from mine. May you never look to Heaven in prayers so hopeless and agonized as in that hour; for never may you, like me, dread being the instrument of evil to someone you truly love.

Chapter 28

Two days have passed. It is a summer evening; the coachman has let me off at a place called Whitcross. He could take me no farther for the money I had given, and I have no more to give. I am alone. At this moment, I discover that I forgot to take my parcel out of the coach. I am now absolutely destitute.

Whitcross is no town, nor even a hamlet; it is a stone pillar, a mere sign, set up where four roads meet. Four arms point to familiar towns, the nearest being ten miles away, the farthest twenty. There are great moors all around me, and waves of mountains far beyond a deep valley at my feet. The population here must be small, and I see no passengers on these roads.

If by chance a traveler passes by, I would wish no eyes to see me; strangers would wonder what I am doing here, evidently lost. I might be questioned; no one would believe my answer. At this moment, I have no ties to human society, no relative but Mother Nature; I will seek peace from her.

I left the road and walked into the heath—scrubby open land as far as I could see. I saw a deep hollow, and waded knee-deep into its dark overgrowth. I sat down under it and felt protected.

Some time passed before I felt calm here. I feared that cattle or bulls might be near, or some hunter might discover me. But as evening came, I felt calmed by the deep silence. Till now, I had no thoughts—I had only listened, watched, and dreaded; now I began to reflect.

What was I to do? Where was I to go? Oh, impossible questions, when I could do nothing and go nowhere! I looked at the sky and saw a kindly star twinkling above; the dew fell softly. Nature seemed kind and good to me; I thought she loved me, outcast as I was. Tonight I would be her guest, as I was her child—my nature mother would lodge me without money and without price.

I had one morsel of bread left, from a roll I had bought with my last penny in a town we passed through at noon. I saw ripe berries gleaming here and there; I gathered a handful and ate them with the bread. My hunger, sharp before, was lessened.

I said my evening prayers, laid down, and spread my shawl over me. A mound of moss was my pillow. My rest might have been happy enough, only a sad heart broke it. My heart trembled for Mr. Rochester and his doom; it moaned with pity; it longed for him.

Worn out with this torture of thought, I rose to my knees. Night had come—a safe, still night, too calm for fear. We know that God is everywhere; but certainly we feel His presence most in the cloudless night sky, where we can see his omnipotence and omnipresence. I had risen to my knees to pray for Mr. Rochester. Looking up with tearful eyes, I saw the mighty Milky Way and felt the might and strength of God. I was sure that He would save what he had made—I grew convinced that neither earth would perish, nor one of the souls it treasured. I turned my prayer to thanksgiving—the Source of Life was also the Saviour of spirits. Mr. Rochester was safe; he was God's; and he would be protected by God. I again laid down and, before long, forgot my sorrow in sleep.

The next day, I got up, and I looked round me. A hot, sunny day on the golden desert of this spreading moor! I looked back at the bed I had left. Hopeless for the future, I wished that my Maker had taken my soul while I slept. Life, however, was still in my possession, with all its needs and pains. The burden must be carried; the want provided for; the suffering endured; the responsibility fulfilled. I set out.

I followed a road which led away from the sun. I walked a long time, and when I thought fatigue would overpower me, I heard the chime of a church bell. I turned in the direction of the sound, and there, amongst the romantic hills, I saw a town and a church spire. The valley on my right hand was full of pasture fields; a glittering stream ran through the green; I heard the wheels of a wagon climbing up a hill. Human life was near. I must struggle on and strive to live.

About two o'clock p.m. I entered the village. There was a little shop with some cakes of bread in the window. I had a small silk handkerchief and my gloves that I could exchange for one of these rolls. I entered the shop; the woman came forward and asked: How could she help me? I was ashamed to offer her the half-worn gloves, the creased handkerchief.

I begged permission to sit down a moment, as I was tired. She pointed to a seat; I sank into it. I wanted to weep, but I held back the tears. I was brought face to face with Necessity. I had no friends, no money. I must do something.

"Do you know of any place where a servant was wanted?"

"Nay, I couldn't say."

A neighbour or two came in; my chair was needed. I took leave.

I passed up the street, looking as I went at all the houses to the right and to the left; but I could discover no reason to enter any. Exhausted, and suffering greatly now for lack of food, I turned aside into a lane and sat down under the hedge. Before many minutes had passed, however, I was again on my feet.

I was so sick, so weak, so hungry, that instinct kept me roaming round houses where there was a chance of food. I drew near houses, I left them, and came back again, and again I wandered away, knowing I had no right to ask for help.

The afternoon advanced, and I saw the church spire before me; I hastened towards it. I saw the parsonage and remembered that strangers can ask the clergyman for help. Renewing my courage, and gathering my feeble strength, I reached the house and knocked at the kitchen door. An old woman opened.

"Is the clergyman in?"

"No, he has been called away by the sudden death of his father. He is at Marsh End now, and would likely be gone a fortnight."

Reader, I could not bear to ask for relief; I could not yet beg, and again I crawled away.

Once more I took off my handkerchief—once more I thought of the cakes of bread in the little shop. Oh, for but a crust, one mouthful!

I turned my face again to the village. I found the shop again, and I went in; and though others were there besides the woman, I asked:

"Would you give me a roll for this handkerchief?"

She looked at me with suspicion. "Nay, I never sell stuff in that way."

Desperate, I asked for half a cake; she again refused.

"Would you take my gloves?"

"No! What could I do with them?"

Reader, it is not pleasant to dwell on these details. Some say there is enjoyment in looking back at painful past experiences; but I can hardly bear to recall those times. I blamed no one who refused me. It was to be expected—an ordinary beggar is an object of suspicion.

A little before dark, I passed a farmhouse. At the open door, a farmer was sitting, eating his supper of bread and cheese. I stopped and said:

"Will you give me a piece of bread? I am very hungry."

He looked at me with surprise; but without answering, he cut a thick slice from his loaf and gave it to me. I imagine he did not think I was a beggar, but only an eccentric sort of lady who had taken a fancy to his brown loaf. As soon as I was out of sight of his house, I sat down and ate it.

That night I slept in the woods, but my night was wretched—the ground was damp, the air was cold, and I had to move again and again as intruders passed by.

Toward morning it rained; the whole next day was wet. I sought work, and was refused. As before, I starved—but food did pass my lips once.

At the door of a cottage, I saw a little girl about to throw a mess of cold porridge into a pig trough.

"Will you give me that?" I asked.

She stared at me. "Mother!" she exclaimed, "there is a woman here who wants me to give her this porridge."

"Well lass," replied a voice within, "give it to her if she's a beggar. The pigs don't want it."

The girl emptied the stiff lump into my hand, and I devoured it ravenously.

After walking an hour or more along a bridle path, the wet twilight deepening, I stopped.

"My strength is quite failing me," I said to myself. "I cannot go much farther. Must I lay my head on the cold, drenched ground? It will be very dreadful, with this feeling of hunger, faintness, chill, and this complete loss of hope. I will most likely die before morning. And why cannot I accept death? Because I know, or believe, that Mr. Rochester is living. Oh, God! Sustain me a little longer! Help me!"

My glazed eye wandered over the dim and misty landscape. I had strayed far from the village; it was quite out of sight. Only a few wild fields lay between me and a dusky hill.

"Well, I would rather die there than on a road," I reflected. To the hill, then, I turned. I reached it. I needed only find a hollow where I could lie down and feel hidden. But the moor was level and even. There was nowhere to hide.

My eye still roved along the moor when, far inside the marshes, I saw a light. I waited to see if it would go out, but it did not.

"It may be a candle in a house," I then guessed, "but if so, I can never reach it. It is much too far away; and besides, what good is it? I would knock at the door to have it shut in my face."

And I sank down where I stood, and hid my face against the ground. I lay still a while. The night wind swept over me, and the rain fell fast, wetting me to the skin. Before long, I rose. The light was still there. I tried to walk again, dragging my exhausted legs slowly toward it. It led me over the hill, through a wide marsh. I fell twice, but rallied myself. This light was my hope—I must reach it.

Across the marsh, I saw a road; it led straight up to the light. As I drew near, I saw a gate; it moved on its hinges as I touched it. Entering the gate, the shadow of a house rose to view—black, low, and rather long.

I crept closer and saw the light coming from a latticed window. When I stooped down, I could see inside. I saw a clean kitchen with a glowing fireplace; a walnut dresser with pewter plates; a clock, a table and chairs. A candle, which had been my beacon, burnt on the table; and by its light an elderly woman, clean but rough-looking, was knitting a stocking.

Near the fireplace sat two young, graceful women—ladies in every way—one in a low rocking chair, the other on a lower stool; both wore black dresses that set off their fair necks and faces. A large old dog rested its massive head on the knee of one girl; in the lap of the other was a black cat.

This humble kitchen was a strange place for such delicate ladies! Who were they? They could not be the daughters of the rustic woman at the table. I had never seen their faces before, and yet, as I gazed on them, they seemed familiar.

I could not call them handsome—they were too pale and serious; they each read a book, and frequently referred to what seemed like a large dictionary on a stand. They were so quiet, I could hear the clock tick; and when they spoke, their voices were clearly heard.

"Listen, Diana," said one of the students. "Franz and old Daniel are together in the nighttime, and Franz is telling a dream from which he has awakened in terror—listen!" And in a low voice she read something, of which not one word was intelligible to me; I later learned it was German.

"That is strong," she said, when she had finished. "I enjoy it."

The other girl, who had lifted her head to listen to her sister, repeated, while she gazed at the fire, a line of what had been read.

Both were again silent.

"Is there any country where they talk in that way?" asked the old woman, looking up from her knitting.

"Yes, Hannah—a far larger country than England."

"Well, if either of you went there, you could tell what they said, I guess?"

"We could probably tell some of it, but not all—for we are not as clever as you think us, Hannah. We don't speak German, and we cannot read it without a dictionary to help us."

"And what good does it do you?"

"We mean to teach it some time—and then we shall get more money than we do now."

"Very likely; but you've done enough for tonight."

"I think we have; at least I'm tired. Mary, are you?"

"Yes. I wonder when St. John will come home."

"Surely he will not be long now; it is just ten. Hannah, will you have the goodness to look at the fire in the parlour?"

The woman rose; she opened a door, through which I dimly saw a passage; she presently came back.

"Ah, children!" said she, "it troubles me to go into that room now; it looks so lonely with the chair empty and set back in a corner."

Hannah wiped her eyes with her apron; the two girls, grave before, looked sad now.

"But he is in a better place," continued Hannah. "Nobody had a quieter death than he had."

"You say he never mentioned us?" inquired one of the ladies.

"He hadn't time; your father was gone in a minute. He had been ailing the day before, but nothing important, and when Mr. St. John asked if he would like either of you to be sent for, he laughed at him. The next day he had a bit of a headache—that was a fortnight ago—and he went to sleep and never wakened; he was almost naked when your brother went into the room and found him. Ah, children! That's the last of the old stock. Your mother was the picture of you, Mary; Diana is more like your father."

I thought the young ladies were so similar that I could not tell where the old servant Hannah saw the difference. Both were fair complexioned and slender; both faces had distinction and intelligence. The clock struck ten.

"You'll want your supper, I am sure," observed Hannah, "and so will Mr. St. John when he comes in."

She prepared the meal as the ladies rose; they seemed about to withdraw to the parlour. Till this moment, I had been so intent on watching them, I had half-forgotten my own wretched situation. It seemed impossible that the women inside would have any concern for me. But I groped for the door, and knocked at it with hesitation. Hannah opened it.

"What do you want?" she inquired, in a voice of surprise, as she surveyed me by the light of the candle she held.

"May I speak to your mistresses?" I said.

"You had better tell me what you have to say to them. Where do you come from?"

"I am a stranger."

"What is your business here at this hour?"

"I want a night's shelter in an out-house or anywhere, and a morsel of bread to eat."

Distrust, the very feeling I dreaded, appeared in Hannah's face.

"I'll give you a piece of bread," she said, after a pause, "but we can't take in a vagrant to lodge."

"Do let me speak to your mistresses."

"No. What can they do for you? You should not be roving about now; it looks very bad outside."

"But where shall I go if you drive me away? What shall I do?"

"Oh, I'm sure you know where to go and what to do. Mind you, don't do wrong, that's all. Here is a penny; now go—"

"A penny cannot feed me, and I have no strength to go farther. Don't shut the door—oh, don't, for God's sake!"

"I must; the rain is driving in—"

"But I will die if I am turned away."

"Not you. I'm afraid you have some ill plans in mind, that bring you about folk's houses at this time of night. If you've any followers—housebreakers or the like—anywhere near, you may tell them we are not by ourselves in the house; we have a gentleman, and dogs, and guns."

Here the servant shut the door and bolted it within. This was the climax. A pain of exquisite suffering and true despair tore my heart. I was, indeed, worn out; I could not move another step. I sank on the wet door-step. I groaned and wrung my hands—I wept in utter anguish. Oh, this vision of death! This last hour, approaching in such horror!

"I can die," I said out loud, "and I believe in God. Let me try to wait for His will in silence."

"All men must die," said a voice quite close at hand, "but not all are condemned to meet a premature doom, as you would if you died here."

"Who or what speaks?" I asked, terrified at the unexpected sound, and unable to have any hope of aid. Someone was near, but in the dark night I could not see him. The stranger gave a long, loud knock on the door.

"Is it you, Mr. St. John?" cried Hannah.

"Yes—yes; open quickly."

"Well, how wet and cold you must be! Come in—your sisters are quite uneasy about you, and I believe there are bad folks about. There is a beggar

Jane Eyre

woman laid down there. Get up! For shame! Move off, I say!"

"Hush, Hannah! I have a word to say to the woman. You have done your duty in excluding her, now let me do mine in admitting her. I was nearby, and listened to both you and her. I think this is an unusual case—I must at least look into it. Young woman, rise, and come into the house."

With difficulty, I obeyed him. I stood within that clean, bright kitchen— trembling, sickening. The two ladies, their brother, Mr. St. John, the old servant, were all gazing at me.

"St. John, who is it?" I heard one ask.

"I cannot tell; I found her at the door," was the reply.

"She does look pale," said Hannah.

"As pale as death," was responded. "She will fall; let her sit."

And indeed my head swam; I dropped into a chair. I still had my senses, though I could not speak.

"Perhaps a little water would restore her. Hannah, fetch some. But she is worn to nothing. How very thin, and how very bloodless!"

"Is she ill? Or only famished?"

"Famished, I think. Hannah, is that milk? Give it to me, and a piece of bread."

Diana broke some bread, dipped it in milk, and put it to my lips. Her face was near mine; I saw there was pity in it, and I felt sympathy in her hurried breathing. In her simple words, too, the same soothing emotion spoke: "Try to eat."

"Yes—try," repeated Mary gently; and Mary's hand removed my soaked bonnet and lifted my head. I tasted what they offered me—feebly at first, then eagerly.

"Not too much at first," said the brother. "She has had enough." And he withdrew the cup of milk and the plate of bread.

"See if she can speak now—ask her name."

I felt I could speak, and I answered, "My name is Jane Elliott." Anxious to avoid discovery, I had already decided to assume an alias.

"And where do you live? Where are your friends?"

I was silent.

"Can we send for anyone you know?"

I shook my head.

"What can you tell us about yourself?"

Somehow, I no longer felt like an outcast, disowned by the whole world. I began to know myself once more. I was far too weak to answer Mr. St. John. After a pause, I said:

"Sir, I can give you no details tonight."

"But what, then," said he, "do you expect me to do for you?"

"Nothing," I replied.

"Do you mean," asked Diana, "that we may now send you out to the moor and the rainy night?"

I looked at her. I thought she had remarkable instinct and goodness. I took sudden courage. Answering her compassionate question with a smile, I said:

"I will trust you. If I were a stray dog, I know that you would not turn me from your home tonight. Do with me as you like; but my breath is short, and my words are few."

All three studied me, and all three were silent.

"Hannah," said Mr. St. John, at last, "let her sit here, and ask her no questions; in ten minutes, give her the remainder of that milk and bread. Mary and Diana, let us go into the parlour and talk the matter over."

They withdrew. Very soon one of the ladies returned—I could not tell which. A kind of pleasant daze was coming over me as I sat by the warm fire. She quietly she gave some directions to Hannah. Before long, with the servant's aid, I climbed a staircase; my dripping clothes were removed; soon a warm, dry bed received me. I thanked God—a glow of grateful joy amidst complete exhaustion—and slept.

Chapter 29

For three days and nights I lay in a narrow bed in a small room; I lay on it motionless as a stone. I paid no attention to the change from morning to noon, from noon to evening. I observed when anyone entered or left the room; I could tell who they were; I could understand what was said; but I could not answer—to open my lips or move my limbs was impossible.

Hannah, the servant, was my most frequent visitor, but I had a feeling that she wished me gone, that she did not understand me or my circumstances, and that she was prejudiced against me. Diana and Mary appeared in the chamber once or twice a day. They would whisper sentences of this sort at my bedside:

"It is very well that we took her in."

"Yes; she would certainly have died had she been left out all night. I wonder what she has gone through?"

"Strange hardships, I imagine—poor, thin, pale wanderer."

"She is an educated person, I think, by her manner of speaking; her accent was quite pure; and the clothes she took off, though splashed and wet, were fine and hardly worn."

"She has an unusual face; thin and tired as it is, I rather like it; and when in good health, I can fancy her appearance would be pleasant."

Never once did they regret taking me in, or of any suspicion about me. I was comforted.

Mr. St. John came in only once; he looked at me and said my condition was the result of extreme fatigue, and decided a doctor was not necessary. Nature, he was sure, would manage best, left to herself. He said every nerve had been frayed, and the whole body must sleep. He thought my recovery would be rapid enough. He spoke these opinions in a few words, in a quiet, low voice; and added, after a pause, "Rather an unusual appearance; she is certainly not low or vulgar."

"Quite the opposite," responded Diana. "To speak the truth, St. John, my heart rather warms to the poor little soul. I wish we may be able to help her permanently."

"That is hardly likely," was the reply. "I imagine she is some young lady who has had a misunderstanding with her friends, and has probably unwisely left them. We may, perhaps, be able to reunite her with them, but I detect lines of force in her face which make me think she can be difficult." He looked at me a few minutes, then added, "She looks sensible, but not at all handsome."

"She is so ill, St. John."

"Ill or well, she would always be plain. The grace and harmony of beauty are quite lacking in those features."

On the third day, I was better; on the fourth, I could speak, move, and rise in bed. Hannah had brought me some porridge and dry toast. I ate eagerly; the food was good. When she left me, I felt fairly strong and revived; before long, I wished to rise, but what could I put on?

On a chair by the bedside were all my own things, clean and dry. In the room were a basin and towel for washing, and a comb and brush to smooth my hair. After a weary process, and resting every five minutes, I managed to dress myself. My clothes hung loose on me, for I was quite wasted, but I was clean and respectable looking.

I left my room and crept down a stone staircase with the aid of the banisters, and found my way to the kitchen. It was fragrant with new bread and the warmth of a generous fire. Hannah was baking. She had been cold and stiff toward me at first; lately she had begun to soften a little; and when she saw me come in, tidy and well-dressed, she even smiled.

"What, you have got up!" she said. "You are better, then. You may sit down in my chair by the fireplace, if you wish."

She pointed to the rocking chair—I took it. She bustled about, examining me every now and then from the corner of her eye. Turning to me, as she took some loaves from the oven, she asked bluntly:

"Did you ever go begging before you came here?"

I was indignant for a moment, but remembering that I had indeed appeared as a beggar to her, I answered quietly, but still not without a certain firmness:

"You are mistaken in supposing me a beggar. I am no beggar, any more than you or your young ladies."

After a pause she said, "I don't understand—you have no house or no money, I guess?"

"The lack of a house or money does not make me a beggar."

"Are you book-learned?" she asked.

"Yes, I was at a boarding school eight years."

She opened her eyes wide. "Why can't you take care of yourself, then?"

"I have taken care of myself and, I trust, shall again. What are you going to do with these gooseberries?" I inquired, as she brought out a basket of the fruit.

"Make them into pies."

"Give them to me and I'll pick them off the vines."

"Nay; I don't want you to do anything."

"But I must do something. Let me have them."

She consented, and even brought me a clean towel to spread over my dress, "lest I should mucky it."

"I see by your hands, you've not been used to servant's work," she remarked. "Have you been a dressmaker?"

"No, and never mind what I have been—don't trouble yourself further about me; but tell me the name of the house where we are."

"Some call it Marsh End, and some call it Moor House."

"And the gentleman who lives here is called Mr. St. John?"

"Nay, he doesn't live here; he is only staying a while. He lives in Morton."

"That village a few miles off?"

"Aye."

"And what is he?"

"He is a parson."

I then recalled the old housekeeper at the parsonage, when I had asked to see the clergyman for some food.

"This, then, was his father's residence?"

"Aye; old Mr. Rivers lived here, and his father, and grandfather, and great grandfather before him."

"Then the name of the gentleman is Mr. St. John Rivers?"

"Aye."

"And his sisters are Diana and Mary Rivers?"

"Aye. And their father is dead—three weeks ago of a stroke."

"They have no mother?"

"The mistress has been dead a year this month."

"Have you lived with the family long?"

"I've lived here thirty years. I nursed all three of them."

"That proves you must be an honest and faithful servant, even though you called me a beggar."

She again regarded me with a surprised stare. "I believe I was quite mistaken about you—but there are so many cheats around, you must forgive me."

"And even though," I continued, rather severely, "you wished to turn me away from the door, on a night when you should not have shut out a dog."

"Well, it was hard; but what can a body do? I thought more of the children than myself, poor things! They've had nobody to take care of them but me. I have to be sharp."

I maintained a grave silence for some minutes.

"You mustn't think too badly of me," she again remarked.

"But I do think badly of you," I said, "and I'll tell you why—not so much because you refused to give me shelter, but because you thought it disgraceful that I had no house or money. Some the best people who ever lived have been as destitute as I am; and if you are a Christian, you ought not to consider poverty a crime."

"No, I ought not," said she. "Mr. St. John tells me so, too; and I see I was wrong—but I've a different idea of you now than what I had. You look like a right decent little creature."

"That will do—I forgive you now. Shake hands."

She put her floury hand into mine; a hearty smile brightened her rough face and, from that moment on, we were friends.

Hannah was evidently fond of talking. While I picked the fruit, and she made the dough for the pies, she gave me many details about her deceased master and mistress, and the children.

Old Mr. Rivers, she said, was a plain enough man, but a gentleman, and from a very old family. Marsh End had belonged to the Rivers family for about two hundred years. The Rivers were gentry in the old days, as anybody might see by looking at the register in the Morton Church vestry. Still, she allowed, the old master was like other folk, fond of hunting and farming.

The mistress was different. She was a great reader, and studied a great deal; and the children had taken after her, and loved learning.

Mr. St. John went to college and became a parson; and the girls, after their schooling, became governesses. Some years ago, old Mr. Rivers had lost a fortune when a man he trusted went bankrupt; and now that he was not rich anymore, they must provide for themselves. They had lived away from home for a long time, and were staying here a few weeks on account of their father's death

They all liked Marsh End and Morton, with the moors and hills. They had been in London, and many other grand cities, but they always said there was no place like home. And they were so agreeable with each other; she never saw such a close family.

Having finished my task of gooseberry picking, I asked where the two ladies and their brother were now.

"Gone over to Morton for a walk; but they should be back in half an hour for tea."

They soon returned, entering by the kitchen door. Mr. St. John, when he saw me, merely bowed and passed through; the two ladies stopped. Mary kindly and calmly expressed pleasure that I was well enough to come down; Diana took my hand and shook her head at me.

"You should have waited for my permission to come down," she said. "You still look very pale—and so thin! Poor child! Poor girl!"

Diana's voice was like the cooing of a dove. Her eyes were delightful and her face was full of charm. Mary's face was equally intelligent, her features equally pretty, but she was more reserved, and her manners, though gentle, were more distant. Diana looked and spoke with authority—she had a strong will. I did not mind complying with an authority such as hers.

"And what business have you here in the kitchen?" she continued. "It is not your place. Mary and I sit in the kitchen sometimes, to be casual, but you are a visitor, and must go into the parlour."

"I am very well here."

"Not at all, with Hannah bustling about and covering you with flour."

"Besides, the fire is too hot for you," interposed Mary.

"To be sure," added her sister. "Come, you must obey." And still holding my hand, she made me rise, and led me into the parlour.

"Sit there," she said, placing me on a chair, "while we take our things off and get the tea ready."

She closed the door, leaving me alone with Mr. St. John, who sat opposite, with a book or newspaper in his hand.

The parlour was small and very plainly furnished, yet comfortable. Antique portraits decorated the walls. Everything looked well-worn and well-preserved.

Mr. St. John Rivers was young, perhaps twenty-eight; tall, slender and very handsome. His face was pure in outline, with a classic nose, mouth and chin. It is seldom, indeed, that an English face comes so close to the Greek model. His eyes were large and blue; his high forehead was partially covered by locks of fair hair.

And yet, there was something about him that indicated a restless, hard, or eager nature. He did not speak one word to me, or even one glance, till his sisters returned.

Diana brought me a little cake. "Eat that now," she said. "You must be hungry. Hannah says you have had nothing but some porridge since breakfast." I did not refuse it, for my appetite was sharp.

St. John now closed his book, approached the table and, as he took a seat, fixed his blue eyes on me. His gaze was direct and searching.

"You are very hungry," he said.

"I am, sir." It was always my way to meet the brief with brevity, the direct with plainness.

"It is well that you have rested. Now you may eat, though still not heartily."

"I trust I shall not be here too long, sir," I replied.

"No," he said coolly, "when you tell us where your friends live, we can write to them, and you may return home."

"That, I must plainly tell you, is not possible; I am without home and friends."

The girls looked at me with curiosity, but not with suspicion. St. John seemed to use his eyes to embarrass rather than to encourage.

"Do you mean to say," he asked, "that you are completely isolated from every friend or relative?"

"I do. Not a tie links me to any living thing."

"A most unique situation at your age!" He looked down at my folded hands, and saw no wedding ring.

"You have never been married? You are a spinster?"

Diana laughed. "Why, she can't be more than seventeen or eighteen years old, St. John."

"I am near nineteen; but I am not married. No."

I felt a burning glow in my face; for bitter memories were awakened by the mention of marriage. They all saw my embarrassment. Diana and Mary turned their eyes elsewhere as I blushed; but the colder and sterner brother continued to gaze, till I began to shed tears.

"Where did you last reside?" he now asked.

"You are too inquisitive, St. John," murmured Mary in a low voice; but he leaned over the table and gave me a piercing look.

"That is my secret," I replied concisely.

"Which, in my opinion, you have a right to keep from St. John and every other questioner," remarked Diana.

"Yet if I know nothing about you or your history, I cannot help you," he said. "And you need help, do you not?"

"I need it, and I hope that someone will help me get work so that I can afford to live."

"I am willing to aid you to the utmost of my power," he said. "First, then, tell me what you have done, and what you can do."

I had now swallowed my tea, and was now refreshed, calming my nerves, and enabling me to address this young judge.

"Mr. Rivers," I said, looking at him, as he looked at me, "you and your sisters have done me a great service—the greatest a man can do his fellow man—you have rescued me from death. I will tell you as much of my history as I can tell without compromising my own peace of mind.

"I am an orphan, the daughter of a clergyman. My parents died before I could know them. I was brought up as a dependant, and educated in a charitable institution—Lowood Orphan Asylum—where I passed six years as a pupil, and two as a teacher. You may have heard of it; the Rev. Robert Brocklehurst is the treasurer."

"I have heard of Mr. Brocklehurst, and I have seen the school."

"I left Lowood nearly a year ago to become a private governess. I obtained a good position, and was happy. I had to leave this place four days before I came here. I cannot and should not explain the reason for my departure—it would be useless, dangerous, and would sound incredible. But no blame is attached to me; the catastrophe that drove me away was strange and awful.

"I am miserable, and must be for a time. I had to leave behind everything I possessed except a small parcel, which I left in the coach that brought me to Whitcross. To this neighbourhood, then, I came quite destitute. I slept two nights in the open air, and I was almost brought to death by hunger, exhaustion, and despair, when you, Mr. Rivers, took me under your roof. I owe your sisters a large debt for their kind, genuine compassion."

"Don't make her talk any more now, St. John," said Diana, as I paused. "Come to the sofa and sit down, Miss Elliott."

I had forgotten my new name and gave a start at hearing it spoken. Mr. Rivers noticed it at once.

"You said your name was Jane Elliott?" he observed.

"I did say so. It is not my real name, but it is the name which I think is best to use at present."

"You will not give your real name?"

"No—I fear discovery above all things."

"You are quite right, I am sure," said Diana. "Now brother, let her be at peace a while."

But after a few moments, St. John continued as calm and sharp as before.

"You would like to be independent of our charity as soon as possible?"

"I do—I have already said so. Show me how to find work, that is all I now ask, then let me go; but till then, allow me to stay here."

"Indeed you shall stay here," said Diana, putting her white hand on my head.

"You shall," repeated Mary.

"My sisters, you see, have pleasure in keeping you," said Mr. St. John, "as they would have pleasure in keeping a half-frozen bird. I shall try to help you, but my influence is narrow. I have a poor country parish. My aid will be humble."

"She has already said that she is willing to do anything honest she can do," answered Diana for me. "And you know, St. John, she is forced to put up with such crusty people as you."

"I will be a dressmaker, a workwoman, a servant, a nurse's girl, if I can be no better," I answered.

"Right," said Mr. St. John, quite coolly. "If that is your attitude, I promise to aid you, in my own time and way."

He now resumed the book which he had been reading before tea. I soon withdrew, for I had talked as much, and sat up as long, as my present strength would permit.

Chapter 30

The more I knew of Diana and Mary, the better I liked them. After a few days, my health had improved so that I could sit up all day, and walk outside sometimes. I could join with Diana and Mary in all their activities; converse with them as much as they wished, and help them when they would allow me. This was the first time I had experienced the pleasure of knowing other young ladies with similar tastes, feelings, and principles.

I liked to read what they read; what they enjoyed, delighted me; what they approved, I liked. They loved their home, and so did I. They loved the purple moors, and the fields, and I shared the strength and truth of the countryside. The strong wind and the soft breeze, the hours of sunrise and sunset, the moonlight and the clouded night, cast the same spell on me that entranced them.

Indoors we agreed equally well. They were better read than I was; but with eagerness I devoured the books they lent me; then in the evening we discussed what I had read. Our thoughts and opinions coincided.

If there was a leader in our trio, it was Diana. She was handsome and full of life. I liked to learn from her—she was the teacher, I was the student and scholar. The result was strong mutual affection.

They discovered I could draw; my skill, greater than theirs, surprised and charmed them. Mary would sit and watch me by the hour; then she would take lessons from me. With all these activities, days passed like hours, and weeks like days.

As to Mr. St John, the intimacy between me and his sisters did not extend to him. One reason was that he was seldom at home—a large portion of his time was devoted to visiting the sick and poor in his parish. Not even bad weather kept him from his work—whether he regarded it as love or duty, I did not know.

But besides his frequent absences, there was another barrier to friendship with him—he seemed to have a reserved, even brooding, nature. Though he was enthusiastic in his clergy work, he did not appear to have that inward content that should be the reward of a sincere Christian.

Moreover, I do not think that Nature held the same delight for him that it did to his sisters. He once spoke of the rugged charm of the hills, but it was said with more gloom than pleasure; and never did he roam the moors for the sake of their soothing silence.

I first got an idea of his nature when I heard him preach in his own church at Morton. It began calm and restrained, and earnestly felt. Then it grew in force—but controlled. Throughout the sermon there was a strange bitterness, a feeling of doom. When he had finished, instead of feeling better, calmer, and more enlightened, I felt sadness.

It seemed that St. John's eloquence came from deep disappointment, from unsatisfied longings and unsettled ambitions. I was sure, then, that St. John Rivers had not yet found that peace of God that passeth all understanding. He had no more found it than I had, with my secret regrets of lost love.

Meanwhile, a month passed by. Diana and Mary were soon to leave Moor House, and return to their life as governesses in a large, fashionable, south-of-England city, for wealthy, haughty families who regarded the sisters only as humble servants.

Mr. St. John had said nothing to me yet about the employment he had promised to obtain for me; yet it became clear that I urgently needed work of some kind.

One morning, I approached his table in the parlour, and was about to speak, when he looked up at me:

"You have a question to ask of me?" he said.

"Yes; I wish to know whether you have heard of any situations for me."

"I found something for you three weeks ago; but as you seemed happy here—my sisters had evidently become attached to you—I decided it was not prudent to mention it until they departed from Marsh End."

"And they will go in three days now?" I said.

"Yes; and when they go, I shall return to my parsonage at Morton; Hannah will accompany me; and this old house will be shut up."

I waited a few moments, expecting he would continue, but he seemed to have another train of thought; so I brought him back to the subject.

"What is the employment you had in mind, Mr. Rivers? I hope this delay will not have hurt my chances of obtaining it."

"Oh, no, because the position depends only upon me to give, and you to accept."

He again paused—he seemed reluctant to continue. I grew impatient; I became restless and stared at him.

"You need be in no hurry to hear," he said. "Let me explain. I am poor; after I pay my father's debts, all I will have left is this crumbling cottage. Rivers is an old name; but of the three remaining descendants, my two sisters are servants, and I feel I am a stranger from my native country—not only for life, but in death. I look to the day when death shall relieve me of this life."

St. John said these words as he pronounced his sermons, with a quiet, deep voice. He resumed:

"And since I am poor and unimportant, I can only offer you a position of poverty and obscurity. You may even think it is degrading, for I see now that you are refined, and your society has been amongst the educated. But I feel that no position is degrading that can help our fellow humans. The harder the Christian labours, the higher the honour."

"Well?" I said, as he again paused. "Proceed."

He looked at me before he proceeded, and seemed to read my face.

"I believe you will accept the post I offer you," said he, "and hold it for a while, but not permanently. For I see in you an element of restlessness."

"Do explain," I urged, when he halted once more.

"I will, and you shall now hear how poor the proposal is. Now that my father is dead, I shall leave Morton in a year; but till then, I will do my utmost to improve the town. When I came to Morton two years ago, it had no school—the children of the poor had no hope of progress. I established a school for boys; I now intend to open a second one for girls.

"I have rented a cottage for that purpose, with two rooms attached to it for the schoolmistress's house. Her salary will be thirty pounds a year. The house has been simply furnished, by the kindness of a lady, Miss Oliver—the daughter of the only rich man in my parish, Mr. Oliver, the owner of a needle factory and iron foundry in the valley. Miss Oliver also pays for the education and clothing of an orphan from the workhouse; this orphan will help the schoolmistress. Will you be this teacher?"

He asked the question rather hurriedly, as if he expected a rejection from me. It was a humble offer, but it was safe and I wanted safety; it was independent, not a servant in a rich house; it was worthy, not degrading; I made my decision.

"I thank you for the proposal, Mr. Rivers, and I accept it with all my heart."

"But do you understand me?" he said. "It is a village school; your schol-ars will be only poor girls—farmers' daughters at best. You will teach knit-ting, sewing, reading, writing, arithmetic—what will you do with your other accomplishments?"

"Save them till they are needed. They will keep."

"You know what you undertake, then?"

"I do."

He now smiled—not a bitter or sad smile, but one that was pleased and deeply gratified.

"And when will you begin your duties?"

"I will go to my house tomorrow and, if you like, open the school next week."

"Very well; so be it."

He rose and walked through the room. Standing still, he again looked at me. He shook his head.

"What do you disapprove of, Mr. Rivers?" I asked.

"You will not stay at Morton long; no, no!"

"What is your reason for saying so?"

"I saw it in your eyes; they are not the kind that promise a steady nature in life."

"I am not ambitious."

He reacted to the word 'ambitious'.

"What made you think of ambition? I know I am ambitious—but how did you find out?"

"I was speaking of myself."

"Well, if you are not ambitious, then you are—" He paused.

"What?"

"I was going to say passionate, but you may have misunderstood. What I mean is—human interaction is important to you. I am sure you cannot be content, for very long, working alone in monotonous labour." Then he added, with emphasis, "Any more than I can be content to live here. Now I contradict myself—I preach contentment among the humble, while my restless nature rages."

He left the room. In this brief hour I had learnt more of him than in the whole previous month—yet still he puzzled me.

Diana and Mary Rivers became more sad and silent as the day approached for leaving their brother and their home. Diana said this would be a different parting from any they had ever known. It would probably, as far as St. John was concerned, be a parting for years—it might be a parting for life.

"He will sacrifice everything to achieve his long-held goal," Diana said. "St. John looks quiet, Jane; but he hides a fever in his veins. The worst thing is, that my conscience wants me to dissuade him from his decision. I certainly cannot blame him for it. It is right, noble, and Christian—yet it breaks my heart!" The tears gushed to her fine eyes.

Mary bent her head low. "We are now without a father; we shall soon be without a home and a brother," she murmured.

At that moment an event happened which proved the old adage that "misfortunes never come singly". St. John entered, reading a letter.

"Our uncle John is dead," said he.

Both the sisters seemed struck—not shocked or appalled; the news seemed important, but not upsetting.

"Dead?" repeated Diana.

"Yes."

She looked at her brother's face with a searching gaze. "And?" she demanded, in a low voice.

"And—what?" he replied, frozen. "And—nothing. Read."

He threw the letter into her lap. She glanced over it, and handed it to Mary. Mary read it in silence, and returned it to her brother. All three looked at each other, and all three shared a dreary, sad smile.

"Well, we are no worse off than before," remarked Mary.

"It only makes us think about what might have been," said Mr. Rivers, "as opposed to what is."

He folded the letter, locked it in his desk, and again went out. For some minutes no one spoke. Diana then turned to me.

"Jane, I am sure you wonder at us and our mysteries," she said, "and think us hard-hearted not to be more moved at the death of so near a relative as an uncle. But we have never seen him or known him. He was my mother's brother. My father and he quarreled long ago. It was by my uncle's advice that my father risked most of his property in the speculation that ruined him. Mutual hatred passed between them; they parted in anger, and were never reconciled.

"My uncle later became prosperous and gained a fortune of twenty thousand pounds. He was never married, and had no near relatives, except for one other person, who was not related any closer than we. My father always hoped that he would atone for his error by leaving his fortune to us; that letter informs us that he has bequeathed every penny to the other relative—except for thirty guineas, for us to purchase mourning rings.

"He had a right, of course, to do as he pleased; yet a damper is cast on our spirits by the receipt of such news. Mary and I would have esteemed ourselves rich with just a thousand pounds each; and such a sum would have been valuable to St. John, enabling him to do much good."

The subject was then dropped, and it was not mentioned again. The next day I left Marsh End for Morton. The day after, Diana and Mary left for their governess positions. In a week, Mr. Rivers and Hannah went to the parsonage. The old cottage was abandoned.

Chapter 31

My home is now a cottage; a little room with whitewashed walls and a bare floor, with four chairs and a table, a clock, a cupboard, with two or three plates and dishes, and a tea set. Upstairs, a bed chamber the size of the kitchen, with a bed and chest of drawers—too big for my scanty wardrobe, though my generous friends have given me some necessary clothes.

It is evening. The little orphan who is my handmaid has left for the day—I gave her an orange as payment, for which she was grateful. I am sitting alone on the hearth. This morning, the village school opened. I had twenty students. Only three of them can read; none can write or do arithmetic. Several knit, and a few sew a little. They and I have difficulty understanding each other's language. Some of them are unmannered and rough, as well as ignorant; but others are quiet, wish to learn, and have a pleasant disposition.

I must not forget that these little peasants are people, just as much as the children of the rich; and their hearts have the same germs of excellence, refinement, intelligence, and kind feeling. My duty will be to develop these germs—surely I shall find some happiness in doing so. I do not expect much enjoyment from my new life; yet it will allow me to live on from day to day.

Was I very happy and content during my hours in the bare, humble schoolroom this morning and afternoon? I must reply—no. I felt degraded. I was saddened by the ignorance, the poverty, the coarseness of the children. But I know these feelings are wrong; I have taken a great step. I will strive to overcome them—a little each day. In a few months, perhaps I will be gratified by the progress in my little scholars.

But which is better? To have surrendered to temptation, listened to passion, and wakened in a luxurious villa in France, as Mr. Rochester's mistress? He would have loved me for a while. He did love me—no one will ever love me so again. I shall never appear beautiful, youthful and graceful to anyone else but him. He was fond and proud of me—no man besides him will ever be. Is it better to be a slave in a fool's paradise in Marseilles, filled with guilt and shame? Or a village schoolmistress, free and honest, in a breezy mountain nook in the healthy heart of England? God directed me to the correct choice; I thank Him for the guidance!

I now rose, went to my door, and looked at the sunset, and the quiet fields before my cottage, which was half a mile from the village. While I looked, I thought I was happy, and was surprised to find myself weeping—why? For the doom which had torn me from my master, whom I would never see again; for his grief which might be leading him down the wrong path.

I turned my face toward the lonely village of Morton—I could see only the spire of the church and the roof of Vale Hall, where the rich Mr. Oliver and his daughter lived.

I leaned against the stone frame of my door, but heard a slight noise near the gate of my garden. A dog—old Carlo, Mr. Rivers' pointer—was pushing the gate with his nose, and St. John himself leant upon it with folded arms—his brow furrowed, his gaze almost angry, staring at me. I asked him to come in.

"No, I cannot stay; I have only brought you a little parcel from my sisters—a colour-box, pencils, and paper."

I approached to take it; a welcome gift it was. He examined my face—the traces of tears were visible upon it.

"Have you found your first day's work harder than you expected?" he asked.

"Oh, no! On the contrary, I think in time I shall get on with my scholars very well."

"But perhaps your cottage is disappointing? True, it is scanty, but—"

I interrupted, "My cottage is pleasing to me. I am thankful, not sad. I am not such a fool as to regret the absence of a carpet, a sofa, and silver plate. Five weeks ago I had nothing—I was a beggar; now I have friends, a home, a position. I wonder at the goodness of God and the generosity of my friends. I do not complain."

"But you feel solitude is harsh? The little house is dark and empty."

"I have hardly had time to enjoy a sense of peace, much less to grow impatient from loneliness."

"Very well; I hope you are content, and not just say you are. Of course, I know nothing about the place you came from, but I advise you to resist looking back. Pursue your present career for a few months, at least."

"It is what I intend to do," I answered.

St. John continued, "God has given us the power to make our own fate; and when we need something we cannot get, we must carve out another road than the one Fortune has blocked against us, even if it is rougher.

"A year ago I was miserable because I thought I had made a mistake by entering the ministry—its tedious duties tired me to death. I yearned for a more active life of the world—to be an artist, author, orator, politician, soldier—anything but a priest. My life was so wretched, it must be changed, or I must die.

"After a season of darkness and struggling, I heard a call from heaven; God had an errand for me, where the talents of soldier, statesman, and orator, were all needed—in a good missionary. From that moment my state of mind changed; the chains dissolved and dropped from my mind, leaving nothing of bondage but its galling soreness—which time only can heal. I have some affairs to settle, and a last entanglement of feelings to cut, then I shall leave England for the East."

He said this in a subdued, yet emphatic voice. Then both of us looked at the setting sun, with our backs to the gate, when we heard a voice, sweet as a silver bell, exclaim:

"Good evening, Mr. Rivers. And good evening, old Carlo. Your dog is quicker to recognize his friends than you are, sir; he pricked his ears and wagged his tail when I was at the bottom of the field, and you have your back toward me now."

It was true. At the first sound of the lady's voice, Mr. Rivers jolted as if a thunderbolt had split a cloud over his head, yet he still stood with his back to her. At last he turned, with deliberate slowness.

She was dressed in pure white—a youthful, graceful form, fine in contour; when she threw back her long veil, there bloomed a face of perfect beauty. Perfect beauty is a strong term, yet in her it was justified. Her eyes were large and dark; her cheeks fresh and smooth; her lips healthy and sweetly formed; her gleaming teeth without flaw; her small dimpled chin; her rich, full hair—all combined in the ideal beauty.

I admired this fair creature with my whole heart. Nature had surely favored her. What did St. John Rivers think of this earthly angel? I naturally asked myself that question as I saw him turn and look at her. I sought the answer in his face, but he now looked down at a group of daisies by the gate.

"A lovely evening, but late for you to be out alone," he said, as he crushed the flowers with his foot.

"Papa told me you had opened your school, and that the new mistress had come; so I put on my bonnet after tea, and ran up the valley to see her—this is she?" pointing to me.

"It is," said St. John.

"Do you think you shall like Morton?" she asked of me, with a pleasing, direct, childlike voice and manner.

"I hope I shall. I have many reasons to."

"Did you find your scholars as attentive as you expected?"

"Quite."

"Do you like your house?"

"Very much."

"Have I furnished it nicely?"

"Very nicely, indeed."

"And made a good choice of an attendant for you in the orphan Alice Wood?"

"You have indeed. She is teachable and handy." Then I realized that this is Miss Oliver, the heiress; what happy combination of the planets presided over her birth, I wondered?

"I shall come up and help you teach sometimes," she added. "It will be a nice change for me to visit you now and then, and I like a change. Last night was so gay, Mr. Rivers—I was dancing till two o'clock in the morning. The regiment is stationed nearby since the riots, and the officers are the most agreeable men in the world—they put all our young knife grinders and scissor merchants to shame."

It seemed to me that Mr. St. John's mouth tightened, and his face was unusually stern and square, as the laughing girl spoke. He lifted his gaze, too, from the daisies, and turned it on her. It was an unsmiling, searching, gaze. She laughed again—laughter well agreed with her youth, her dimples, her bright eyes.

As he stood, mute and grave, she caressed Carlo.

"Poor Carlo loves me," said she. "He is not stern and distant to his friends; and if he could speak, he would not be silent."

As she patted the dog's head, I saw St. John's face blush and glow. His solemn eyes melted with sudden desire. He looked nearly as beautiful for a man as she for a woman. His chest heaved, as if his heart expanded and wanted to be free to express his feelings. But he curbed it. He neither spoke nor moved toward her gentle advances.

"Papa says you never come to see us now," continued Miss Oliver, looking up. "You are quite a stranger at Vale Hall. He is alone this evening, and not very well; will you return with me and visit him?"

"It is not a seasonable hour to intrude on Mr. Oliver," answered St. John.

"Not a seasonable hour! But I declare it is. It is just the hour when papa most wants company. Now, Mr. Rivers, do come. Why are you so very shy, and so very somber?"

Before he could reply, she exclaimed, "I forgot!" and shook her beautiful curled head, as if shocked at herself. "I am so giddy and thoughtless! Do excuse me. It had slipped my mind that you have good reasons for not joining in my chatter. Diana and Mary have left you, and Moor House is shut up, and you are so lonely. I am sure I pity you. Do come and see papa."

"Not tonight, Miss Rosamond, not tonight."

Mr. St. John spoke almost like a machine. Only he knew the effort it took to refuse her.

"Well, if you are so stubborn, I will leave you; for I dare not stay any longer. Good evening!"

She held out her hand. He just touched it.

"Good evening!" he repeated, in a voice low and hollow as an echo. She began to leave, but in a moment returned.

"Are you well?" she asked. Well might she have asked the question—his face was as pale as her gown.

"Quite well," he said, and with a bow, he left the gate. She went one way; he another. She turned twice to look back at him as she tripped fairy-like down the field. He, as he strode firmly across the field, never turned at all.

This spectacle of his suffering and sacrifice turned my thoughts from my own situation. Diana Rivers had called her brother "unchangeable as death". She had not exaggerated.

Chapter 32

I continued my work at the village school as actively and faithfully as I could. It was truly hard work at first. With no previous schooling, the girls seemed at first to be hopelessly dull and lazy; but I soon found I was mistaken. Some were different, and when I got to know them, and they me, this difference rapidly became clear.

Once their amazement at me—my language, my rules, my ways—lessened, I found that some of these dumb-looking rustics woke up into sharp-witted girls. Many became friendly, and some possessed natural politeness, self-respect, and excellent ability that I admired. These girls soon took pleasure in doing their work well, keeping themselves neat, learning their tasks, and developing quiet, orderly manners. The speed of their progress, in some instances, was even surprising; and I took an honest and happy pride in it; besides, I began to personally like some of the best girls, and they liked me.

I had amongst my scholars several farmers' daughters—young women, almost. They could already read, write, and sew; and to them I taught grammar, geography, history, and fine needlework. I found them eager to improve themselves, and spent many pleasant evening hours in their own homes. Their parents—the farmers and their wives—paid me great attention. I enjoyed accepting their simple kindnesses, and repaying them with great respect—something they had not been accustomed to receiving from anybody. This respect charmed them and made them eager to earn more of it.

I felt I became a favourite in the neighbourhood. Whenever I went out, I heard friendly greetings and was welcomed with friendly smiles. To be regarded this way, though it came from working people, is like "sitting in sunshine, calm and sweet".

And yet, reader, in the midst of all this calm, I had strange dreams at night—stormy, anxious dreams of unusual scenes, charged with adventure and romantic chance, where I again and again met Mr. Rochester, always at some exciting crisis; and then being in his arms, hearing his voice, meeting his eyes, touching his hand and cheek, loving him, being loved by him—the renewed hope of spending a lifetime at his side, with all its force and fire.

Then I awoke. I remembered where I was, and rose up on my bed, trembling and quivering; and then, in the still, dark night I had convulsions of despair and tears of passion. Then by nine o'clock the next morning I was punctually opening the school—peaceful, settled, prepared for the steady duties of the day.

Rosamond Oliver kept her word about coming to visit me, usually during her morning ride. She would canter up to the door on her pony, followed by a mounted livery servant. One can scarcely imagine anything more exquisite than her appearance, in her purple riding clothes, with her black velvet cap placed gracefully above the long curls that kissed her cheek and floated to her shoulders—and she would glide into the rustic building, among the dazzled village children.

She generally came during the hour when Mr. Rivers was giving his daily scripture lesson. I felt that the eyes of Miss Oliver sharply pierced the young pastor's heart. When she appeared at the door, his cheeks would glow, and his marble-like features, though they did not change, had a subdued passion in them.

Of course, she knew her power—he did not conceal his feelings from her, because he couldn't. When she smiled fondly in his face, his hands would tremble and his eyes burn. He seemed to say, with his sad and determined look, "I love you, and I know you love me. If I offered my heart, I believe you would accept it. But that heart is already laid on a sacred altar."

And then she would pout like a disappointed child, withdraw her hand quickly from his, and turn away from his martyr-like face. St. John, no doubt, would have given the world to follow her, but he would not give up his hope of the true, eternal Paradise.

Besides, loving Rosamond would limit all the aspects of his personality—the rover, the achiever, the poet, the priest. He could not, and would not, give up his missionary warfare for the parlours and the peace of Vale Hall.

Miss Oliver had already made frequent visits to my cottage. I had gotten to know her well. She was flirtatious, but not heartless; indulged from birth, but not spoiled; vain, but not affected or proud; honest; sufficiently intelligent; lively and charming. But she was not very interesting or truly impressive. Her mind was very different from that of St. John's sisters, for example.

She had taken a sudden liking to me. She said I was like Mr. Rivers, only "not one-tenth so handsome; I was a nice, neat, little soul, but he was an angel." I was, however, good, clever, calm, and firm, like him. She said that I didn't quite fit as a village schoolmistress—she was sure my previous history would make a delightful romance novel.

One evening, she was rummaging through my cupboard, with her usual childlike activity. She discovered two French books, a volume of Schiller, a German grammar and dictionary, and then my drawing materials and some sketches, including a pencil drawing of one of my pretty little scholars, and several sketches of the moors. She was, at first, stunned with surprise, and then electrified with delight.

"Did you do these pictures? Do you know French and German? What a love—what a miracle you are! You draw better than my master from school. Would you sketch a portrait of me, to show to papa?"

"With pleasure," I replied; and I felt a thrill of the artist—delight at the idea of drawing so perfect and radiant a model. She had on a dark blue silk dress; her arms and neck were bare; her only ornament was her chestnut hair, which waved over her shoulders. I took a sheet of fine paper and drew a careful outline. I wanted the pleasure of colouring it and, since it was getting late, I told her she must come and sit another day.

She made such a glowing report of me to her father, that Mr. Oliver himself accompanied her next evening—a tall, massive, middle-aged, grey-headed man. He appeared to be reserved, and perhaps proud, but he was very kind to me. The sketch of Rosamond's portrait pleased him highly; he said I must make a finished picture of it. He insisted, too, that I visit the next evening at Vale Hall.

I went. I found it a large, handsome residence, showing much evidence of wealth. Rosamond was full of glee and pleasure; her father was friendly. After tea, he told me he strongly approved of what I had done at Morton school, and said he only feared that I was too good for the place, and would soon quit for one more suitable.

"Indeed," cried Rosamond, "she is clever enough to be a governess in a high family, papa."

I thought I would much rather be where I am, than with any high family in the land. Mr. Oliver spoke of Mr. Rivers—and of the Rivers family—with great respect. He said it was a very old name in that neighbourhood; that the ancestors were wealthy; that all of Morton had once belonged to them.

He thought it a pity that so fine and talented a young man should become a missionary—it was throwing a valuable life away. It appeared, then, that her father would desire Rosamond's marriage to St. John. The young clergyman's good birth, old name, and sacred profession evidently compensated for his lack of a fortune.

It was the 5th of November, and a holiday. My little servant, after helping me clean my house, was gone, well-satisfied with the penny I gave her. I now had the afternoon to spend as I wished.

I spent an hour translating a few pages of German; then I got my palette and pencils, and fell to the more soothing task of completing Rosamond Oliver's miniature. The head was finished already, and only the details remained. I was absorbed in my work when, after one rapid knock, my door opened, admitting St. John Rivers.

"I have come to see how you are spending your holiday," he said. "Not, I hope, in thought—no, I see all is well. When you draw, you will not feel lonely. You see, I mistrust you still, though you have held up wonderfully so far. I have brought you a book for the evening," and he laid on the table a new book of poems—"Marmion" by Sir Walter Scott—from the golden age of modern literature. Alas! The readers of our era are less favoured. I know poetry is not dead, nor genius lost; nor has money gained power over art. No! Without art's influence, you would be in the hell of your own mediocrity.

While I was eagerly glancing at the bright pages of the book, St. John stooped to examine my drawing. Suddenly, his tall figure sprang erect again with a start—he said nothing. I looked up at him; he avoided my eyes. I knew his thoughts well, and could read his heart plainly; at the moment I felt I could do him some good.

He locks every feeling inside, I thought, expressing nothing, confessing nothing. I am sure it would benefit him to talk a little about this sweet Rosamond, whom he thinks he ought not to marry—I will make him talk.

I said, "Take a chair, Mr. Rivers."

But he answered, as he always did, that he could not stay. Very well, I thought, stand if you like; but you shall not go just yet; solitude is just as bad for you as it is for me. I'll try to find an opening in your marble breast, and give it one drop of feeling.

"Is this portrait a good likeness?" I asked bluntly.

"Of whom? I did not observe it closely."

"You did, Mr. Rivers."

He was astonished at my sudden directness. Oh, that is nothing yet, I thought. I'm prepared to go to considerable lengths.

I continued, "You observed it closely and distinctly; but I have no objection to your looking at it again." And I rose and placed it in his hand.

"A well-executed picture," he said. "Very soft, clear colouring; a very graceful and correct drawing."

"Yes, yes; I know all that. But what of the resemblance? Who is it like?"

After some hesitation, he answered, "Miss Oliver, I presume."

"Of course. And now, sir, to reward you for the accurate guess, I promise to paint you a faithful duplicate of this very picture, if you would like. But I don't wish to throw away my time and trouble if you would deem it worthless."

He continued to gaze at the picture—the longer he looked, the more he seemed to prize it.

"It is a very good likeness!" he murmured. "The eyes are well done—the colour, light, expression, are perfect. It smiles!"

"Would it comfort you, or would it wound you, to have a similar painting? Tell me that. When you are in Madagascar, or at the Cape, or in India, would the sight of it relieve your distress?"

He now secretly glanced at me, disturbed; he again surveyed the picture.

"It is certain that I should like to have it; whether it would be wise is another question."

Since I had determined that both Rosamond and her father desired a marriage, I felt strongly inclined to promote the match. It seemed to me that St. John could do as much good with Mr. Oliver's fortune, as he could by withering under a tropical sun. I answered:

"As far as I can see, it would be wiser for you to take the original at once."

By this time he had sat down; the picture laid on the table, and he hung fondly over it. I felt he was now neither angry nor shocked at my boldness. I even saw that to freely discuss such a subject was, for him, a pleasurable relief. Reserved people often really need a frank discussion of their feelings—they are human, after all.

"She likes you, I am sure," said I, standing behind his chair, "and her father respects you. She is a sweet girl—not many thoughts, but you would have enough thoughts for both of you. You ought to marry her."

"Does she like me?" he asked.

"Certainly—better than she likes anyone else. She talks of you continually; there is no subject she enjoys so much or touches upon so often."

"It is very pleasant to hear this—very," he said. "Go on for another quarter of an hour." And he actually took out his watch and laid it upon the table to measure the time.

"But what is the use of going on," I asked, "when you are probably preparing fresh objections?"

"Don't imagine such hard things. Imagine me melting—love rising like a fountain and overflowing. I see myself stretched on a sofa in the drawing room at Vale Hall, at the feet of my bride, Rosamond Oliver. She is mine—I am hers—this present life is enough for me. My heart is full of delight—my senses are entranced—let the quarter hour pass in peace."

I humoured him—the watch ticked on. He breathed fast and low; I stood silent. Amidst this hush the quarter hour sped; he put his watch away, laid the picture down, rose, and stood.

"Now," said he, "that short time was given to delirium and delusion. I laid on the breast of temptation; I tasted her cup. The wine has a bitter taste; her promises are hollow; her offers are false. I see and know all this."

I gazed at him in wonder.

"It is strange," pursued he, "that while I love Rosamond Oliver so wildly, I calmly realize that she would not make me a good wife; that she is not the partner suited to me; that I would discover this within a year after marriage; and that after twelve months of rapture I would have a lifetime of regret. This I know."

"Strange indeed!" I could not help exclaiming.

"While I see her charms," he went on, "I also see her defects—she could not sympathize with my missionary work. Rosamond a sufferer, a labourer, a female apostle? Rosamond a missionary's wife? No!"

"But you don't need to be a missionary. You could give up that plan."

"Relinquish my vocation? My great work? My foundation laid on earth for a mansion in heaven? My hopes of bringing knowledge into the realms of ignorance, of substituting peace for war, freedom for bondage, religion for superstition, the hope of heaven for the fear of hell? It is dearer than the blood in my veins. It is what I have to look forward to, and to live for."

After a considerable pause, I said, "And Miss Oliver? Her disappointment and sorrow are of no interest to you?"

"Miss Oliver is always surrounded by suitors and flatterers; in less than a month, she will forget me, and will probably marry someone who will make her far happier than I could."

"You speak coolly enough; but you are suffering—you are wasting away."

"No. If I get a little thin, it is because I am anxious. My departure has been postponed again. Only this morning, I received news that the priest who will replace me cannot come for three to six months yet."

"You tremble and become flushed whenever Miss Oliver enters the schoolroom."

Again he was surprised—he could not imagine that a woman would dare to speak to a man this way. For me, I felt at home in this sort of conversation.

"You are an original," said he, "and not timid. There is something brave in your spirit, as well as penetrating in your eyes. But you misinterpret my emotions. When I blush before Miss Oliver, I am angry at my weakness. I know it is a mere fever of the flesh—not a movement of my soul. That is fixed as a rock. Know me as I am—a cold, hard man."

I smiled with disbelief.

"I am simply," he continued, "a cold, hard, ambitious man. Reason, not feeling, is my guide; my ambition is unlimited; my desire to rise higher, to do more than others, insatiable. I honour endurance, perseverance, hard work, talent; because these are the means by which men achieve great deeds. I watch your career with interest, because I consider you an orderly, hard working, energetic woman, not because I deeply feel for what you have gone through, or what you still suffer."

"You are describing yourself as a mere pagan philosopher," I said.

"No, I believe the Gospel. I am not a pagan, but a Christian philosopher—a follower of the sect of Jesus. As His disciple, I adopt His pure, merciful, kind doctrines. I am sworn to spread them."

Having said this, he took his hat, which lay on the table beside my palette. Once more he looked at the portrait.

"She is lovely," he murmured. "and well-named. Rosamond—Rose of the World."

"And may I not paint one like it for you?"

"To what good? No."

To prevent the drawing from being smeared, he took the thin sheet of paper, on which I rested my hand while drawing, and placed it over the picture. What he suddenly saw on this blank paper, I could not tell—but something had caught his eye.

He snatched it up; he looked at the edge; then shot a glance at me, peculiar and quite beyond understanding—a glance that seemed to scan my shape, face, and dress—quick and sharp as lightning. His lips parted, as if to speak; but he said nothing.

"What is the matter?" I asked.

"Nothing in the world," was the reply and, replacing the paper, I saw him skillfully tear a narrow slip from the margin. It disappeared into his glove and, with one hasty nod and "good afternoon", he vanished.

"Well!" I exclaimed, using a local expression, "that caps the globe!"

I studied the paper, but saw nothing on it except for a few dingy stains from where I had tried out the tint in my pencil. I pondered the mystery a minute or two, but finding it unsolvable, and being certain it could not be important, I soon forgot it.

Chapter 33

When Mr. St. John left, it was beginning to snow; the whirling storm continued all night. The next day a sharp wind brought blinding snowfalls; by twilight the valley was almost impassable. I had closed my shutter, laid a mat to the door to keep the snow from blowing in under it, lit a candle, and began reading "Marmion".

I heard a noise; I thought the wind shook the door. No—it was St. John Rivers, who lifted the latch and came in out of the frozen hurricane, the howling darkness, and stood before me. His cloak was as white as a glacier. I was concerned, for I had not expected a guest that night.

"Any ill news?" I demanded. "Has anything happened?"

"No. How very easily alarmed you are," he answered, removing his cloak and, hanging it up against the door, he stamped the snow from his boots.

"I shall soil the purity of your floor," said he, "but you must excuse me for once." Then he approached the fire. "It has been hard work to get here, I assure you," he observed, as he warmed his hands over the flame. "One snowdrift was up to my waist; happily the snow is still quite soft yet."

"But why have you come?" I could not help saying.

"Rather an inhospitable question to put to a visitor; but since you ask, I answer simply—to have a little talk with you. I got tired of my quiet books and empty rooms. Besides, since yesterday I have had the excitement of hearing half a tale, and I am impatient to hear the rest."

He sat down. I recalled his conduct from yesterday, and really I began to fear he was insane. A very cool and collected insanity, however; I had never seen that handsome face look more like chiseled marble than it did just now, but pale and hollow, with a trace of sorrow. I waited, but his hand was now at his chin, his finger on his lip—he was thinking. It struck me that his hand looked wasted, like his face. I was moved to say:

"I wish Diana or Mary would come and live with you; it is too bad that you should be quite alone; and you are reckless about your own health."

"Not at all," said he. "I care for myself when necessary. I am well now. What do you see wrong with me?"

I was silenced.

He still sat quietly, thinking. I asked him if he felt a cold draft from the door.

"No, no!" he responded testily.

"Well," I reflected, "if you won't talk, then you may sit still. I'll let you alone now, and return to my book."

So I resumed my reading of poetry. He soon stirred; my eye was instantly drawn to his movements; he only took out a pocket-book, removed a letter, which he read in silence, folded it, put it back, and returned to meditation. It was useless to try to read, nor could I continue to be silent. He could rebuff me if he liked, but I would talk.

"Have you heard from Diana and Mary lately?"

"Not since the letter I showed you a week ago."

"Has there has been any change in your arrangements? Will you leave England sooner than you expected?"

"I fear not, indeed; such luck is too good to come to me."

Baffled, I decided to talk about the school and my scholars.

"Mary Garrett's mother is better, and Mary came back to the school this morning, and I shall have four new girls next week—they would have come today but for the snow."

"Indeed!"

"Mr. Oliver pays for two of them."

"Does he?"

"He intends to give the whole school a treat at Christmas."

"I know."

"Was it your suggestion?"

"No."

"Whose, then?"

"His daughter's, I think."

"It is like her; she is so good-natured."

"Yes."

Again came a pause. The clock struck eight. He uncrossed his legs, sat erect, and turned to me.

"Leave your book a moment, and come a little nearer the fire," he said.

Wondering, I complied.

"Half an hour ago," he said, "I spoke of my desire to hear the rest of a tale. However, I believe it will be better if I am the narrator and you are the listener. Before I begin, it is only fair to warn you that the story will sound somewhat stale to your ears—you may have heard it before—but stale details often become fresh when told from new lips.

"Twenty years ago, a poor clergyman—never mind his name for the moment—fell in love with a rich man's daughter. She also fell in love with him, and married him, against the advice of all her friends, who disowned her after the wedding. Two years later, the couple was dead. I have seen their grave. They left a daughter, now an orphan, which Charity brought to the house of its rich maternal relations; it was raised by an aunt-in-law, called Mrs. Reed of Gateshead.

"You gave a start, Jane—did you hear a noise? I daresay it is only a rat; this was a barn before I had it altered, and barns are generally haunted by rats.

"To continue. Mrs. Reed kept the orphan ten years—whether it was happy or not with her, I cannot say, never having been told. Then she transferred it to a place you know—the Lowood School, where you so long resided yourself. It seems her career there was very honorable; from a pupil, she became a teacher, like yourself—it really strikes me that there are parallels in her history and yours. She left the school to be a governess; there, again, your fates were similar—she undertook the education of the ward of a certain Mr. Rochester."

"Mr. Rivers!" I interrupted.

"I can guess your feelings," he said, "but restrain them for a while; I have nearly finished—hear me to the end. I know nothing about Mr. Rochester's character, except that he offered honourable marriage to this young girl, and at the altar she discovered he had a wife yet alive, though a lunatic. One can only guess what his subsequent conduct was, but the next day it was discovered that she was gone—no one could tell when, where, or how. She had left Thornfield Hall in the night; the countryside was searched far and wide, but no information could be gathered about her.

"And yet, it has become a matter of serious urgency that she be found; advertisements have been put in all the papers; I have received a letter from a lawyer, Mr. Briggs, communicating the details I have just shared. Is it not an odd tale?"

"Just tell me this," said I, "and since you know so much, you surely can tell me—what about Mr. Rochester? How and where is he? What is he doing? Is he well?"

"I know nothing about Mr. Rochester—the letter never mentions him except to narrate the fraudulent and illegal attempt at marriage. You should instead ask me the name of the governess—and the reason her whereabouts are sought."

"Did no one go to Thornfield Hall, then? Did no one see Mr. Rochester?"

"I suppose not."

"But they wrote to him?"

"Of course."

"And what did he say? Who has his letters?"

"Mr. Briggs implies that the answer to his letter came not from Mr. Rochester, but from a lady—it is signed 'Alice Fairfax.'"

I felt cold and saddened. My worst fears, then, were probably true; he had in all probability left England and rushed in reckless desperation to the Continent. And what relief for his severe sufferings—what object for his strong passion—had he sought there? I dared not answer the question. Oh, my poor master—once almost my husband—whom I had often called "my dear Edward"!

"He must have been a bad man," observed Mr. Rivers.

"You don't know him—don't pronounce an opinion on him," I said, with warmth.

"Very well," he answered quietly, "and indeed, I have my tale to finish. Since you won't ask the governess's name, I must tell you. Stay! I have it here—it is always better to write down important points in black and white."

And Mr. Rivers again produced the pocket-book, opened it and, from one of its compartments, removed a shabby slip of paper, hastily torn off. I recognized it to be the cover page of my portrait of Miss Oliver.

He got up, held it close to my eyes, and I read, traced in Indian ink, in my own handwriting, the words 'Jane Eyre'—which I had no doubt scribbled in some absent moment.

"Briggs wrote to me of a Jane Eyre," he said. "The advertisements demanded a Jane Eyre. I knew a Jane Elliott. I confess I had my suspicions, but it was only yesterday afternoon they were at once resolved into certainty. Do you own the name and reject the alias?"

"Yes—yes; but where is Mr. Briggs? He perhaps knows more of Mr. Rochester than you do."

"Briggs is in London. I doubt his knowing anything at all about Mr. Rochester; he is not interested in Mr. Rochester. Meantime, you are pursuing details while forgetting the essential point—you do not ask why Mr. Briggs sought you—what he wanted with you."

"Well, what did he want?"

"Merely to tell you that your uncle, Mr. John Eyre of Madeira, is dead;

that he has left you all his property, and that you are now rich—just that, nothing more."

"I! Rich?"

"Yes, you, rich—quite an heiress."

There was silence.

"You must prove your identity of course," resumed St. John, "but that will not be a problem; then you can have immediate possession. Your fortune is invested in English funds; Briggs has the will and the necessary documents."

Here was a new card turned up! It is a fine thing, reader, to be lifted in a moment from poverty to wealth—a very fine thing; but not a matter one can comprehend, or therefore enjoy, all at once. Other chances in life, such as love, are far more thrilling and give more rapture. This is solid—an affair of the actual world, nothing dreamy about it—solid and sober.

One does not jump and shout hurrah! at hearing one has got a fortune; one begins to consider responsibilities, and to consider business; certain grave cares arise, and we contain ourselves with a solemn brow.

Besides, the words Legacy and Bequest go side by side with the words Death and Funeral. I had heard my uncle was dead—my only relative. Ever since learning of his existence, I had cherished the hope of one day seeing him. Now, I never would.

And then, this money came only to me—not to me and a rejoicing family, but just to me. It was grand, and independence would be glorious—yes, I felt that; the thought swelled my heart.

"You relax at last," said Mr. Rivers. "Perhaps now you will ask how much you are worth?"

"How much am I worth?"

"Oh, a trifle! Nothing, of course, to speak of—twenty thousand pounds—but what is that?"

"Twenty thousand pounds?"

Here was a new stunner—I had figured four or five thousand. This news actually took my breath for a moment. Mr. St. John, whom I had never heard laugh before, laughed now.

"Well," said he, "if you had committed a murder, and I had told you your crime was discovered, you could scarcely look more aghast."

"It is a large sum—don't you think there is a mistake?"

"No mistake at all."

"Perhaps you have read the figures wrong—it may be two thousand!"

"It is written in letters, not figures—twenty thousand."

I again felt rather like someone sitting down to feast at a table wit...
for a hundred. Mr. Rivers rose now and put his cloak on.

"If it were not such a wild night," he said, "I would send Hannah down
to keep you company—you look too desperately miserable to be left alone.
But Hannah, poor woman! could not walk through the snowdrifts; so I
must leave you to your sorrows. Goodnight."

He was lifting the latch; a sudden thought occurred to me. "Stop one
minute!" I cried.

"Well?"

"It puzzles me why Mr. Briggs wrote to you about me; or how he knew
you, or could think that you, living in such an out-of-the-way place, had
the power to aid in my discovery."

"Oh! I am a clergyman," he said, "and the clergy are often asked about
odd matters." Again the latch rattled.

"No, that does not satisfy me!" I exclaimed; and indeed, there was something in the hurried reply that piqued my curiosity more than ever.

"It is a very strange coincidence," I added. "I must know more about
it."

"Another time."

"No! Tonight! Tonight!" And as he turned toward the door, I placed
myself between it and him. He looked rather embarrassed.

"You certainly shall not go till you have told me all," I said.

"I would rather not just now."

"You shall! You must!"

"I would rather Diana or Mary informed you."

Of course these objections brought my impatience to a climax; it must
be gratified without delay, and I told him so.

"But I told you that I was a hard man," said he, "difficult to persuade."

"And I am a hard woman—impossible to put off."

"I am cold," he pursued, "I am cold—no passion affects me."

"I am hot, and fire dissolves ice. The snow has thawed from your cloak
and soaked my floor. If you ever hope to be forgiven, Mr. Rivers, from the
crime of ruining my sanded floor, tell me what I wish to know."

"Well, then," he said, "I surrender—if not to your sincerity, then to
your determination. Besides, you must know some day. Your name is Jane
Eyre?"

"Of course; that was all settled before."

"You are perhaps not aware that I was christened—St. John Eyre
Rivers?"

eed! I remember now seeing the letter E. in your initials, writ-
s you have lent me. But what then? Surely—"
d, and thought; the disconnected links of my family chain were
; every ring was perfect. The connection was complete in my
as St. John explained it:
:her's name was Eyre. She had two brothers. One was a clergyman, who married Miss Jane Reed, of Gateshead; the other was John Eyre,
a merchant, of Madeira. Mr. Briggs, being Mr. Eyre's lawyer, wrote to us last
August to inform us of our uncle's death, and to say that he had left all his
property to his clergyman-brother's orphan daughter. He left me and my
sisters out of his will because of a quarrel between him and my father that
was never forgiven. Mr. Briggs wrote again a few weeks later, to say that the
heiress was lost, and asking if we knew anything of her. Your name, casually
written on a slip of drawing paper, enabled me to find you. You know the
rest." Again he was going, but I set my back against the door.

"Do let me speak," I said. "Let me have one moment to draw a breath
and reflect."

I paused. He stood before me, hat in hand, looking composed enough.
I resumed:

"Your mother was my aunt?"

"Yes."

"And so you, Diana, and Mary are my cousins?"

"We are cousins, yes."

I studied him. It felt as if I had found a brother, one I could be proud
of—one I could love; and two sisters, whose qualities were such that, when
I knew them as mere strangers, they had inspired me with genuine affection and admiration. These three, who had found me almost dying at their
threshold, were my blood relatives.

What a glorious discovery to a lonely wretch! This was wealth indeed!
Wealth to the heart! A gold mine of pure affection. This was a blessing—
bright, vivid, and exhilarating. Not like the gift of gold that was rich and
welcome enough, in its way, but bulky from its weight. I now clapped my
hands in sudden joy—my pulse bounded, my veins thrilled.

"Oh, I am glad! I am so glad!" I exclaimed.

St. John smiled. "Again, you ignore important points to focus on trivial
ones," he said. "You were serious when I told you about your fortune; and
now, you are excited about something that doesn't matter."

"What can you mean? It may not matter to you—you have sisters and
don't care about a cousin. But I had nobody, and now three relatives—or

two, if you don't choose to be counted—are born into my world full-grown. I say again, I am glad!"

I paced quickly around the room. I stopped, barely breathing with the thoughts that came faster than I could comprehend them—thoughts of what might have been, and would be now.

My three cousins who had saved my life, I could now benefit. They were under a yoke—I could free them. They were scattered—I could reunite them. The independence and wealth that was mine could be theirs, too. Were we not four? Twenty thousand pounds shared equally would be five thousand each.

Justice would be done, mutual happiness would be certain. Now, the wealth did not weigh on me; now it was not a mere bequest of money, it was a legacy of life, hope, and enjoyment.

To Mr. Rivers, I must have appeared greatly excited while these ideas were taking shape, for he placed a chair behind me, and was gently trying to make me sit down. He also advised me to be calm. I shook off his hand and began to walk around again.

"Write to Diana and Mary tomorrow," I said, "and tell them to come home at once. Diana said they would both consider themselves rich with a thousand pounds, so with five thousand, they will do very well."

"Let me get you a glass of water," said St. John. "You really must try to calm your feelings."

"Nonsense! And what effect will the wealth have on you? Will it keep you in England, induce you to marry Miss Oliver, and settle down like an ordinary mortal?"

"Your head is confused. I have been too quick in telling you the news; it has excited you beyond your strength."

"Mr. Rivers! You quite try my patience. I am rational enough—it is you who misunderstand, or rather pretend to misunderstand."

"Perhaps if you explained yourself a little more fully, I should comprehend better."

"Explain! What is there to explain? You cannot fail to see that twenty thousand pounds, divided equally between the nephew and three nieces of our uncle, will give five thousand to each? What I want is, that you write to your sisters and tell them of the fortune that has come to them."

"To you, you mean."

"I have told you how I see the situation. I would be pleased to have five thousand pounds; I would be tormented to have twenty thousand—which, besides, could never be mine in fairness, though it might by law. I am incapable of taking more. I am not selfish, unjust, or ungrateful. Besides, I am determined to have a home and family. I like Moor House, and I will live at Moor House; I like Diana and Mary, and I will attach myself for life to Diana and Mary. I give to you and your sisters what is absolutely unnecessary to me. Let there be no opposition, and no discussion about it; let us agree amongst ourselves, and decide the point at once."

"This is acting on first impulse; you must take several days to consider such a matter."

"Do you see the justice in my decision?"

"I do see a certain justice, but it goes against all custom. Besides, the entire fortune is your right—my uncle earned it by his own efforts, and he was free to leave it to whomever he wished. He left it to you. Justice permits you to keep it for yourself."

"With me," said I, "it is as much a matter of feeling as conscience. I must indulge my feelings—I have so rarely had a chance to do so. I cannot do without the delicious pleasure of repaying, in part, a huge debt and winning lifelong friends."

"You think so now," rejoined St. John, "because you do not know what it is to possess and enjoy wealth. You cannot imagine how important twenty thousand pounds would make you—of the place you could take in society; of the opportunities it would open to you; you cannot—"

"And you," I interrupted, "cannot imagine the craving I have for brotherly and sisterly love. I never had a home, I never had brothers or sisters. I must, and will, have them now—you are not reluctant to be my brother, are you?"

"Jane, I will be your brother—my sisters will be your sisters—without your sacrificing what is rightfully yours."

"How could we truly be brothers and sisters if I was wealthy with gold I never earned, you were penniless and living a thousand miles away, and my sisters were slaving amongst strangers? That is a close union? An intimate attachment?"

"But, Jane, your desire for family ties could be achieved a different way—you could marry."

"Nonsense, again! Marry? I don't want to marry—and I never shall marry."

"That is saying too much—it is proof of the excitement you are experiencing."

"It is not saying too much. I know what I feel. No one would love me, except for my money. I want my family. Say again you will be my brother—when you spoke those words, I was happy; repeat them, if you can; repeat them sincerely."

"I think I can. I know I have always loved my own sisters; I respect them and admire their talents. Your tastes and habits resemble Diana's and Mary's; I find you agreeable to be with; your conversations give me comfort. I feel I can easily and naturally make room in my heart for you, as my third and youngest sister."

"Thank you—that satisfies me for tonight. Now you had better go; for if you stay longer, you might irritate me again with some new concern."

"And the school, Miss Eyre? It must now be closed, I suppose?"

"No. I will continue as mistress till you get a replacement."

He smiled his approval; we shook hands, and he left.

I need not narrate in detail the hard work that followed to settle the estate as I wished. My cousins finally realized my mind was unchanged about the division of property; and they must have realized that they would have done precisely the same thing.

And so, the documents were drawn up, and St. John, Diana, Mary, and I became equal heirs to the fortune.

Chapter 34

*I*t was near Christmas, and the holiday season approached. I closed up Morton school, and as my rustic scholars and I parted, they showed their strong affection for me. I was deeply grateful to know that I really had a place in their unsophisticated hearts. I promised them that never a week should pass in the future that I did not visit them, and give them an hour's teaching in their school.

St. John arrived and watched as the sixty girls filed out of the schoolroom. I said a special farewell to half a dozen of my best scholars—as decent, modest, and well-informed young women as could be found in the ranks of the British peasantry. And that is saying a great deal; for after all, the British peasantry are the best taught, best mannered, most self-respecting of any in Europe.

"Have you received pleasure from your few months of work?" asked Mr. Rivers, when they were gone.

"Without a doubt."

"And wouldn't an entire life devoted to helping women be well spent?"

"Yes," I said, "but I could not go on forever; I am ready to enjoy a full holiday."

He looked grave. "What sudden eagerness is this? What are you going to do?"

"To be as active as I can. And first, I must beg you to free Hannah, and get somebody else to wait on you."

"Do you want her?"

"Yes, to go with me to Moor House. Diana and Mary will be home in a week, and I want to have everything in order for their arrival."

"I understand. Hannah shall go with you." Then he said, "I don't understand what you propose to do as a replacement for teaching. What purpose do you have in life now?"

"My first aim will be to clean down Moor House from chamber to cellar; then to rub it with beeswax and oil till it glitters; third, to arrange every piece of furniture with mathematical precision; afterwards I shall keep good fires in every room; and lastly, Hannah and I will beat eggs, grate spices, and make Christmas cakes and mince pies. My purpose, in short, is to give Diana and Mary a beautiful ideal of a welcome when they come."

St. John smiled slightly; still he was dissatisfied.

"It is all very well for the present," said he, "but seriously, I trust that when the holiday is over, you will look for something else to do. I excuse you for the present—I give you two months' grace to enjoy yourself; but then, I hope you will begin to look beyond Moor House and Morton, and sisterly companionship, and the selfish comfort of wealth."

I looked at him with surprise. "St. John," I said, "I think you are almost wicked to talk so. Why do you try to stir me up?"

"To use the talents which God has given you, and of which He will surely one day demand a strict account. Jane, I shall watch you closely and anxiously. Try to limit your pleasures and save your energy for a good cause. Do you hear, Jane?"

"Yes, just as if you were speaking Greek. I feel I have reason to be happy, and I will be happy. Goodbye!"

I was happy at Moor House, and hard I worked, and so did Hannah. She was charmed to see how happy I could be to dust, clean and cook. I had previously purchased some new carpets, curtains, mirrors, and china vases to freshen up the house. But I left the parlour and bedrooms alone, for I knew Diana and Mary would feel more comfortable with the homely old tables, chairs, and beds. When all was finished, I thought Moor House was a model of bright snugness inside.

The eventful Thursday came at last. My cousins were expected to arrived around dusk—fires were lit, the kitchen was perfect, Hannah and I were dressed, and all was in readiness.

St. John arrived first. He found me in the kitchen, baking cakes for tea. Approaching the hearth, he asked, "Are you finally satisfied with house-maid's work?"

I answered by inviting him on a tour of the house. He merely looked in as I opened each door; and when we had finished, he said I must have gone to a great deal of trouble to make so many changes in so short a time—but not one syllable of pleasure about the improved appearance of his house.

This silence discouraged me. I thought perhaps the alterations had upset him. I inquired whether this was the case.

"Not at all; on the contrary, I fear you must have expended more effort than it was worth."

Then he asked me where a certain book was. I showed him the volume on the shelf; he took it down, withdrew to his usual chair, and began to read it.

Now, I did not like this, reader. St. John was a good man; but I began to feel he had spoken the truth when he said he was hard and cold. The pleasures of life had no attraction for him. Literally, he lived only to aspire to greatness, but he would never approve of others resting round him. As I looked at his lofty forehead, still and pale as a white stone, I understood all at once that he would not make a good husband, and that it would be a trying thing to be his wife.

I understood how he despised himself for his love for Miss Oliver, and how he wished to stifle and destroy it. I saw that he was like a steadfast wall, the kind that heroes were made of. But at home, by the fireside, he was a cold, white column, gloomy and out of place.

This parlour is not his world, I reflected; the Himalayan mountains or even the Guinea Coast swamp would suit him better. The calm of domestic life is not his element. He will thrive where there is danger—where courage is proven and strength is tested. He is right to choose a missionary's career—I see it now.

"They are coming! They are coming!" cried Hannah, throwing open the parlour door, as old Carlo barked joyfully. Out I ran. It was now dark, but I heard a rumbling of wheels. Hannah lit a lantern. The coach stopped at the gate, and my cousins stepped out. In a minute, I had my face under their bonnets, first kissing Mary's soft cheek, then Diana's flowing curls. They laughed and kissed me, then Hannah; patted Carlo, who was half wild with delight; asked eagerly if all was well; and hastened into the house.

They were stiff from their long and jolting drive from Whitcross, and chilled with the frosty night air; but their pleasant faces warmed to the cheerful firelight. While the driver and Hannah brought in the luggage, they asked for St. John. At this moment he came in from the parlour. They both threw their arms round his neck at once. He gave each one a quiet kiss, said in a low tone a few words of welcome, talked a while, and then withdrew to his place of refuge in the parlour.

Diana and Mary followed me upstairs. They were delighted with the renovation and decorations of their rooms; with the new drapery, and fresh carpets, and rich tinted china vases. I was pleased that my changes met their wishes exactly, and that I had added a vivid charm to their joyous return home.

Sweet was that evening. My cousins were so full of excitement that their conversation made up for St. John's silence. He was sincerely glad to see his sisters, but he could not share their flow of joy. The return of Diana and Mary pleased him, but all the talkative glee irked him.

About an hour after tea, a knock was heard at the door. Hannah answered, then entered the parlour to say that "a poor lad had come to fetch Mr. Rivers to see his mother, who was dying."

"Where does she live, Hannah?" he asked.

"Up at Whitcross Brow, almost four miles away."

"Tell him I will go."

"Sir, you had better not. It's the worst road to travel after dark—there are no tracks, and it is such a bitter night. You had better send word, sir, that you will be there in the morning."

But he was already putting on his cloak, and without one objection, one murmur, he departed. It was then nine o'clock.

He did not return till midnight. Though starved and tired, he looked happier than when he left. He had performed an act of duty, felt his own strength to accomplish something good, and was on better terms with himself.

I am afraid the whole week tried his patience. It was Christmas week, and the air of the moors, the freedom of home, and the dawn of prosperity, filled Diana and Mary's spirits. They were happy from morning till noon, and from noon till night. They talked constantly; and their witty, pithy, original conversation was so charming to me, that I preferred it to anything else.

St. John did not criticize our liveliness, but he escaped from it. He was seldom in the house—his parish was large, the population scattered, and he found daily business in visiting the sick and poor.

One morning at breakfast, Diana, after looking a little thoughtful for some minutes, asked him "if his plans were still unchanged."

"Unchanged and unchangeable," was the reply. And he informed us that his departure from England was now set for the following year.

"And Rosamond Oliver?" asked Mary, the words having slipped out; for no sooner had she uttered them, than she made a gesture of wishing to take them back. St. John had a book in his hand—it was his unsocial custom to read at meals—he closed it, and looked up.

"Rosamond Oliver," said he, "is about to be married to Mr. Granby, the very social and respected grandson and heir of Sir Frederic Granby; I received the news from her father yesterday."

His sisters looked at each other and at me; we all three looked at him; he was calm and clear.

"The match must have been made hastily," said Diana. "They cannot have known each other long."

"Only two months; they met in October at the county ball. But when the marriage is in every way desirable, delays are unnecessary. They will be married as soon as Sir Frederic's mansion, which he is giving them, can be renovated."

After breakfast, when I found St. John alone, I felt tempted to ask if this event distressed him; but he seemed to need so little sympathy that I did not venture to offer him more. Besides, I was out of practice in talking to him—his reserve was again frozen over.

He had not kept his promise of treating me like his sisters; he continually pointed out chilling little differences between us. In short, now that I was recognized as his cousin, and lived under the same roof with him, I felt the distance between us to be far greater than when he had known me only as the village schoolmistress. When I remembered how far our friendship had once progressed, I could hardly understand his present coldness.

Such being the case, I was quite surprised when he raised his head suddenly from his desk and said:

"You see, Jane, the battle is fought and the victory won."

Startled, I did not immediately reply; after a moment, I answered:

"But has your triumph cost you too much? Would another love not ruin you?"

"I think not. I shall never again be called upon to compete for another. My way is now clear; I thank God for it!" Then he returned to his book and his silence.

After the holidays, we resumed our usual habits and regular studies. St. John stayed more at home—he sat with us in the same room, sometimes for hours together. While Mary drew, Diana pursued a wide range of reading, and I toiled away at German, St. John studied some kind of Eastern language which he thought necessary to his work.

He sat in his own nook, quiet and absorbed, but his blue eyes had a habit of wandering over to us with curious observation. If caught staring, he would instantly look away. I wondered what that meant.

I also wondered about his satisfaction at my weekly visits to Morton school. I was still more puzzled when, on rainy or snowy days, and his sisters urged me not to go, he would make light of their concern and advise me to accomplish my task.

"Jane is not such a weakling as you would make her," he would say. "Her constitution is sound—better able to endure bad climate than many who are more robust."

And when I returned, sometimes quite tired and weather-beaten, I never dared complain, so as not to annoy him.

One afternoon, however, I was allowed to stay home because I really had a cold. His sisters went to Morton in my place. I sat reading Schiller, while he translated some difficult Oriental scrolls. I happened to look his way, and found myself under the gaze of his ever-watchful blue eyes. His stare was so sharp, and yet so cold, it felt inhuman.

"Jane, what are you doing?"

"Learning German."

"I want you to give up German and learn Hindu."

"You are not serious?"

"I am so serious that it must be done, and I will tell you why."

He explained that Hindu was the language he was studying for his missionary work; that it would greatly assist him to have a pupil with whom he might study; that his choice was between me and his sisters, but he decided on me because I could sit at a task the longest of the three. Would I do him this favour? It would not be a long sacrifice, for he was only three months from departure.

St. John was not a man to be lightly refused—I consented. When Diana and Mary returned, Diana laughed, and both she and Mary agreed that St. John could never have persuaded them to take on such a task. He answered quietly, "I know it."

I found him a very patient, yet exacting, master. He expected me to do a great deal; and when I pleased him, he, in his own way, fully approved. Little by little, he gained a certain influence over me that took away my freedom.

I could no longer talk or laugh freely when he was near, because I knew that he disliked cheerfulness—only serious moods were acceptable. I fell under a freezing spell. When he said "go", I went; "come", I came; "do this", I did it. But I did not love being his servant—many times I wished he had continued to ignore me.

One evening when, at bedtime, his sisters and I stood round him, bidding him goodnight, he kissed each of them, as was his custom; and, as was equally his custom, he shook hands with me. Diana—who was not painfully controlled by his will, for hers was as strong—exclaimed:

"St. John! You used to call Jane your third sister, but you don't treat her as such; you should kiss her too."

Diana pushed me toward him. I was uncomfortable and confused; then

St. John bent his head, his Greek face came toward mine, his eyes questioned my eyes—and he kissed me.

There are no such things as marble kisses or ice kisses—his was an experimental kiss. After he kissed me, he looked at me to see the result—I am sure I did not blush. I might have turned a little pale, for I felt as if this kiss sealed my bonds to him. He kissed me every evening afterwards, and seemed to be charmed by it.

Every day I wished to please him more; but to do so, I felt more and more that I must disown half my nature, stifle half my abilities, change my tastes, and force myself to pursue studies for which I had no natural calling. He wanted to bring me to a level I could never reach. It was as impossible as molding my irregular face to his classic Greek one, or change my green eyes to his blue ones.

But it wasn't just his power over me that caused my sadness lately; there was an evil in my heart that drained my happiness—the evil of suspense.

Perhaps you think I had forgotten Mr. Rochester, reader, amidst all these changes of place and fortune. Not for a moment. The craving to know what had become of him followed me everywhere. When I was teaching at Morton, I entered my cottage every evening to think of him; and now at Moor House, I worried over it each night in my bedroom.

I asked Mr. Briggs if he knew anything about Mr. Rochester's present residence and state of health, but he was quite ignorant of all concerning him. I then wrote to Mrs. Fairfax, expecting a quick reply. I was astonished when a fortnight passed without an answer. After two months of not hearing, I became extremely anxious.

I wrote again—there was a chance my first letter never arrived. Renewed hope followed for several weeks, then it faded. Not a line, not a word reached me. When half a year passed, my hope died out, and then I felt dark indeed.

Spring came—a fine spring which I could not enjoy. Summer approached; Diana tried to cheer me; she said I looked ill and wished to take me to the seaside. St. John opposed this. He said I did not need rest, I needed employment—my present life had no purpose. And so, he continued my Hindu lessons. I, like a fool, never thought of resisting him—I could not resist him.

One day I came to my studies in lower spirits than usual. Hannah had told me, earlier that morning, that there was a letter for me. I was almost certain it contained news of Mr. Rochester. But it was only an unimportant note from Mr. Briggs. Now, as I laboured over Indian scrolls, alone in the parlour with St. John, tears filled my eyes.

He asked me to read, but my voice was lost in sobs. St. John did not act surprised or question me. He only said:

"We will wait a few minutes, Jane, till you are more composed."

And while I smothered my sudden outburst, he sat calm and patient, leaning on his desk. Wiping my eyes, and muttering something about not feeling well that morning, I resumed my task, and completed it. St. John put away my books and his, locked his desk, and said:

"Now, Jane, you shall take a walk with me."

"I will call Diana and Mary."

"No, only you. Put on your things; go out by the kitchen door. Take the road toward Marsh Glen; I will join you in a moment."

In dealing with people, I have always either completely submitted to them, or determinedly revolted against them. And since, in my present mood, I was not inclined to disobey him, I did as he ordered. Ten minutes later, we walked side by side.

The breeze came over the hills, sweet with scents of spring flowers; the sky was stainless blue; the stream from the ravine was clear, catching golden gleams from the sun. As we left the road, we walked on emerald green moss, covered with tiny white and yellow blossoms.

"Let us rest here," said St. John, as we reached a group of rocks. I took a seat; St. John stood near me. He looked up at the unclouded heaven, removed his hat, and let the breeze stir his hair and kiss his brow. He seemed, with his eyes, to bid farewell to something.

"And I shall see it again," he said aloud, "in dreams when I sleep by the Ganges River, and again when another slumber takes over me, on the shore of a darker stream!"

Strange words! He sat down, and for half an hour we never spoke. Then he said:

"Jane, I go in six weeks; I have taken my berth in an East India ship which sails on the 20th of June."

"God will protect you, for you have undertaken His work," I answered.

"Yes," said he, "it is my glory and joy. I am the servant of an infallible Master. It seems strange to me that everyone does not join in the same enterprise."

"Not everyone has your powers, and it would be foolish for the weak to march with the strong."

"I do not speak to the feeble. I speak only to those who are worthy of the work and able to accomplish it."

"They are few in number, and difficult to find."

"True—but when they are found, it is right to stir them up; to urge them on; to show them what their gifts are, and why they were given; to speak Heaven's message in their ear; to offer them, direct from God, a place in the ranks of His chosen."

"If they are really qualified for the task, will not their own hearts tell them?"

I felt as if an awful charm was circling round me and gathering over me.

"And what does your heart say?" demanded St. John.

"My heart is quiet—my heart is quiet," I answered, terrified.

"Then I must speak for it," continued the deep, relentless voice. "Jane, come with me to India; come as my helper and fellow labourer."

The sky spun round; the hills moved! It was as if a summons from Heaven, a visionary messenger, had announced, "Come over and help us!" But I was no apostle—I could not receive his call.

"Oh, St. John!" I cried. "Have some mercy!"

But I was appealing to someone who knew neither mercy nor guilt. He continued:

"God and nature intended you for a missionary's wife. They have given you mental, not personal, powers. You are made for labour, not for love. A missionary's wife you must—you shall—be. You shall be mine. I claim you—not for my pleasure, but for my Sovereign's service."

"I am not fit for it. I have no training," I said.

He had expected me to object, and was not irritated. Indeed, as he leaned back against the rock, folded his arms on his chest, and fixed his gaze, I saw he was prepared for a long and trying discussion—confident, however, that he would win me over.

"Humility, Jane," said he, "is the groundwork of Christian virtues. You are correct that you are not fit for the work—but who is? I, for instance, am but dust and ashes. Along with St. Paul, I am the worst of sinners; but I do not let my personal vileness daunt me. I know my Leader and, though He has chosen a feeble instrument to perform a great task, He will give me the means to the end. Think like me, Jane—trust like me. Lean on the Rock of Ages—it will bear the weight of your human weakness."

"I do not understand a missionary life; I have never studied missionary work."

"I can give you the help you need, from hour to hour; stand by you always in the beginning. I know your powers—soon you would be as strong as myself, and would not require my help."

"But my powers—where are they for this undertaking? I do not feel them. Nothing speaks to me, or stirs in me, while you talk. I see no great light, no quickening of my pulse. My mind is like a dark dungeon, with one fear—the fear of being persuaded by you to attempt something I cannot accomplish!"

"I have an answer for you—hear it. I have watched you ever since we first met—I have studied you for ten months. In the village school, you performed your work punctually, correctly, well, and with tact. You were calm when you learnt you had become suddenly rich—money had no undue power over you. When you readily and willingly divided your wealth into four parts, I recognized a soul that found pleasure and excitement in giving and sacrifice. You gave up studying what interested you, and studied what I requested, because it interested me—and showed great energy in the face of difficulty. These are the qualities I seek. Jane, you are, diligent, faithful, and courageous; gentle and heroic. As a teacher of Indian schools, and a helper amongst Indian women, your assistance will be invaluable to me."

Slowly, surely, his persuasion advanced. Shut my eyes as I would, these last words of his succeeded in making the way clear. He shaped my work, which had seemed so vague, into a definite form. He waited for an answer. I demanded a quarter of an hour to think, before I gave him a reply.

"Very willingly," he said and, rising, he walked up the hill, threw himself down, and there lay still.

I can do what he wants me to do, I meditated; I must acknowledge that. But I feel I could not live long under the Indian sun. What then? He does not care; when my time came to die, he would give me up to God.

The case before me is very clear. In leaving England, I would leave a loved but empty land; Mr. Rochester is not there; and if he were, what can that ever mean to me? My business is to live without him now, not to drag on from day to day, waiting for some impossible change that might reunite us.

Of course I must find another interest in life to replace the one that is lost. Isn't the occupation he now offers me truly the most glorious that God can assign? The one to best fill the void left by ruined love and demolished hopes? I believe I must say 'yes'—and yet I shudder. Alas! If I join St. John, I abandon half myself; if I go to India, I go to premature death.

And how will I fill my time between leaving England and certain death? That, too, is very clear—by satisfying St. John, till my bones ache, to his fullest expectations. If I do go with him, I will throw my all onto the altar—heart, vitals, everything. He will never love me, but he shall approve of me; I will show him energies he has not yet seen, resources he has never suspected. Yes, I can work as hard as he can, and with as little complaining.

I can consent to his demand, but for one dreadful item—he asks me to be his wife. But he has no more of a husband's heart for me than a rock. He prizes me as a soldier would value a good weapon—and that is all.

But can I go through with the wedding ceremony? Can I receive from him the bridal ring, and complete our marriage vows when the spirit was absent? No, I will never do it. As his sister, I might accompany him—not as his wife. I will tell him so.

I looked toward where he lay, still as a white column; his face turned to me, his eyes beaming and watchful. He stood up and approached me.

"I am ready to go to India, if I may go free."

"Your answer requires an explanation," he said. "It is not clear."

"You have, till now, been my adopted brother—I, your adopted sister. Let us continue as such; you and I had better not marry."

He shook his head. "That will not do in this case. If you were my real sister it would be different. But either our union must be consecrated and sealed by marriage, or it cannot exist. Do you not see it, Jane? Consider a moment—your strong sense will guide you."

I did consider; and still my sense told me that we did not love each other as man and wife should; and therefore we ought not to marry. I said so.

"St. John," I returned, "I regard you as a brother—so let us continue."

"We cannot—we cannot," he answered, with short, sharp determination. "It would not do. You have said you will go with me to India. Remember—you have said that."

"Conditionally."

"Well—well. You are willing to cooperate with me in my labours—now we must see how it can best be done. Simplify all your feelings, wishes, thoughts and goals, and merge them with one purpose—serving your great Master. To do so, you must have a husband—not a brother. I do not want a sister; a sister might be taken from me any day. I want a wife—the sole helper I can influence and keep till death."

I shuddered as he spoke—I felt his influence in my bones—his hold on my body.

"Seek one elsewhere than in me, St. John; seek one who fits you."

"One who fits my purpose, you mean. I do not wish to marry just any individual—it is the missionary I wish to mate."

"And I will give you my energies—it is really all you want—but not myself."

"You cannot—you ought not. Do you think God will be satisfied with half a commitment? Will He accept a mutilated sacrifice? It is for the cause of God I marry you. I cannot accept on His behalf a divided allegiance—it must be entire."

"Oh! I will give my heart to God," I said. "You do not want it."

I will admit, reader, that there was a bit of sarcasm in my remark. I had silently feared St. John till now, because I had not understood him. But he had revealed his nature to me this afternoon. I saw his faults. He was a man, as caring as I. I felt his imperfections and took courage. He was my equal—one with whom I could argue, and one whom I could resist.

He was silent after I had uttered the last sentence, then soon he said:

"I trust, Jane, you are serious when you say you will serve your heart to God—it is all I want. Once you give your heart to God, you will see how much better our efforts will be if we are united in marriage."

"Will I?" I said briefly; and I looked at his features, beautiful but still severe; at his brow, commanding but not open; at his eyes, bright and searching, but never soft; at his tall imposing figure; and imagined myself his wife.

Oh! It would never do! As his comrade, all would be right—I would cross oceans with him, toil under Eastern suns and Asian deserts, admire and imitate his courage and devotion and vigor.

I would no doubt suffer often; my body would be under strict control, but my heart and mind would be free. I would still have myself to turn to, my natural feelings to talk to in moments of loneliness, places in my mind which would be only mine, that his warrior march could never trample down.

But as his wife—always at his side, always restrained, to force the fire of my nature to burn inwardly and never utter a cry—this would be unendurable.

"St. John!" I exclaimed.

"Well?" he answered icily.

"I repeat—I freely consent to go with you as your fellow missionary, but not as your wife. I cannot marry you and become part of you."

"A part of me you must become," he answered steadily, "otherwise the whole bargain is void. How can I, a man not yet thirty, take with me to India a girl of nineteen, unless she is married to me? How can we be forever together—sometimes in private, sometimes amidst savage tribes—and unwed?"

"Very well," I said shortly. "Quite as well as if I were either your real sister, or a man and a clergyman like yourself."

"It is known that you are not my sister; I cannot introduce you as such. To attempt it would be to cast dangerous suspicions on us both. And for the rest, though you have a man's vigorous brain, you have a woman's heart and—it would not do."

"It would do," I affirmed, "perfectly well. I have a woman's heart, but not where you are concerned. For you, I have only a fellow soldier's frankness, fidelity, fraternity—nothing more, don't fear."

"Jane, you would not regret marrying me—be certain of that; we must be married. I repeat—there is no other way. And I am sure that enough love would grow between us, after our marriage, to make it right, even in your eyes."

"I reject your idea of love," I could not help saying, as I rose up and stood before him, leaning my back against the rock. "I reject the false sentiment you offer—yes, St. John, and I reject you when you offer it."

He fixed his gaze on me, his lips tightening while he did so. Whether he was angered or surprised, or what, it was not easy to tell—he could thoroughly control his expression.

"I scarcely expected to hear that from you," he said. "I do not think I have said and done anything to deserve scorn."

I was touched by his gentle tone, and awed by his calm demeanor.

"Forgive me those words, St. John; but it is your own fault that I have spoken so freely. You have introduced a topic on which we disagree—a topic we should never discuss. The very name of love is an apple of discord between us. My dear cousin, abandon your plan of marriage—forget it."

"No," said he, "it is a long-cherished plan; but I shall press you no further at present. Tomorrow, I leave home for Cambridge; I have many friends there to whom I wish to say farewell. I shall be absent a fortnight—take that time to consider my offer. And do not forget that if you reject it, it is not me you deny, but God. Through my means, He opens to you a noble career; only as my wife can you have it. Refuse to be my wife, and you limit yourself forever to a life of selfish ease and empty obscurity."

As I walked by his side homeward, his silence revealed his disappointment in me. He was a severe tyrant, who met resistance when he expected submission. With his cold, rigid judgment, he disapproved of my feelings and views, and had no power to sympathize with them. As a man, he would have forced me into obedience; it was only as a sincere Christian that he was patient with my unreasonable behaviour and gave me time to reflect and repent.

That night, after he had kissed his sisters, he forgot to even shake hands with me, leaving the room in silence. I was hurt—so hurt, that tears came to my eyes.

"I see you and St. John have been quarrelling, Jane," said Diana, "during your walk. But go after him; he is now lingering in the hallway, expecting you—he will make up."

I do not have much pride under such circumstances—I would always rather be happy than dignified; and so I ran after him; he stood at the foot of the stairs.

"Goodnight, St. John," said I.

"Goodnight, Jane," he replied calmly.

"Then let us shake hands," I added.

What a cold, loose touch, he gave my hand! He was deeply displeased by what had occurred that day—friendliness would not warm him, nor tears move him. No happy reconciliation was to be had with him—no cheering smile or generous word.

But still, the Christian was patient and calm; and when I asked him if he forgave me, he answered that he had not been offended, and so he had nothing to forgive.

And with that answer he left me. I would much rather he had knocked me down.

Chapter 35

St. John did not leave for Cambridge the next day, as he had said he would; he delayed his departure a whole week. During that time, I experienced the severe punishment that a good, yet stern, man can inflict on someone who has offended him.

He had forgiven me for saying I rejected him and his love, but he had not forgotten; and as long as he and I lived, he never would. I saw by his look, and heard in his voice, that those words were always there.

He continued to call me to his desk each morning to study; but he had become no longer flesh, but marble; his eyes were cold, bright, blue gems; his tongue was an instrument to speak—nothing more.

All this was torture to me—a slow fire that harassed me and crushed me. I felt that, if I were his wife, he would soon kill me without drawing a single drop of blood. He had no desire to settle our differences; and though, more than once, my tears fell on the page we studied, they had no more effect on him than if his heart was made of stone.

Meantime, he was somewhat kinder than usual to his sisters—as if he were afraid that coldness toward me would not be punishment enough.

The night before he left home for Cambridge, I saw him walking in the garden about sunset. As I looked at him, I remembered that this man had once saved my life, and that we were cousins. I made one last attempt to regain his friendship. I went out and approached him as he stood leaning over the little gate.

"St. John, I am unhappy because you are still angry with me. Let us be friends."

"I hope we are friends," was the stiff reply, while he stared at the rising of the moon.

"No, St. John, we are not friends, as we were. You know that."

"Are we not? That is wrong. For my part, I wish you no ill and all good."

"I believe you, for I am sure you are incapable of wishing anyone ill; but, as I am your cousin, I would desire a bit more affection than you extend to mere strangers."

"Of course," he said. "Your wish is reasonable, and I do not regard you as a stranger."

This, spoken in a cool, tranquil tone, was humiliating. Had I listened to my pride, I would immediately have left him. But his friendship was of value to me—to lose it would be painful. I tried once again to regain it.

"Must we part in this way, St. John? And when you go to India, will you leave me without any kinder words than this?" He now turned from the moon and faced me.

"When I go to India, Jane, will I leave you? What! Are you not coming to India?"

"You said I could not come, unless I married you."

"And you will not marry me? You adhere to that resolution?"

Reader, do you know, as I do, what terror those cold people can put into the ice of their questions?

"No. St. John, I will not marry you. I adhere to my resolution."

The avalanche had shaken and slid a little forward, but it did not yet crash down.

"Once more, why this refusal?" he asked.

"I refused before," I answered, "because you did not love me. Now, I refuse because you almost hate me. If I were to marry you, you would kill me. You are killing me now."

His lips and cheeks turned white—quite white.

"I would kill you—I am killing you? Your words should not be used—violent, unfeminine, and untrue. They reveal an unfortunate state of mind; they are inexcusable, but it is the duty of a man to forgive his fellow man even until seventy and seven times."

I was finished now. In trying to erase my former offense, I had now offended him further and deeper.

"Now you will indeed hate me," I said. "It is useless to attempt to bring us together. I see I have made an eternal enemy of you."

My words touched on the truth. His white lip quivered to a temporary spasm. I knew I had sharpened his steely anger. It twisted my heart.

"You completely misinterpret my words," I said, taking his hand. "I have no intention to grieve you or pain you."

Most bitterly he smiled, as he withdrew his hand from mine. "And now you retract your promise, and will not go to India at all, I presume?" said he, after a considerable pause.

"Yes, I will, as your assistant," I answered.

A very long silence succeeded. He spoke at last.

"I proved to you, before, the absurdity of a single woman of your age accompanying me abroad. I regret—for your sake—that you have mentioned it again."

I interrupted him. "You are talking nonsense, St. John. You pretend to be shocked by what I have said, but you are not really shocked. I say again, I will be your assistant, if you like, but never your wife."

Again he turned deathly pale, but controlled his feelings perfectly. He answered emphatically but calmly:

"It seems, then, you cannot go as my wife."

He paused a moment. "However, I know of a married missionary in town; his wife needs an assistant; I will speak to him. And thus, you may still honour your promise of going to India."

Now I never had, as the reader knows, either given any formal promise or entered into any engagement. I replied:

"I am not under the slightest obligation to go to India, especially with strangers. I would have risked a great deal with you, because I admire you and, as a sister, I love you. But I am convinced that, whomever else I went with, I would not live long in that climate."

"Ah! You are only afraid of yourself," he said, curling his lip.

"Yes. I am. God did not give me my life to throw away; and to do as you wish would almost be committing suicide. Moreover, before I ever think of leaving England, I must know for certain whether I can be of greater use by remaining here than by leaving."

"What do you mean?"

"It would be pointless to try to explain; but there is a matter about which I have long endured a painful doubt, and I can go nowhere till that doubt is removed."

"I know where your heart turns, and to what it clings. The thing you cherish is illegal and unholy. You ought to have crushed it long ago. Now you blush when you mention it. You think of Mr. Rochester?"

It was true. I confessed it by silence.

"Are you going to seek Mr. Rochester?"

"I must find out what has become of him."

"Then I will remember you in my prayers," he said, "and to ask God that you do not become a castaway. I had thought I saw you as one of the chosen. But God does not see what man sees—His will be done."

He opened the gate and walked down the glen. He was soon out of sight.

On entering the parlour, I found Diana standing at the window, looking very thoughtful. She put her hand on my shoulder and examined my face.

"Jane," she said, "you are always anxious and pale now. I am sure there is something the matter. Tell me what you and St. John have discussed. I have watched you for half an hour from the window; you must forgive my being such a spy, but for a long time I have imagined—I hardly know what. St. John is a strange being—"

She paused; I did not speak. Soon she resumed:

"That brother of mine has long shown you an interest he never showed to anyone else. I wish he loved you—does he, Jane?"

I put her cool hand to my hot forehead. "No, Die, not one whit."

"Then why does he watch you and keep you at his side? Mary and I had both concluded he wished you to marry him."

"He does—he has asked me to be his wife."

Diana clasped her hands. "That is just what we hoped and thought! And you will marry him, Jane, won't you? And then he will stay in England."

"Far from that, Diana; his sole idea in proposing to me is to acquire a fellow labourer for his work in India."

"What! He wishes you to go to India?"

"Yes."

"Madness!" she exclaimed. "You would not survive three months there, I am certain. You shall never go—you have not consented, have you, Jane?"

"I have refused to marry him—"

"And have therefore displeased him?" she suggested.

"Deeply—he will never forgive me, I fear: yet I offered to accompany him as his sister."

"That was folly, Jane. Think of the constant fatigue, where fatigue kills even the strong, and you are weak. St. John—you know him—would have you do the impossible. And unfortunately, I have noticed, whatever he demands, you perform. I am astonished you found the courage to refuse his offer of marriage. You do not love him then, Jane?"

"Not as a husband."

"Yet he is a handsome fellow."

"And I am so plain, you see, Die. We would never suit each other."

"Plain! You? Not at all. You are much too pretty, as well as too good, to be roasted alive in Calcutta." And again she begged me to give up all thoughts of going with her brother.

"I will indeed," I said, "for when I repeated my offer to serve him as an assistant, he was shocked that I would accompany him unmarried."

"And what makes you say he does not love you, Jane?"

"He has again and again explained that he wishes to marry me, not for

Jane Eyre   289

love, but for his work. He has told me I am made for labour, not for love—which is probably true. But if I am not made for love, it follows that I am not made for marriage. Wouldn't it be strange, Die, to be chained for life to a man who thought of me as a useful tool?"

"Unnatural—out of the question!"

"And then," I continued, "if forced to be his wife, he would not want me to love him; and if I showed him love, he would make me realize that he did not require it. I know he would."

"And yet St. John is a good man," said Diana.

"He is a good and a great man. But he forgets, without pity, the feelings and rights of little people in pursuing his own large views. It is better, therefore, for us to keep out of his way, so he does not trample us down. Here he comes! I will leave you, Diana." And I hurried upstairs as I saw him entering the garden.

But I was forced to meet him again at supper. He was as composed as usual. I thought he would not speak to me, and I was certain he had given up the idea of marriage—but I was wrong on both points.

He addressed me with careful politeness. No doubt he had asked the Holy Spirit to help him subdue his anger, and now I believed he had forgiven me once more.

For the evening reading before prayers, he chose the twenty-first chapter of Revelation. It was always pleasant to hear him read from the Bible; and tonight his voice was more solemn, as he sat there, bending over the great old Bible, and described how God would wipe away all the tears from men's eyes, and promised that there would be no more death or pain, because those things would be passed away.

The next words affected me strangely, as I felt that his eyes had turned on me:

"The fearful, the unbelieving, shall have their part in the lake which burneth with fire and brimstone, which is the second death." With those words, I knew what fate St. John feared for me.

In reading the last verse, his voice blended a calm, subdued triumph with a sincere longing. St. John believed his name was already written in God's book, and he yearned for the hour which should admit him to heaven.

In the prayer following the chapter, all his energy and zeal awoke. He asked for strength for the weak-hearted; guidance for wanderers from the fold; a return, even at the eleventh hour, for those whom the temptations of the world and the flesh were luring from the narrow path.

As I listened to that prayer, I was touched by his sincerity and, finally, awed by it. He felt the greatness and goodness of his purpose so sincerely—I could not help but feel it, too.

The prayer over, we left him. He was to leave very early in the morning. Diana and Mary kissed him and left the room—at his request, I think. I then offered my hand, and wished him a pleasant journey.

"Thank you, Jane," said St. John. "I shall return from Cambridge in a fortnight. I leave you to reflect. If I listened to my pride, I would say no more about marriage; but I listen to my duty, and keep my goal before me—to do all things to the glory of God. My Master was long-suffering—so will I be. I cannot give you up to hell. Repent—while there is still time. Remember the fate of he who has riches in this life. God give you strength to choose the right path!"

He laid his hand on my head as he spoke the last words. He had spoken mildly and sincerely; his look was not a lover beholding his love, but a guardian angel watching over a soul for which he is responsible. All men of talent have their sublime moments.

I felt respect for St. John—respect so strong that I was tempted give in to him. I think now, when I look back at that moment, I was unaware of my folly.

I stood motionless under his touch. I forgot my refusals and overcame my fears. The Impossible—my marriage to St. John—was fast becoming possible. Everything was changing with a sudden sweep. Religion called—Angels beckoned—God commanded—Eternity was revealed beyond. It seemed that, for happiness hereafter, I might sacrifice everything on earth in a second. The room was full of visions.

"Can you decide now?" asked the missionary. The question came in gentle tones; he drew me to him just as gently. Oh, that gentleness! How much stronger it is than force! I could resist St. John's anger—but I grew limp under his kindness.

"I could decide if I were certain," I answered. "If I were convinced it is God's will that I should marry you, I could vow to marry you here and now!"

"My I prayers are heard!" exclaimed St. John. He pressed his hand firmer on my head, as if he claimed me. He put his arms around me, almost as if he loved me—I say almost, for I knew the difference; I had felt what it was to be loved. But, like him, I had now put love out of the question, and thought only of duty.

I sincerely, deeply, fervently longed to do what was right—and only that. "Show me, show me the path!" I begged of Heaven. I was excited more than I had ever been—and whether what followed was the effect of excitement, the reader shall judge.

The house was still, for I believe everyone except St. John and myself were now in bed. The one candle was dying out; the room was full of moonlight. My heart beat fast; I heard it throb. Suddenly my heart stood still to an indescribable feeling that shocked through it, and then to my head and limbs. My eyes and ears waited, expectantly, while my flesh quivered.

"What have you heard? What do you see?" asked St. John.

I saw nothing, but I heard a voice somewhere cry:

"Jane! Jane! Jane!"

"O God! What is it?" I gasped.

I might have said, "Where is it?" for it did not seem to come from the room, or the house, or the garden. Nor did it come from the air, the earth, or the sky.

It was the voice of a human being—a known, loved, well-remembered voice—that of Edward Fairfax Rochester; and it spoke in pain and woe, wildly, eerily, urgently.

"I am coming!" I cried. "Wait for me! Oh, I will come!"

I flew to the door and looked into the hallway; it was dark. I ran out into the garden; it was empty.

"Where are you?" I exclaimed.

The hills beyond Marsh Glen echoed faintly back—"Where are you?"

I listened. The wind sighed low in the trees; all was midnight hush.

"This is not a ghost, or witchcraft," I said. "This is the work of nature. She was awakened, and did her best."

St. John had followed me outside. I broke from him—he would have held me back. It was my time to assume power; my powers were in play and in force. I told him not to question me; I asked him to leave me; I must and would be alone. He obeyed at once.

I went to my bedroom, locked myself in, fell on my knees, and prayed in my way—different from St. John's, but effective. I seemed to touch a Mighty Spirit; and my soul rushed out in gratitude at His feet. I rose from the thanksgiving, made a decision and lay down—fearless, enlightened, and eager for the daylight.

Chapter 36

The daylight came and I rose at dawn. I busied myself for an hour or two with arranging my things for a short journey. Meantime, I heard St. John leave his room. He stopped at my door—I feared he would knock. He did not, but a slip of paper was passed under the door. I picked it up and read these words:

"You left me too suddenly last night. Had you stayed a little longer, you would have laid your hand on the Christian's cross and the angel's crown. I shall expect your clear decision when I return in a fortnight. Meantime, watch and pray that you enter not into temptation. The spirit, I trust, is willing, but the flesh, I see, is weak. I shall pray for you hourly. Yours, ST. JOHN."

My spirit, I answered mentally, is willing to do what is right; and my flesh, I hope, is strong enough to accomplish the will of Heaven, once that will is known to me. At any rate, it will be strong enough to find an answer from this cloud of doubt.

It was the first of June, yet the morning was chilly and rainy. I heard the front door open and St. John leave. Looking through the window, I saw him cross the garden, walking over the misty moors toward Whitcross—there he would meet the coach.

In a few more hours, cousin, I thought, I too shall meet a coach in Whitcross. I too have someone to ask after in England, before I depart for India forever.

It was yet two hours until breakfast. I filled the time walking softly about my room and thinking of last night's visitation, which had formed today's plans. I recalled the voice I had heard; it seemed to come from within me—not from the external world. It had wakened my soul out of its sleep, then vibrated in my quaking heart and through my spirit.

Soon, I thought, I will know something of him whose voice seemed to summon me last night. Letters have proved to no avail—personal inquiry shall replace them.

At breakfast, I announced to Diana and Mary that I was going on a journey, and should be absent at least four days.

"Alone, Jane?" they asked.

"Yes, to see or hear news of a friend about whom I have for some time been uneasy."

They might have said that they believed I had no friends, but with their natural delicacy, they made no comment. Diana asked if I was well enough to travel. I looked very pale. I replied that only anxiety ailed me, which I soon hoped to cure.

I left Moor House at three o'clock, and soon after four I stood at the Whitcross signpost, waiting for the coach which was to take me to distant Thornfield. It was the same vehicle from which, a year ago, I had stepped onto this very spot—desolate and hopeless!

The coach stopped and I entered—and this time, the price of the journey was not my entire fortune.

It was a journey of thirty-six hours. I had set out from Whitcross on a Tuesday afternoon, and early on the following Thursday morning, the coach stopped to water the horses at a wayside inn, situated in the midst of familiar scenery.

"How far is Thornfield Hall from here?" I asked the innkeeper.

"Just two miles, ma'am, across the fields."

My journey is done, I thought to myself. I got out of the coach, gave my trunk to the innkeeper, and paid my fare to the coachman.

The sun gleamed on the gilded sign of the inn, "The Rochester Arms". My heart leapt up—I was already on my master's very lands. Then my heart fell again, and I thought:

"Your master may be across the British Channel, for all you know; and if he is at Thornfield Hall, who else is there? His lunatic wife. And then you can have nothing to do with him. Ask information of the people at the inn—they can solve your doubts at once. Go up to that man, and inquire if Mr. Rochester is at home."

The suggestion was sensible, and yet I could not force myself to act on it. I so dreaded a reply that would crush me with despair. To prolong doubt was to prolong hope.

There was the fence in front of me—the very fields through which I had hurried on the morning I fled Thornfield.

I knew which fields to cross. How fast I walked! How I ran sometimes! How I looked forward to catch the first view of the well-known woods! How I welcomed glimpses of familiar meadows and hills!

At last, another field crossed, a lane threaded, and there were the courtyard walls—the house itself.

My first view of it shall be in front, I determined, where I can see my master's very window; perhaps he will be standing there—he rises early; perhaps he is now walking in the orchard, or on the road in front.

But if I see him, surely I should not be so mad as to run to him? And if I did—what then? God bless him! What then? Who would be hurt by my once more tasting the life his glance can give me? But I am raving—perhaps he is not at Thornfield at all, but watching the sun rise over the Pyrenees, or on the southern sea.

I walked along the lower wall of the orchard, and turned the corner. There was the gate, between two stone pillars. From behind one pillar I could peep round quietly at the full front of the mansion. I advanced my head with precaution—.

Now an illustration, reader.

A lover finds his mistress asleep on a mossy bank; he wishes to catch a glimpse of her fair face without waking her. He advances softly over the grass, careful to make no sound; he bends over her; a light veil rests on her face; he lifts it, but how he starts! He gazes on her wildly, and cries, because he finds she is stone dead.

I looked with timid joy toward the stately Thornfield Hall—I saw only a blackened ruin.

The lawn, the grounds were trodden and waste. The front was an empty shell of a wall—no roof, no chimneys—all had crashed in.

And there was the silence of death about it. No wonder that letters addressed to people here had never received an answer. The grim blackness of the stones told that the Hall had fallen by fire—but how? What story belonged to this disaster? Had life been lost as well as property? If so, whose? Dreadful question, and there was no one here to answer it.

Wandering round the shattered walls and through the devastated interior, I realized the disaster was not recent. Winter snows and winter rains had come; spring had brought grass and weeds here and there between the stones and fallen rafters.

And oh! Where was Mr. Rochester? In what land? My eyes wandered to the grey church tower near the gates, and I thought, "Is he buried there, in the Rochester family vault?"

There must be answers to these questions. I could find it nowhere but at the inn, and there I returned.

The host himself brought my breakfast into the parlour. I asked him to shut the door and sit down. But when he did, I scarcely knew how to begin—such horror had I of the possible answers. And yet the charred ruin

I had just left, prepared me somewhat for a tale of misery.

The host was a respectable-looking, middle-aged man.

"You know Thornfield Hall, of course?" I managed to say at last.

"Yes, ma'am; I lived there once."

"Did you?" Not in my time, I thought—you are a stranger to me.

"I was the late Mr. Rochester's butler," he added.

The late! I received, with full force, the blow I had been trying to avoid.

"The late!" I gasped. "Is he dead?"

"I mean Mr. Edward's father," he explained. I breathed again; my blood resumed its flow, fully assured by these words that Mr. Edward—my Mr. Rochester—was at least alive. Glad words! It seemed I could hear all that was to come now, with relative calmness.

"Is Mr. Rochester living at Thornfield Hall now?" I asked, knowing, of course, what the answer would be, but still hoping to delay the news of where he really was.

"No, ma'am—Oh, no! No one is living there. I suppose you are a stranger in these parts, or you would have heard what happened last autumn—Thornfield Hall is quite a ruin. It was burnt down just about harvest time. A dreadful calamity! Such an immense quantity of valuable property destroyed—hardly any of the furniture could be saved. The fire broke out in the dead of night, and before the engines arrived from Millcote, the building was one mass of flame. It was a terrible spectacle; I witnessed it myself."

"At dead of night!" I muttered. Yes, that was always the fatal hour at Thornfield. "Do they know how it started?" I demanded.

"They guessed, ma'am. Indeed, I should say it was determined beyond a doubt. You are not perhaps aware," he continued, edging his chair a little nearer the table, and speaking low, "that there was a lady—a lunatic—kept in the house?"

"I have heard something of it."

"She was kept confined, ma'am; for some years, people were not even absolutely certain of her existence. No one saw her; they only knew by rumour that such a person was at the Hall; and who or what she was, no one could guess. They said Mr. Edward had brought her from abroad, and some believed she had been his mistress. But a queer thing happened a year ago—a very queer thing."

I feared now to hear my own story. I tried to bring him back to the main topic.

Jane Eyre

"And this lady?"

"This lady, ma'am," he answered, "turned out to be Mr. Rocheste
The discovery was brought about in the strangest way. There was
lady, a governess at the Hall, that Mr. Rochester fell in—"

"But the fire," I suggested.

"I'm coming to that, ma'am—that Mr. Edward fell in love with. The servants say they never saw anybody so much in love as he was; he was after her continually. They used to watch him—servants will, you know, ma'am—and nobody but him thought her so very handsome. She was a small little thing, they say, almost like a child. I never saw her myself; but I've heard Leah, the housemaid, tell of her. Leah liked her well enough. Mr. Rochester was about forty, and this governess not twenty; and you see, when gentlemen of his age fall in love with girls, it is often like they are bewitched. Well, he wanted to marry her."

"You shall tell me this part of the story another time," I said, "but now I wish to hear all about the fire. Was it suspected that this lunatic, Mrs. Rochester, had any hand in it?"

"You've hit it, ma'am. It's quite certain that it was her, and nobody but her, that set the fire. She had a woman to take care of her called Mrs. Poole—an able woman, and very trustworthy, except for one fault—she kept a very private gin bottle beside her, and now and then she took a drop too much.

"When Mrs. Poole was fast asleep after the gin, the mad lady, who was as cunning as a witch, would take the keys out of her pocket, let herself out of her chamber, and go roaming about the house, doing any wild mischief that came into her head. They say she had nearly burnt her husband in his bed once, but I don't know about that.

"However, on this night, she set fire first to the curtains in the room next to her own, and then she got down to a lower story, and made her way to the chamber that had been the governess's, and she ignited the bed there; but there was nobody sleeping in it, fortunately.

"The governess had run away two months before; and though Mr. Rochester sought her like she was the most precious thing in the world, he never found her; and he grew savage—quite savage in his disappointment. He never was a wild man, but he got dangerous after he lost her. He would be alone, too. He sent Mrs. Fairfax, the housekeeper, to her friends far away; but he gave her a handsome income for life. Miss Adele, a ward he had, was sent away to school. He broke off his acquaintances with all the gentry, and shut himself up like a hermit at the Hall."

"What! He did not leave England?"

"Leave England? Bless you, no! He would not leave the house, except at night, when he walked like a ghost about the grounds and in the orchard as if he had lost his senses—which in my opinion he had. He was a bold, spirited gentleman before that governess crossed him. In my opinion, I have often wished that Miss Eyre had been sunk in the sea before she came to Thornfield Hall."

"Then Mr. Rochester was at home when the fire broke out?"

"Yes, indeed he was. And he went up to the attic when all was burning above and below, and got the servants out of their beds and helped them down himself, and went back to get his mad wife out of her cell. And then they called out to him that she was on the roof, waving her arms, and shouting. I saw her and heard her with my own eyes. She was a big woman, and had long black hair.

"I witnessed, and several more witnessed, Mr. Rochester climb through the skylight onto the roof; we heard him call 'Bertha!' We saw him approach her; and then, ma'am, she yelled and jumped, and the next minute she lay smashed on the pavement."

"Dead?"

"Dead! Ay, dead as the stones on which her brains and blood were scattered."

"Good God!"

"You may well say so, ma'am. It was frightful!" He shuddered.

"And afterwards?" I urged.

"Well, ma'am, afterwards the house was burnt to the ground; there are only some bits of walls standing now."

"Were any other lives lost?"

"No—but perhaps it would have been better if there had."

"What do you mean?"

"Poor Mr. Edward!" he ejaculated, "Some say it was God's judgment on him for wanting to take another wife while he had one living; but I pity him, for my part."

"You said he was alive?" I exclaimed.

"Yes, yes, he is alive; but many think he would be better off dead."

"Why? How?" My blood was again running cold. "Where is he?" I demanded. "Is he in England?"

"Ay, ay—he's in England; he can't get out of England, I suppose—he's a fixture now."

What agony was this! And the man seemed determined to prolong it.

"He is blind," he said at last. "Yes, he is stone blind, is Mr. Edward."

I had dreaded worse. I had dreaded he was mad. I summoned the strength to ask what had caused this calamity.

"It was all his own courage, and his kindness, in a way, ma'am. He wouldn't leave the house till everyone else was out before him. As he came down the great staircase at last, after Mrs. Rochester had flung herself from the roof, there was a great crash—everything fell. He was taken out from under the ruins, alive, but sadly hurt; a beam had fallen in such a way as to partly protect him—but one eye was knocked out, and one hand so crushed that Mr. Carter, the surgeon, had to amputate it. The other eye inflamed, and he lost the sight of that also. He is now helpless, indeed—blind and a cripple."

"Where is he? Where does he now live?"

"At Ferndean, a manor house on a farm he has, about thirty miles away—quite a desolate spot."

"Who is with him?"

"Old John and his wife—he would have no one else. He is quite broken down, they say."

"Do you have a carriage?"

"Yes, ma'am, a very handsome one."

"Let it be gotten ready instantly; and if your driver can take me to Ferndean before sunset today, I'll pay both you and him twice the fare you usually demand."

Chapter 37

The manor house of Ferndean was an old, moderately sized house of simple design, buried deep in the woods. I had heard of it before. Mr. Rochester often spoke of it and sometimes went there. His father had purchased the estate for the sake of his hunting. Mr. Rochester would have rented the house, but due to its remote location, he could find no tenants. Ferndean had then remained vacant and unfurnished, except for several rooms.

I came to this house just before dark on an evening marked by a sad sky, cold wind, and steady rain. I walked the last mile, after dismissing the carriage with the double fare I had promised. Even close to the house, you could see nothing of it, so thick and dark were the woods around it. Iron gates between granite pillars showed me where to enter and, passing through them, I followed the tracks, on and on, though no sign of the house was visible.

I thought I had taken a wrong track and lost my way. But as dusk gathered over me, the way opened at last, and I saw a railing, then the house. It was barely distinct from the trees, so dank and green were its decaying walls. Entering a gate, there were no flowers. The windows were latticed and narrow, as was the door. It was, as the host of the inn had said, "a desolate spot".

"Can there be life here?" I asked myself.

Yes, for I heard a movement—the front door was opening, and some shape was about to come out of the house.

It opened slowly; a figure came out into the twilight and stood on the step; a man without a hat; he stretched forth his hand to feel whether it rained. Though it was dusk, I recognized him—it was my master, Edward Fairfax Rochester, and no other.

I stopped, almost held my breath, and stood to watch him, unseen, and alas! invisible to him. My rapture was kept in check by the pain of his appearance.

His figure was as strong and stalwart as ever—still erect, his hair still raven black. His athletic features were not altered after one year's time.

But in his face, I saw a change that looked desperate and brooding—it reminded me of some wronged and chained wild beast, dangerous to approach.

And, reader, do you think I feared him in his blind ferocity? If you do, you little know me. I had a soft hope that soon I could dare to place a kiss on that brow of rock, and on those lips so sternly sealed beneath it—but not yet. I would not approach him yet.

He descended the step and moved slowly, groping toward the grass. Where was his daring stride now? Then he paused, as if he knew not which way to turn. He lifted his hand and opened his eyelids—and gazed blankly into the darkness.

He stretched out his right hand—he kept the mutilated left arm hidden in his shirt. He seemed to want to get an idea of what lay around him, but he met only air. He then gave up the effort, folded his arms, and stood quietly in the rain. At this moment, John approached him from inside the house.

"Will you take my arm, sir?" he said. "There is a heavy shower coming on; had you not better go in?"

"Let me alone," was the answer.

John left without having observed me. Mr. Rochester now tried to walk about, vainly—all was too uncertain. He groped his way back to the house and, entering it, closed the door.

I now drew near and knocked. John's wife opened the door. "Mary," I said, "how are you?"

She started as if she had seen a ghost.

"Is it really you, miss, come at this late hour to this lonely place?"

I calmed her by taking her hand; and then I followed her into the kitchen, where John now sat by a good fire. I explained to them, in few words, that I had heard all about what had happened since I left Thornfield, and that I had come to see Mr. Rochester. I asked John to go down to the turnpike house, where I had dismissed the carriage, and bring my trunk, which I had left there.

Then, while I removed my bonnet and shawl, I asked Mary if I could stay at the manor house for the night; she said that would be possible. Just at this moment the parlour bell rang.

"When you go in," said I, "tell your master that a person wishes to speak to him, but do not give my name."

"I don't think he will receive you," she answered. "He refuses everybody."

When she returned, I asked what he had said.

"You are to send in your name and your business," she replied. She then proceeded to fill a glass with water and place it on a tray, together with candles.

"Is that what he rang for?" I asked.

"Yes, he always has candles brought in at dark, though he is blind."

"Give the tray to me. I will carry it in."

I took it from her hand; she pointed out the parlour door. The tray shook as I held it; some water spilt from the glass; my heart beat loud and fast. Mary opened the door for me, and shut it behind me.

This parlour looked gloomy—a neglected fire burnt low in the hearth and, leaning over it, with his head against the mantelpiece, was Mr. Rochester. His old dog, Pilot, lay on one side, out of the way, coiled up as if afraid of being stepped on. Pilot pricked up his ears when I came in; then he jumped up with a yelp and a whine, and bounded toward me. He almost knocked the tray from my hands. I set it on the table, then patted him and said softly, "Lie down!"

Mr. Rochester turned mechanically to see what the commotion was; but as he saw nothing, he returned and sighed.

"Give me the water, Mary," he said.

I approached him with the glass; Pilot followed me, still excited.

"What is the matter?" he inquired.

"Down, Pilot!" I said again. As he drank the water, he seemed to listen, then put the glass down.

"This is you, Mary, is it not?"

"Mary is in the kitchen," I answered.

He put out his hand with a quick gesture, but not seeing where I stood, he did not touch me.

"Who is this? Who is this?" he demanded, trying to see with those sightless eyes—a vain attempt!

"Answer me—speak again!" he ordered, demanding and loud.

"Will you have a little more water, sir?" I said.

"Who is it? What is it? Who speaks?"

"Pilot knows me, and John and Mary know I am here. I came only this evening," I answered.

"Great God! What delusion has come over me? What sweet madness has seized me?"

"No delusion—no madness. Your mind, sir, is too strong for delusion, your health too sound for madness."

"And where is the speaker? Is it only a voice? Oh! I cannot see, but

I must feel, or my heart will stop and my brain will burst. Whatever—whoever—you are, let me touch you, or I cannot live!"

He groped; I stopped his wandering hand, and held it in both of mine.

"Her very fingers!" he cried. "Her small, slight fingers! If so, there must be more of her."

The muscular hand broke from mine; he seized my arm; he entwined and gathered my shoulder—neck—waist—to him.

"Is it Jane? What is it? This is her shape—this is her size—"

"And this her voice," I added. "She is all here—her heart, too. God bless you, sir! I am glad to be so near you again."

"Jane Eyre! Jane Eyre," was all he said.

"My dear master," I answered, "I am Jane Eyre—I have found you—I have come back to you."

"In truth? In the flesh? My living Jane?"

"You touch me, sir, you hold me—I am not cold like a corpse, nor vacant like air, am I?"

"My living darling! These are certainly her limbs, and these are her features; but I cannot be so blest, after all my misery. It is a dream; such dreams as I have had at night when I have clasped her once more to my heart, as I do now, and kissed her, and felt that she loved me, and trusted that she would not leave me."

"Which I never will, sir, from this day."

"Never will, says the vision? But I always woke and found it an empty mockery, and I was desolate and abandoned—my life dark, lonely, hopeless; my soul thirsty but forbidden to drink; my heart famished but never fed. Gentle, soft dream, nestling in my arms now, you will leave, too. But kiss me before you go—embrace me, Jane."

"There, sir—and there!"

I pressed my lips to his once brilliant and now dark eyes—I swept his hair from his brow and kissed that, too. He suddenly seemed to arouse himself—belief in the reality of all this seized him.

"It is you—is it, Jane? You are come back to me then?"

"I am."

"And you do not lie dead in some ditch under some stream? And you are not a beggar amongst strangers?"

"No, sir! I am an independent woman now."

"Independent! What do you mean, Jane?"

"My uncle in Madeira is dead, and he left me five thousand pounds."

"Ah! Now this is real!" he cried. "I could never dream that. Besides, there is that peculiar voice of hers, so animating and spicy, as well as soft—it cheers my withered heart, it puts life into it. What, Janet! You are an independent woman? A rich woman?"

"If you won't let me live with you, I can build a house of my own, close to your door, and you may come and sit in my parlour when you want company in the evening."

"But as you are rich, Jane, you no doubt have friends who will look after you, and not force you to devote yourself to a blind, lame man like me?"

"I told you I am independent, sir, as well as rich—I am my own mistress."

"And you will stay with me?"

"Certainly—unless you object. I will be your neighbour, your nurse, your housekeeper. You are lonely; I will be your companion—to read to you, to walk with you, to sit with you, to wait on you, to be eyes and hands to you. Cease to look so melancholy, my dear master; you shall not be left desolate, so long as I live."

He did not reply; he seemed serious, distracted; he sighed; he half-opened his lips as if to speak, then closed them again. I felt a little embarrassed. Perhaps I had too quickly overstepped my bounds.

I had made my proposal, assuming that he would ask me to be his wife. But he had not mentioned it and, his face now becoming darker, I suddenly realized that I might have been all wrong, and perhaps was being a fool. I began to gently withdraw myself from his arms—but he eagerly snatched me closer.

"No—no—Jane; you must not go. No—I have touched you, heard you, felt the comfort of your presence, the sweetness of your comfort. I cannot give up these joys. I have little left in myself—I must have you. The world may laugh, may call me absurd and selfish, but it does not matter. My very soul demands you, and it must be satisfied."

"Well, sir, I will stay with you; I have said so."

"Yes—but staying with me might mean something different for you than for me. You, perhaps, could wait on me as a kind, little nurse, and that ought to satisfy me. I suppose I should now have only fatherly feelings for you—do you think so? Come, tell me."

"I will think what you like, sir. I am content to be only your nurse, if you think it better."

"But you cannot always be my nurse, Janet. You are young—you must marry one day."

"I don't care about being married."

"You should care, Janet. If I were what I once was, I would try to make you care—but—a sightless block!"

He relapsed again into gloom. I, on the contrary, became more cheerful, and took fresh courage—these last words gave me an insight as to where the difficulty lay. And since it was no difficulty with me, I felt quite relieved from my previous embarrassment. I spoke in a lighter tone.

"It is time someone re-humanized you," said I, parting his thick and long uncut locks, "for I see you are changing into a lion, or something of that sort. Your hair reminds me of eagles' feathers; and your nails are grown like birds' claws."

"On this arm, I have neither hand nor nails," he said, drawing the mutilated arm from his shirt, and showing it to me. "It is a mere stump—a ghastly sight! Don't you think so, Jane?"

"It is a pity to see it; and a pity to see your eyes—and the scar of fire on your forehead. And the worst of it is, one is in danger of loving you too well for all this, and making too much of you."

"I thought you would be revolted, Jane, when you saw my arm and my scarred face."

"Did you? Don't tell me so—lest I should question your judgment. Now, let me make a better fire. Can you tell when there is a good fire?"

"Yes; with the right eye I see a glow—a ruddy haze."

"And you see the candles?"

"Very dimly—each is a bright cloud."

"Can you see me?"

"No, my fairy; but I am only too thankful to hear and feel you."

"When do you eat supper?"

"I never eat supper."

"You shall have some tonight. I am hungry; so are you, I daresay, only you forget."

Summoning Mary, I soon had the room in more cheerful order. I prepared him a comfortable meal. My spirits were excited, and I talked to him with pleasure and ease during supper, and for a long time after. He showed no restraint, no subdued glee. With him I was at perfect ease, because I knew I suited him; all I said or did seemed either to console or revive him.

He brought to life and light my whole nature; in his presence, I thoroughly lived, and he lived in mine. Blind as he was, smiles played over his face, joy dawned on his forehead; his face softened and warmed.

After supper, he began to ask me many questions—where I had been, what I had been doing, how I had found him out. But I gave him only very partial replies—it was too late to enter into particulars that night. Besides, I did not wish to open a fresh well of emotion in his heart; my sole aim was to cheer him. And cheered he was. And yet, if a moment's silence broke the conversation, he would turn restless, touch me, then say, "Jane."

"There is enchantment, Jane," he said, "in the very hour I am now spending with you. Who can tell what a dark, dreary, hopeless life I have dragged on for months past? Doing nothing, expecting nothing, merging night into day, feeling cold when I let the fire go out, hunger when I forgot to eat, and then a ceaseless sorrow, and a delirium of desire to behold my Jane again. Yes, I longed for her, far more than for my lost sight. How can it be that Jane is with me, and says she loves me? Will she not depart as suddenly as she came? Tomorrow, I fear I shall find her no more."

I passed my finger over his eyebrows, and remarked that they were scorched, and that I would apply something which would make them grow as broad and black as ever.

"What is the use of doing me any good when, at some fatal moment, you will again desert me?"

"Have you a comb, sir?"

"What for, Jane?"

"Just to comb out this shaggy black mane. I find you rather alarming; you talk of my being a fairy, but you are more like a goblin."

"Am I hideous, Jane?"

"Very, sir; you always were, you know."

"Humph! The wickedness has not been taken out of you, wherever you have journeyed."

"Yet I have been with good people, far better than you, a hundred times better people; with ideas and views you never entertained; quite more refined."

"Who the deuce have you been with?"

"If you twist that way, you will make me pull the hair out of your head."

"Who have you been with, Jane?"

"You shall not get it out of me tonight, sir; you must wait till tomorrow. To leave my tale half-told will assure you that I will appear at your breakfast table to finish it."

"Jane, you make me feel as I have not felt these twelve months!"

"There, sir, you are made decent. Now I'll leave you; I have been traveling these last three days, and I believe I am tired. Goodnight."

"Just one thing, Jane. Were there only ladies in the house where you have been?"

I laughed and made my escape, still laughing as I ran upstairs. A good idea, I thought with glee. I see I have the means to worry him out of his melancholy for some time to come.

Very early the next morning I heard him up, wandering from one room to another. As soon as Mary came down, I heard him ask:

"Is Miss Eyre here? Which room did you put her in? Was it dry? Is she up? Go and ask if she wants anything, and when she will come down."

I came down as soon as breakfast was ready. Entering the room very softly, I had viewed him before he discovered my presence. It was sad, indeed. He sat still in his chair, expectant, but not at rest. Lines of permanent sadness marked his strong features. His face reminded me of a lamp waiting to be re-lit.

I had meant to be happy and careless, but the powerlessness of this strong man touched my heart; still, I approached him with what cheerfulness I could.

"It is a bright, sunny morning, sir," I said. "The rain is gone; you shall have a walk soon."

I had wakened the glow—his features beamed.

"Oh, you are there, my skylark! Come to me. You are not gone? Not vanished? I heard a bird singing this morning, but its song had no music for me. All the melody on earth is in my Jane's tongue to my ear. All the sunshine I can feel is in her presence."

Tears came to my eyes as I heard this vow of his dependence upon me. But I wiped them away and busied myself with preparing breakfast.

Most of the morning was spent in the open air. I led him out of the wet and wild woods into some cheerful fields. I described to him how brilliantly green they were, how the flowers and hedges looked, and how sparklingly blue was the sky. I found a seat for him on the dry stump of a tree; and I let him place me on his knee. Pilot lay beside us; all was quiet. While clasping me in his arms, he suddenly broke out:

"Cruel, cruel deserter! Oh, Jane, what did I feel when I discovered you had fled Thornfield, and when I could not find you and, after searching your bedroom, realize that you had taken no money! A pearl necklace I had given you lay untouched in its little box; your bridal trunks were left locked. What could my darling do, left destitute and penniless? And what did she do? Let me hear now."

Thus I began the story of my experience for the last year. I softened considerably what happened during the three days of wandering and starvation, because to have told him would have caused unnecessary pain. The little I did say pierced his faithful heart deeper than I wished.

He said that I should not have left him without taking any money—I should have told him my intention. I should have confided in him; he would never have forced me to be his mistress. Violent as he had seemed in his despair, in truth he loved me far too well and too tenderly to be a tyrant. He would have given me half his fortune, without demanding so much as a kiss in return, rather than have me fling myself, friendless, on the wide world. He was certain that I had endured more than I had confessed.

"Well, whatever my sufferings have been, they were very short," I answered. I then told him how I had been taken in at Moor House; how I had obtained the position of schoolmistress; the receipt of my fortune; and the discovery of my relatives. Of course, St. John Rivers' name came up frequently during my tale. When I had finished, that name was immediately brought up.

"This St. John, then, is your cousin?"

"Yes."

"You have spoken of him often—do you like him?"

"He was a very good man, sir; I could not help liking him."

"A good man. Does that mean a respectable, well-mannered man of fifty? Or what does it mean?"

"St. John was only twenty-nine, sir."

"Is he a person of low stature, dull, and plain? A person whose goodness is lack of vice, rather than abundance of virtue?"

"He is untiringly active. He lives to perform great and exalted deeds."

"But his brain? Is it rather soft? He means well, but he is boring?"

"He talks little, sir. What he does say is always to the point. His brain is first-rate and vigorous."

"Is he an able man, then?"

"Truly able."

"A thoroughly educated man?"

"St. John is an accomplished and profound scholar."

"But his manners, I think you said, are not to your taste? Prudish and clerical?"

"I never mentioned his manners; but they are polished, calm, and gentlemanlike."

"His appearance—I forget what description you gave of his appearance—a sort of raw priest, half-strangled with his white neckcloth, and stilted up on his thick-soled shoes, eh?"

"St. John dresses well. He is a handsome man—tall, fair, with blue eyes, and a Grecian profile."

"Damn him! Did you like him, Jane?"

"Yes, Mr. Rochester, I liked him; but you asked me that before."

Of course, I understood his drift. Jealousy had gotten hold of him and stung him—but the sting gave him a break from his melancholy. I would not, therefore, immediately charm the snake.

"Perhaps you would rather not sit any longer on my knee, Miss Eyre?" was his next, somewhat unexpected, observation.

"Why not, Mr. Rochester?"

"Your words describe a graceful Apollo—tall, fair, blue-eyed, and with a Grecian profile. But your eyes look upon a Vulcan—a real blacksmith, brown, broad-shouldered, blind and lame."

"I never thought about it before, sir, but you certainly are rather like Vulcan."

"Well, you can leave me, ma'am. But before you go," he said, holding me firmer than ever, "please answer me a question or two." He paused.

"What questions, Mr. Rochester?"

Then followed this cross-examination.

"St. John made you schoolmistress of Morton before he knew you were his cousin?"

"Yes."

"You would often see him? He would visit the school sometimes?"

"Daily."

"He would discover many things in you he could not have expected to find? Some of your accomplishments are not ordinary."

"I don't know about that."

"You had a little cottage near the school, you say—did he ever come there to see you?"

"Now and then."

"In the evening?"

"Once or twice."

A pause.

"How long did you reside with him and his sisters after the cousinship was discovered?"

"Five months."

"Did Rivers spend much time with the ladies of his family?"

"Yes; the back parlour was both his study and ours; he sat near the window, and we by the table."

"Did he study much?"

"A good deal."

"What?"

"Hindu."

"And what did you do?"

"I learnt German, at first."

"Did he teach you?"

"He did not understand German."

"Did he teach you nothing?"

"A little Hindu."

"Rivers taught you Hindu?"

"Yes, sir."

"And his sisters also?"

"No."

"Only you?"

"Only me."

"Did you ask to learn it?"

"No."

"He wished to teach you?"

"Yes."

A second pause.

"Why did he wish it? Of what use could Hindu be to you?"

"He wanted me to go with him to India."

"Ah! Here I reach the root of the matter. He wanted you to marry him?"

"He asked me to marry him."

"That is fiction—a rude lie to annoy me."

"I beg your pardon, it is the truth. He asked me more than once, and was as stern about urging his point as ever you could be."

"Miss Eyre, I repeat, you can leave me now. How often am I to say the same thing? Why do you remain perched on my knee, when I have given you notice to leave?"

"Because I am comfortable here."

"No, Jane, you are not comfortable here, because your heart is not with me—it is with this cousin, this St. John. Oh, till this moment, I thought my little Jane was all mine! I believed she loved me even when she left me. As long as we have been parted, the tears I have wept over our separation—I never thought that while I was mourning you, you were loving another! But it is useless grieving. Jane, leave me—go and marry Rivers."

"Shake me off then, sir—push me away, for I'll not leave you of my own accord."

"Jane, I always like your tone of voice—it still renews hope, it sounds so truthful. When I hear it, it carries me back a year. I forget that you have formed a new tie. But I am not a fool—go."

"Where must I go, sir?"

"Your own way—with the husband you have chosen."

"Who is that?"

"You know—this St. John Rivers."

"He is not my husband, nor will ever be. He does not love me—I do not love him. He loves a beautiful young lady called Rosamond. He wanted to marry me only because he thought I would make a suitable missionary's wife, which she would not have done. He is good and great, but severe; and, for me, cold as an iceberg. He is not like you, sir. I am not happy at his side, or near him, or with him. He has no fondness for me. He sees nothing attractive in me, not even youth—only a few useful mental powers. So then, I must leave you, sir, to go to him?"

I shuddered, and clung instinctively closer to my blind but beloved master. He smiled.

"What, Jane! Is this true? Is this really the state of matters between you and Rivers?"

"Absolutely, sir! Oh, you need not be jealous! I wanted to tease you a little to make you less sad. I thought anger would be better than grief. But if you wish me to love you—if you could see how much I do love you, you would be proud and happy. All my heart is yours, sir; it belongs to you; and with you it would remain, even if fate kept me from you forever."

Again, as he kissed me, painful thoughts darkened his face. "My scarred vision! My crippled strength!" he murmured regretfully.

I caressed him to soothe him. I knew what he was thinking, and wanted to speak for him, but dared not. As he turned his face aside a minute, I saw a tear slide from under the sealed eyelid, and trickle down the manly cheek. My heart swelled.

"I am no better than the old lightning-struck chestnut tree in Thornfield orchard," he said before long.

"You are no ruin, sir, no lightning-struck tree. You are green and vigorous. Plants will grow about your roots, whether you ask them or not, because they take delight in your bountiful shadow; and as they grow they will lean toward you, and wind round you, because you offer them such strength."

Again he smiled; I gave him comfort.

"You speak of being friends with me, Jane?" he asked.

"Yes, of friends," I answered rather hesitatingly, for I knew I meant more than friends, but could find no other words to use. He helped me.

"Ah! Jane. But I want a wife."

"Do you, sir?"

"Yes. Is it news to you?"

"Of course—you said nothing about it before."

"Is it unwelcome news?"

"That depends on your choice, sir."

"Which you shall make for me, Jane. I will abide by your decision."

"Choose then, sir, her who loves you best."

"I will at least choose her I love best. Jane, will you marry me?"

"Yes, sir."

"A poor blind man, whom you will have to lead about by the hand?"

"Yes, sir."

"A crippled man, twenty years older than you, whom you will have to wait on?"

"Yes, sir."

"Truly, Jane?"

"Most truly, sir."

"Oh! My darling! God bless you and reward you!"

"Mr. Rochester, if ever I did a good deed in my life, if ever I thought a good thought, if ever I prayed a sincere and blameless prayer, if ever I wished a righteous wish, I am rewarded now. To be your wife is, for me, to be as happy as I can be on earth."

"Because you love to sacrifice."

"Sacrifice! What do I sacrifice? To be privileged to put my arms round whom I value, to press my lips to whom I love, to rest on whom I trust—is that to make a sacrifice? If so, then certainly I delight in sacrifice."

"And to bear with my flaws, Jane—to overlook my deficiencies."

"Which are none to me, sir. I love you better now, when I can really be useful to you, than I did in your state of proud independence, when you scorned every role but giver and protector."

"Until now, I have hated to be helped—to be led. From now on, I feel I shall hate it no more. I did not like to put my hand into a nurse's, but it is pleasant to feel it circled by Jane's little fingers. I preferred loneliness to the constant attendance of servants; but Jane's soft attention will be a perpetual joy. Jane suits me—do I suit her?"

"To the finest fiber of my nature, sir."

"That being the case, we have nothing in the world to wait for—we must be married instantly."

"Mr. Rochester, the sun is setting, and Pilot has actually gone home to his dinner. Let me look at your watch."

"Fasten it into your girdle, Janet, and keep it there; I have no use for it."

"It is nearly four o'clock in the afternoon, sir. Don't you feel hungry?"

"We shall be married in three days, Jane. Never mind fine clothes and jewels."

"The sun has dried up all the rain, sir. The breeze is still; it is quite hot."

"Do you know, Jane, I have your little pearl necklace at this moment fastened round my neck? I have worn it since the day I lost my only treasure, as a memento of her."

"We will go home through the woods; that will be the shadiest way."

He pursued his own thoughts without paying me attention.

"Jane! I daresay, you know I am not religious, but my heart swells with gratitude to God just now. He sees not as man sees, but far clearer; judges not as man judges, but far more wisely.

"I did wrong—I would have soiled you, my innocent flower. God snatched you from me. I, in my stubborn rebellion, almost cursed God for it. Instead of bending to His will, I defied Him. Divine justice pursued its course—disasters came thick on me. I was forced to pass through the valley of the shadow of death.

"His punishments are mighty, and He has humbled me forever. You know I was proud of my strength—but what is it now? Lately, Jane, only lately, I began to see and acknowledge the hand of God in my doom. I began to experience remorse and repentance, the wish to reconcile with my Maker. I began sometimes to pray—very brief prayers they were, but very sincere.

"Four days ago, last Monday night, a mood of sorrow and gloom came over me. I had long assumed that, since I could find you nowhere, you must be dead. Late that night, perhaps around midnight, I appealed to God that I might soon be taken from this life, and admitted into Heaven, where there was still hope of rejoining Jane.

"I was in my own room, sitting by the window. I longed for thee, Janet! Oh, I longed for thee both with soul and flesh! In pain and humility, I asked God, "Have I not been desolate, afflicted, and tormented long enough? And might I not soon taste bliss and peace once more?" I acknowledged that I deserved all that I endured, and that I could scarcely endure any more.

"I pleaded; and the beginning and end of my heart's wishes broke from my lips in the words—'Jane! Jane! Jane!'"

"Did you speak these words aloud?"

"I did, Jane. If anyone had heard me, he would have thought me mad—I said them with such frantic energy."

"And it was last Monday night, near midnight?"

"Yes, but what happened next is the strange point. You will think me superstitious, but as I exclaimed 'Jane! Jane! Jane!' a voice—I cannot tell from where the voice came, but I know whose voice it was—replied, 'I am coming, wait for me.' And a moment later, the words 'Where are you?' went whispering on the wind.

"Those words seemed spoken amongst the mountains; for I heard an echo repeat the words. I could have believed that, in some wild scene, Jane and I were meeting. In spirit, I believe we must have met. At that hour, you were no doubt asleep, Jane. Perhaps your soul wandered here to comfort mine—for that voice was yours. As certain as I live, it was yours!"

Reader, it was on Monday night, near midnight, that I too had heard the mysterious call—those were the very words I replied to. I listened to Mr. Rochester's tale, but said nothing. The coincidence struck me as too mysterious to be discussed. I kept these things to myself, then, and pondered them in my heart.

"You cannot now wonder," continued my master, "that when you appeared so unexpectedly last night, I had difficulty believing you were anything other than a mere voice and vision. Now, I thank God! I know it to be otherwise. Yes, I thank God!"

He gently took me off his knee, rose, and reverently removing his hat, and bowing his head, he stood in quiet prayer. Only the last words could I hear:

"I thank my Maker that, in the midst of judgment, he has remembered mercy. I humbly beg my Redeemer to give me strength, from now on, to lead a purer life than I have done up to now!"

Then he stretched his hand out to be led. I took that dear hand, held it a moment to my lips, then put it round my shoulder. We entered the woods, and walked homeward.

Jane Eyre

Chapter 38

*R*eader, I married him. A quiet wedding we had—he and I, the parson and clerk, were present. When we got back from the church, I went into the kitchen of the manor house, where Mary was cooking the dinner and John cleaning the knives, and I said:

"Mary, I have been married to Mr. Rochester this morning." The housekeeper and her husband were both the sort of decent people who would not shriek at a remarkable piece of news. For three minutes, Mary looked up and stared at me, her ladle suspended in the air, and John ceased polishing the knives. Then Mary, bending again over the roast, said only:

"Have you, Miss? Well, for sure!"

A short time later she said, "I saw you go out with the master, but I didn't know you were gone to church to be wed," and she basted away. John, when I turned to him, was grinning from ear to ear.

"I told Mary how it would be," he said. "I knew what Mr. Edward would do, and I was certain he would not wait long; and he's done right, for all I know. I wish you joy, Miss!"

"Thank you, John. Mr. Rochester told me to give you and Mary this." I put into his hand a five-pound note. Without waiting to hear more, I left the kitchen. In passing by the door later, I caught the words:

"She'll be better for him than any of those grand ladies." And again, "If she had been one of the handsomest, she would not be very good-natured; and in his eyes, she's fair and beautiful—anybody may see that."

I wrote to Moor House and to Cambridge immediately, to say what I had done, fully explaining why. Diana and Mary approved the marriage completely. Diana announced that she would come and see me after the honeymoon.

"She had better not wait till then, Jane," said Mr. Rochester, when I read her letter to him. "If she does, she will be too late, for our honeymoon will last our whole life long; its beams will only fade over your grave or mine."

How St. John received the news, I don't know—he never answered my letter. Yet six months later, he wrote to me, without, however, mentioning

Mr. Rochester's name or alluding to my marriage. His letter was very serious, but calm and kind.

He has maintained a regular, though not frequent, correspondence ever since. He hopes I am happy, and trusts that I am not one of those who live without God in the world, and only care about earthly things.

You have not forgotten little Adele, have you, reader? I had not; I received permission from Mr. Rochester to go and see her at the school where he had placed her. Her joy at seeing me again touched my heart. She looked pale and thin; she said she was not happy. I found the rules of the school were too strict and its course of study too severe for a child of her age—I took her home with me.

I meant to become her governess once more, but I soon found this impractical; my husband needed all my time and care. So I found a school that was kinder, and near enough to permit my visiting her often, and bringing her home sometimes. I made certain that she should always be comfortable. She soon settled into her new school, became very happy there, and made fair progress in her studies.

When she grew up and left school, I found her to be a pleasing companion—quiet, good-tempered, and well-principled. By her grateful attention to me, she has long since repaid the kindness I ever gave her.

My tale draws to its close; one word about my married life, and one brief glance at the fortunes of those whose names have most frequently recurred in this narrative, and I am done.

I have now been married ten years. I know what it is to live entirely for, and with, the person whom I love best on earth. I hold myself supremely blessed—blessed beyond what language can express, because I am my husband's life as fully as he is mine.

No woman was ever nearer to her husband than I am. I never tire of my Edward's company, nor he of mine, and so we are always together. To be together is, for us, to be free and happy. We talk all day long. All my trust is bestowed on him, all his trust is devoted to me. We are precisely suited in character—perfect harmony is the result.

Mr. Rochester continued to be blind for the first two years of our marriage—perhaps that was the circumstance that drew us so very near, that knit us so very close; for I was his vision, as I am still his right hand.

I was, literally, the apple of his eye. He saw nature, he saw books, through me; and never did I weary of gazing on his behalf, and of putting into words the vision of field, tree, town, river, cloud, sunbeam—of the landscape before us, of the weather round us. Never did I weary of reading to him, or leading him where he wished to go, or doing for him what he wished to be done.

One morning, after two years, I was writing a letter as he dictated, and he came and bent over me, and said:

"Jane, do you have a glittering ornament round your neck?"

I wore a gold watch chain. I answered, "Yes."

"And have you a pale blue dress on?"

I had. He informed me then, that for some time he had sensed that one eye was becoming less clouded, and that now he was sure of it.

He and I went up to London. He had the advice of an eminent doctor, and he eventually recovered the sight of that one eye. He cannot now see very distinctly—he cannot read or write much, but he can find his way without being led by the hand. The sky is no longer a blank to him—the earth no longer a void.

When his first-born was put into his arms, he could see that the boy had inherited his own eyes—large, brilliant, and black. On that occasion, he again, with a full heart, acknowledged that God had balanced judgment with mercy.

My Edward and I, then, are happy; and the more so, because those we most love are happy as well. Diana and Mary Rivers are both married; once a year, they come to see us, and we go to see them. Diana's husband is a captain in the navy, a gallant officer and a good man. Mary's is a clergyman, a college friend of her brother's and, from his achievements and principles, worthy of the marriage. Both Captain Fitzjames and Mr. Wharton love their wives, and are loved by them.

As to St. John Rivers, he left England and went to India. He entered on the path he had marked for himself, and pursues it still. Firm, faithful, and devoted, full of energy, zeal and truth, he labours for his fellow humans. He may be stern, exacting, and ambitious, but his is the sternness of a warrior who guards his pilgrims.

His is the life of the apostle, who speaks for Christ when he says, "Whosoever will come after me, let him deny himself, and take up his cross and follow me." His is the ambition of those who stand before the throne of God—the chosen and faithful.

St. John is unmarried; he never will marry now. His work draws near its close, his glorious sun hurries toward its setting. The last letter I received from him brought tears to my eyes, and yet filled my heart with divine joy.

I know that a stranger will write to me soon, to say that the good and faithful servant has been called into the joy of his Lord. And why weep for this? No fear of death will darken St. John's last hour. His mind will be clear, his heart will be strong, his hope will be sure, his faith steadfast. His own words from his letter are a pledge of this:

"My Master," he says, "has forewarned me. Daily He announces more distinctly, 'Surely I come quickly!' and hourly I more eagerly respond, 'Amen; even so, come, Lord Jesus!'"